# COWBOY
## ANGELS

# COWBOY

Paul
McAuley

# ANGELS

an imprint of **Prometheus Books**
**Amherst, NY**

Inquiries should be addressed to
Pyr
59 John Glenn Drive
Amherst, New York 14228–2119
VOICE: 716–691–0133
FAX: 716–691–0137
WWW.PYRSF.COM

15  14  13  12  11     5  4  3  2  1

Library of Congress Cataloging-in-Publication Data

McAuley, Paul J.
    Cowboy angels / by Paul McAuley.
        p. cm.
    First published: London : Gollancz, an imprint of Orion Publishing Group, 2007.
    ISBN 978–1–61614–251–3 (pbk.)
    1. Intelligence officers—United States—Fiction. I. Title.

PR6063.C29C68  2011
823'.914—dc22

2010044350

Printed in the United States of America

For **GEORGINA**

and

for **JACK WOMACK**

*We ought to look in a mirror and get proud and stick out our chests and suck in our bellies and say: "Damn, we're Americans."*

Lieutenant General Jay Garner

"They're Americans, Adam. Americans like you and me. Americans who want to rid their homeland of communist tyranny. Americans who are laying their lives on the line to return liberty and freedom to their version of the US of A. Their government may not be the perfect model of democracy, I'll give you that, but they uphold the Constitution, they've kept the flame of liberty burning for fifty years, they sure as hell deserve our full support. And here you are, got up like an undertaker, ready to sell them out."

"Go easy on me, Tom. I'm just the messenger."

"Just the messenger, huh? And I guess you're just obeying orders too, like all those bloodless nine-to-five office workers who've taken over the Company. Jesus, Adam. I'd be happier to hear that you side with Jimmy Carter and his merry band of quitters. At least it would mean you still believed in something."

The two men were sitting on either side of a government-issue steel desk. Adam Stone in a black wool overcoat and a black suit, the briefcase on his lap handcuffed to his left wrist; Tom Waverly in a brown leather jacket and combat fatigues, greying hair caught up in a loose ponytail and pulled through the clip of his baseball cap, cradling a half-empty bottle of Jack Daniel's. Trucks roared past the makeshift office every couple of minutes, shaking its plywood walls. A space heater blew baked air and the smell of burnt wiring. Music thumped out of a battered mini-system.

"You want to know what I believe?" Stone said. "I believe that the time for crude interventions like SWIFT SWORD has passed. I believe that these so-called Free Americans don't have a chance of winning their war unless we back them up with a lot more than a secure resupply line. And the country's tired of war, Tom. It doesn't want to be dragged into another quagmire. That's what the election was all about, in case you didn't notice."

"So you *are* siding with the quitters. Adam Stone has turned peacenik. I never thought I'd see the day."

"And I never thought you'd take something like this so personally."

"How else am I supposed to take it? How are General Baines and his men supposed to take it? Jesus Christ, Adam, we've been working on this for six months, we're all tooled up and ready to go, and at the very last moment, only a couple of hours before the show kicks off, we're told that we aren't going to get the tactical support we need. Okay, I admit it's hardly a surprise. Carter slid into office on an antiwar ticket, Senate delayed implementation of SWIFT SWORD until after the election, and Baines has been taking calls from the Joint Chiefs of Staff and the secretary of state all week. But it's still a callous and cowardly act, and I'm as sorry as hell to see you fronting for it."

Tom Waverly took a sip of Jack Daniel's. He was red-eyed and drawn, and looked as if he hadn't slept for a week. "How did it ever come to this? Here we are, two of the first guys to have been shot through a Turing gate. Key players in the first operation to organize a coup d'état in an alternate America. The fall of the American Bund? They teach eager new recruits all about it. We're in the fucking textbooks, Adam, and what have they got us doing? You're about to deliver history's worst Dear John letter, and I've just wasted three months running SWIFT SWORD's training and morale programme. Fact is, Baines's troops were trained and ready to go *before* they came through the mirror. They're good, disciplined soldiers who don't need to be told which end of a rifle is which, or how to run an assault course in full pack. And they certainly don't need me to tell them that the communists are the bad guys. My so-called training programme consisted of making sure they got hot meals three times a day, running back-to-back movie shows, and giving their officers access to all the liquor and whores they could handle. Which was plenty, believe you me. Those boys were so hot-blooded I had to bring in working girls from as far away as New Orleans to take care of them. I admit it was kind of fun to organize, but it wasn't what you could call real action."

"It looks like you're dressed up for action now," Stone said.

When Stone had arrived at SWIFT SWORD's camp, he'd been warned by Bruce Ellis, the colonel in charge of perimeter security, that Tom Waverly was in a bad way. "Baines will take his own sweet time organising an escort to his HQ," Bruce had said. "While you're waiting, you could maybe talk to Tom, try to calm him down." But Tom had already been half in the bag when Stone had found him, and he'd been getting steadily drunker ever since, alternating between self-lacerating bitterness and blustering bravado. And he kept identifying with the Free Americans, too, saying things like *we*'re ready to go. . . .

Saying now, "You miss it, Adam? Being in action?"

"Not a bit."

"Don't try to bullshit a bullshitter. I know you miss it as much as I do." Tom Waverly leaned back in his chair and crossed his boots on top of the desk. The wings of his brown leather jacket, a scuffed antique with fleece collar and cuffs, fell open, revealing the .357 Smith & Wesson revolver and the throwing knife hung on his customised shoulder rig. "You and me, Adam, we're not the kind of guys who end up pushing paper across a desk, signing off reports on aid programmes and friendship initiatives, tootling around golf courses in those little buggies at weekends, shooting the shit at the nineteenth hole while we wait for our first heart attacks. Don't you think we should go out on our own terms? Wouldn't it be better to burn out than fade away?"

"I think you're drunk, Tom. You always get this way when you've had a few too many."

"Yeah? What way is that?"

"Sentimental, mostly. Maudlin. Listen, I'll be happy to share that bottle with you and talk about the good old bad old days, but I have to get this little job done first. Why don't you use that phone on your desk and find out where my escort has got to?"

"He'll be here soon enough. Ease back, my man. Relax. You're not in the DCI's office now. This here's *my* house. You want a drink? Loosen your tie and *have* a goddamn drink. We can shoot the shit and listen to Bobby Dylan until your man gets here."

"I thought I recognised the voice," Stone said, grabbing at the chance to change the subject, "but the songs are like nothing I remember."

"It's a new album. A friend of mine black-bagged a cassette tape through the mirror, and I had one of the wizards in Technical Services transfer it to disk. Bobby Dylan has had himself some kind of midlife crisis and turned to evangelical Christianity, but he can still make a point when he wants to."

"He sounds pretty funky."

"'Funky,' huh? Where did a straight-arrow guy like you pick up a word like that?"

"I believe it was in the Nixon sheaf, that time we worked together."

"Oh yeah. You buried yourself in the New York Public Library, doing your sociopolitical research, and I got to hang out with those zippies or yippies or whatever the hell they called themselves. Happy times." Tom toasted Stone with his bottle and took a sip. "Tell me something, and don't lie. Bruce Ellis put you up to this little visit, didn't he?"

"He mentioned you were here. And because I have to wait for this damned escort, I thought I'd stop by and catch up."

"Colonel Bruce Ellis," Tom said, with a teasing lilt. "As I recall, he was a brand-new lieutenant when you two went through the mirror. It was the first time for both of you, wasn't it? A couple of virgins lost in the wild woods of that wild sheaf. And look at you now, all grown up and working for the DCI's office, thinking it gives you the right to meddle in other people's business. Well, it doesn't. And besides, there's no need."

"This is the first time I've seen you in a couple of years—"

"First time, I believe, since I saved your life."

"I hadn't forgotten. Do you want me to thank you all over again?"

"It was embarrassing enough at the time. You don't owe me anything, Adam. Don't you ever think you *owe* me, that you have to somehow pay me back."

"What I'm trying to say is that it's been a long time. I stopped by because I wanted to see how things are working out for you."

"Well I guess you can see where my career's headed—straight into the crapper, like my fucking marriage. How *that* worked out, thanks for asking, is I got to keep the clothes I was wearing when I walked out, and the car I drove off in. Brenda got the house and everything else when the divorce was finalised, she threatens to use my disks as skeet-shooting targets every time it looks like I'm gonna step out of line, and now her boyfriend has moved in, the slick son of a bitch. Fucker wants Linda to call him Daddy, like he's part of the family, but Linda isn't having any of that. She calls him Robert to his face, Mr. Hair Oil when she's with me." Tom's expression softened for a moment. "My little girl's grown up strong and smart, Adam. And she's not so little anymore. She'll be twenty this April and wants to join the Company as soon as she graduates from NYU. You can imagine what Brenda has to say about that."

"Nothing good, I bet."

Tom's ex-wife was employed by the analytical arm of the Company, turning raw data into finished intelligence: she'd always had a pretty good idea about what his clandestine work in Special Ops had involved. Her attempts to persuade him to transfer to a safer position had sparked a series of spectacular and legendary rows that had eventually led to their divorce.

"You still going out with that photographer?" Tom said. "Nora what's-her-name?"

"It didn't work out. I guess I'm kind of in between relationships at the moment."

"Sorry to hear it. I know I'm no advertisement for marriage, but I always thought you'd make the ideal all-American father. Clean-cut, hardworking, loyal. . . . I guess we should strike out 'loyal,' given why you're here."

Stone let that one go.

Tom put his head to one side, listening to Dylan sing about naming animals in Eden. "I guess he does sound a little bit funky. But it doesn't matter what the man chooses to do, he's always cool. Always has been, always will be. He doesn't care what other people think. He just does his own thing." He took a sip of Jack Daniel's and said, "These poor guys are going to get slaughtered if they don't have any backup." He suddenly sounded tired and sober and sad.

"That's not the idea," Stone said.

"Maybe it isn't. But that's what going to happen."

A horn blared outside, long and loud.

Tom checked his watch and said, "That'll be the guy come to take you up the hill."

Stone's pang of relief was immediately tempered by guilt. "As soon as I've seen the general, I'll come straight back here and have that drink with you."

"It stinks, Adam. Jimmy fucking Carter is going to let Baines's men go back through the mirror and commit suicide because that's easier than finding some way of standing down and repatriating five thousand soldiers. You know what this reminds me of? The Bay of Pigs."

"I don't know it."

"It's part of the same history as 'funky,' and this particular doppel of Bobby Dylan. Look it up. One thing I'll tell you now, the only thing we've learnt from all the different Americas we found through the mirror is that we haven't learnt anything at all." Tom Waverly screwed the top onto the bottle of Jack Daniel's and stood up, saying, "Let's go, compañero."

Stone hesitated for a moment. On the one hand, he had a politically sensitive delivery to make, and didn't really want to have Tom Waverly around when he made it in case Tom got it into his head to cause some kind of scene. On the other, he felt that he should keep his old friend under close watch in case he was working himself up to do something reckless. . . .

He said, "If you want to ride along, be my guest."

"You bet. I'm all done here."

Adam Stone's Free American escort, Captain Gene Lewis, drove his Jeep with reckless speed, overtaking a string of trucks lumbering toward the staging area, barely slowing when he swung onto the dirt track that climbed to the farmhouse where General Wendell Baines had his headquarters.

Tom had taken the shotgun seat. He turned to Stone, gestured at the wide valley spread below the ridge, and said, "Ain't that something?"

Two thirty-foot-diameter Turing gates—clones of the primary, which had been opened onto the Free America sheaf at Brookhaven in 1978—stood under a raked steel canopy at one end of the huge concrete apron where trucks, half-tracks, and light tanks were drawn up in neat rows like the audience for the world's biggest drive-in cinema. The low winter sun glowered through a haze of diesel smoke, and in this apocalyptic light soldiers were lining up to receive ammunition and grenades from quartermasters, standing in front of a field altar where a military chaplain elevated the host, or sitting around oil-drum braziers among piles of equipment.

In the Free America sheaf's version of history, the USA had fallen to a communist revolution in 1929, and a cabal of disenfranchised politicians, bankers, and businessmen, backed by loyal elements of the army and navy, had occupied Cuba and Haiti and established a government-in-exile. Operation SWIFT SWORD, approved by President Floyd Davis just before he'd been defeated by Jimmy Carter in an election so close there had been recounts in fifteen states, had been set up to help the Free Americans strike at the communist heartland. It had brought a division of Free American troops into the Real through a Turing gate at Guantánamo Bay and transported them to a camp a few miles outside Gettysburg, where they had been equipped with modern weaponry and trained in its use.

According to the original plan of campaign, the Free Americans would have reentered their sheaf at Gettysburg, and the Real would have defended the Turing gates and built up resupply routes while the Free Americans staged a fast, hard march across Pennsylvania and Maryland to Washington, DC, destroying the seat of the communist government, inciting a popular uprising, and bringing another version of America to the Pan-American Alliance. But because the centrepiece of Carter's campaign had been a promise to end the so-called wars for freedom that Davis and three Republican presidents before him had fought across a dozen versions of America, and scaling down support for SWIFT SWORD was the first step in making good on that promise, the Free Americans would now either have to fight their war on their own or return to their version of Cuba.

"We do not give up," Captain Lewis told Stone, bellowing over the roar of the Jeep's engine. He was a muscular young man with shaggy black hair and a dark, contemptuous gaze. "This is what we dream of for fifty years. You break your word, but we do not care. We fight anyway. We fight and we win."

Tom clapped Captain Lewis on the shoulder. "You believe the balls on this guy?"

"If you don't help us, we fight on our own," the Free American said. "What else can we do?"

They passed through a security check into a compound where Jeeps and powder-blue sedans with military plates were parked in front of a fieldstone farmhouse. A line of soldiers carried stacks of accordion files and sacks of shredded paper out of the farmhouse to feed fires burning in a row of oil drums. Ashy curls and flecks sifted out of the cold air like snow. Off to one side, a small black helicopter squatted beneath its drooping rotor blades.

Tom Waverly told Stone that the helicopter had brought in the Old Man about an hour ago.

"What's Knightly doing here?"

The Old Man, Dick Knightly, had been in charge of the Central Intelligence Group's Directorate of Special Operations ever since it had been set up in 1968. He'd lost his job two days ago, when President Carter had been sworn into office and his reorganisation of the CIG—the Company—had taken effect.

"He delivered four helicopters to Baines," Tom said. "Crop dusters rigged with rocket launchers and machine guns."

"Jesus, Tom. They could put him in jail for a stunt like that."

"He has paperwork showing they were donated by a wealthy patriot. Watch out for him," Tom said, as Stone climbed out of the Jeep. "He might try to feed you a line about how us old-school guys will need to stick together because bad times are coming down. Don't believe a word of it."

"I quit Special Ops, remember?"

"Yeah, and the Old Man got himself fired. But he still thinks he can call on his cowboy angels whenever he needs some help."

"What kind of help? What is he into?"

Tom shook his head. "I'm just giving you a little friendly advice, Adam. Don't try to take advantage."

"Why don't you come inside with me? This thing I have to do won't take long. Then we can talk—"

"I have some business of my own," Tom said, and gave Stone a sloppy salute. Before Stone could say anything, Captain Lewis popped the handbrake and the Jeep sped off with a slippery squeal of tires.

Stone pulled out his cell phone, called Bruce Ellis, and told him that he was worried that Tom was planning to do something spectacularly stupid. "He just rode away from Baines's HQ with one of the Free American officers."

"I don't have any jurisdiction inside the camp," Bruce said.

"You have security camera coverage. Can you keep track of him for me? I want to talk to him again as soon as I've finished with Baines."

General Baines's aide was waiting on the porch of the farmhouse, flanked by two soldiers. He insisted on patting Stone down for concealed weapons and asked him to open the briefcase.

"What's in the briefcase is for General Baines's eyes only," Stone said.

The aide stared at Stone and said with frosty disdain, "It is not necessary for me to see, because I know already what you bring."

"So how about letting me do my job," Stone said. "Or are we going to stand out here in the cold and keep your general waiting?"

With the soldiers at his back, he followed the aide into the farmhouse's front parlour. Blinds pulled down over the windows glowed with the last of the sunlight. Lamps dropped pools of light at a table where men talked in low voices over a tiling of maps, on a steel desk where a sergeant was typing with two fingers on an IBM Selectric. A grey cumulus of cigarette and cigar smoke drifted under the sagging horsehair plaster ceiling. The air was hot and oppressive, stale with the weary sense of failed intrigue.

General Wendell Baines was sitting in an armchair in a corner of the crowded room. A short, straight-backed man with a lined and deeply tanned face and crew-cut white hair, dressed in neatly pressed camouflage fatigues, he studied Stone and said at last, "I've seen you before, son."

"We met at a briefing at the State Department, sir. Two weeks ago."

Stone was sweating inside his overcoat, but he couldn't take it off because his briefcase was cuffed to his wrist.

"I remember now," Baines said. "You were with the incoming director of Central Intelligence, Admiral Turner. How do you like your new boss, by the way? Is he the right man for the job?"

"It's too early to say, sir."

"The impression I took away from our brief meeting is that he's the kind of unimaginative martinet more interested in the state of the cutlery in the canteen than in the morale of his men. Well, I suppose we must get this thing done. In the last week I have many meetings with members of your government and armed forces, and I talked on the telephone to your Admiral Turner this morning. He confirmed his government's position and told me to expect you. He told me what you would be carrying. Show me, please. Let us complete this formality."

Everyone in the room was watching them. The sergeant had stopped typing, and Stone's former boss, Dick Knightly, was standing in the doorway, lean and tough as whipcord in his trademark Harris tweed suit and yellow waistcoat. He looked straight at Stone, then inclined his head and whispered something to the muscular man who stood just behind him.

Stone unlocked the handcuffs, set the briefcase on a side table, worked its combination locks, and took out a thick cream envelope printed with the presidential seal. The aide intercepted the envelope and slit it open in a single fluid motion, extracted and unfolded the single sheet of paper, and with a click of his heels presented it to Baines.

The general glanced at it, then told Stone, "I have great respect for Floyd Davis. He is a man of vision and integrity. He sees an eternal chain of Americas connected to each other by your Turing gates, each freed of oppression, each spreading its democratic influence to other histories. This operation, which means everything to me and my men, was part of that vision. Your new president, I don't know him too well, but I see that he is at least a man of his word. He promised that he would withdraw tactical support for this thing of ours if he was elected, and this letter confirms it."

The men in the room gave a kind of murmuring sigh.

"He requests that we consider standing down the entire operation," General Baines said. He was speaking to everyone in the room, but his gaze was still locked on Stone's face. "He offers us repatriation. I say what I have been saying this past week. I say the hell with him. I say that we take orders from *our* president, not from this spineless upstart. And our president honoured me with the task of leading my men into war, not away from it."

Several officers began to clap. The general silenced them with a raised hand.

"Mr. Stone, you may tell your new director of Central Intelligence that we'll strike at twenty hundred hours, as already agreed. I will not betray the loyalty of my men; nor will I throw away this opportunity. Besides, I already have guerrillas in place. They are preparing to knock out much of the local air force and military, and they are under a radio blackout. I can't recall them."

From the door, Knightly said, "The gates will be opened on schedule, General. Carter doesn't have the guts to cancel the entire operation."

"Of course they'll be opened," General Baines said. "We are unwelcome guests, and it is the easiest way to be rid of us."

"I'll see that they'll remain open as long as possible," Knightly said.

"That's very good of you, Dick, and I hope you won't get into any trouble for it. But I do not intend to come back." General Baines looked at Stone and said, "I believe you have my answer. Go tell your boss."

*

Knightly's bodyguard intercepted Stone on his way out of the farmhouse and told him that Mr. Knightly wanted to have a word.

"Mr. Knightly and I have nothing to say to each other."

"He told me to tell you that it's about Tom Waverly." The bodyguard was stuffed into a black suit and had about six inches and a hundred pounds on Stone.

Stone pictured the Jeep carrying Tom and the Free American captain speeding down the hill toward the Turing gates, and said to the bodyguard, "What's your name?"

"Flynn. Albert Flynn."

"Are you with the Company, Albert?"

"No, sir. I resigned when they fired Mr. Knightly."

"So you work for Mr. Knightly now."

"Yes, sir. But if you're going to ask me what this is about, I don't know."

"Does Tom Waverly work for Mr. Knightly?"

"Not that I know of."

Albert Flynn had a pretty good poker face.

Stone thought for a moment, told Flynn that he would talk to Knightly once he'd made a couple of phone calls, and walked outside into the cold, floodlit compound.

He talked to Bruce Ellis first, then made an encrypted call to Bud Goodrich, the special assistant responsible for the disposal of SWIFT SWORD. He told Goodrich that the letter had been delivered, gave a summary of Baines's response, and said that the general was committed to the invasion.

"You can stand down," Goodrich said. "I'll expect a report on my desk oh nine hundred tomorrow, but there's no need to pad it."

"There's something else," Stone said. "Dick Knightly is here. He was with Baines when I delivered the letter, and I believe he brought four modified helicopters to help the Free American cause."

"I know. Some gung-ho cattle baron fronted the papers."

"Do you know what he's up to? Is he being watched?"

"He's showboating, making a political point about honouring promises. Don't worry about it, Stone. It's none of your business. Your work is done."

"Right," Stone said, although he knew that it wasn't.

Albert Flynn was waiting on the porch of the farmhouse. Stone walked up to him and said, "Take me to your leader."

Dick Knightly stood at the edge of a steep drop beyond the farmhouse, hands clasped at his back as he studied the army assembled in front of the Turing gates down in the valley. "I'm sorry to see you reduced to running errands for chair-warming bureaucrats like Bud Goodrich," he said. "You deserve better."

"With respect, sir, that's a cheap shot," Stone said.

"It's my honest opinion. I know you had a hard time of it on your last mission for Special Ops, and I don't blame you for opting for a nice easy job in the DCI's office. But frankly, son, you'd be better off in an insurance company. It's the same kind of work, and at least you'd get a gold clock at the end of it. Speaking of retirement, I hope you're not too attached to your new job. Stansfield Turner was a classmate of Carter's at Annapolis, and Carter put him in office for just one reason: to cut us off at the knees. Word is, he's going to open the Company's cupboards and ransack the family jewels. Clandestine operations, black ops, executive orders—they'll smear us with everything we had to do for the good of the Real and all the other Americas. And don't think that your new position is going to save your lily-white ass from a reckoning for your past sins. If he thinks it expedient, Turner will throw you to the wolves without a second thought."

"Is that a warning, sir?"

"It's sound advice," Knightly said, and extracted a cigar and a silver penknife from the breast pocket of his tweed jacket and sliced off the end of the cigar and plugged it into his mouth.

Down in the valley, one of the pair of giant Turing gates blinked on, its circular maw suddenly lit by the reflected light of the setting sun. The familiar deep hum of the gate filled the dark air and sharpened Stone's anxiety, but he knew it would do no good to ask straight out about Tom Waverly. Knightly would come to that in his own sweet time, or not at all. So Stone stepped on his impatience and waited quietly while his old boss returned the penknife to his pocket and took out a Second Infantry Zippo lighter and snapped it open and bathed the end of the cigar in its flame. The little finger and ring finger of Knightly's right hand were missing, lost to frostbite during the Battle of Moscow. Like many senior Company men, he was a veteran of the Russian Campaigns.

"I must have seen hundreds of gates open," Knightly said, "but it still makes my blood race."

"I thought this wasn't kicking off until twenty hundred."

"That's when the main force goes through. But the gates have been opening and closing all day, retrieving scouts and sending in advance parties."

A Jeep shot out of the bloodred mirror and swerved to a halt at the bottom of the ramp. On the other side of the gate, in an alternate version of America under communist rule, an observer would have seen the same vehicle vanishing into a shining circle of light hung in thin air. A moment later, the mirror vanished like a burst soap bubble and the deep, ground-shaking hum faded away as technicians returned the Turing gate to its resting state.

"The poor bastards," Knightly said. "They spent fifty years in exile, hoping all the while that the communist government would somehow collapse so that they could return home. And then we appeared out of nowhere and told them that we were willing to give them the chance to take the fight directly to the communists, that if things went wrong they could disappear back into our reality, regroup, and try again. Who could resist a deal like that? We were the answer to their prayers. So we brought them through the mirror, we armed and trained them, and we helped them gather intel and work up a credible Order of Battle. And then, just when they're fired up and ready to go, we turn around and kick 'em square in the ass."

He drew on his cigar, looking down at the army arrayed in the floodlit dusk.

"Baines is an exceptional soldier, but this isn't like George Washington and Valley Forge. He isn't trying to evict an overextended colonial power. He's going toe-to-toe with an entrenched government that exercises complete control over an entire nation. Even if he and his men manage to melt into the countryside and start up a guerrilla campaign, it isn't likely anything'll come of it."

"'If anything can happen in the multiverse, it will happen somewhere.'"

"No use quoting that at me, son. I may have invented that little *bon mot* to screw funding out of the Senate, but it doesn't mean I believe it. Oh, I don't deny it's possible that SWIFT SWORD will split history into a hundred separate sheaves, and Baines may defeat the commies in one or two of them. But mostly he won't. The bad outcomes will outnumber the good outcomes. The sum of human happiness will be diminished." Knightly blew a plume of smoke into the cold dark air. "Did you follow the election?"

"I know who won, sir."

"It was a true contest of thesis and antithesis. Davis is a visionary; Carter is an opportunist. Davis supports continued expansion, locating new Americas in need of aid and enlightenment, going to war to bring them the freedom they deserve, carrying the flame of freedom to every corner of the known multiverse. Carter wants an end to what he calls military adventurism, an end to exploration of anything but so-called wild sheaves. The difference is as clear as day and night, right and left, good and bad. Do you know who I supported?"

"I don't suppose it was Carter."

"The fact is, I think both of them are wrong. Carter is wrong about ending exploration, and Davis is wrong about using military force to expand our influence. War is a blunt tool, it's costly, and if it goes badly there are huge political costs. In short, as Davis has so recently discovered, no democratic government can maintain a permanent war state. The sad thing is, it should never have come to this. We didn't need to fight those wars. I've always argued that the best way to topple a government is by covert action. With just a few good men applying force at exactly the right place, you can do anything. And if you fail, no one has to know about it. It's how we started out, it's what the Company does best, it's what we should be doing right now. How about you, son? Do you still have fire in your belly? Are you still ready to lay down your life for your country?"

"If I didn't know better, sir, I'd think that you were trying to recruit me for some kind of covert op," Stone said.

Knightly looked straight at him, the same heavy-lidded stare that Stone had endured when he'd first reported for duty in the makeshift headquarters of the newly created Directorate of Special Operations, some fourteen years ago. Marsha Mason, the only woman in the first batch of Special Op field officers, had once said that it was like having your soul x-rayed.

"You always were the smart one, Adam. Not the most intelligent of my little band of cowboy angels, not by any means, but the most savvy. As a matter of fact, I *do* need your help, but not for any operation, covert or otherwise. No, I want you to go to the assistance of your friend Tom Waverly. He went through the mirror about half an hour ago with one of the advance units. . . . You don't seem surprised."

"I talked to Tom before I came up here. I was pretty sure that he'd try something like this, so I asked perimeter security to keep an eye on him."

"Ah yes, your old friend Colonel Ellis." Knightly smiled around his cigar. "It's a small world, isn't it? What would you say if I gave you the chance to go after Tom and bring him back?"

"Is that an order, sir?"

Stone was having a hard time hiding his relief. When Bruce Ellis had told him that Tom had gone through the mirror, he'd immediately decided to try to rescue him from the consequences of his stupid bravado, even if it meant chasing after him through the middle of a battlefield. He'd agreed to talk to Knightly only because he needed all the help he could get, and suspected that the Old Man wanted to save Tom for reasons of his own.

"You don't work for Special Ops anymore," Knightly said, "and neither do I. So how on God's good green Earth could I give you an order? What I *am* giving you is a chance to save the life of the man who once saved your life. You won't be able to go through until after Wendell Baines has led his troops into battle, but as long as Tom sticks with that advance unit I know exactly where you can find him. You can take Albert with you—he's a useful man in a tight spot—and I'll make sure that at least one of the gates is kept open until you return. How about it? Are you game?"

General Baines's speech to his troops was short and punchy. He quoted Shakespeare, the old chestnut about Saint Crispin's day from *Henry V*. He made much of the fact that Gettysburg was just a few miles down the road, and told his troops that they were lighting a flame of freedom that would drive communism's evil works from their native land.

Stone watched the general's performance on a monitor in an Airstream trailer that housed one of Bruce Ellis's surveillance teams. Bruce was talking on a telephone in a cubbyhole at the far end, jammed between the chemical toilet and a kitchen nook where a pot of coffee simmered on a hot plate. Half a dozen technicians in roller chairs hunched over keyboards and CCTV monitors. One of them had shown Stone footage of the advance platoon passing through one of the Turing gates. Captain Gene Lewis had been driving the lead Jeep. The man in the shotgun seat next to him had been wearing a fleece-trimmed leather jacket and a baseball cap pulled low over his face.

Baines got a big cheer at the end of his speech. A bugler in a cavalry hat blew the Charge; several hundred engines revved up, pumping plumes of black smoke into the floodlit air. For a long moment, nothing else happened. Then the floodlights around the apron dimmed, the air filled with a low rumble that the turning axis of the world might make, and the mirrors of the two Turing gates flicked on, giving back the dazzle of the headlights of the vehicles facing them.

Bruce Ellis handed Stone a mug of coffee. "I guess you still take it black."

"Have you found out how long the gates will stay open?"

"I still have a few people to call. Hang in there," Bruce said, and went back to his cubbyhole.

Stone sipped coffee and watched a rack of monitors that showed different views of two orderly lines of vehicles moving through the pair of gates. The coffee was pretty good, but it burned like acid in his jittery stomach and he couldn't finish it. Two by two, vehicles moved toward the silvery mirrors of the gates and were swallowed by their reflections. Only a couple of dozen trucks were left when Bruce came back down the narrow corridor between the techs and racks of monitors and electronics.

"I just got word that Knightly has been pulling strings back at Third Div headquarters. We're supposed to shut down the gates as soon as the last of Baines's men go through, but Knightly managed to get that changed. They'll stay open for another three hours. Will that be long enough?"

"I think so. If Tom isn't where he's supposed to be, I'm coming straight back."

"If you're going into combat, you need to get kitted out," Bruce said. "Let's start by losing that nice suit."

Stone stripped to his underwear and pulled on a set of khaki coveralls and a flak vest with ceramic plates front and back. He borrowed a pair of combat boots from one of the technicians; Bruce gave him an olive-green parka with wolf-fur lining, a Kevlar-lined resin composite helmet, a Browning Hi-Power pistol, and a .22 pocket auto in an ankle holster.

"As you once told me, always carry some kind of backup in Indian Territory," Bruce said. "It's small, but it fires high-velocity hollowpoints with plenty of stopping power."

"Thanks, Bruce. I owe you big time."

"That parka's a vintage item. If you get blood on it, don't bother coming back."

Stone carried a spare flak vest and helmet outside. Albert Flynn was leaning against the hood of the Jeep he'd requisitioned, smoking a cigarette. When Stone handed him the combat gear, he said, "You take the wheel, I'll tell you exactly where to go."

Stone said, "Do you have combat experience?"

"Five years in the Marines. I can handle myself."

"What rank?"

"Sergeant."

"Let me make it clear, Sergeant Flynn. I'm in charge. If you don't like that you can stay here."

"I don't like any of it," Flynn said. "But I have my orders, just like you."

"I'm not doing this because I was told to do it. I'm doing it because I want to help out an old friend."

"Did this guy really save your life?"

"Once upon a time, in a place far away from here."

Stone drove as fast as he could down the road into the valley and across the empty, floodlit apron of the staging area. He braked and shifted down as the Jeep climbed the broad ramp, and couldn't help holding his breath as the arch of the gate swept overhead like a scythe. There was the usual moment of blackness, as if every neuron in his brain had short-circuited, and then the Jeep thumped down on a steel-mesh trackway laid over mud.

They were on the other side of the mirror, in a version of America where the course of history had diverged from that of the Real more than fifty years ago.

Stone had passed through the mirror more times than he cared to remember. He was used to the idea of moving from one landscape to another in a single step. But he had never before driven straight into the middle of a war.

The gates had been opened in the middle of a collective farm. Their two silvery circles hung side by side with no visible means of support. The ground level here was a little higher than in the Real, and cut chords out of their bottom edges. A vast muddy field stretched away into darkness, rutted by vehicle tracks. The night seemed colder than in the Real, but perhaps that was just Stone's imagination. A cluster of buildings was burning on the ridge above the valley. The black sky strobed with huge red flashes. The crackle of small-arms fire sounded from several points in the middle distance.

As Stone drove past the empty low-loaders that had transported Dick Knightly's helicopters through the gates, Flynn reached under his seat and pulled out a radio with a whip aerial. He gave the call sign of Captain Lewis's platoon and asked for an update, repeating the question three times without getting a response, then clicking through channels until someone answered. After a brief conversation, he told Stone, "The guy I talked to is with the main column. They're under heavy fire just a few miles away, a little place called Catocin Furnace. No one has heard from Lewis's platoon."

"Let's hope it's still where it's supposed to be. Point me in the right direction, Sergeant Flynn."

"See that clump of trees?"

It was at the edge of the huge fields, silhouetted by a small fire.

"There should be a country road leads straight to a railroad," Flynn said. "Lewis's platoon was supposed to secure it."

A Jeep was burning beyond the clump of trees. It sat in the middle of the road, a chalice of yellow flame with dead men lying all around, some in camo gear, some in heavy woollen coats. As Stone drove past, a plane roared overhead and something screeched down and exploded on the ridge and lit up the whole valley. Stone crouched low as the Jeep was rocked by a solid thump of air and clods of hot earth rattled all around.

"I thought the guerrillas were supposed to have sabotaged the local airfields," he said. His ears were ringing and he felt as if he was speaking under half a mile of water.

"Looks like this thing is coming apart," Flynn said. "Maybe you could get this heap of junk moving. I feel kind of vulnerable sitting here."

Stone drove as fast as he dared down the dark road, headlights off. It climbed a small rise, dropped down, and there were lights up ahead, shimmering through a scrim of leafless trees, moving to and fro along the length of a train of cattle cars halted on a single-track railroad. Soldiers were hauling back the doors of the cars and yelling at men crowded inside, telling them to jump down, telling them they were liberated. A massive brute of a locomotive stood at the head of the train, clouds of steam leaking from the joints of its pistons, a big red star splashed across the riveted flank of its tender. A small group clustered below its cab. Soldiers, three men in bib overalls— Stone guessed that they must be the train crew—and a burly man in a fleece-trimmed leather jacket.

Stone told Flynn to stay frosty, and they both sat still and kept their hands in plain sight as Captain Lewis and three soldiers trotted toward the Jeep. Tom Waverly followed right behind them. He had lost his baseball cap and a bandage was wrapped around his head and spotted with blood over his right ear, but he was cheerful and animated, saying, "You're just in time, Adam. We're going to use this train to outflank the unfriendlies and punch right through their lines."

Captain Lewis pulled the Browning from Stone's holster, told him to put his hands on his head and step down. "What you think you doing here?"

"What were *you* thinking, Captain, letting Mr. Waverly ride along with you?"

On the other side of the Jeep, Flynn was telling the two soldiers patting him down to take it easy, he was on their side.

Captain Lewis said, "We are friends. He ask me for a favour, I should refuse him?"

"If you really are his friend, yes, you should."

Tom put his hand on Captain Lewis's shoulder and said, "Let me handle him, Gene."

"You will be responsible for him?"

"You bet."

"Then you are also responsible for Mr. Stone's friend. If Mr. Stone tries anything, his friend dies."

Albert Flynn said, "Wait a fucking minute. . . ."

Captain Lewis told Stone, "I move out in ten minutes no matter what. Do we understand each other?"

"I'm here to talk with my friend, Captain, not cause you any trouble."

Captain Lewis held Stone's gaze for a moment, then turned and walked back to the locomotive, following the soldiers who were escorting Flynn at gunpoint.

Tom said, "We're gonna ride this train all the way to Washington. It'll be a lot of fun."

"You won't get five miles." Stone's ears were still ringing. Nothing seemed quite real and he had a claustrophobic sense of time passing too quickly, of the narrowing window before the gates were shut down and he was trapped here for good.

Tom said, "We're going all the way, old buddy."

"You're going straight to hell if you don't come back with me."

"You came through the mirror because you wanted to, Adam, why don't you admit it? Admit that you miss the action."

"I came through to ask you to come back with me, Tom. This isn't our war, and you know it."

"Let me show you something," Tom said, and led Stone along the side of the train.

Soldiers were hauling men out of the cattle cars. They were manacled in pairs by wrist cuffs welded to short iron bars, or shackled in groups of four or five. Soldiers in the cars pushed them to the open door. Soldiers on the track reached up and grabbed their legs and pulled them down. Men fell and tried to get up and other men fell on top of them. The soldiers worked in a fever, hauling men from the recesses of the cars, screaming at them, pushing them out. A soldier kicked a man square in the crotch and he fell to the ground and the four men chained to him fell down too. Men fell out of the cars and lay in heaps. Only a few managed to get to their feet. Soldiers swore at them and tried to shove them out of the way, but they took only a few steps and stood still again, blinking stupidly.

Stone caught the arm of a soldier who was about to strike a skinny man with his rifle butt and pushed him away. "What are these men? Slaves?"

"Political prisoners. Remember the American Bund? This is worse," Tom said, and grabbed the shoulders of the man Stone had rescued, turning him around.

He wore a ragged shirt and filthy trousers that ended in tatters around his calves. He was barefoot and there were welted scars around his wrists and ankles. He stank horribly. His gaze flicked here and there, not resting on anything or anyone for more than a second. He looked as if he might bolt at any moment, if only he could figure out how to do it.

Tom plucked a penlight from the pocket of his leather jacket and shone it in the man's face. His teeth were black with decay and he had no tongue, just a stump that jumped like a frog at the back of his mouth.

"The commies cut out the tongues of political prisoners and lobotomise them or treat them with a chemical cosh to make them docile," Tom said. "Send them to work in factories, steel mills, mines, farms. They only last a year or two, but there are always more prisoners. This is what this is all about, Adam. This is what we're going to destroy."

He patted the man on the back and told him he could go, he was free, but the man just stood there, smiling a stupid ingratiating smile.

Stone said, "How about the slaves the Free Americans use on their farms and plantations in Cuba? Are you going to free them, too?"

Tom pulled a hip flask from the pocket of his leather jacket. "Know what we should have done here? Brought a nuke through, set it off in the middle of Washington. The commies don't have nukes. If we nuked Washington and told 'em New York or San Francisco was next, they'd cave in the very same day."

Stone shook his head when Tom offered him the flask. "Commit an atrocity to end an atrocity—it's no way to win a war."

"Look around you! Look at these poor fuckers! The whole fucking country is an atrocity!"

The two men were standing toe-to-toe in the near dark while soldiers hauled men out of the cattle cars. Shouts, the sound of rifle butts on flesh, on bone. Stone took a breath and put his hand on Tom's shoulder. "You want to do something useful? Come back with me. Tell me why the Old Man needs you."

Tom knocked Stone's hand away. "You don't have clue one, do you? Why I'm here, the Old Man made me the kind of offer you can't refuse."

"If you're in trouble, Tom, I swear I'll do my best to straighten it out."

"I'm better off here. Better to burn out, bro, than fade away."

They stared at each other for a few moments, Tom Waverly mulishly stubborn, Adam Stone angry and frustrated. Then gunfire started up somewhere beyond the head of the train, the snap of rifles, the heavy rattle of a machine gun. Rounds sparked off the boiler, sparked off spoked driving wheels. Tom ran toward the locomotive and Stone chased after him, into the roar of an incoming plane. Soldiers were returning fire. Stone saw Captain Lewis walk up to the three men in overalls who knelt on the ground, saw him shoot two in the head, one after the other, saw him haul the third to his feet and shove him toward the cab of the locomotive. Albert Flynn stood to one side of this, hands raised to his shoulders, two soldiers aiming their rifles at him.

The plane tore low overhead. Leafless trees threshed in its wake. It climbed and turned back and came in again. Captain Lewis's soldiers started up a ragged fusillade and the plane's guns flashed along the edge of its wings, tearing long furrows out of the embankment. Then it was gone again, making another turn out in the darkness.

Tom Waverly ran to a Jeep and lifted a fat cylinder from the back seat—the launch tube of an M-288 smart missile, totally forbidden to locals in any sheaf. No doubt it was another of Knightly's gifts. Tom flipped open the tube front and back and shouldered it, and Stone yanked the .22 from his ankle holster and shouted Tom's name.

Tom grinned at him. "That won't do much against a plane, but I appreciate the gesture."

"It's time to go home, Tom."

The plane was making a rising noise out in the dark as it swung back toward the train.

Stone cocked the .22. "Put that thing down, Tom. Come with me."

"Fuck you," Tom said and threw the launch tube at Stone and reached inside his jacket for his revolver.

Stone shot him in the right shoulder, ran forward as Tom dropped to his knees, and clipped him on the point of his chin and laid him out.

The plane made another roaring pass. Something slanted down with a piercing whistle and flame burst on the other side of the locomotive and a blast of hot air knocked Stone down. He took a little while to get to his feet. The locomotive was venting jets of steam from its broken boiler. Most of the cattle cars were on fire. A few soldiers and prisoners were stirring; many more lay still. Stone saw Albert Flynn stoop over a body and pick up a rifle, saw a soldier fire a burst that kicked dirt around the big man, saw him spin around and fall down.

Stone got his hands under Tom's shoulders and hauled him into the back seat of the Jeep. Soldiers were staggering out of the steam and smoke. One of them was Captain Gene Lewis.

The young officer was covered in dirt and soot and he was bleeding from his nose and ears, but he was aiming his pistol straight at Stone. He screamed something lost in the howl of venting steam and the ringing in Stone's ears, and fired. The shot crazed the Jeep's windshield and Stone snatched Tom's knife from his shoulder rig and threw it in a flat arc. Captain Lewis took a step, his hand reaching for the handle of the knife that protruded from his breastbone, and then his gaze lost focus and he collapsed.

Stone swung behind the wheel and gunned the Jeep and pulled a U-turn, scattering soldiers. Something big was on fire a mile away and heavy artillery was lighting the horizon beyond it, making thunder under the black sky. Stone swerved past the burning Jeep and rattled over a smashed fence. One of the Turing gates was still open, a circle of beautiful silver light shining at the end of the trackway like a tethered moon. Stone accelerated, saw a smoking crater that bisected the trackway, swerved to avoid it, and got bogged down in mud. He gathered Tom's dead weight into his arms and slogged around the crater and walked into the glow of the gate.

Black lightning flared inside his skull, and then he was walking down a broad, floodlit ramp. Dick Knightly was waiting at the bottom, in front of the open doors of an army ambulance. Stone staggered past his old boss and allowed two medics to take Tom from him. When he turned, Knightly was right behind him, asking a question. He had to say it three times to make himself understood; Stone's ears were still ringing.

"Where's my man? Where's Albert?"

"Sergeant Flynn is dead. One of Captain Lewis's soldiers shot him. If you want his body, you'll have to go get it yourself," Stone said, and brushed past Knightly and walked away across the empty stage of the apron.

Behind him, the mirror of the Turing gate winked out.

# Part One

# WORLD WAR THREE BLUES

# 1.

When the Company came for him, Adam Stone was tilling the narrow half acre where corn had been harvested a few weeks ago. Barechested in faded blue jeans and a frayed straw hat, steering the yoke of a scratch plough behind a plodding mule, he heard a rattling roar heading toward him and saw a Jeep speeding along the ridge beyond the patchwork of small fields. It was an old Willy M-38, its air-cooled radial engine loud as a low-flying aircraft on a strafing run as it dragged a long tail of dust down the rough track everyone here called Broadway because it ran more or less where Broadway ran in the Real, the real Manhattan, the real America, heading toward the stand of shade trees and the farm's whitewashed log cabin.

As Stone unhitched the mule and turned it loose to graze, Petey scrambled over the rough stone wall at the far end of the field. A sturdy straw-haired little boy in dungarees, he ran pell-mell across the litter of unploughed corn stalks, shouting breathlessly that a soldier had come visiting.

"I saw him."

Stone lifted Petey up and set him on his shoulders and started toward the cabin. The boy locked his legs around Stone's neck and planted his hands on the crown of Stone's hat. "He came all the way from the gate."

"I bet he did."

"He came to see you. Can I ride in his wagon?"

"I believe it's called a Jeep."

"Can I ride in his Jeep?"

"You'll have to ask your mother." Stone raised Petey over his head and set him on top of the wall. "And you'd better be quick about it. After I've had a word with him, I'm pretty sure he'll be going straight back to where he came from."

The Jeep was parked a little way beyond the red barn, close to the manure heap where pumpkins swelled among a sprawling tangle of leaves and vines. The olive-green paint job and the white star painted on the hood didn't fool Stone, and he felt something kink in his stomach when he saw the man in army uniform sitting with Susan at the picnic table by the cabin's back door. It was David Welch, one of the original cowboy angels.

Stone put on a shirt and walked Welch toward the marshy shore. He didn't want to talk Company business around Susan and Petey.

"This is a nice place," Welch said. "I should have stopped by sooner."

"I'm kind of glad you didn't."

"A nice kid, too. How old?"

"He just turned six."

"Mmm. You moved here two years ago, I believe. Right after you quit the Company."

"You're wondering about his father," Stone said. "Jake died this February. A hunting accident."

Stone's friend and business partner, out shooting duck in the salt marshes on the east side of the island, had fallen through a thin spot in the ice and broken his leg at the thigh. He'd lost his shotgun and cell phone, too, couldn't call for help, couldn't get back to his boat. Susan had rallied the neighbours and organized a search party after she had realised that her husband was overdue, but wolves had found him first. He'd killed two with his knife before the rest killed him.

"Tough for the kid, losing his father at such a young age," Welch said.

"Yeah."

"So how do you fit into this?"

"I first met Jake when he was in the army, back in the American Bund sheaf. He invited me to become a partner in his hunting business when I moved here. Right now, Susan and I are trying to keep that going, and I'm helping out with chores around the place, too."

Welch glanced sideways at Stone. "Does your pretty young widow know about your colourful past, Adam? Have you been telling her tall stories to while away the evenings?"

Stone's unease abruptly deepened. "She doesn't even know I used to work for the Company. I was under military cover back when I first met her husband."

"You were a major in one of the aid-supply companies, according to your file. Winning hearts and minds with crackers and cheese. Are you maintaining that cover here?"

"What is this, David, a security check? Even if the people here knew I worked for the Company, which they don't, I don't have any secrets worth keeping. Not after the Church Committee got through with me."

They came out of the trees and the sun was in their faces. It was one of those perfect fall days, the sun golden in a cloudless sky, a fresh breeze from the Hudson walking through the treetops, when everything seemed lifted clean out of its ordinary self into some purer realm.

Welch shaded his eyes and looked around at the vista of grassy marshland and river and blue sky. He was a tall, stoop-shouldered man with a clever face and a glib manner. His khaki jacket and pants were crisply pressed and his combat boots were brand new. The knot of his tie was precisely centred over the top button of his green shirt. He took a deep breath and said, "This air is something else. You can feel it doing good all the way down to the bottom of your lungs. How many people live here?"

"Around a hundred fifty here on the island, maybe twenty thousand along the whole of the East Coast, mostly veterans and winners of the settler lotteries. There's the usual oil business in Texas and Oklahoma and Alaska, the usual exploitation of gold, silver, copper, and uranium reserves, but otherwise it's pretty much pristine. There used to be a maximum-security prison near First Foot, but Carter closed it down, and we've managed to keep out resorts and industrial ranches, and rich megalomaniacs who want to carve out personal empires."

"I believe you scouted it back in '67. Your first time through the mirror."

"Me and a couple of squads of gung-ho Army Rangers. Did you come all this way to talk about the good old days, David?"

Like Stone, David Welch had been one of the first Special Operations field officers. One of Dick Knightly's cowboy angels. He'd served a hitch in the 82nd Airborne before joining the Company, but preferred administration to action in the field. He'd been washing dirty money in the Directorate of Financial Management when Knightly had recruited him, and after five years with Special Ops had moved sideways into the Directorate of Diplomatic Support, hadn't been touched when the Church Committee's exhaustive investigation uncovered evidence of the Company's clandestine operations, unauthorised assassinations, mind-control experiments, and all the other dirty little secrets.

He lifted a pack of Dunhills from the breast pocket of his fatigues and shook out a cigarette and lit it with a slim gold lighter, bending to the transparent flame, exhaling smoke. "We're, what? Somewhere in Greenwich Village, if this was the Real?"

"A little lower than that—around North Church Street, under the footprint of the Pan-American Trade Center. The farmhouse is about where St. Paul's Chapel would be."

"That little church they have in the big plaza? I guess the shoreline has been extended into the river in the Real. Is that your boat I see down there?"

The fourteen-foot clinker-built dinghy was tied up to a short jetty at the end of a long channel cut through the reed beds. Stone had put it together his first summer here, between spells working on the Long Island Railroad.

He said, "It's for hire if you want to go fishing."

"I just might take you up on that sometime. I bet the fishing is fantastic."

"You name it, we have it. Striped bass, trout, shad, all kinds of coarse fish. I caught a sturgeon a couple of weeks ago. A hundred forty pounds."

"You're kidding."

"We have lobsters that run to six feet. Plenty of oysters too, and cod and herring and mackerel out in the harbour."

"Yeah? How about the hunting?"

"There are white-tailed deer and woodland caribou and mule deer. Wolves and black bears, and short-faced bears too—those are as big as grizzlies. A few panthers."

"Pretty good hunting for Manhattan."

"We call the island New Amsterdam here," Stone said. He was trying to picture David Welch in a camo jacket and hunter's peaked cap, following a trail through the deep woods with a Winchester .3030 slung on his shoulder. It wasn't easy. "If you want to hunt something exotic, a mastodon or a ground sloth, you'll have to go inland. In fact, I'm due to take a party over there in a few days. You're lucky you found me."

"Is that how you've been supporting yourself, Adam? Playing the great white hunter to jaded businessmen who want to bag an extinct animal for their den? When you're not playing at being a farmhand, that is."

"I don't ask anything of Susan but bed and board."

"I bet."

Stone let that go.

Welch blew a riffle of smoke from his finely figured nostrils. "You know, I never figured you for the backwoodsman type."

"We have electricity—solar and wind power. We have antibiotics, cell phones, computers. . . ."

"And you plough fields with a mule. Like something in one of those old paintings."

"That's how we choose to farm here. The idea is to sit lightly on the land."

"A painting with a mythic tone. Something by Homer Winslow or

Thomas Hart Benton, celebrating the foolish notion of frontier utopianism. Man and beast taming the great American wilderness. You look good on it, at any rate. A nice colour, too. Like a Red Indian."

Welch had the even tan of someone who had put in a lot of time by a country club pool.

Stone said, "Farmwork will do that for you."

"You haven't let yourself go. You look ready for action," Welch said, and took an envelope from inside his uniform jacket and offered it to Stone, his half-smoked cigarette dangling from the corner of his smile.

"I'm retired, David."

Stone had the sudden feeling that something very big and completely unstoppable was rushing toward him at a thousand miles an hour.

"All you have to do is look at this, give me your opinion."

"It better not be a subpoena."

"Just take a look."

There were five photographs inside, two in black and white and three in colour, all different sizes, all of the same woman. In each photograph she had a different hairstyle and wore different clothes, and in each one she was dead. In three she had been shot in the head; in the fourth she had been garrotted; in the fifth she didn't have a mark on her but she was dead all the same, sprawled on a tile floor, dry eyes staring into infinity.

Welch said, "He's killed her six times. Six times that we know about, anyway. I thought I'd spare you the one where he got her with a car bomb."

"These are all doppels of the same woman?"

Doppels were doppelgängers—alternate versions of the same person, living different lives in different sheaves, different alternate histories. It had been a long time since Stone had used the word.

Welch nodded. "Name of Eileen Barrie."

"You said 'he.' These six doppels were all murdered by the same guy?"

"We think so."

"You think he used to work for the Company, too. For Special Ops."

"It's good to see that farmwork hasn't softened your brain."

"It's an easy reach. He can travel between sheaves. He knows how to hit a target cleanly. He knows how to get in and how to get out. You've been trying to catch him for a while, and you've come up dry—you have to be desperate or you wouldn't have come here. When did he start?"

"The first one was killed just two weeks ago. He killed three more before someone finally worked out what was going on."

"But you're protecting her now. The Real version and the surviving doppels, I mean."

"I don't know the full extent of this operation, but I do know that he managed to make two hits after we started taking measures."

"You're watching the gates, you're watching the doppels, and he's still taking them out. It must be frustrating."

"Thousands of soldiers and ancillary personnel move through the gates every day. Not to mention relief and reconstruction supplies, diplomatic parties, trade parties, businessmen, journalists, all those humanitarian workers Carter is so fond of. . . . The whole system would grind to a halt if we had to check everyone on every train."

Stone shuffled through the photographs. He was beginning to be interested. He was wondering where this was leading. "This guy is moving between sheaves, he made his last two hits while the targets were under protection, he used to work for the Company. Does he have inside help?"

"Not that we know of." Welch dropped his cigarette butt and stepped on it. "Let's cut to the chase. After he killed the last one, he got clean away from the scene, but he didn't get out of the sheaf. The locals locked down their version of Brookhaven interchange within thirty minutes, and at the moment it's the only way in and out. The other gate in the sheaf, at San Diego, was blown up a couple of weeks ago by a suicide bomber driving a truck stuffed with ammonium nitrate and diesel fuel. We know he didn't get out, Adam. We know he's still there. I've been sent to ask you to help find him."

"He's someone I know, isn't he?"

"It's Tom Waverly."

Stone felt as if someone had sapped him. "No way. Tom's MIA, presumed dead."

Tom Waverly had resigned from the Company directly after the SWIFT SWORD debacle. When he'd recovered from his gunshot wound, he'd joined a private security company and gone to work in the American Bund sheaf. He'd disappeared two months later, and an obscure insurgent group had released video footage of him, claiming to have kidnapped and executed him.

Welch pulled a photograph from inside his jacket and handed it to Stone. "They got that off a surveillance camera in the Brookhaven interchange after he killed her the fourth time."

"It's pretty grainy."

But the man in army uniform, cap pulled low over his face as he walked past a crowd of aid workers, looked a lot like Stone's old friend and comrade-in-arms.

Welch said, "PHOTINT had to blow it up and enhance it to hell and back, but it hit twenty-one of the twenty-eight points of the face-recognition system. And crime-scene techs lifted a partial thumbprint from a fragment of the car bomb's trigger mechanism, and also found his prints at the scene where he'd garrotted her. It's Tom, all right."

"And you think, what? He was captured and brainwashed? He allowed himself to be turned? Come on."

"We don't know what happened to him in the past three years, or why he's surfaced now. We also don't know why he's killing Eileen Barrie's doppels, but there it is."

"It could be a doppel of Tom that someone's using to smoke the trail."

"Tom's an orphan with no known mother or father, just like you and me and all the other cowboy angels. Who'd know where to find one of his doppels?"

"It would be hard, but not impossible," Stone said, remembering something that Tom Waverly had once told him.

"It's easier to believe he was turned or that he's working on some unsanctioned action of his own," Welch said. "He always did have a wild streak."

"Who is Eileen Barrie? Does she work for the Company?"

"In the Real she's a mathematician. And so are her doppels."

"Every one of her? That's pretty stable."

"There are a couple of sheaves where she doesn't exist, or where she died young. But in every other sheaf she's a mathematician, usually working on some aspect of quantum theory. She's more stable than Elvis."

"Is she working on something important? Something someone might not want her to work on?"

"Forget the woman, Adam. We want to find Tom and bring him in, safe and well. We think you can help us."

Stone let that *we* go for the moment. He said, "Why me? Nathan Tate worked with Tom on more operations that I did. Jimmy McMahon worked alongside Tom and me in the American Bund sheaf—"

"Jimmy McMahon retired last year after he suffered a heart attack and had a triple bypass. And Nathan Tate *was* working the case, until yesterday evening. The Cluster used a travelling-salesman program to work out which doppels of Eileen Barrie were most likely to be targeted next. Nathan was working protection for one of the candidates. She was living in New York, the Johnson sheaf. Tom planted an incendiary device in her house. It started a fire that drove everyone outside, and Tom shot and killed Eileen Barrie and Nathan Tate with a .308 rifle from about two hundred yards."

"Tom killed Nathan?"

Welch nodded. "Yesterday evening, New York City, the Johnson sheaf. Like I said, there's only one functional gate, and we have it locked up. But there's a complication. In addition to Eileen Barrie and Nathan Tate, Tom also killed a cop who happened to be the nephew of the mayor of New York. The local police have been authorised to use terminal force against him. I want you to come back with me. I want you to help us find him. If the locals get to him before we do, they'll shoot him down like a dog."

"Who sent you? Was it Knightly?"

"Not hardly. The Old Man is still wearing a diaper and drooling out of one side of his mouth. He hasn't even learnt how to talk again."

After the Church Committee had presented its findings to a closed session of Senate, Dick Knightly had been tried on charges of conspiracy to conceal the involvement of Special Operations in clandestine activity against governments in other sheaves. He'd suffered a massive stroke after he'd been sentenced, and was serving a twenty-year term in the hospital ward of a minimum security facility in the Florida Everglades.

"Why I'm here," Welch said, "I happen to be working for the Directorate of Diplomatic Support in the sheaf where Tom made his last hit, where he's locked in right now. The guy in charge of the investigation, Ralph Kohler, asked me to reach out to you because one of his men found a note at the scene."

"Tom left a note?"

"Carved in the bark of the tree he used as a sniper's position: *I'll talk to Stone.*"

"That's it? You came all the way out here because someone who may or may not be Tom Waverly carved my name on a tree?"

"I came here because Tom Waverly wants to talk to you, Adam. I know you and Tom had a bad falling-out over SWIFT SWORD, but I also know that he saved your life, once upon a time. Are you willing to try to save his?"

Susan said, "After I sent Petey to find you, I asked Colonel Welch point blank why he was here, but the slippery son of a gun wouldn't give a straight answer."

Stone said, "It's how he is. Don't take it personally."

"One minute you're ploughing, the next you're packing. So forgive me for being kind of curious."

Susan, slender and tousled in jeans and one of her dead husband's shirts, its tails tied in a knot above her navel, had just climbed the ladder into Stone's temporary living quarters in the barn's hayloft. There was a single bed and a kitchen chair and a raw pine chest, and an unglazed window that looked out across treetops toward the broad sweep of the Hudson and the Jersey shore. It was warm under the slanting ribs of the rough-hewn roof beams and smelled pleasantly of the straw stacked below. Stone had washed up and put on his Sunday chinos and his best checked shirt. He'd been packing, folding T-shirts into neat squares, when Susan had climbed into the loft. Now he smiled at her and said, "Are you mad at me?"

"I understand why you couldn't talk about this in front of your friend. And I'll try to understand if you can't tell me everything, but how about a hint or two?"

"It really isn't anything. They want me to help find someone."

"Someone . . . ?"

"An old friend who's gotten himself into a little trouble. I want to help him, if I can. Not because I want to help David Welch."

Stone felt bad because he couldn't tell Susan about the woman who had been murdered six different ways, about Nathan Tate and the policeman who'd been the nephew of the mayor of New York, about the manhunt. Less than an hour after David Welch had turned up, he was back inside the old world of evasion and half-truths, legends and lies.

"And you're going, just like that," Susan said. "He must be a very good friend."

"Actually, I'm not sure if we're still friends. The last time we saw each other, we had a falling-out."

"Over some *femme fatale*, I hope."

"As a matter of fact, it was over foreign policy."

"Not quite as romantic."

"Sorry to disappoint. But we *were* good friends once upon a time, and I sort of owe him a favour."

"Is it going to be dangerous?"

"He wants to talk to me. That's all I'm going to do."

"This is what Welch told you?"

"Your Mr. Welch is definitely a slippery son of a gun, but I think he told me the truth, as far as it goes."

Susan pushed a strand of hair behind her ear. She'd cut it short at the beginning of summer, and now the dirty-blonde curls cascaded around her shoulders. "I've never asked about what you were doing when you met Jake, Adam, and I'm not going to start now. But I can't help worrying that this is a lot more dangerous than making sure aid packages get to the right place, or whatever it was you did back then."

"This friend of mine wants to talk to me. That's all it is."

A silence stretched between them, heavy with evasions and things unspoken, while Stone swiftly packed folded clothes, a wash-bag, and his Colt .45 automatic and shoulder rig inside his kitbag. As he was stuffing socks into nooks and crannies, Blackie, the farm's Border collie, started to bark out in the yard. A few moments later, Stone heard the roar of the Jeep's engine. David Welch was back from taking Petey for a ride.

Susan said, "How long is this going to take?"

"I don't know. A couple of days if I'm lucky."

"Mr. Wallace and his son are due Saturday."

"They want to bag a sabre-toothed cat. I haven't forgotten, and I promise I'll be back in time."

Susan narrowed her eyes, put her hands on her hips, and said in a playful, mock-tough voice, "You'd better be back, mister, or I'm going to have to find myself another partner."

"I'll come back as soon as I can."

"Take care of yourself around that slippery Colonel Welch."

"You bet."

Petey was making a lot of noise below, calling to Susan, telling her that the Jeep had gone as fast as anything.

Susan told her son that she'd be right down, and smiled at Stone. "I guess we can manage without you for a little while."

Stone smiled back. "I know you can."

David Welch pretended not to watch when Susan hugged Stone and told him again to take care. Stone slung his kitbag into the back of the Jeep and climbed into the shotgun seat beside Welch, and the Jeep drove off down Broadway, laying white dust over the goldenrod and tall grasses that grew on either side.

Stone didn't look back. He believed that it would be bad luck if he did.

# 2.

Astreamlined, aluminium-skinned railcar coupled to a flatbed wagon was waiting in the little station on the far side of the East River ferry crossing. Stone helped David Welch lash the Jeep to the wagon, and the railcar rattled along the ninety-odd miles of single-track railroad that cut through the woods and bogs of Brooklyn and Long Island, past the settlements of Jamaica Bay, Rockville, Wantagh, Bay Shore, and New Patchogue, to First Foot and the Turing gate. Stone had plenty of time to work through the file Welch had given him. He ate the packed lunch Susan had provided—home-baked biscuits, home-cured ham and pickles, hard-boiled eggs, and an apple, one of the season's first—read reports by field officers and local police, and studied photographs and forensic documentation. He wanted to have all the facts at his fingertips. If he was going to talk to Tom Waverly, he wanted to know everything the man had done.

The first four assassinations had been staged to look like street robberies or home invasions gone bad. Eileen Barrie had been killed by shots to the head from a small-calibre handgun, by a knife-thrust to the heart, by garrotting: murders that were up close and personal. Then, after someone in the Company had put two and two together and every surviving version of Eileen Barrie had been given protection, the subsequent murders had been textbook examples of executive actions. The car bomb that had killed her outright but had left the officer sitting next to her unharmed except for superficial burns and burst eardrums. And the latest killing which, with its combination of careful planning, patience, and split-second action, had Tom Waverly's fingerprints all over it.

When he'd been working for the Company, Tom had specialised in assassination. He'd once hiked through a forest and set up a position in a tree and for three days had focused on the window of a house, waiting for his target to show for just a second. One summer day in Florida, he'd lain all afternoon on the flat roof of an office building, still as a basking snake under the ghillie blanket that had hidden him from police helicopters while he'd watched the front of the Miami-Dade County Courthouse, killing his target with a single shot as a phalanx of bodyguards had hustled the man across the sidewalk toward his limo. Stone wondered if Tom had turned freelance and was killing Eileen Barrie's doppels to order, or if he was working off some kind of massive personal grudge. But although the file contained comprehensive summaries of the circumstances and methodology of each murder, there was nothing, not so much as a single speculative sentence, about possible motivations for attempting to eliminate Eileen Barrie from every known sheaf.

The railcar sounded its horn. Stone glanced out of the window and saw a familiar cluster of wind generators standing proud on a low hill, their sixty-foot triple-bladed props lazily revolving. He glimpsed the roofs of the little town of First Foot through a scrim of pine trees. The railcar rattled past the station's single platform, entered the long loop that led to the Turing gate, and began to pick up speed: trains always ran through gates as fast as possible, to minimise the power expenditure needed to keep them open. Two white horses in a field briefly chased after it, heads down, manes rippling, and it left them behind and sped past a coal-black locomotive with a flared chimney and cowcatcher that stood on a spur, rushed down a steep grade in a cutting, and plunged into the tunnel at the far end.

Although Stone braced for it, the black flash that pounded in his head, the knockout punch of collapsing probability functions, was every bit as bad as he remembered. Then the railcar emerged into daylight, drawing away from a row of two dozen artificial mounds, each mound turfed over and pierced with a short tunnel, each tunnel the entrance to a Turing gate, each gate a portal to a different sheaf, a different alternate history.

There were bigger interchanges at Chicago, San Diego, and White Sands, but the Brookhaven interchange was the oldest. It was where the Many Worlds theory had been experimentally validated when the first Turing gate, a mere hundred nanometers across, had been forced open in the high-energy physics laboratory in 1963, where the first man to travel to another sheaf had taken his momentous step in 1966, and where the first cloned gate had been produced in 1969.

Cloning gates using symmetry-breaking technology based on the Feynman-Schwinger-Dyson $n$-manifold manipulation was the only way of providing multiple points of entry into any sheaf. The physicists and mathematicians who had developed the first Turing gates had quickly discovered that each time a gate accessed a new sheaf, a stochastic energy-horizon phenomenon created a unique quantum state or signature that no other gate could ever reproduce. This so-called quantum censorship principle meant that only one gate could link the Real with a particular sheaf, and that link would be lost forever if the gate was shut down. Although it was theoretically possible to produce secondary links via an intermediate sheaf—to travel from the Real to the First Foot sheaf via the Nixon sheaf, for instance—it was impossible in practice, because locating a particular sheaf in a multiverse of possible sheaves was, as Murray Gell-Mann, one of the leaders of the original Brookhaven Project, had put it, like finding a needle in a haystack the size of the universe. Before cloning technology had been developed, there had been only a single, fragile link between the Real and any other sheaf. Afterward, primary gates were locked away in a facility more secure than Fort Knox, cloned copies were deployed in large interchanges and clandestine facilities, colonies were established in a dozen wild sheafs, and the Real was able to take control of the destiny of other, less fortunate Americas and establish the Pan-American Alliance.

There were more than a hundred cloned gates in the Brookhaven interchange, linking twenty-two different sheaves to the Real. Stone saw a long freight train drawing out of a grassy mound like a chain of scarves from a magician's sleeve, and saw other trains waiting in sidings or on loop roads or loading bays of the marshalling yard. Strings of passenger cars and strings of freight cars, well wagons loaded with shrouded tanks and helicopters and APCs, reefers, grain hoppers, tank cars.

AH-6 "Little Bird" helicopters, quick and manoeuvrable as humming birds and armed with rockets and .50-calibre machine guns, swooped and hovered overhead, checking each arriving train. More than three years after President Carter had put an end to empire building and declared that the business of the Pan-American Alliance was not war but reconciliation and reconstruction, the Real was still vulnerable to terrorist attacks by misguided patriots and militias and fanatics loyal to former regimes in client sheaves.

The railcar rocked over a gleaming web of rails under signal catenaries, gaining speed as it headed toward a tunnel set in the grassy mound covering another gate. Again the sudden plunge, the sharp judder, the momentary black headache, and then the railcar was slowing under a sky sheeted with low clouds, sliding into a station under a geodesic dome of grimy white Teflon.

The air under the dome was hot and wet, and tasted of diesel smoke. Crowds moved everywhere beneath banners hung from scaffold towers.

*BROOKHAVEN: GATEWAY FOR RECONSTRUCTION AND*
*RECONCILIATION.*
*DEMOCRACY AND SOVEREIGNTY FOR ALL AMERICANS.*
*ONE NATION UNDER MANY SKIES.*

Soldiers in all kinds of uniforms (Stone wondered if most were recruits from post-nuclear-war sheaves, as in the old days) were outnumbered by gaggles of fresh-faced Reconstruction and Reconciliation Corps volunteers in jeans and *Planning for Peace* T-shirts. A team of wisecracking construction engineers sat on their tool boxes, watching the human parade. A column of troops in black coveralls and what looked like silver motorcycle helmets marched past at double time. Soldiers and civilians milled around kiosks where girls in Stars-and-Stripes T-shirts were handing out free cigarettes and coffee and sandwiches. As he followed Welch toward a turnstile checkpoint tucked under the dome's white curved flank, Stone thought that the noise under the dome was like the cackling of the sky-blotting flocks of geese that flew down the Hudson ahead of the first winter blizzards.

At the checkpoint's steel and glass booth, Welch pushed the sheaf of travel order papers into a slot. The marine inside the booth checked the papers and returned them through the slot with two square white plastic badges—dosimeters. A light overhead turned from red to green, the turnstile unlocked with a heavy clunk, and Stone and Welch walked out into grey light, warm gritty air, and the smell of recent rain. Aid workers were climbing into a long line of yellow school buses. In the distance, the superstructures of troop ships and cargo ships rose above cranes and warehouses.

A black stretch Cadillac equipped with smoked bulletproof glass and antimine flooring drove them down the Long Island Expressway toward Manhattan. Welch handed one of the dosimeters to Stone. "We've done a lot of rebuilding, but we can't do much about the radiation."

"What happened here?"

The file hadn't given Stone much information about the Johnson sheaf's precontact history.

"They had themselves a Second World War in the middle of the century," Welch said. "The US, Britain, and Soviet Russia defeated Nazi Germany and Japan; then a cold war developed between the free world and the Soviets. In 1962, the Soviets stationed missiles in Cuba, which was part of the communist bloc. After a standoff, their premier, a fellow by the name of Khrushchev, agreed to withdraw the missiles, but a bunch of high-ranking military officers assassinated him and staged a coup. The Soviet navy tried to break a shipping blockade around Cuba and the president, one of the Kennedys, responded by sinking several of their ships and threatening to invade. The Soviets took out Guantánamo Bay and Miami with tactical nukes, and it stepped up from there." Welch was examining the cut-glass decanters in the little drinks cabinet. "We have generic whiskey, generic brandy, generic gin, but no ice, and no mixers. I guess we'll have to rough it."

"Nothing for me."

"It helps sluice the radiation out of you," Welch said, and slopped an inch of amber whiskey into a tumbler.

"I guess New York got hit," Stone said.

"Plenty of places got hit. The Soviets threw everything they could from Cuba before the US nuked it down to bedrock. Short-range missiles took out most of Florida, New Orleans, and Atlanta; sub-launched missiles hit Washington, DC, and most of the West Coast. And a fair number of long-range bombers got through a defensive line above the Arctic Circle, too. They hit Detroit and Chicago, they hit Boston, and two of them hit New York. One dropped its load on the Brooklyn Naval Yard, but the bomb didn't go off. The second was shot up by a fighter plane, blew itself up over the Hudson, and took out most of downtown. The bomb it was carrying wasn't big, twelve kilotons or so, but it was dirty, jacketed with iodine-125 and cobalt-60. And that's why we're wearing dosimeters more than twenty years later."

The limo overtook a column of army trucks. It sped past a gang of shaven-headed men in orange coveralls lengthening a trench alongside the Expressway under the watchful gaze of soldiers with assault rifles.

Stone said, "It looks like they're still at war here."

"A little local difficulty with the European Economic Community, and Australia and Japan. The Soviets came off worst in WW3. A good deal of Russia is still uninhabitable, and the rest is a bunch of outlaw states run by criminals and warlords. But America is in pretty bad shape too. The Europeans and Japanese provided aid, but it came with all kinds of strings, and we arrived in the middle of a resurgence of isolationist politics and some serious sabre-rattling on both sides. The locals were as grateful as hell to get help from fellow Americans, but the Europeans took serious exception, especially when we set up trade barriers and seized their assets in the States. Right now, we're fighting a nasty little war for control of Texas and the Gulf. Canada's staying out of it, and so is China—we're feeding China a little technology in exchange for neutrality—but despite our best diplomatic efforts, the Europeans aren't backing down. There's some internal opposition against us, too. Secessionists in the South, Midwest survivalists. . . . In short, the usual set of grudges." Welch took a sip of whiskey, made a face, and said, "I guess I should tell you about rules of procedure. The guy in charge of our side of the investigation, Ralph Kohler, told me to make sure you got anything you want. I assume you have no problem with that. As for the locals, we had to inform Ed Lar, the local FBI officer in charge of the manhunt, that you were being brought in. These days, protocol demands full and frank cooperation with the locals."

"He knows I'm the guy Tom Waverly wants to talk to."

Welch nodded.

"Does he know that I'm working for the Company?"

"A lot of things have changed since you quit, but we still maintain cover for all operatives. We told Mr. Lar that you're a forensic psychologist employed by our FBI, and you and Tom have history from working together on serious crimes in the Real. I doubt that Ed Lar believes it for a second, but he can't question it publicly without causing a diplomatic incident."

"We have to pretend to be something we're not, and the locals have to pretend that they don't know we're pretending."

"It's a wicked old world."

"Do I need to talk to Ralph Kohler? Or to this local guy, Ed Lar?"

Welch shook his head. "Ralph's an attorney, a political guy. He's done a lot of good work toward preventing this thing from turning into a full-blown diplomatic crisis, but he'd be the first to admit that he doesn't know anything about pounding the bricks. As for Mr. Lar, we promised to keep him informed about the progress of your investigation, and to share any hot leads."

"And has he promised not to interfere?"

"Not in so many words. But we made it clear that you're an independent operator, and in any case he's already badly overstretched by the manhunt. The locals are eager to catch Tom before we do. It's not just the political fallout because Tom shot the mayor's nephew; it's also a matter of pride. They've set up running roadblocks, and checkpoints at train and bus stations. They're making random stops in public places, they're searching every hotel and rooming house in the area, and empty apartments and business places. . . . They've even sent squads of Port Authority police to help us check every piece of luggage and freight due to go through the Turing gate."

"Even so, Mr. Lar knows that Tom wants to talk to me. That makes *me* a hot lead, and he'd be a fool if he didn't put a tail on me."

"Let's worry about that when you need to get close to Tom."

"I want to work this as I see fit."

"Absolutely."

"And you're, what? My partner, my line manager?"

"My job is to deliver you safe and sound, and see that you get what you need to do the job. Other than that, I'm happy to keep out of your way. I gave up active service a while back."

"So did I," Stone said.

Welch had booked him into the Plaza Hotel, a corner room on the fifth floor that overlooked the trees of Central Park. The horse-drawn carriages were plying their immemorial trade here as in all the other versions of New York that Stone had visited. A gallows—this was something he hadn't seen before—stood in front of the Grand Army Plaza. He counted fifteen corpses, barefoot in grey pyjamas, placards with block printing he couldn't quite read hung around their necks. Shaved heads, swollen faces black with congested blood. Two sailors posed in front of them while a third took their photograph.

"The locals' idea of justice," Welch said. He was sitting on the edge of the bed, using his handkerchief to remove dried mud from his combat boots. "Spies and black-marketeers, mostly. They hang 'em on the Great Lawn in the park. Night rallies with flaring torches, speeches, loyalty pledges, marching bands, Girl Scouts selling cookies . . . the whole nine yards. Afterward, they display the bodies *pour encourager les autres*. They'll hang Tom Waverly there if they get the chance. Why don't you try on the suit, get rid of that hick-from-the-sticks look."

A black suit and a white shirt were laid out on the king-size bed, alongside black lace-up shoes, black socks, a cell phone, a billfold containing two thousand local dollars, ID and documentation that backed up Stone's FBI cover story, a local driver's licence, and an NYC Military Zone pass.

Stone checked that the cell phone worked and asked if he could use it to contact the local office if he needed information.

"My cell number is on speed-dial," Welch said. "Call me if you need to know anything."

"You aren't coming with me?"

"I have a meeting with General Grover, the local who's in charge of security in the New York Military Zone. Ralph Kohler wants me to smooth his feathers, feed him bullshit about cooperation and full and frank exchange of information. As I said, this isn't like the old days when we could do whatever the hell we wanted and make up some story to tell the locals afterward. We don't coerce; we cooperate." Welch watched Stone take his Colt .45 and shoulder rig out of the kitbag, and added, "Are you seriously going to carry that?"

"You bet."

"Jesus. Try to remember that you're not working for Special Ops now, Adam. You have diplomatic cover, but you don't have *carte blanche*. If you start shooting at people, I won't be able to keep Ed Lar off your back."

Stone shrugged out of his checked shirt. "Back when you were working for Special Ops, I remember that you liked to boast that the only time you fired your weapon was on the ranges."

"I'm proud to say that's still the case."

"I guess you don't need to carry a piece into an embassy reception or a courtesy meeting with some local general, but I'll be moving in different circles. Don't worry, I promise I won't shoot at anyone unless they start shooting at me." Stone buttoned up the white shirt. "Your file didn't have anything about the Real version of Eileen Barrie. About whether or not Tom tried to make a hit on her."

"I haven't been told everything about this operation, Adam. You know how it is—compartmentalization and all the rest of that horseshit."

"Tom seems to be trying to kill off every doppel of the woman. So why wouldn't he go after the Real version too? If he had any sense, he would have hit her first." Stone pulled on the suit trousers and sat down on the bed beside Welch to lace up his shoes. "Unless, that is, he's trying to intimidate her. Or draw attention to her. Does he know her? Have they ever worked together on the same project?"

"You read everything in the file?"

"Cover to cover."

"Then you know as much about that as me. And all I know is that the Company has decided that we don't need to know."

"Because her work is classified, and we aren't on the bigot list."

"I don't know. Truly. I do know that the DCI's office wants to limit blowback from this little fiasco. Tom is hiding out somewhere in this sheaf. You're here to help find him. To help bring him in alive. Don't get sidetracked by trying to figure out his motivation, or every angle of the operation."

"His motivation might lead me to him. She's a scientist. A mathematician," Stone said, shrugging into his shoulder rig. "In the Real, and in all the sheaves where she was killed. That can't be a coincidence."

"Maybe you can ask Tom, when you find him."

Stone stood up and pulled on the suit jacket. "I intend to."

"That's the spirit. How's the fit?"

"A little tight around the shoulders, but otherwise not bad. Let's go. I'd like to check out the murder scene before it gets dark."

In the elevator, Welch examined the knot of his tie in a mirror and said, "I have to scoot off and placate General Grover, but I've arranged for a driver to take you anywhere you need to go."

"I can drive myself."

"You think you can handle Manhattan traffic after three years in that back-to-nature sheaf? Also, if Ed Lar does have people dogging your tail, you'll need someone with local knowledge to shake them if you want to go somewhere you don't want them to know about. Walk over to Madison Avenue and go a block north to the corner of East Sixtieth Street. There'll be a yellow taxi parked with its sign unlit, a woman driver. Climb in, she'll take you where you want to go."

"A taxi? That's cute, David."

"Wait until you see the driver," Welch said, and blew into his cupped hand and sniffed his palm to check his breath.

"As long as she keeps out of my way while I check the scene."

"She'll do whatever you ask her to do. It goes without saying, by the way, that if you do find anything the locals missed, I want to hear about it before the locals do."

The elevator stopped and its door slid open to reveal the marble-floored lobby.

Stone said, "Why would I want to tell the locals anything?"

"I think I'm going to enjoy working with you again, Adam. You're still a cowboy at heart, aren't you?"

Was he?

Stone thought about that as he walked toward his rendezvous. Like all of Dick Knightly's cowboy angels, he'd been trained to work in deep cover in precontact sheaves, to blend in, to live as invisibly as possible while accumulating data for historical, political, and economic profiles. Once, in the early days of Special Ops, before the first overt contact with the government of an alternate America, a woman at a party in Washington, DC, had walked up to Stone and said that she'd just bet fifty dollars with a girlfriend that he was a spy, and Stone had told her, no lie, that he spent most of his time in libraries. That was exactly what he'd done, back in the day. He'd gone through the mirror and ransacked libraries for all kinds of data: the failure rate of start-up companies, price and wage inflation, the ratio of the highest and lowest salaries in key companies, unemployment rates among white males between the ages of eighteen and twenty-one, the annual yields of cotton crops, winter wheat, soy beans. He'd tabulated prison terms for a variety of crimes, compared school-leaving ages of urban and rural whites and blacks, used fake academic or journalistic credentials to obtain interviews with CEOs and Ivy League professors about the state of the economy, identified prominent lawyers and preachers and political commentators. That was how all the cowboy angels in Special Ops had rolled in the early days, before the Real made its first overtures to governments in other sheaves. Before the covert actions, before the wars and revolutions, before the insurrections and terrorist reprisals.

"You like to watch," Susan had told Stone, a few months ago. They'd been walking home from a church social, Petey trailing a little way behind, singing one of his nonsense songs, cutting at weeds with a stick he'd picked up somewhere. "When you're around other people, you like to watch what's going on, don't you?"

"If you've been watching me, who is it that likes to watch?"

"I've been taking notice of you," Susan said. "Noticing how you behave when you hang out with the other guys."

"Yeah? How do I behave?"

"On the whole, you're pretty quiet. Self-contained. The other guys like to show off to each other; they always have an opinion about whatever it is they're talking about. But you don't say anything unless you have something to say. I don't mean you're afflicted with Allan King's famous Yankee taciturnity; the man thinks every word costs him a dime. I mean you don't bullshit."

"Mommy swore," Petey said.

"And Mommy's sorry for it, sweetie. She spent far too much of the afternoon talking with Nora Partridge, who has a kind heart but can never quite get to the point of what she's trying to say. Adam isn't like that, is he? When he says something, he says what he means, no more and no less."

"He likes to think about things," Petey said, and swiped the head off a milk-weed plant.

Stone said, "Is this criticism or observation?"

Susan smiled. "If I said you were aloof, maybe it would be a criticism. But you're not. You're watchful."

"I don't know about that. Maybe I like to be aloof, but I don't like to be watchful."

"The way you like trees, but not bushes?"

"I like grass too. Flowers I can live without."

"*Mom!* You're doing it *again*," Petey said. All summer he'd been driven to distraction by this word game, an open secret he wanted desperately to share, a code he couldn't quite crack. That evening, Susan and Stone had teased and tantalised him all the way home with their preference for books over magazines, bulls over cows, hills over mountains.

Watchful—Stone could live with that. Tom Waverly, though, was the poster boy for the dark side of the cowboy angels. He preferred overt action to undercover research, flamboyance to restraint. He liked to push regulations and convention as far as they would go, and then push them a little further.

"You're a deep man pretending to be shallow," Marsha Mason had once told him, and he'd laughed, not at all offended. This had been at one of the infamous barbecues at the little house in the Maryland woods where Tom had lived with his wife and daughter. Its back yard had run down to a lake. One night, Tom had rowed out into the middle of the lake and let off fireworks while the "Nessun dorma!" aria from *Turandot* played on speakers he'd set up among the trees. He'd stood up in the little boat with rockets and Roman candles exploding from his hands, whooping with glee.

At age thirteen, Tom had spent a year in juvenile prison in California for stealing a car; at sixteen he had enlisted in the army, training as a sniper and taking courses in parachuting, martial arts, and cryptography; at twenty-six he had been recruited by Dick Knightly into the CIG's brand-new Directorate of Special Operations. He liked to play up his reputation as a hellraiser. He wore blue jeans and biker boots and a leather jacket with the sleeves ripped off. He rode a motorbike everywhere, a Norton Commando he'd restored himself. He did handstands on the backs of chairs, once did a backflip from a motel balcony into the swimming pool two storeys below. He read Rilke and Thoreau and Barth, sang along with tuneless gusto to opera and the folk music he'd discovered in the Nixon sheaf, the very same sheaf in which, a few years later, Stone had been supposed to kill a novelist in the middle of a popular uprising against an unpopular war in Southeast Asia.

It had been one of twenty hits that had targeted counterculture lawyers, liberal politicians, journalists, and radical civil rights workers. . . . And this novelist, who'd once run for mayor of New York, a sometime journalist and rabble-rouser with powerfully expressed opinions, but still, Stone had wondered at the time, what could be so important about a man who wrote books for a living? But the Cluster crunched the data and constructed its probability models, the Company set up its covert actions, and its cowboy angels went to work without questioning their orders. In the end, Stone hadn't made the hit after all; the whole operation had unravelled after one of the locals they were running, a bomb maker, had managed to blow up a house in Greenwich Village. Six months later, work toward contact in that sheaf had been suspended indefinitely. The Nixon sheaf's version of America had been well on its way to becoming the world's only superpower, and the Cluster had calculated that the advantages of contact would be either negligible or negative.

All officers in Special Ops had been trained to take the initiative, but Tom Waverly had possessed a bravura recklessness that had set him apart. And he still had it, Stone thought. Even though he must have known that the game was up when he saw that Nathan Tate was guarding the target, he'd gone right ahead with his plan. He'd shot and killed the doppel of Eileen Barrie, he'd shot and killed Nathan Tate, and he'd gotten clean away from the scene. He still had it. Tracking him down wasn't going to be easy, especially as the locals were going balls-out to find him first. The only edge Stone had was that Tom wanted to talk to him.

A yellow taxi was parked where David Welch had said it would be. Stone walked around the block, moving with the flow of the crowd, looking in shop windows and using his peripheral vision to try to spot likely tails, seeing only civilians with pinched faces and shuttered expressions, rowdy little groups of soldiers and sailors. He was conscious of the weight of the Colt .45 in the holster under his left armpit. He passed a beggar being hassled by a pair of cops—the ragged guy, shiny burn scars disfiguring his face and scalp, kept trying to sidle away from the cops and they kept pushing him back against the wall with their nightsticks. People stepped past, eyes fixed elsewhere. A team of skeletal, shaven-headed men in orange coveralls hauled a wagon among the stop-and-go rush of military trucks, buses, taxis, bicycles. A lot of people were riding bicycles. Stone, grown used to a pace of life based on unmediated animal and human muscle, felt that everything was slightly speeded up, like one of those old hand-cranked silent movies.

He crossed the street and doubled back the way he'd come. Although he hadn't seen anyone dogging him, he was pretty sure that he was being followed. Probably by a tag team, almost impossible to spot. He walked to where the taxi was parked and climbed into the back. The driver, a young woman with a pale face and a mass of curly red hair, turned to look at him through the scratched plastic divider.

Stone hadn't seen her for more than ten years, but he recognised her at once.

Linda Waverly, Tom's daughter.

# 3.

"Welch put you up to this, didn't he?" Stone said. "The slick son of a bitch brought you through the mirror because he thought you might flush out your father."

"It isn't like that at all," Linda Waverly said, and started the taxi and pulled away from the curb. "When my father shot that woman, I was already working here. In this sheaf, in New York. I was taken off my job and grilled by Ralph Kohler's people for six hours straight. They were going to send me home, but David Welch persuaded them to let me help out."

"Welch likes to play games, Linda. He's using you."

"There's a good chance my father will try to make contact with me if I'm out on the street in plain view. What's wrong with that?"

"You can let me out right here. Then you can turn this taxi around, find David Welch, and tell him that I think he's crazy." Stone tried the door; it was locked. He rapped on the plastic partition and said, "That wasn't a suggestion, by the way. Stop right here."

Linda looked at him in the rearview mirror with cool defiance. "What are you going to do if I don't? Shoot me?"

Stone felt a little pang of guilt, and wondered if Tom had broken one of the golden rules of clandestine service and told his daughter about what had happened when SWIFT SWORD had fallen apart. "I came here because your father asked for me. Because I'm his friend, and because he saved my life once upon a time, and I still owe him. I don't know why he's been doing what he's been doing, but I do know that you don't want to get caught up in it."

Linda said, "I thought my father died three years ago, Mr. Stone. Now I know he didn't, I want to help find him and bring him in safe and sound."

"You're being used, Linda."

"We're both of us being used, Mr. Stone. Maybe we can figure out how to make the best of it."

Stone had to admit that it was a good point. Linda definitely had a stubborn streak a mile wide, just like her father, but she also appeared to be sensible and level-headed, and she had been working right here. She had local knowledge. Maybe he could turn this around, Stone thought. Pay back Welch in his own coin. He leaned forward and spoke into the cluster of holes drilled in the partition. "You can drive me to the scene. When I've finished there, we can try to work something out."

"You won't regret it, Mr. Stone."

"And you can slow down, too. Before we get a ticket."

"You don't like my driving?"

"I guess it has been a long time since I was in a New York taxi. A long time since I last saw you, too. What were you doing, before David Welch brought you into this thing? I take it you're working for the Company now."

"I'm part of a team that's liaising with the local FBI, trying to break up criminal gangs that are smuggling deserters out of the country. The desertion rate among our troops is three percent and rising. A few want to find their doppels, or the doppels of their wives or sweethearts, but most of them want to get to Canada. Canada is neutral in this sheaf. Once they're over the border, they're gone. The gangs help them get across, and then squeeze them for interest payments on the fee."

"So you're a field officer, just like your father."

"Actually, at the moment, I'm more on the analytical side of things. I was seconded from DI to help run a data-management system—computer work, basically. But I get to sit in on interviews with suspects, and I've been on a couple of raids, too."

"How do you like it, out in the field?"

"I was working with the forensic crew both times. I didn't come in until after the assault teams had taken out the bad guys. But it was still a buzz."

"I guess it must be," Stone said, remembering his first field actions. How it had all seemed like good clean fun until he'd had to shoot someone.

"I majored in anthropology at NYU before I joined the Company," Linda said. "This is my first time through the mirror, and I end up back in New York. It's different, but not *that* different. There's the aftermath of the war, of course, and the Dodgers and the Giants are still here, they didn't move to the West Coast. But it isn't like it's a foreign country. Apart from downtown, the streets are more or less the same. They have NYU, they have guys playing chess in Washington Square, they have yellow taxis and hot dog carts. . . . It reminds me of the time I went to Arizona with Mom and Dad. I was four-teen, they'd just got back together after their first big bust-up, and we took a trip to Arizona for a good old-fashioned family vacation. We visited with my aunt, my mother's sister, in Phoenix. We drove all around. We saw the Grand Canyon. We saw Sedona. You want to talk about another world, there it is. Sedona. All those red rocks, it's like nowhere else on Earth. Like Mars.

But it was still America, all the same. You travel a thousand miles to somewhere completely different, and you find the same TV shows, Coke, McDonald's. . . ."

"There are all kinds of different Americas, but they're all America."

"One nation under many skies. I remember seeing a man in a restaurant in Arizona who kept on his hat while he was eating. An expensive one, white, with a strip of snakeskin around the crown. He had these cowboy boots with little pointy toes, too. That was different, watching a man dressed like a cowboy spoon soup under his hat brim." Right in front of them, a truck swerved across two lanes. Linda hit her horn. "Army drivers, I swear none of them have licences."

Stone remembered the last time he'd seen Linda. It had been at one of Tom's parties. A little girl in a black bathing suit, screaming with laughter as she ran through the spray of the sprinklers in the vegetable patch behind the house. She'd been, what, ten or eleven. . . . A few weeks after that party, Stone had gone through the mirror again, had spent a couple of years working on a clandestine operation to overthrow the government in the American Bund sheaf. Toward the end, with everything lined up and the final stage of the operation about to kick off, Tom had turned up to help out, and the first thing he'd said to Stone was that he'd split up with his wife. He'd gone back to her that time, the marriage had staggered on for a few more years, but there had been no more barbecues at the little house in the woods. Stone hadn't seen Linda Waverly since that party, and now here she was, driving him toward the scene of a double murder committed by her father. It was the kind of thing, he thought, that made a man feel the years in his bones.

Linda broke the silence that had grown between them. "Did he really save your life, once upon a time?"

"He was given a medal for it."

"The Intelligence Star?"

"That's the one."

"I went to the ceremony, but he never explained what he'd done. He liked to tell tall stories about travelling in other sheafs, but he never once talked about his work. His real work, I mean, not the cover stories. Even after I joined the Company, he used to say that if he ever told me anything about his actions, he'd have to kill me afterward. With that look that meant you could never tell if he was joking or not."

"I remember that look."

"Of course, I picked up a few bits and pieces during my training. Some

55

of the stuff you old-school guys were involved in is in the text books, and one of my instructors knew my father. I get the impression he was something of a rogue operator."

"He always had a reason for everything he did. And I'm sure there has to be a reason for this."

Stone wasn't about to tell her that her father might have sold out, or gone bug-eyed crazy.

"There's a rumour that the Company has an internal situation. That there's been a purge, there was some kind of problem at White Sands . . . ?"

"I'm retired, Linda. I'm no longer plugged into the rumour circuit."

"I thought Mr. Welch might have told you something."

"Welch likes to play games, remember? Withholding information or giving out partial information is part of it. Who was purged?"

"There aren't any hard facts, but something's definitely going on. Where I work, a couple of people due to go on leave have had their leave cancelled, and a couple more haven't come *back* from leave—"

"In case they're infected with rumours."

"There's been a hitch in communications through the mirror, too. Also, the station chief gave us a little pep talk a few days ago. Something's going on for sure, and I can't help thinking that it might have something to do with whatever it is my father has gotten himself into."

North Meadow swung by. The sky was growing dark beyond a line of trees. A chain of streetlights flickered on one by one. Stone thought of the whitewashed cabin set on the ridge above the wild, untravelled Hudson, and wondered what Susan was doing at that precise moment, several miles and two sheaves away. All they shared now was time. Whenever history split, time rolled on at the same speed, one second per second, in the two daughter sheaves. In every version of America, in every known and unknown sheaf, it was September 15, 1984, six thirty-two p.m. Stone thought of Susan moving about in the kitchen where Petey's crayon drawings were tacked to the plank wall by the sash window, steam rising from a pot on the wood-burning stove, the cozy, familiar domestic clatter, and felt a sudden yearning ache.

He'd met Susan's husband, Jake Nichols, in the American Bund sheaf some ten years ago. Stone and his fellow Special Ops officers had helped to incite a revolution; Jake had been part of the peacekeeping force that had come in immediately afterward. Stone had hit it off from the start with straight-talking, can-do Lieutenant Nichols, and had been one of the first to visit Jake in the VA hospital a year later, after Jake had lost two fingers on his left hand, the calf muscle of his left leg, and five feet of his small intestine to a roadside bomb. Afterward, Jake walked with a limp and had to take painkillers and steroids twice a day, but he didn't let his disabilities slow him down. He quit the army and went to work for the American Red Cross, which was where he met and married Susan. Stone was the best man at their wedding.

When Susan became pregnant, Jake invoked the right, granted by the Veterans' Bill to every honourably discharged member of the armed forces, to move to a wild sheaf. He and Susan bought a farm in the First Foot sheaf from a lottery winner who'd had enough of the frontier life, and Stone followed them there after he resigned from the Company. He paid his community dues by working on the railroad, then took a job as a guide for the Nichols' hunting outfit, leading rich clients through the pine forests and marshes to the west of the Hudson in search of mastodon, giant sloths, sabre-toothed cats, and other megafaunal species that in the absence of native human beings still flourished there. Susan handled the paperwork and Jake had forgotten more about hunting than Stone would ever learn, but they insisted on making Stone an equal partner in the business.

After Jake's fatal accident out on the ice, Stone did all he could to help Susan keep both the farm and the hunting business going, and when the snows melted and the growing season began, with fields to plough and crops to plant and tend, it seemed sensible to leave the little cabin he'd built near the shore of the East River and live on the farm. Just for the summer, he and Susan agreed. Just for the summer, and then for the harvest. Their discussions about the future were strictly practical. They talked about dismantling Stone's cabin and rebuilding it closer to the farm, about hiring help, about how they could improve the hunting business. They talked about everything except the mutual feeling that grew between them that summer, furtive and patient and strong as a flower pushing through the concrete slabs of a side-walk. There were moments—one hot, still evening when they sat together and watched the sun set over the Hudson, the day they went fishing for striped bass in Stone's little boat, a long ramble through the woods, picking mushrooms—when Stone had been ready to confess to Susan that he'd fallen in love with her. But it was still too soon after Jake's death. It felt too much like the low subterfuges and betrayals of adultery.

Now, remembering what he and Susan had said to each other in the barn and what had hung unspoken in the air, Stone knew that they would have to sit down and have themselves a heart-to-heart talk when he returned to New Amsterdam. It was time he bit the bullet.

The taxi had stopped at a red light at the western border of the park. Stone told Linda Waverly to take a right.

"Quicker if I go straight across."

Stone was looking out of the taxi's rear window at the vehicles in line behind it. "Go right, then take Duke Ellington Boulevard, or whatever they call it here."

"They call it Duke Ellington Boulevard." The light changed. Linda turned right. "If the guys following us know where we're going, what's the point of trying to lose them?"

"I want to show them that we know they're there," Stone said.

When Linda turned the taxi onto Duke Ellington Boulevard, he saw the sedan that had followed them through Central Park make the same manouevre.

"You see it?" Linda said. "The white Ford four cars back?"

"I see it."

"He took over from a red Chrysler on Madison and East Eighty-Fifth."

"I guess I'm out of practice," Stone said.

This girl who'd once scampered about in summer twilight wearing a white taffeta dress with fairy wings pinned to the back calmly telling him about a switch he hadn't seen.

"Who do you think they are?" she said. "Locals, or Company?"

"Does it matter?"

Up in the low hundreds, things didn't look that different from Stone's memories of New York in the Real. A little less neon, the storefronts shabby but homelier. Not as many high-rise apartment blocks, that was for sure. Most of the pedestrians were civilians, and there seemed to be more white people here than in the Real. They were heading home, buying fruit and bottled water in superettes, walking their dogs. A fat man in an undershirt stood at the doorway of a dry-cleaning place, smoking a cigar with the placid, absolute authority of the Emperor of all Time and Space. Then the taxi turned onto Riverside Drive, with brownstones and taller apartment buildings facing the long park, and glimpses of the river through the trees.

This sheaf's doppel of Eileen Barrie must have been doing well: she owned a turn-of-the-century brownstone right on Riverside Drive, a few blocks south of her workplace at Columbia University. Sawhorses blocked off the sidewalk and a uniformed cop stood by the railings at the bottom of the steps up to the front door. Most of the windows were broken, and smoke had blackened their lintels.

Stone told Linda to wait in the taxi. She said she didn't mind, she'd already scoped the scene.

"Welch brought you here, I bet."

He'd shown her what her father had done, Stone thought, and put her on the spot, in plain sight. David Welch and his insincere charm, his smoke and mirrors, his sly little tricks.

Linda said, "I can walk you through it, show you how it went down."

"I read the report. Stay there while I figure a few things out. It shouldn't take long."

Stone didn't want to discuss the murders with Linda and talk about the different ways her father had killed six doppels of the same woman. Also, he wanted her to sit right in front of the house. If Tom Waverly was hiding close by, she might draw him out or at least make him careless. When it came down to it, Stone thought as he swung out of the taxi, he wasn't any better than Welch.

He showed his ID to the cop, borrowed the man's flashlight and the keys to the house, and told him to go find a cup of coffee. The splintered front door was chained and padlocked, and sashed with yellow crime-scene tape. There were spray patterns of blood on its green paint, spots and spatters of blood on the columns on either side, and plenty of smears and boot prints left by police, paramedics, and firefighters who'd stepped in pools of blood that were now dried to flaky crusts on the steps.

According to the preliminary report in the file Welch had given Stone, the hit had happened just before dawn. Tom Waverly had climbed onto the roof, removed the protective mesh from the top of one of the disused chimneys, and lowered into it a flexible plastic tube containing a mix of gasoline and liquid soap. When this homemade napalm had ignited, probably sparked by a timed charge, it had blown out most of the windows and started a fire in the kitchen at the rear of the house. Nathan Tate had brought Eileen Barrie out the front, sandwiched between two police from the mayor's protection squad, and that had been where they'd both died, shot by a .308 rifle from a position across the road in Riverside Park. Nathan Tate had been right in front of Eileen Barrie when he'd been shot. And before he'd hit the ground, before the police officers had cleared their weapons from their holsters, Eileen Barrie had been shot too, once in the chest, once in the head, and then a burst of fire from a machine pistol had sent everyone diving for cover, and two smoke grenades had ignited in the middle of the street. It had been all over in less than a minute. Quick, brutal, thoroughly planned, calmly executed.

Stone crossed the street and stepped into the park. Trees sloped down toward the river. His new, thin-soled shoes slipped on leaf mulch. He could hear the warm wind moving through the trees, the hum of traffic on the Hudson Parkway.

Twenty minutes before the bomb had gone off, Tom Waverly had knifed one of the uniformed cops who had been patrolling the park, the mayor's nephew, and dragged his body under a laurel bush. And then he'd taken up his position in a tall oak that was now ringed off by police tape, whiling away the time before his napalm bomb went off by whittling a message into the bark of the tree.

*I'll talk to Stone.*

The undergrowth around the tree had been trampled flat. Tom Waverly had taken the machine pistol with him, but the bolt-action Winchester .308 had been found at the foot of the tree, and the rope he'd used to slide to the ground after the hit was still in place.

Stone hooked his suit jacket on a branch and used the rope to climb as high as he could. Splintered rips in the tree trunk suggested that Tom had worn spiked overshoes to help him climb through the canopy, almost to the top of the tree. Stone couldn't get that high, but thirty feet up he had a pretty good view of the brownstone. The yellow taxi was parked right in front, Linda Waverly dimly visible through the side window, sitting there like a target. Stone realised that he should have asked her if she was carrying a pistol before he left her there, just in case Tom took the bait—but even if she was armed, she was hardly likely to draw down on her own father.

He straddled a branch and thought about angles, figured that if he climbed another twenty feet he would have been able to look over the top of the moving truck Nathan Tate had used to screen the front door of the brownstone from the street. Tom must have scoped out the scene sometime before he made the hit. He'd brought rope and spiked overshoes because he'd known that he would have had to climb this high to make the hit. And he'd known that there was a way out through the back yard, so he'd set the fire in the kitchen to force everyone in the house out the front door. Stone smiled. Tom might have gone crazy, but he could still set up a hit with meticulous precision. Leave anything to chance, he used to say, and you'll most likely end up in a box like Schrödinger's cat, wondering when you're going to start smelling almonds.

Dick Knightly's cowboy angels had learnt about the fundamental principles of the Many Worlds theory during their training. Their physics instructor,

Fred Lehman, introduced the concept with Schrödinger's "ridiculous case," a thought experiment designed to challenge the assertion that measurement forced a quantum system to adopt a specific state, and any observer making measurements could not be isolated from the system he observed. In Schrödinger's thought experiment, a cat was placed in a box equipped with a flask of cyanide gas, a mechanism that would break the flask if a detector was triggered by the random decay of an atom, and a source of radioactivity so weak that there was only a fifty percent chance that a single atom would decay in any given hour. The cat and the mechanism were sealed inside the box, and the experiment ended after exactly an hour, when the box was opened again.

"Schrödinger's question was this," Fred Lehman said. "With a fifty percent chance that an atom has decayed and triggered the mechanism that releases the cyanide, what's the state of the cat immediately before the box is opened?"

Tom Waverly raised his hand, saying that he had a question of his own. What, he wanted to know, did this Schrödinger guy have against cats?

This was in the lecture theatre at Brookhaven. Fifteen young men and one young woman were scattered across tiers of seats, some assiduously taking notes, some hopelessly lost, all of them feeling the same electric thrill of participating in something tremendously secret and important. Tom Waverly was sprawled in a seat in the front row, his arms stretched across the backs of the seats to either side, smiling while he waited for Fred Lehman's answer.

"We're not talking about a real cat in a real experiment," the physicist said. "The cat is a metaphor Schrödinger used to ridicule the suggestion that quantum theory could be used to make a complete description of physical reality. He claimed that before the box is opened, the cat must be in some indeterminate state, half dead, half alive. Since no living creature can be alive and dead at the same time, there must be something wrong with quantum theory."

"Of course it can't be a real experiment," Tom Waverly said. Looking around, taking his time, building to his punchline. "I mean, have you ever tried to get a cat inside a box?"

In the warm dark, high above the ground in the branches of the oak tree, Stone smiled, remembering that Fred Lehman had waited out the laughter before explaining that the premise on which the thought experiment had been based was wrong, that the cat in the unopened box did not exist an indeterminate state, neither wholly alive nor wholly dead, as Schrödinger had asserted. Instead, the experiment caused the state of the observer to split into two—and it didn't matter if the observer was the experimenter, the cat, or the radiation detector, as long as something or someone took a measurement that forced the quantum system of cat and box and cyanide apparatus to adopt a definite state. In one universe the observer opened the box and discovered a live cat; in the other, the box contained a corpse.

And this happened with every choice we ever make, Fred Lehman had told his class. In most cases the split was trivial and the two sibling universes quickly recombined. But if the observation caused a change big enough to affect other observers, recombination was delayed, and more and more differences accumulated in the states of the sibling universes until the split became permanent. A single probability sheaf split into two; history went in two different directions. In one the cat was alive; in the other, it was dead. In one, Khrushchev was assassinated and the Soviet generals ordered an atomic strike against the United States; in another, the assassination attempt failed or was stillborn, and Khrushchev withdrew the Soviet missiles and battlefield atomic weapons from Cuba. Each sheaf was woven from billions of closely related microhistories that branched and recombined and branched again as billions of observers made their trivial choices. But although most microhistories recombined almost immediately, a significant number did not, and in a few of those the split eventually became permanent.

Tom Waverly had loved the weirdness of quantum theory, but on a job he'd always done everything he could to avoid the dichotomous fate of Schrödinger's cat, planning his hits to the last detail. It was pure bad luck that the cop had stumbled across him when he was moving into position. If he had shot only Eileen Barrie and Nathan Tate, the locals would have requested that a couple of NYPD murder detectives liaise with the Company team, purely as a formality, and left it at that. But Tom had killed a cop, the cop had been the mayor's nephew, and now every one of New York's finest was looking for him. Because one of their own had been murdered, they had permission to shoot on sight, and they were ready and willing to take care of business.

*I'll talk to Stone.* But where, and when? Stone knew that he would have to think hard and fast, and hope for a lot of good luck, if he was going to catch up with Tom before the locals did.

He slid down the rope, put on his jacket, and walked back to the edge of the park and stood there for a few moments, looking at Eileen Barrie's brownstone and the identical brownstones on either side, their bow windows, the balustrades that ran along the edges of their flat roofs. He slapped a lone, late mosquito and walked across the street. When he reached the taxi, Linda cranked down her window and asked if he had found anything.

"The report said that he got onto the roof of the house from one of the neighbouring brownstones."

"The one on the right. He got in through the back, picked the lock of the fire door in the basement, then picked the lock of the access door to the roof. The forensic team found fresh scratches on both of them. You think they missed something?"

"I'm wondering why he didn't stay up on the roof after he planted the napalm. He had an easy shot of the front door from across the street, but he had to evade police patrols to get into position. And in fact he *didn't* evade them—he ran into that cop. If he'd stayed up on the roof, the shot would have been harder, but he wouldn't have had to take the risk of moving into the park."

"He couldn't stay up there because there were men posted on the roof of Dr. Barrie's brownstone."

"There were? How many?"

It hadn't been in the report.

"Two sharpshooters. They were watching the back yards and the roofs on either side."

"Were they in position all the time?"

"Only when Dr. Barrie was at home. When she went to work, a couple of officers stayed behind in her apartment, but the rest of the protection squad went with her. When she wanted to go home, the squad moved into position and checked everything out before they let her come back."

"She came home at around half-eight in the evening," Stone said. "So Tom had plenty of time to get up on the roof and plant the bomb and get out. But how did he know when she'd be coming home?"

"He didn't have to know the exact time. She always worked late."

"Are you sure?"

"I tracked down one of the guys who'd been part of the protection squad and had a little chat with him. He said that the assignment was a nightmare because Dr. Barrie kept crazy hours. Where are you going?"

"I'm following a train of thought. Wait there. It won't take long."

Tom Waverly had left a message at his sniper's position. He'd also spent some time on the roof of Eileen Barrie's house, so he might well have left a message there, too. Stone unlocked the padlock and stripped away police tape, switched on the borrowed flashlight, and stepped into the dark hallway. The ceiling had come down and there was a strong smell of smoke and burnt paint and charred wood. He picked his way through fallen plaster and puddles of water to the staircase and climbed all the way to the top, where the door to the building's flat roof hung on a single hinge.

The cluster of brick chimneys had been collapsed by the explosion and the roof had caved in around them, exposing blackened beams. Stone skirted the hole, played the beam of the flashlight over the waist-high brickwork at the front of the roof but found nothing of interest, then clambered onto the roof of the neighbouring brownstone, the one that Tom Waverly had broken into.

Stone paced the perimeter of the roof, shoes crunching on gravel, and flicked the beam of the flashlight this way and that. There were fresh cigarette butts and a crumpled soft-drink can by the dividing wall, probably dropped by the police sharpshooters. There was a junked air conditioner. And there was an aluminium lawn chair set beside the balustrade at the front of the roof.

Although there could be a perfectly ordinary reason why there was a chair up here—perhaps someone liked to sit on the roof on fine summer days, taking in the view across the river to New Jersey and catching some rays—Stone got a little chill when he saw it. He walked over to the balustrade and looked down at the road, the chain of streetlights, the sawhorses blocking off the sidewalk in front of the brownstone, the taxi parked in front. In the sodium lamplight its roof was the colour of an old bruise. He sat in the chair and looked at the trees in the long narrow park, the streetlights of the Hudson Parkway, the New Jersey shore twinkling across the river . . . and remembered Tom Waverly sitting in a similar chair on his lawn at one or another of his barbecues, a drunkenly benevolent potentate watching his daughter search on her hands and knees for the coins he'd hidden in the grass. The chair set in what Tom claimed to be his favourite spot on Earth, where he liked to drink beer while watching the sun go down beyond the little lake; the search for coins scattered around it a little game that he and Linda loved to play.

A treasure hunt.

Stone trailed his fingers in the gravel on either side of the chair, then dug deeper, his fingertips scraping tar paper beneath the gravel, finding nothing. But Tom had hidden coins *under* his chair too. Stone set the chair to one side and started to sift through the patch of gravel. Almost immediately, he found a scrap of thin card: the cover torn off a book of matches. It must have been placed there recently, because it was unwrinkled by time and weather. Chills chased up and down Stone's spine when he held it in the beam of the flashlight and saw what was written there.

# 4.

"Is it your father's handwriting?"

"Definitely."

Linda Waverly was examining the matchbook cover by the taxi's interior light, holding it by its edges between thumb and forefinger. Printed in blue ballpoint on red card, half obscuring the logo of a bar, were a New York telephone number, the next day's date, and *9.30 a.m.* On the reverse, in the same blue ink: *Adam—be there.*

"How could he be sure you'd find it?" she said.

"He knows how I work. He knew I would want to check out the scene, and guessed I'd spot that lawn chair and remember the game he used to play with you. It's an easy reach," Stone said, and took the matchbook cover from her and dropped it into the breast pocket of his jacket.

He was excited and also—this he hadn't expected—happy. Happy to be back in the field, happy to discover that his tradecraft wasn't as rusty as he'd feared. Although he had only been in this sheaf for a few hours, he'd confirmed that Tom Waverly wanted to make contact, and had found a way of reaching out to him. Perhaps Tom wanted to turn himself in. Perhaps, in a day or two, Stone would be able to go back to New Amsterdam, and Susan and Petey.

Linda said, "We could call that number right now. See if he's at home."

"It doesn't say 'Call me.' It says, 'Be there.'"

"How can you go visit a telephone number? Wait—it's a pay phone, isn't it? He wants to put you in some public place, so he can see if you've brought along company before he makes contact."

"That's one possibility," Stone said. "Another is that he'll call me and tell me where to go next. In any case, what I need to do now is find the location of the phone the number belongs to."

"The local office will have a reverse directory," Linda said. "I could call them right now—"

"We'll go check it out in person," Stone said. "The fewer people who know about this the better."

"And then what?"

"Then you can take me back to my hotel."

"I want to be there when he calls you," Linda said. "I *should* be there."

"He asked to talk to me, Linda. I'm sorry, but that's the only way—"

A couple of blocks down the dark street, two white sedans veered around a corner in a squeal of tires, straightened out, and sped toward the taxi.

"Friends of yours?" Stone said.

"Locals," Linda said, squinting into the glare of two sets of headlights. "I should call Mr. Welch."

She seemed angry and determined, not at all scared. She was her father's daughter, all right.

"Let's see what they want first," Stone said, watching men in suits spill from the sedans, drawing guns as they went left and right, up the steps into the brownstone or across the street to the park. Locals, putting on a show.

A tall man in a brown chalk-stripe suit walked up to the taxi, knocked on the window by Stone's head, and spoke his name, stepping back when Stone swung the door wide and climbed out.

"Ed Lar," the man said. "We haven't met, but I bet David Welch mentioned my name. And I surely know who you are. Mind showing me what you found?"

"Mind showing some ID?" Stone's heart was beating quickly, but he felt calm and cool; he had been half expecting this.

Lar flipped his badge case in front of Stone's face. The FBI officer was in his early forties, hair of no particular colour slicked back from a lean face with sharp cheekbones and bright blue eyes. "I know you found something up on that roof that my men missed, Mr. Stone. I'm impressed. Truly."

"How were you keeping watch?"

Lar jerked a thumb at the black sky. "Technology borrowed from you guys. A couple of stealthed drones equipped with cameras that can count every hair on your head, parabolic dishes that can hear your every breath."

"It would have been easier to bug the taxi."

"Not as much fun, though. You can hand over that thing you found directly, or we can waste time downtown. Your call."

"In the spirit of cooperation," Stone said, and lifted the matchbook cover from his breast pocket with two fingers and held it out. "Be careful—there could be fingerprints."

Lar took the scrap of cardboard from him and held it up in the glare of the headlights of the sedans. "I guess we both know who left this little love note."

"You'll notice it's addressed to me."

"Yeah, and you found it so easily I can't help wondering if you and Waverly have something going on."

"He wanted me to find it. That's why he left it where he did. And I can't help wondering, Mr. Lar, why his daughter is involved in the search for him."

Lar glanced at Linda Waverly, who was watching them through the taxi's open door, and said, "What do you mean?"

"Was it David Welch's idea to use her to try to flush out Tom Waverly, or did you two dream it up together?"

"As far as I'm concerned, we don't need either of you to find the son of a bitch," Lar said. He called over one of his officers, gave him the matchbook cover, and told him to find out who the phone number belonged to.

Stone said, "Tom Waverly wants to talk to me, Mr. Lar, no one else. He wants me to be at that phone tomorrow, at nine thirty. If I don't answer, he'll hang up. We'll lose the chance to find out what he wants."

Lar looked off at the park on the other side of the street. Flashlight beams danced in the darkness beneath the trees. "He wants to jerk our chains. To waste our time and resources by setting up a rendezvous he has no intention of keeping, because while we're busy with his little diversion he'll be attempting to slip past the security at Brookhaven."

"You could be right. But we can't take the chance, can we?" Stone said.

Lar pressed his eyes shut with the thumb and forefinger of his right hand. After a few moments, he said, "I'll talk to Welch, and then I'll want to talk to you and Miss Waverly. I'll get you a ride back to your hotel."

"Thanks for the offer, but I already have a ride."

As they drove off, Stone asked Linda to call the local Company office and find the location of the phone that belonged to the number her father had written on the matchbook.

"I thought you wanted to check it out in person?"

"That was before Mr. Lar muddied the water."

Linda wedged her cell phone between her shoulder and ear as she drove, gave her name and the day code, then recited the telephone number. Adding, "I think you should pull up the phone company's listings before you check the subscriber reverse directory."

She listened for a few moments, then thanked the person at the other end of the line, switched off her phone, and told Stone, "It's a pay phone, all right. One of six consecutive numbers in Duffy Square. Want to go check it out?"

"Is Duffy Square north of Times Square here?"

Linda nodded. "Apart from the damage caused by the atomic bomb, everything's more or less where it is in the Real. It's good, isn't it? That my father wants to talk, I mean."

"Of course it is." What else could he say? Besides, he wanted to believe it, too. He added, "I guess you'd better take me back to my hotel. I need to talk to Welch, get this thing with the locals straightened out."

Linda said, "The bar where he got that matchbook—"

"Your father is hardly likely to go back to it, Linda. Although I bet Mr. Lar will put it under surveillance, just in case."

"It's down in Alphabet City and features live music every night—the kind of old-time stuff my father likes. There are a few other places like that, too. I was thinking of checking them out."

"Are you asking my permission, or are you asking me to come along?"

"You could help me canvass bar staff. Our friends in the white Dodge, by the way, they're following us again. One lane over, three cars back."

Stone thought for a moment. Now that the locals were all over him, it might not be a bad idea to have someone who could help him evade their attention. And while there was virtually no chance of picking up Tom's trail, he would be able to see how Linda handled herself, and get an idea of how things worked in this sheaf. . . .

He said, "If I go barhopping with you, I don't want to be looking over my shoulder all the time."

"So you'll come along?"

"Isn't that what I said? But only if you can lose our friends."

"Let's wait until we get to Atom City," Linda said. "They'll have a hard time blending in there. Actually, so will you, in that suit and tie. The first thing we have to do is find you something else to wear."

When the atomic bomb had exploded over the Hudson, two-hundred-and-fifty-mile-an-hour winds and firestorms had levelled every building on the west side of Manhattan below Houston Street. East of Broadway, the upper storeys of surviving buildings were still printed with black scorch marks, and many were derelict, standing stark and windowless in wastelands of rubble. Linda Waverly told Stone that the social geography of Manhattan was reversed here. Survivors with money and influence had moved as far as they could from Ground Zero, displacing the poor from Harlem and the Bronx, who had been resettled in high-rise blocks of social housing built on the ruins of Greenwich Village as part of the European-funded reconstruction plan. She pointed out a tall, slender tower outlined in red and green lights, about where the Pan-American Trade Center stood in the Real, and where reed beds grew along the shore at the edge of Susan's farm.

"The Atlantic Friendship Tower," she said. "It carries New York's TV and radio traffic. Before we came through the mirror, it was popular with European tourists. They used to ride to the top to get a good view of Ground Zero."

The Lower East Side, renamed Atom City, was mostly intact, although many buildings were propped up by massive wooden braces. Avenues A, B, and C had been renamed Alpha, Beta, and Cobalt 60. Cars and taxis crawled nose to tail along the potholed streets, reflections of neon signs sliding over their windshields, and pedestrians overflowed the crowded sidewalks. Most were under thirty, dressed in what looked like their grandparents' clothes, men in hats and suits with wide lapels, women in A-line dresses or beaded sweaters and knee-length skirts. Young toughs in leather jackets or T-shirts and jeans lounged on stoops, sizing up the crowds with insolent eyes. Little knots of soldiers or sailors called to each other. Street vendors sold hot dogs and doughnuts, pretzels and Chinese noodles. A guy in a red jacket was beating the hell out of a stack of cardboard boxes and plastic crates with a pair of drumsticks.

After Linda found an empty spot and parked the taxi, the white Dodge nosed past. Two men in it, their gazes fixed straight ahead.

"Take off your jacket," Linda told Stone. "We need to dress you down. It'll help us lose those guys, and in the places where we need to go you could get in a lot of trouble if you're wearing that suit."

"I was told the locals were friendly here."

"We have good relations with the government, but out on the street there are plenty of people who aren't so happy with our presence. Street gangs, students. . . . People who hang around student bars and pubs but aren't actually students, if you know what I mean."

They found a used-clothing store, a whitewashed basement crammed with racks of tuxedos and Hawaiian shirts, cotton dresses and sweaters and woollen overcoats. Linda helped Stone choose a red wool shirt with long, pointed lapels, and a loose-fitting navy-blue cord jacket that more or less hid his shoulder holster, then stepped back and studied him, her head tilted to one side. She was almost his height, dressed in a green needlecord shirt and knee-length khaki shorts. She'd caught up her mass of red curls under a shapeless old Homburg. Tom Waverly's little girl, all grown up.

Stone said, feeling amused and slightly foolish in his disguise, "How do I look?"

"Like an undercover cop who got out of bed in a hurry," Linda said. "But in a dim light and a crowded bar, you'll just about pass for an ordinary human being."

They hopped from bar to bar, buying drinks they didn't touch, scoping out the customers, showing bartenders and waitresses a photograph of Tom Waverly that Linda had brought along, moving on. No one seemed to be following them. In a club that occupied a converted bus garage, where strings of coloured lights dangled from the steel trusses of the high roof and a three-piece band played a ragged blues, Linda persuaded one of the bartenders to let her and Stone leave through the fire door. They walked away quickly and circled around Tompkins Square and the tent city for the homeless that was laid out under the trees.

"I think we lost our friends," Stone said.

"You're enjoying yourself."

"I guess it reminds me of the good old days."

For a moment, the ghost of a young, exuberant, recklessly brave Tom Waverly touched both of them.

Linda said, "There's one more place I'd like to check out."

It was on the second floor of an old tenement building hidden behind a forest of wooden props. Stone followed Linda up a narrow flight of stairs into a space made out of three or four rooms knocked through, crowded with young people in old-fashioned clothes who were drinking beer and wine from paper cups and making a lot of noise under the pressed-tin ceiling. Most of them were smoking. In the big room at the end, on a small, low stage in front of windows shuttered with corrugated iron painted bright red, a man and a woman perched on bar stools with their acoustic guitars in their laps. Their audience sat on broken-down sofas and kitchen chairs, listening to the woman sing about how her morphine would be the death of her.

Stone stood with Linda at the back of the audience. The singer played rhythm guitar and wore a calf-length flowered dress and tooled leather cowboy boots, her pale face framed by auburn hair parted down the centre, her dark eyes grave and steady. Her partner was dressed in a grey suit, black hair falling across his handsome Irish face as he bent over his guitar, putting some Spanish into his phrasing. They played a song about John Henry. They played a pretty song about a brave little flower called the acony bell. They played a song about the coo-coo bird, that sings as it flies. Songs that put a shiver in Stone's blood, reminding him of the Harvest Home dance at the Ellison place two weeks ago, of tunes played at christenings, barn-raisings, and Fourth of July picnics. The singer and her partner were like travellers from distant blue hills, come down into the city with the mythic cargo of a lost, half-forgotten America.

In a break in the set, while the two musicians retuned their guitars and chatted with friends in the audience, Linda told Stone that this bar was the centre of the revivalist scene.

"When we first came through the mirror, all they had was European pop, European heavy metal, European dance hall. But after we made contact, there was a cultural flowering, a rediscovery of American roots. They have gospel, all kinds of blues, dozens, grunge. . . ."

"Grunge?"

"It's like heavy metal, but played real fast. There's acid grunge, apocalypse grunge, garage grunge . . . all kinds. It's what teenage white kids play in their bedrooms to annoy their parents, if they aren't playing dozens."

"How about Bob Dylan? If we found him—"

"We'd find my father." Linda smiled at Stone from under the brim of her Homburg. They were leaning close to make themselves heard over the noise of the crowd. He could feel the heat of her body. A faint scent of patchouli oil. She said, "I looked around for Bobby D., a.k.a. Robert Zimmerman, but I don't think he took up the guitar in this sheaf."

"Maybe he's out there somewhere, walking the back roads. He just hasn't made himself known yet. How about Elvis Presley?"

"He's strictly a movie actor here. He started out as a singer, but after the war he went into the movies. I saw him in one—*Judgement Day*. He played a corrupt Southern Senator."

"I'd say it gives this sheaf a good six out of ten on the Elvis scale."

"I remember how you and my father used to joke about things like that."

"Back in the good old days."

Stone didn't entirely trust Linda. She was inexperienced and naive, and David Welch was almost certainly using her to get close to him, but he was pretty sure that he was going to need some help tomorrow and, at bottom, they both wanted the same thing. They both wanted to find Tom Waverly before the locals did, and bring him in alive.

He said, "When did you last see your father?"

"Three years ago. Just before he went through the mirror for the last time. He disappeared, those insurgents claimed to have captured him, and then he was officially declared dead."

"How did he seem?"

"A little quieter than usual, a little preoccupied, but maybe that's only hindsight. You know how he was. It was always hard to know what he was really thinking."

"Did you happen to see his apartment after he disappeared?"

"It was cleared out by the Company, in case he'd left sensitive information lying around. They sent on a few of boxes of personal stuff, mostly clothes and disks."

"No computer stuff? Notebooks? Files? Letters?"

Linda shook her head. "We had a couple of phone conversations just before he disappeared. He talked about a motorbike he was thinking of buying, a long road trip he wanted to make. I can't help thinking that what happened to him, the reason he disappeared, wasn't something planned. He could have gotten caught up in something against his will. He could have been brainwashed."

"It's possible."

"But you don't think so."

Stone smiled. "I plan to ask him about it, first chance I get."

The two musicians took to the stage again. The woman told the audience they had but one number left, and in the expectant hush began a long, yearning song about dreaming of a highway that would take her home, take her back to her lost love. A highway like a winding ribbon, a winding ribbon with a band of gold. For a little while, everything except the music seemed to stop; only the music kept time moving forward.

Stone was so caught up in its spell that he didn't at first realise that the trilling noise was coming from the cell phone in the pocket of his pea jacket. He pulled it out, saw that Welch was calling him, pressed the *yes* button and said, "Wait up," and walked through the crowd to the restroom in back, disturbing a couple of teenagers in ruffled silk shirts and eyeliner who were sharing a marijuana cigarette. Stone locked himself in a vacant cubicle and told Welch to go ahead.

Welch's voice scratched in his ear. "What are you doing down in Atom City?"

"Did Linda Waverly tell you where we were going, or do you have goons following me too?"

"The phone tells me where you are."

The strong sweet smell of pot coiled through the stink of urine and disinfectant. Stone said, "Does it also tell you I'm off duty?"

72

"I don't think you are. I think you're following up a lead from that little clue you found tonight."

"I guess Mr. Lar got around to telling you about it."

"I thought we had an agreement, Adam. Anything you found, you'd tell me first."

"The locals were tailing me. They pounced as soon as they realised I'd found something. And maybe I'm just a little pissed off at you, David, because you gave Tom's daughter the job of driving me around town."

"I forgot to ask. How's that working out?"

Stone heard the amusement in Welch's voice and pictured his sly smile.

"Tom hasn't tried to get close to her, if that's what you mean."

"She's no more bait than you are, Adam."

"We need to talk about that. Get it straightened out."

"Good idea. I'll meet you for breakfast at the hotel tomorrow, six thirty. Ed Lar will be stopping by at seven. You can thank me for persuading him to let you stake out the phone."

"The one in Duffy Square? Of course I'm going to stake it out. Tom expects me to be there tomorrow morning. Me, and no one else. If he sees that I'm being shadowed by the local law, he'll call the whole thing off."

Stone was certain that Tom wouldn't be anywhere near Duffy Square, but he didn't want to waste time evading local surveillance after he found out where Tom wanted him to go.

Welch said, "We have to cooperate with the locals, Adam. That's how it is now."

"If you can't call off Lar and his men, things could go bad very quickly."

"I'm sure you'll be able to find a way around it. We'll talk tomorrow and see what we can come up with."

"Maybe you can tell me something now. Why are so many of the old gang involved? There's Tom, of course, and you and me, Nathan Tate. . . . I wonder how many more. I wonder if it has something to do with the Old Man."

"Most of Knightly's brain is shut down. He couldn't plot his way out of his diapers."

"The last time I talked to him, in the middle of that mess over SWIFT SWORD, he told me that he was in need of a few good men. He never got around to explaining what he wanted them for, but I can't help wondering now if some of his cowboy angels might still be working for him. And I also can't help wondering if this might have something to do with the Company's current internal problem."

"We can ask Tom about it, when we bring him in," Welch said, and cut the connection.

Linda was waiting outside the restroom. Stone said, "I'm sorry I missed the rest of that song."

He was, too.

"You attracted some attention," Linda said. "Only Men in Black carry cell phones."

"Men in Black?"

"It's what unfriendly locals call us. Like the guy who got in my face just now, asking why I was hanging out with the enemy. It's okay, he was just some drunk, easy enough to deal with. But I think we should get out of here before someone decides to start some real trouble."

They'd gone less than a block when a battered four-door sedan with fat chrome bumpers and rocket-ship fins sharked up onto the sidewalk. Three young men climbed out. With their shaven heads, chests bare under army-surplus camo jackets, and black jeans tucked into heavy combat boots, they looked like brothers from an unfavoured family. The tallest had a tattoo of the Confederate flag on the side of his neck and flicked open a butterfly knife as he walked toward Stone; the other two circled wide, beating the ends of their aluminium baseball bats on the sidewalk while the kid with the knife told Stone that he was going to find out what colour his guts were.

"If you're going to do it, son, do it," Stone said.

He stepped inside the knife's wild swing, caught the kid's wrist, and spun him around, bearing down on his arm and twisting it until the shoulder joint gave with a sharp click. The kid squealed and dropped his knife; Stone shoved him away and pulled out his Colt .45.

Linda had also drawn her pistol. The two boys with the baseball bats were backing away from her. Stone watched the kid with the dislocated arm stumble after them. He watched as they fell into their car and squealed away with a defiant blare of their horn.

"You did all right," Stone told Linda.

She had a little trouble sliding her pistol, a sleek little Beretta, into the holster under the hem of her green shirt, and her smile was shaky. "At least we know we really did blow off Mr. Lar's people. They would have been all over those idiots."

"Why don't you take me somewhere where we can have a quiet drink? We need to talk about what we have to do tomorrow."

# 5.

"It sounds like you had a run-in with representatives of the local version of the Minutemen," David Welch said, after Stone had finished telling him about the brief tussle with the three thugs. "They used to be a gang of white supremacists. Now they're a self-styled patriotic movement that's taken to targeting anyone from the Real—they claimed responsibility for nail-bombing a Red Cross walk-in clinic in Newark a couple of days ago. Frankly, no one would have made any fuss if you'd terminated them right there on the sidewalk."

They were in the hotel's dining room. The lights in the crystal chandeliers seemed too bright at this early hour. Waiters were laying silverware on tables spread with white linen. Welch was working his way through a stack of pancakes with a side order of Canadian bacon, pausing every now and then to take a drag from the cigarette burning in the crystal ashtray by his elbow.

"You'll regret that heavy breakfast if we have to go chasing after Tom," Stone said. He'd eaten half a grapefruit and was sipping black coffee laced with sugar.

"I don't plan to go chasing after anyone," Welch said, "and I don't expect you to go chasing after anyone either. All that's going to happen: Tom is going to phone you, and you're going to talk to him and work out a way of bringing him in alive."

"Tom wants to talk to me, that much we can agree on. But how do you know he wants to talk about surrendering himself?"

Welch dabbed a forkful of pancake in the pool of maple syrup on the side of his plate and pushed it into his mouth. "Tom was a good field officer in his day, one of the best, but he's no Superman. He knows he can't get out of this sheaf and he knows the net is closing around him. That's why he left that message at the scene of the crime. He wants to talk to someone he knows and trusts because he wants to work out a way of coming in safely."

"I hope you're right."

"Of course I'm right. Ed Lar will have had his psychologists up all night, working out ways to play Tom, writing scripts for different scenarios. But you're his friend, Adam. You don't need any scripts or coaching. All you have to do is let him talk. Encourage him, be sympathetic, agree to anything he demands. Above all, convince him that you're on his side. It shouldn't be that difficult. After all, he took some trouble to reach out to you. It was unfortunate Ed Lar found out about the matchbook, but the important thing is that you found it in the first place. It's a bona fide cry for help if ever I saw one."

"The locals had me under close surveillance," Stone said, resenting the way Welch had twisted things around. "They knew I'd found something and I wasn't in a position to deny it."

Welch folded another forkful of pancake into his mouth and said around it, "Ed Lar will want you to keep Tom on the line long enough to get a trace. He'll want you to get Tom to agree to a meeting, and he'll probably suggest a couple of possible venues. Cooperate with him as far as you can, but remember that the locals don't have Tom's best interests in mind. They don't want to bring him in alive. They want to put him in clear view of one of their sharpshooters."

Stone was worried that David Welch—or the people for whom Welch was working—didn't have Tom Waverly's best interests in mind either. He had already decided that he would meet up with Tom on his own terms, no one else's. See what his old friend had to say for himself, and take it from there.

He said, "I guess you have a plan to get around the locals."

Welch picked up his cigarette and took a drag. His smile so white in his tanned face, so sly. He was in his element, playing one side against another. Stone was sure that he knew a lot more about Tom Waverly's killing spree than he'd so far let on, but was also sure that, if challenged, Welch would deny everything without altering his smile by so much as a fraction of an inch.

"There's a farm out in the sticks we used for covert entry into this sheaf before we made ourselves known to the government," Welch said. "The gate's no longer there, but we still own the place. Tom knows all about it. When he calls you at this pay phone, you should suggest meeting him there—at the old farm. He'll know exactly what you mean, but the locals won't have clue one. Tell him you'll be there for him, alone and unarmed. Tell him you'll go in bare-ass naked if that's what he wants. And if he insists on another venue, make sure he understands that you can't guarantee that it won't be compromised by the locals."

Stone said, because he knew that Welch would be suspicious if *he* didn't seem suspicious, "Will this old farm be compromised? Will there be Company sharpshooters waiting for Tom to show?"

"Remember what the Old Man used to say about working in the field? That thing he claimed to have borrowed from Kipling?"

"'Not to trust anyone: that is the whole of the law.'"

"There you go. I understand why you're anxious, Adam. I don't blame you. But you have to believe me when I say that the Company really does want Tom to come in safely."

"Is that because he knows something about this internal problem that's causing so much trouble right now?"

Welch skated right past that. "Listen to what Tom has to say. He'll probably assume the phone line is tapped, but make sure he knows it anyway. Float the idea of meeting at the old farm. And if you have to abort the call for any reason, make sure that Tom knows why. Make sure he knows you'll be waiting for him to get back in contact."

"Or I could tell him I'm holding a gun to his daughter's head. Tell him she'll get it if he doesn't surrender himself."

"I guess you're still sore about my little surprise. Listen, Adam, if I thought threatening Linda would bring Tom in from the cold, I'd be happy for you to do it, and I'm sure Linda would agree to it, too. But Tom *wants* to come in, so it isn't necessary. What we have to do is make sure he can do it safely." Welch looked at something behind Stone, then glanced at his Rolex and said, "He's a little early. Anxious to get in his five cents' worth, I bet."

Stone turned and saw Ed Lar bearing down on them, leading a small group of civilians and men in police uniforms through the ranks of empty tables.

"Listen to what they have to say, but don't take any shit from them," Welch said.

"I don't plan on taking shit from anyone," Stone said.

The number Tom Waverly had written on the matchbook cover was for one of the pay phones that stood in a short row on the triangular traffic island of Duffy Square, at the northern end of Times Square. Stone sat on the plinth of the life-sized statue of George M. Cohan, right in front of the phones, leafing through a copy of the *New York Times*. He was wearing his black suit, an earpiece, and a throat microphone. A radio transmitter was clipped to his belt. As he turned pages, the idle chatter of Ed Lar's chase team whispered in his earpiece. Traffic shuddered past on either side, a stop-go avalanche of metal and exhaust fumes and braying horns. Yellow taxis, buses, army trucks repainted in the blue-and-white livery of the Reconstruction and Reconciliation Corps, a scattering of private vehicles. Swarms of cyclists blew whistles and rang bells as they wove through stationary lines of vehicles, shot red lights, and skimmed past clots of pedestrians.

This version of Times Square had an old-fashioned, down-at-heel look. The façades of old theatres were not yet hidden behind video displays, news headlines still chased around the famous zipper sign, and the *New York Times* had not yet quit the elegant Italianate building at the southern end. Stone flashed on another time, another sheaf—bodies scattered among rubble and craters across a wide plaza fringed by massive Greek-revival buildings, half of them in flames, all of them badly damaged by fire and tank shells, grey air tasting of cordite and rotten meat. Better to think of the birch woods of New Amsterdam. Better to think of Susan. She was probably ploughing that half acre right now, slim and strong and capable in jeans and one of her dead husband's shirts. . . .

Stone wanted to believe that in a few days he'd be back in the First Foot sheaf, back with Susan and Petey. That he'd never have to leave again. He didn't have David Welch's cockeyed optimism, but he did have Linda waiting for him in a car downtown, and last night in his room he'd worked out three different ways of escaping the locals' surveillance, their sharpshooters and heavy squads. All he had to do was drop out of sight, arrange a face-to-face with Tom Waverly, and, if Welch was right, if Tom was looking for an exit strategy, find a way to bring him in under the radar. There were a lot of holes in the scheme, most especially Tom's motivation for wanting to contact him in the first place, but Stone had a good feeling about this. He was pumped up and tamped down. He was in his element, doing what he'd been trained to do. A player back in the game.

From his perch at the feet of Broadway's Yankee Doodle Dandy, he could see two of Ed Lar's men dressed as Con-Ed workers busily doing no work whatsoever around a manhole flagged off from the traffic. The jump-out crew were inside a van with Con-Ed decals parked nearby, watching Stone through the two-way glass in the back windows and the periscope hidden in the roof ventilator. The guy selling roasted nuts from a cart on the corner of Forty-Fifth Street was one of Ed Lar's men too; so was the panhandler pestering passers-by under the Shubert Theater's awning. Ed Lar, David Welch, the police psychologist, and two police captains were in the coffee shop of the Edison Hotel, nursing two-way radios and a feed from the phone tap.

Stone, the focus of all this attention, passed the time by working out this sheaf's recent history from the newspaper headlines. He didn't need to read much beyond the front-page leads, which were all about the ongoing war in

Texas. A diagram showed the state of the battle lines. Arrows bent toward Austin. Apparently there was a good chance that combined American forces could push the European Community Army into Mexico by Christmas. There were wars in Saudi Arabia and Persia, too. *Shah commits tanks, fifty thousand men to the Northern Front.*

The same old same old. Jimmy Carter was trying to bring peace to Americas in a dozen sheaves, but in most of them he was having a hard time making it stick.

Although primary Turing gates accessed new sheaves at random, so far they had only opened onto those where history had diverged sometime in the last fifty years, or where there were no humans at all, only apemen—so-called wild sheaves, where the ancestors of modern humans had long ago died out, and other primate species had begun to evolve a limited form of intelligence instead. No one had ever come up with a convincing theory to explain why no gate had ever accessed a sheaf where America was still a British colony, or where it had been settled by the Chinese or the Spanish, much less truly exotic sheafs where dinosaurs still ruled the Earth, say, or where intelligent squid gardened the oceans. Some historians suggested that there were no exotic histories because truly global history hadn't emerged until the twentieth century, and only global history could affect the minds of a majority of the human population and cause change on the scale needed to create a new sheaf. They pointed to the variety of alternate Americas that had suffered atomic war and claimed that it was the effect of history on mass consciousness that mattered, not the actions of any single individual; that so-called great men were shaped by history, not the other way around; that histories accessed by Turing gates were variations on a limited number of themes because their histories were those most likely to happen.

Physicists disagreed. They said that quantum theory did not distinguish between the path of a photon and the course of an atomic war; that while most divergent histories lasted less than a picosecond, a random few would always survive, accumulating differences until collapse back to their original state was no longer possible. Anything that *could* happen *would* happen, somewhere or other, but access to an infinite variety of sheaves was limited by a mapping problem. The multiverse was like a rubber sheet that had been stretched and warped and crumpled into a ball; it wasn't surprising that all the Turing gates opened so far connected with sheaves that were either similar to the Real or devoid of human occupation, because those two types of sheaf happened to enjoy a close topological relationship with the Real, and so were the easiest to reach. In time, as the volume of computational space explored by quantum computers increased, new Turing gates would be able to connect to more distant and more exotic sheaves.

Some people believed that this had already happened: there were plenty of rumours of secret facilities where gates opened onto sheaves beyond human imagination or understanding. But this was the stuff of pulp fiction, a pseudoscientific fantasy on a par with the crackpot theories that access to new sheaves was controlled by aliens or by quantum computers that had secretly evolved self-awareness, or that reality was nothing more than a game spun by inhuman hyperintelligences living in the distant future, our children's children's children reaching back into their past and manipulating their ancestors, jealously guarding their time line. . . .

Stone checked his watch and turned a page of the newspaper. It seemed that Elvis Presley and his fourth wife were separating.

Lar's voice said in his ear, "He's late."

"Maybe your fake Con-Ed workers scared him off," Stone said, and the pay phone rang.

Lar said, "Stations, everyone. Go ahead, Mr. Stone. Answer the damn thing."

As soon as Stone spoke his name into the receiver, Tom Waverly said, "Corner of Forty-Fourth and Eighth. You have three minutes."

Stone ran, dodging through bumper-to-bumper traffic with Lar yelling in his ear and the beggar and two men from the jump-out crew chasing after him. The Con-Ed van sounded its horn, trying to force its way past a column of R&R Corps trucks; Forty-Fourth Street was one-way, and Stone was running against the direction of the traffic. Lar was still yelling in his ear. Stone ripped out the earpiece and peeled off the throat mike as he rounded the corner and spotted a phone booth. The phone inside was ringing. He snatched it up and took a breath that hurt his throat and said, "I'm here."

"You're out of condition," Tom Waverly said. "Do you have friends or are you alone?"

One of the jump-out guys caught up with Stone, breathing hard. His partner and the fake beggar were some way behind.

"I have a few friends, nothing serious," Stone said into the phone.

"Tell them to stay back for the next leg or that's it."

"Okay."

"Inside the bus terminal," Tom Waverly said. "By the men's restroom on the second floor. It's only a couple of blocks. A former high school running-track star like you should be able to make it inside two minutes."

"Tom—"

"The clock's started," Tom Waverly said, and the line went dead.

Stone caught the jump-out guy's arm. "He's playing telephone tag. If you follow me, the deal's off."

The man repeated this into his cell phone, listened for a moment, then shook his head. "I'm sorry, Mr. Stone, I have to—"

Stone's uppercut caught the man on the side of the jaw and he reeled back and sat down hard. Stone shook the sting from his knuckles and took off along Eighth Avenue, running between slow-moving, nose-to-tail lanes of trucks and cars and taxis. He could feel his shirt sticking and unsticking to his back. The soft tar of the road slapped the thin soles of his shoes. Soldiers packed into the back of a flatbed truck cheered him on. A cyclist swerved to avoid him and slammed into the back of a taxi. Stone jerked the transmitter from his belt and dropped it in a trash basket as he ran through the intersection at Forty-Second Street and charged into the grimy monolith of the Port Authority Bus Terminal.

The second-floor concourse was full of buses and lines of soldiers and civilians. Stone, breathing like a broken steam engine, sweat stinging his eyes, saw the sign for the restrooms and bulled his way through the crowd and the noise of buses backing up, the harsh stink of diesel fumes. A young soldier was talking into one of the phones. Stone grabbed the receiver from him and heard only the dial tone. The soldier got in his face, Stone pulled his pistol and told him to get lost, and another phone started to ring.

Stone snatched it up and said, "It wasn't anyone. Some soldier."

Tom Waverly said, "Remember our last job together, in the McBride sheaf?"

Stone's blood was thumping in his head. His entire body was slippery with sweat. "It's kind of hard to forget."

"Remind me of the name of the guy who whispered in Jack Walker's ear."

"It was a blind woman, she went by the name of Molly Gee. Listen to me a minute," Stone said, speaking quickly because he was scared that Tom would hang up before he got it all out. "David Welch wants me to tell you to meet up at the old farm, but I know he'll have a snatch squad lying in wait there. So I've made arrangements to get out from under and blow off any tail. We can arrange to meet anywhere you want, Tom. All you have to do is name a time and place and I'll be there. No wire, no backup, just you and me for as long as you like."

"I knew I could rely on you, Adam. You always were an honest soldier."

"I made you a serious offer, Tom. If this is about having fun, playing me, playing the Company, maybe we should forget about it."

Stone had his back to the phone booth, the steel-wrapped cord over his shoulder and the receiver jammed against the side of his face as he scanned the grimy, crowded concourse. Buses idling under the low concrete ceiling. People boarding buses, people climbing off buses, people sitting behind the windows of buses. No sign of Tom Waverly. No sign of any of Lar's soldiers either, but Stone knew that they wouldn't stay back forever.

Tom Waverly's voice said in his ear, "This is about making sure things come out right. Let's get back to the McBride sheaf. After I came for you, while we were waiting to be brought out, I told you something I've never told anyone else. Remember?"

Stone blanked for a moment. "What is this, Tom, you don't know who you're talking to?"

"If you can't remember what I told you before the helicopters came to extract us, I'll have to hang up."

"We talked about a lot of things. I was lying on the ground, bleeding hard, and you were telling me to hold on, that everything was going to be okay. Which worried the hell out of me, because I thought you thought I was dying. Listen, Tom—"

"I told you about the orphanage, and that's the only clue you're going to get."

A memory surfaced. Stone said, "You broke into the orphanage office one time, and looked up your file. You found out who your mother was."

"I found out where she lived, too. Remember that? Where she lived, where I was born. Don't say the name of the place, just tell me that you remember."

"I remember."

"In this sheaf, my father did the right thing and married my mother. They still live in that little town. My doppel, too. I want you to go there right now, Adam. There's a motel, the Crest Inn, just north of the railroad tracks. Wait for me there. If you're alone, I'll come talk to you."

"I'll be there. One more thing—"

But Stone was talking to the dial tone, and there was a commotion by the stairs on the far side of the concourse. The fake beggar and a posse of uniformed cops were pushing through the crowds, heading toward him. He dropped the phone and ran in the opposite direction.

# 6.

Stone took the A train to Penn Station. In the Real, the station's original Belle Époque building, an elaborate reworking of the Roman Baths of Caracalla, had been demolished to make way for an expansion of Madison Square Gardens, but it was still intact in this sheaf. An upscale outdoor sports store anchored one corner of the grand arcade. Stone purchased two sets of clothing, two pairs of hiking boots, and a canvas rucksack, and changed into a brown cord shirt, blue jeans, and an imported, eye-wateringly expensive waterproof jacket, then dumped his suit and shoes in a trash basket and rode the subway four stops along Seventh Avenue.

He emerged in a bleak plaza surrounded on three sides by housing project high-rises, loitered by the subway stairs for a few minutes but saw nothing suspicious, and then ambled toward Fourteenth Street. Relief washing through him when he saw Linda Waverly step out of the white Dodge parked at the curb, red hair blowing back from her pale face in the cold, faintly radioactive wind.

# 7.

There were no roadblocks on the Hudson Parkway; the police radio under the car's dash crackled with nothing more than routine chatter about routine crimes. After they had gone past White Plains and he was certain that they had evaded the local law enforcement agencies, Stone relaxed into the leather upholstery and told Linda about the business with the pay phones, told her that her father had sounded sane and in control.

Linda said, "Did he tell you where he's at?"

"He pointed me toward a place where we can meet up."

"I don't suppose you're going to tell me where that is."

"Not yet."

It occurred to Stone that Tom Waverly might have told his daughter that he'd found out where he'd been born. If he had, and if the Company knew about it, this simple plan for making contact might turn out to be not so simple after all.

"Judging by your new outfit, it's somewhere out in the sticks," Linda said. "Someplace where you expect to do some hiking."

She was speaking slightly too loudly, as if there was someone else in the car.

Stone said, "See that gas station up ahead? We'll stop there for a moment."

"We have a full tank."

"Stop anyway."

Stone bought a sheaf of local maps, studied them while Linda drove, and told her they'd stick to the back roads as much as possible.

"If we're heading north, the Taconic will be faster. Or if we're heading west or east, we should take the Interstate."

"We're not in a hurry. And the back roads will be quieter."

"You don't trust me," Linda said flatly, as if commenting about something incontrovertible, like a change in the weather.

"It's nothing personal."

"Do I sound like I'm taking it personally?"

"As a matter of fact, you sound very calm."

"You don't trust me, you don't trust Mr. Welch, but I guess you must trust my father, or you wouldn't be here."

"I came here to help him. That's what I'm doing."

"Because he saved your life, once upon a time."

"Because he's my friend."

A couple of miles passed.

Linda said, "Maybe you could tell me about it—the time my father saved your life."

"I shouldn't have mentioned it. I had a weak moment."

"If you don't want to talk about it, if it's too embarrassing or whatever, I'll understand. But I'd like it if you did, if only to fill in these awkward silences on this long drive to wherever it is we're going."

"You remind me of your father," Stone said.

"I do?"

"When he wanted you to tell him something, he'd keep at it until you gave it up."

"Where was it he helped you out?"

"The McBride sheaf. Do you know it?"

"I hear it's pretty bad. They had a cold war between America and the Soviets, just like here, but it blew up into a worldwide nuclear conflict, not a relatively limited exchange like they had here."

"Global spasm," Stone said. "Both sides threw everything they had at each other. Every large city in America was hit at least once. Three and a half billion people died. That was in 1968. Eight years later, when we opened a gate into the sheaf, there was nothing left anywhere but gangs fighting over rubble."

"And you guys went in to help bring back civilisation."

"Not exactly. We went in to eliminate the sworn enemy of a crazy man who'd become president of the United States by default."

General E. Everett McBride had been inside Strategic Air Command's command site at Colorado Springs when World War Three began. The Soviets dumped a stick of hydrogen bombs on the mountain under which the command site was buried, reducing its height by several hundred feet, turning a vast swathe of countryside to vitreous slag, and incidentally vaporising Denver. But the hardened command site survived, and so did most of its personnel: six months later, they emerged to take control of a country that now existed only in General McBride's imagination.

McBride was an air force technocrat with no combat experience, and a Christian fundamentalist who was convinced that the nuclear war had been nothing less than Armageddon. All true believers and the risen dead had been translated directly into Heaven as a prelude to the Last Battle between Satan and the Risen Christ, and McBride and his soldiers and technicians had been left behind because they were of insufficient faith. Now they had to prove themselves worthy of redemption by destroying the enemies of the Lord; in particular, they had to identify and defeat the Antichrist, who even now would be plotting to take control of all the nations of the Earth, probably through the agency of the United Nations.

As soon as it was safe to leave the command site's deep bunkers, McBride led his men on a crusade toward the eastern seaboard, but within days of setting out he ran into a ferocious and well-armed group of survivors. Most of his little army were slaughtered, and the survivors were chased back into the mountains. When the Company opened a Turing gate into his sheaf eight years later, he was no more than a petty warlord struggling to hold on to a few hundred square miles of territory. But despite his lowly status, and although he was suffering from tuberculosis and tertiary syphilis, and his soldiers were given to raping captured women and torturing and ritually cannibalising captured men who refused to convert to his cause, General E. Everett McBride was still, according to the rules of succession, president of the United States.

Aided by detailed scenarios provided by the Company's supercomputer cluster, the National Foreign Intelligence Board decided that McBride would be a suitable figurehead for the reunification of the United States of America, and acted accordingly. Several hundred Special Forces troops took out McBride's local rivals and helped him to establish a form of government in the little city of Las Vegas, New Mexico, but attempts to open routes to the west and south (the territory to the north, covered by the footprint of the radioactive fallout from the massive nuclear strike on Colorado Springs, would be uninhabitable until the middle of the next century) were hindered by hit-and-run attacks on supply columns and assaults on settlements that received aid from the new government. The guerrillas even managed to shoot down several helicopters with modified rocket-propelled grenades. When hot interrogation of captured unfriendlies revealed that this resistance was controlled by one man, Adam Stone and Tom Waverly were sent into the McBride sheaf to take him out.

Two weeks later, Stone was taken prisoner by a guerrilla patrol while riding up into the Sangre de Cristo Mountains to obtain intelligence from a

Native American village. It was winter, and bitterly cold. A steady wind blew snow dry as polystyrene pellets into Stone's face as he followed his two guides through a steep forest of aspen and ponderosa pine. He didn't like to think what this northern bone-cutter might be carrying from the plateau around Colorado Springs and the multiple craters of what had once been Los Alamos, but it was good to get away from the squalid chaos of Las Vegas.

Although it had been declared the capital of the United States more than a year ago, the little city was still mostly in ruins. The historic city centre had been burned and looted in riots immediately after the war, and the extremes of postnuclear weather had left its suburbs in little better condition. The army base that sprawled next to the railhead, with its runway and hangars, bunkers and razor-wire perimeter, was surrounded by growing camps of refugees. Trench sewers ran alongside mud roads, there was one standpipe for roughly every hundred people, and the only health clinic was regularly overwhelmed by epidemics of typhoid, yellow fever, and dysentery. President McBride lived in a concrete bunker and spent most of his time drunk, while his soldiers raced around the city in imported Jeeps. Although they were supposed to be keeping the peace, they routinely ransacked the refugee camps, stole medicines and food, and kidnapped women. Nights in Las Vegas crackled with gunfire, and every morning two or three mutilated corpses were discovered around the perimeter of the army camp.

In the mountains, the only vestiges of nuclear war were a few north-facing slopes where regrowth had not yet hidden the trunks of trees smashed flat by overpressure of the strike on Los Alamos. Everywhere else, pines and aspen thickened in every direction, half buried in deep drifts. Snow hazed the sky and blew between the trees and muffled the hooves of the horses of Stone and his two taciturn guides as they followed an old road.

The ambush was sudden, swift, and ruthless. A horse snickered among trees to one side of the road, and before Stone or his guides could draw their pistols a quick burst of gunfire flamed through the blowing snow. Stone's horse pranced and reared. By the time he had it under control, his guides lay dead and the guerrillas had ridden onto the road in front of him.

There were eight of them, mostly lean wolfish teenagers with long hair greased up in stiff spikes or tied back in pigtails stuck with feathers dyed red or yellow. They were mounted on nimble ponies with plaited manes and tails and wore a ragged motley of uniforms and furs and hides. Two of them went straight past Stone, their ponies kicking up puffs of snow as they galloped away down the trail; two more trained M-16 rifles on him as their leader caught at the snaffle of his horse and told him to climb down and take off his clothes; the rest dismounted and began to strip the bodies of the guides.

The leader was a black man whose face was a piebald patchwork of old burn scars. He wore a fur cap and a long coat stitched from a dozen dog hides. He watched closely, leaning on the pommel of his saddle, as two of his teenage soldiers searched Stone's clothes and his saddlebag. He examined the radio transmitter one of them handed to him, and asked Stone if he could use it to talk to the people in Las Vegas.

"Sure." Stone stood at the centre of a loose circle of ponies and riders, wearing only a T-shirt, thermal underpants, and wool socks. Frozen pellets blew in his eyes. He was trying not to shiver in the cutting wind. He was trying not to look at the bodies of his guides sprawled naked and bloody on the snow.

One of the teenagers said, "Ain't it the rule we don't bring back any electrical gear? Stuff can be used to track us."

"If it isn't switched on, it can't do anything. And Jack needs to talk to this man's kin," the piebald man said, and told Stone to get dressed.

"Where are you taking me?"

Stone's fingers were white with cold. He was having trouble doing up the buttons of his shirt.

The piebald man's grin showed toothless gums. "Into the mountains."

The pair who had ridden down the trail came back and conferred briefly with their leader. Stone was allowed to climb back on his horse, and rode in the middle of the pack along a path of trampled snow that climbed through the forest. Each man rode as if alone, no sound but the muffled step of the ponies and the chink of bit rings. At some point it stopped snowing. The trees gave way to a bare rock ridge swept clean of snow by a tireless wind that blew into the faces of the riders as they mounted the crest and rode down into the valley beyond. They forded a swift-moving river and turned to follow it as light faded from the sky.

No fire was lit when the guerrillas at last made camp. In the iron dusk they drank water dipped from the river and ate cold K-rations taken from Stone's saddlebag and twisted strings of dry deer meat tough and tasteless as bootlaces. Two men were posted to keep watch. The rest slept in a close huddle; slept as innocently as animals, as if they were the first men in a world where no sin had yet been committed.

Stone dozed fitfully, waking once to the plangent music of wolves, feeling cold to the marrow of his bones even though he was padded out in all his clothes and wrapped in his silvery thermal blanket. At daybreak, the guerrillas did not pay especial attention to him while they made ready to leave, and he rode with them unhindered as they followed the course of the river to the head of the valley, where water fell in a smooth rush from a steep notch in a tall cliff, thickly fringed with icicles taller than any man. They dismounted and followed a winding path through boulders capped with clear ice, walking in single file and leading their mounts like penitent pilgrims approaching a shrine. At the top, they remounted and rode on across a stony slope caught about with wind-sculpted drifts. Stripped and shattered trunks of dead trees all leaned south. In the far distance mountains stood against the edge of the pale sky, serene and remote as a celestial city.

At around noon, the piebald man rode up close on the left side of Stone's horse and told him that he would have to travel the rest of the way blindfold. A hood of black cloth was pulled over his head and cinched tight around his neck. It was hard to breath through the hood's clammy weave, and Stone clung to the saddle's pommel as his horse was led down a steep slope through thick-growing trees. Fragrant pine boughs slapped at his legs and chest and hooded face, and he almost fell off when the horse stumbled in deep snow. They crossed a swift river, the current pushing hard against the side of Stone's horse as it stepped uneasily and tossed its head. Stone clamped his legs to its flanks and clutched his saddle; bitterly cold water filled his boots and soaked his trousers. One of the young guerrillas said something that he couldn't quite catch, two more laughed, and that was all the noise they made until the end of the journey. It was a discipline that he admired and feared.

At last, with the horses' hooves thumping regularly on packed snow, the leader spoke up from behind and said that he reckoned it was safe for Stone to unmask. Stone pulled off the hood and took deep breaths of fresh cold air as he looked around. Sweat cooled on his face. The boy who had been leading his horse flipped the reins to him. He was in the middle of the file of mounted men, riding up a path with a wall of red sandstone on one side and on the other a steep drop to a box canyon in which the tops of leafless bushes showed like half-buried spiders among pure white untrodden snow. Then the path made a sharp turn and revealed a wide cliff face where a huddle of small, square, flat-roofed adobe houses of great age leaned in teetering stacks of three and four. Above these rude snow-capped huts, a long ledge cut deeply into the face of the cliff, sheltered by a bulging overhang. Ragged people stood along its edge; behind them, houses were scattered under the rock roof like the nests of swallows.

The guerrillas riding in front of Stone whooped and spurred their ponies, standing up in their stirrups as their mounts cantered away up the narrow path. Stone and the rest of his captors went in single file around a stack of adobe houses to the shelter of the ledge. Following the lead of his captors, Stone swung down from the saddle and stood holding the reins of his horse, his feet pinched and throbbing with incipient frostbite inside his wet boots and the cold smoking off his clothes. A little crowd of men and women and children crept up to him, parting to allow two people to step through.

One was an old woman wrapped in layers of drab and tattered clothes, her face horribly scarred, a twist of cloth tied over her eyeless sockets. A tame crow stood on her shoulder, cocking its sleek head this way and that. The other was a tall young man with a sharp blue gaze, long black hair, and a casually imperious bearing. Stone knew at once that here was the man that he and Tom Waverly had come to kill: the leader of the guerrillas, Jack Walker.

Stone found it hard to describe the impact of Jack Walker's presence. He said to Linda Waverly, "Have you ever met anyone with real charisma?"

"I met President Davis once, at the ceremony where my father was awarded the Intelligence Star. We were sitting in this little room with a podium up front, waiting with a bunch of other recipients and their families, and when the president walked in everyone stood up and started to applaud. You could feel the excitement in the air. It was as if the lights had been turned up. Afterward, the president worked the room. He exchanged a few words with my father, and my father introduced me to him. He had this way of grasping your wrist instead of your hand and sort of hanging on, looking you right in your eyes while he talked to you. For those few second he made you feel that, as far as he was concerned, you were the only person in the world," Linda said, smiling at the memory.

"That's how it was with this guy, Jack Walker. He was just a kid, but he was a natural leader. He commanded attention."

"The only time I ever saw my father blush was when the president handed him that medal."

"He got a kick out of it, huh?"

"Wouldn't you?"

"I was awarded the Exceptional Service Medallion about the same time.

They give it for injury or death resulting from service in an area of hazard. Some middle-ranking staffer dropped it off while I was in hospital—I guess that's the difference between being rescued and being the rescuer."

Linda glanced over at him and said, "I do believe you're a cynic, Mr. Stone."

They were four hours beyond New York now. They had skirted around Albany and were still driving north. Stone had his cell phone in his lap. He'd been checking its signal every ten minutes. Now he checked it again, and said, "We need to pull over for a moment."

Linda looked at him.

"See that fire road up ahead? Pull over there."

There was no other traffic on the road, but Linda looked in the rearview mirror and put on the car's blinkers before she brought it to a stop. When Stone took out his Colt .45 and told her to drive a little way down the fire road, she set her jaw and said, "I don't think so."

"This is a necessary precaution, Linda. Nothing will happen to you, I swear. Drive nice and easy down into the trees. It looks pretty dry in there, so you shouldn't have any trouble."

"And if I don't?"

"Then I guess this is where you get out."

Linda squared her shoulders and released the emergency brake and set the selector to *Drive*. The big car wallowed like a boat along the corrugated surface of the unmade road, under the dense canopy of the pines. Half a mile in, Stone told Linda to park in a turnout, told her to take out her pistol by its barrel and toss it out the window.

"All right," he said, when she'd thrown the Berretta away. "Your watch, does it have sentimental value?"

"My mother gave it to me the day I graduated from NYU."

"Take it off and put it in the glove compartment. Put your cell phone in there too. Don't worry. I doubt anyone will find the car before our tail does."

"Our tail? Don't you think you're being a little a paranoid, Mr. Stone?"

"I've been wondering if it was David Welch's idea for you to take a car from the Company motor pool. It has a police radio and we were followed by the same model white Dodge last night. . . ."

Linda Waverly looked him in the eye and said, "I borrowed it."

"I bet you did." Stone gestured with the Colt and said, "Lose your watch, your jewellery, the phone. You can keep your driver's licence and ID."

After Linda had done as she was told, Stone plucked the keys from the ignition and climbed out, and told her to step out too. He popped the trunk, hurled the keys into the undergrowth, checked his cell phone again, and threw it after the keys, then told Linda, "Take the rucksack out of the trunk. We're going for a little hike."

He walked Linda at gunpoint away from the road, following a narrow deer path that cut through thick stands of ferns. The ground began to slope downward and the ferns gave way to a carpet of old needles spread thickly between the pines. Boulders broke through here and there. A bird sang somewhere in the shadows between the pines.

After a little while, Linda said, "I don't see how is this is going to help my father. They'll set up a grid search when they realise that we've gone missing, and when they find us they'll take us back to New York."

"Either they were tracking our cell phones or they fixed a transponder to the car. In any case, reception is pretty patchy out here. I lost the signal for my cell phone a mile before we turned off the highway; it was still out when we stopped. If we're lucky, the signals from anything they planted in the car will have trouble getting through, too. Our friends will probably overshoot and have to backtrack. By the time they find the car, we'll be long gone."

"So we become fugitives. How is that going to help my father?"

"We'll be able to talk freely with your father when we meet him. We'll be able to work out how to bring him in on his own terms. We might even find out why he got himself in this jam in the first place. Meanwhile, it'll make things a lot easier if you don't take this personally."

"That's getting kind of hard."

They walked through the heavy silence of the woods until they reached the edge of a steep slope that dropped to a stream running between mossy rocks and banks of ferns. Stone told Linda to set the rucksack down, told her to turn around nice and slow.

Linda did as she was told, her face set tight. She was wearing a black jacket and black trousers, the shades of black not quite matching, a white shirt, and black, flat-heeled shoes. Her hair, loose around her shoulders, was as vivid as freshly spilled blood in the green shadows under the trees. She said, "Whatever you want to do, let's get it over with."

"I want you to take off your clothes."

"You have got to be kidding."

Stone raised the Colt. "Take everything off. Nice and slowly, in case you've got a surprise hidden away somewhere."

After a moment, Linda said, "Okay, you win. There's a transponder in the heel of my shoe. The left one."

"The one you want me to know about."

"I swear it's the only one."

"Maybe there's another bug stuck somewhere in your clothes. Welch or someone else could have planted one on you and you wouldn't know about it. If you want to come the rest of the way, if you want to see your father, I have to be sure you're clean."

"I remembered you being a nice guy, but you're really a son of a bitch, aren't you?"

Linda shrugged off her jacket and started to undo the buttons of her shirt. When she had stripped down to her underwear, she stood looking at Stone with her arms crossed over her breasts, pale and pliant as a wood elf.

Stone said, "You'll have to lose the underwear too."

"Will you shoot me if I refuse?"

"I could leave you here, Linda, let you make your way back to the highway. By the time Welch's people find you, I'll be a hundred miles away. And you'll never find out why your father was killing these women, or why he wants to talk to me."

"At least point the gun the other way. Make it look a little less like rape."

"Right."

"And don't watch. I promise I won't try to hit you over the head with a rock."

Stone looked away, but was aware of Linda bending and straightening in the periphery of his vision. He said, "There are clothes in the rucksack. I think I got your size about right, but they're the kind of clothes that don't need to fit exactly."

She pulled on blue jeans and a red checked shirt, and cinched the jeans with a brown leather belt. She sat down on a rock, pulled on one of the hiking boots, and said, "These are a little too big."

"There's an extra pair of socks."

She put on the socks, laced the boots, and stood up. "I might have a transponder somewhere on my body. Under the skin, or in my stomach. Or in my vagina. Did you think of that, Mr. Stone? Want to check it out?"

Stone knew that she could allow herself to be angry now it was over. "I'll live with the risk. Pick up your clothes. We'll take them down to the stream."

He made Linda push her jacket and trousers and blouse and underwear under the stream's clear water. The clothes spread out as they sank. He knocked open the heel of her left shoe against a boulder, extracted the button-sized transponder from its pocket and dropped it into a foamy pool under the exposed roots of a birch tree, then tossed the shoes and Linda's shoulder holster in after it.

Linda said, "This isn't going to work, Mr. Stone. You've bought yourself a little time, but if the Company people don't find you, Ed Lar's people will. And if the locals find you, you won't have any backup. You won't be able to protect Dad from them."

"I think your father wants to tell me something, Linda. I want to hear what it is, and I want you to hear it too. Maybe he's gone crazy and wants to tell us that the Man in the Moon made him do it, but I don't think so."

"I want to talk to him too," Linda said, after a moment. "I want to know why he's been . . . doing what he's been doing."

"We'll find out soon enough." Stone took a bearing from the sun. "There's a town about two miles northeast of here. It'll be dark in a couple of hours, so we better get moving."

The little town was clustered around the place where a highway and a single-track railroad crossed a river at the bottom of a broad valley. The tall brick chimney of an old mill feathered white smoke into the clear sky. A neon sign on top of a bar put a radioactive glow in the darkening air.

As they approached the bar, Linda Waverly said, "Is this where Dad told you to meet him?"

"This where we're going to pick up some transport," Stone said, and told her to choose one of the cars and pickup trucks parked in the dirt lot beside the bar.

She picked a green Chevy with a bumper sticker that declared *Work is the curse of the drinking class*, and an empty half-pint of Wild Turkey on the back seat. Stone broke the window on the driver's side with a rock, slid inside and reached across and opened the passenger door. As Linda climbed in beside him, he pulled down the sun visor, and a spare set of keys slid into his hand.

Stone drove slowly out of the parking lot, turned left at the four-way, and drove uphill past clapboard houses, past an automobile cemetery in the woods at the edge of town. A junkyard dog chased the car's red lights a little way, stood in the middle of the road, and barked defiantly as they vanished over the top of the ridge.

# 8.

The stolen car's radio was a predigital fossil. Linda had to turn a knob to dial through music and sports stations, weather and local news reports, a phone-in about farm subsidies, a preacher promising healing for the faithful and hellfire for everyone else. She finally settled on a station playing bluegrass, but after a few minutes the signal broke up and she switched off the radio and they drove in silence for a while, following a road that switch-backed through hilly forest into Vermont. At last, Linda asked Stone if he would finish his story and explain how her father had rescued him from the guerrillas in the McBride sheaf.

"It'll help pass the time, and it'll help me get to know you a little better, too."

She was sitting sideways in the roomy front seat, her back against the door and one leg tucked beneath her.

"I don't know if I want you to know me."

Stone had spoken lightly, but Linda took his remark seriously. "You're just like my father. Whenever he came home, it was as if he had shut a door on that part of his life. Not that he came home very often, he was never what you could call a regular father. But we did manage to have a lot of fun together when I was growing up."

"I can imagine."

"He didn't like to sit around. He'd do chores around the house or work on one of his bikes, good old Bobby Dylan or some kind of old-time music blasting from the stereo he'd rigged up in the garage. What he most liked to do was tool around in this '55 Chevy he'd rebuilt, or ride the back roads on his motorcycle. When I was old enough, he'd take me on road trips. He taught me how to fish and shoot. He gave me a hunting crossbow for my six-teenth birthday—he and Mom had a huge fight about it."

Linda was putting up a good front, but Stone could tell that his move, losing the Company tail and more or less kidnapping her at gunpoint, had shaken her up more than she cared to admit: her thoughts were bouncing around like hornets in a jar.

She said, "When you were working in other sheaves, were you ever tempted to find out about any of your doppels?"

"Not once. For one thing, I was ordered not to. For another, I'm an orphan, like your father and every other field officer in Special Ops back in the early days. The idea was that we wouldn't be tempted to search out our doppels and blow our covers because none of us knew anything about our families, or where we'd come from."

By now, Stone was fairly certain that Linda didn't know that her father had discovered where he'd been born—if she did, she would surely have mentioned it by now. But he wasn't quite ready to tell her where they were heading, not while there was still a chance that she could, with the best of intentions, betray the rendezvous to the Company.

He said, "It's different for civilians, of course. I remember there was this TV show about doppels—"

"The one about ordinary people or the one about celebrities?"

"When I left the Real, there was only the one about ordinary people. *This Could Be Your Life.*"

It had been a cynical freak show that claimed First Amendment protection while courting cheap sensation by confronting terminal cancer patients with healthy doppels, losers with doppels who were millionaires in some other sheaf, God-fearing ordinary folk with doppels who were prostitutes or dopers.

"There's a bunch of them now," Linda said. "There's one where people vote on whether the doppel of a movie actor or a pop singer is better than the original, another where minor celebrities are confronted with their John Q. Public doppels. But the show that draws the biggest ratings is the one where the grieving relatives get to meet the doppels of their dead loved ones."

"Frankly, I never saw the point. Your doppel is a completely different person who happens to share a bit of common history with you. It's what you and your doppel *don't* share that's important."

"And that's exactly why people are curious about their doppels. They want to know how much of their life is shaped by who they are, and how much by contingency. They want to know if there's such a thing as destiny."

"I guess it depends on the person. Some swim against the tide, others are content to float along."

"Which are you, Mr. Stone? A swimmer or a floater?"

"Lately I've been content to live in a place where there aren't any tides."

A silence fell. Trees stood close together along one side of the winding road; the other dropped away to a small river barely visible in the blue bloom of the night. Cool night air blew through the broken window. Stone could hear the noise the river made as it ran over and around rocks.

Linda said, "This isn't getting the story told."

"What story?"

"The story about the last time you and Dad worked together. The operation in the McBride sheaf. The time he saved your life."

Stone smiled. "You aren't going to let it go, are you?"

"You started to tell me the story, Mr. Stone. It's only fair you finish it. There'd been a nuclear war. Civilisation had collapsed. You were captured by guerrillas, and my father was sent to rescue you. What happened after that? How did he get you out? Did he infiltrate the place where you were being held, and kill your captors one by one? Or did he pull off something highly dangerous and utterly spectacular?"

"Is that what you think we did? Kill everyone who got in our way?"

"There are all kinds of stories about you old-school guys."

"What I mostly used to do was work in libraries."

"Is that what my father used to do, too?"

"I guess he was a little more proactive."

"And he rescued you that time. He saved your life. You were taken prisoner. You were brought before this hugely charismatic guy. . . ."

"Jack Walker."

"Right. And then what happened?"

Stone steered the car around a long bend, headlights raking trees that stood up along the edge of the road like soldiers surprised in an ambush. "Jack Walker was charismatic, all right. He could talk to a man and convince him to murder his own mother, talk to a crowd and carry everyone with him. But charisma is dangerous because it has no moral dimension. It doesn't have anything to do with the character of the man who possesses it. Saints and tyrants, they're equally charismatic."

"And what was Jack Walker? Was he a saint or a tyrant?"

"He was on a crusade," Stone said, remembering the way Jack Walker had moved among his people, princely and insane. "He believed that he was the saviour of America. He had a utopian vision of a world without cities or agriculture, without any technology above the level of the bow and arrow and the stone axe. He wanted to turn the clock back to the Neolithic era, turn America into a pristine wilderness inhabited by small tribes of hunter-gatherers. And he was prepared to slaughter anyone who stood in his way. We became the focus of his crusade after we came through the mirror and started to interfere with local politics, but he'd been waging war against other survivors of the nuclear war long before we arrived. Families trying to settle down and make a new life for themselves would find a patch of unclaimed land and start to farm it, and Jack Walker and his ragtag band of guerillas would come along and offer them a very simple choice: join his cause, or die. Other warlords took food from the settlers, a little ammunition if they had it, maybe a horse or two, and in return promised protection against other warlords and bandits and gangs of crazy people. But Jack Walker wanted their souls, and he killed everyone who refused to yield to him. One of the settlements had rigged up a truck motor to give themselves electric lighting and run a refrigerator. Jack Walker's people rode down from the hills and killed them all, even the children and babies. He told me all about it. He was proud of the massacre, claimed that it was a great victory against the evil that had nearly destroyed the land. That's another thing about people with charisma, by the way. The first person they convince of the incorruptible righteousness of their vision is themselves. They are consumed by their own conviction."

"Why didn't he kill you?"

"He wanted to use me in a stunt to demonstrate his belief in absolute war. He was going to negotiate my release in exchange for some prisoners, then strap explosives to me and a couple of volunteers, and turn us into human bombs that would go off when I was handed over. I think he would have done it, too, if your father hadn't tracked me down. One of the men who captured me kept my radio because Jack Walker needed it for his negotiations. He didn't know that it put out a signal even when it wasn't switched on. It didn't have much range, but your father got close enough to pick it up. He went against standing orders, he didn't have any help from the army or the Company, but he found me."

After Stone was brought into the camp, Jack Walker sat him down and interrogated him for six hours straight. The guerrilla leader wanted to know about the disposition of army forces in and around Las Vegas, the health of the refugees crowded into the camps, the morale of McBride's men, the general's health and sanity. Stone stuck to his cover story, claimed that he was a Red Cross worker supervising a vaccination programme among outlying settlements, and gave harmless or incomplete answers to every question. Walker listened carefully and attentively, and never seemed to forget anything. He asked the same question a dozen different ways, pursuing flaws and inconsistencies and contradictions in Stone's answers with unflagging zeal. He had the sharpest mind Stone had ever encountered, but he had one crippling flaw: he was flat-out crazy.

At the end of the session, Stone was shoved into a tiny windowless room with two guards at the door, and given a bowl of thin corn gruel flecked with fatty gristle. Jack Walker came for him soon after daybreak and led him up to the ridge above the caves where his people had made their winter camp. Possessed by the unwavering solipsism of the true tyrant, he believed that he could convince Stone that his cause was true and righteous by the sheer force of his own personality.

The top of the ridge was a wind-blown sweep of rocks and snow and yellow grass. Low stone walls ran here and there, remnants of little houses built by the Anasazi about two thousand years ago. There was a tremendous view of mountains stepping away southward under a clear blue sky, their peaks hidden by clouds grey with unfallen snow.

In those mountains, Jack Walker told Stone, was the spot where he'd hidden out with his father while the world ended. His father had been an ecologist working for the National Park Service. He and Jack's mother had split up several years before the war, and Jack had seen little of him after the divorce had been finalised, but after a political crisis in Germany blew up into a full-scale confrontation between America and the Soviets, he turned up at Jack's school in Santa Fe one day and told him they were going on a little trip.

They drove into the mountains, left the car at a picnic area, and hiked through the forest to the remote valley where Jack's father had dug a deep shelter into a slope above a river, and hidden caches of food, guns, ammunition, tools, medicine, and clothing round and about. Jack and his father spent most of their time fishing, making an inventory of their stores, and listening to news bulletins and the president's speeches to the nation on the radio. The first report of full-blown war in Europe came three days after they moved into the shelter. A few hours later, the radio cut out in the middle of a prerecorded civil defence message.

It was just after noon. The flawless summer sky was suddenly crisscrossed with white contrails. Jack Walker and his father sealed the shelter's three sets of doors and hunkered down among boxes of canned and dry goods and bottled water. The clicking of the radiation counter grew into a steady roar. The radio picked up snatches of music, screaming rants, plaintive calls for help, a confusion of military and civil defence traffic. One by one the signals faded into a dismal universal hiss.

After they emerged from their shelter, Jack Walker and his father made no attempt to contact other survivors. They kept away from roads and houses. They hunted with bows and arrows, stitched coats and boots from hides, wove fish traps from willow switches, drove waterfowl into pens woven from reeds. Jack's father taught him everything he knew about the mountains, told him about the wonderful variety of plants and animals and the intricate web of checks and balances that kept them in ecological harmony, told him about the culture and history of the native people, the Anasazi, who had lived in the mountains and the desert to the south before Europeans stole the land and made it part of the great lie they called America.

Two years after the war, Jack's father died from blood poisoning after he pulled out an abscessed tooth. Jack gave him a sky burial on a platform raised on a high, rocky crest and set out into the new world. He remembered everything he'd been taught: it became the foundation of his belief that the war was both a punishment for man's hubris and a chance to begin afresh. Now, on the ridge above the guerrilla camp, looking out across the winter landscape toward the snow-capped mountains, Jack Walker told Stone about the lesson that could be learned from the sudden failure of the civilisation that the Anasazi had built across the Southwest.

"The climate changed," he said. "It became drier, their crops failed, and they could no longer feed themselves. There were too many people and there was not enough food. War broke out between the settlements—that's why the last of the Anasazi lived on the tops of mesas, and on ridges like this one, places that were easily fortified. They became so desperate they turned to cannibalism. If you dig through the middens of late-period Anasazi settlements, you'll find human bones with marks on them that show they were processed for meat, just like animal bones. You'll find skulls split open with stone axes, too, and skulls with scorch marks that show they were set on fires to roast them. Like the Anasazi, every society that relies on agriculture lives on the edge of catastrophe. All it takes is a couple of bad summers. It was because we relied on agriculture and technology that most of the survivors died after the war. They did not know how to live off the land, and in any case there were too many of them for the land to support."

The bitter wind plucked at the blanket Stone had wrapped around his shoulders and blew Walker's hair back from his face. His trousers and tunic were sewn from tanned deer hides that had been scraped with stone knives until they were as soft as butter. His deer-hide boots were lined with dry grass. He looked heroic. He looked frighteningly young.

Molly Gee, the old blind woman who followed him everywhere, crouched a little way off, a black blot in the snow. Her crow was perched on her shoulder, shrugging its wings to keep its balance in the wind. She seemed to be the only person Walker deferred to. He believed that she could see into the future.

"I love this land," he said. "I have sworn that no more harm will come to it. I told my father that, on his deathbed. When he could no longer stand the pain, I killed him and carried him to a high place and cut up his body so the crows and turkey vultures would take it back into nature. I was sixteen. That was when I became a man."

Walker was silent for a while. Stone clutched the blanket around his shoulders. The wind cut him to the bone.

"Before the war, we lived our lives out of balance," Walker said. "The war was a blessing. It was a great cleansing. We can't afford to make the same mistakes again, and that's why we will never surrender to your people. That's why we will drive you back through your gate and destroy it. You are a strong-willed and determined man. You haven't told me half as much as I need to know, and much of what you have told me is at best only half true. I could try to torture the truth from you, of course, but I think you would lie to me even under torture, and I have a better use for you. I will tell your bosses that I will exchange you for several of my people who were captured and are being held prisoner in Las Vegas."

For a moment Stone felt a pang of hope, felt that he might live through this after all. But then Walker explained the plan to turn him into a human bomb and told him that he should be happy, because his death would help to end the war.

"It will show your people that they cannot afford to fight us. It will prove to them that we will stop at nothing to drive them from our land, that we will never negotiate, and never submit. Yours will be a glorious death—a martyr's death! We will always remember and honour it."

The next day, a party of whooping warriors brought a new prisoner into the camp, a sturdy Native American on foot among the riders, his wrists bound and a cord looped around his chest and tied to the saddle of one of his captors. He had a gunshot wound in his shoulder but walked with straight-backed dignity, looking neither right nor left at the people who jeered and spat at him.

Jack Walker questioned the prisoner in front of Stone. He wanted to know where the man had come from, how many people lived there, how many had been born that year, how many had died, what crops they grew, what they had salvaged from the ruins of the old towns, but the man refused to answer any of the questions, saying only that he was the brother of one of the guides who had been leading Stone into the mountains, that he'd sworn to revenge his brother's death and had been tracking Walker's men when they had caught him.

When it was clear that the man wasn't going to give up any useful information, Walker handed him over to the mob. They stripped him naked and hung him by his heels over a fire and slowly roasted him by lowering him inch by inch toward the hot coals. The prisoner began to scream and thrash. A vile stink of burnt hair and roasting flesh filled the air. Black blood burst from his ears and nostrils.

Stone begged Walker to give the man a clean death. At first, the guerrilla leader feigned indifference to both Stone's pleas and the prisoner's screams, but after a few minutes he signalled to the youngest of his warriors and told him to finish it. The teenager strolled across the cave, pushed through the crowd around the fire, and cut the prisoner's throat with a single stroke.

"I gave him release because he told the truth and he was on an honourable quest," Walker said to Stone. "Also, if he did not come here alone, as he claimed, his screams would have brought his friends to us by now. Still, we will have to move on from here at first light. If he could find us, so could others. It will delay your martyrdom, my friend, but only by a day or so."

Stone tried once more to convince the young guerrilla leader that he had started a war he could not win, that instead of fighting against the new government he should become part of it and help shape the new America.

"This isn't about power," Walker said. "This is about ideas. I have studied your people. I have listened to their propaganda broadcasts and read the pamphlets they hand out to settlers. I know that they want to spread the same idea through all the different Americas, to impose a single way of life and obliterate everything else in the name of freedom. Have you never thought how wrong that is? Ideas are like trees. They are shaped by the place where they take root. And they can only take root in the right kind of place, the right kind of soil. Everywhere else, they wither and die."

"Frankly, I don't think much of your ideas. They mostly involve murdering people to prove yourself right."

Walker's smile showed all his teeth. "Is it murder when the wolves take down a deer?"

"Is that how you see yourself? As a wolf?"

Behind Walker, the old woman stirred and said in a voice dry as dust, "He is the will of the land."

That night, Tom Waverly launched his attack on the guerrillas' camp.

The emplacement where guards kept watch over the entrance to the canyon went up in a showy fireball fuelled by plastic explosive and jellied gasoline; charges planted above the long, wide ledge brought a dusty avalanche crashing down; smaller bombs set fire to trees and dry brush. Inside the roofless room where he'd been confined for the night, Stone was jerked awake by the explosions. He felt the bare rock quiver beneath him and saw light cast by burning trees flicker across raw rock slabs high overhead. The guard who'd been sitting outside the entrance was gone. Stone sat up, palming the shard of flint he'd spent most of last night flaking to a razor edge. He was sawing at the rawhide that pinioned his wrists behind him when Jack Walker strode into the room.

He kicked Stone in the chest and knocked him flat, pointed a Colt revolver at him and said, "Tell me who it is and I'll give you a quick death."

Stone felt rawhide part beneath him. He coughed as if winded and mouthed nonsense words. Walker took the bait. He knelt beside Stone, grabbed a handful of his hair, and pulled his head up and repeated the question, and Stone rolled sideways and punched the shard of flint into the soft flesh under the hinge of the boy's jaw, severing the carotid artery. Walker's gun went off and hot gases scalded Stone's cheek and the shot sparked off the floor an inch from his face. He caught Walker's wrists and threw him onto his back and straddled him, but the boy managed to fire another shot. The round hit Stone in the abdomen, just above the crest of his left hip bone, drilled through fat and muscle, clipped the descending flexure of his large intestine, exited beneath his left kidney, and lodged in the pocket of his quilted jacket, where he found it much later, after he'd been discharged from hospital back in the Real.

At first, Stone didn't know that he'd been shot. Something kicked him hard in the belly and knocked him onto his back, and then the old woman's crow was smashing its wings in his face. He cuffed it away, but it came for him again in a fierce frantic flurry, its naked feet clawing his chest as it pecked at his fingers and face, trying for his eyes. Stone managed to catch hold of it with both hands and it gave a hoarse cry and tried to break free, but he tightened his grip on its body with his left hand and closed his right around its head and snapping beak, and yanked and twisted until its neck broke.

When he struggled to his feet, he felt a burning wire pull through his belly and knew that he was badly hurt. Jack Walker lay in a spreading pool of his own blood, his legs twitching as he bled out. Wild bursts of gunfire hammered outside. People shouted to each other. A man was laughing hysterically. A child was crying out for its mother. And the old woman was suddenly standing in the doorway, as if she'd coagulated from firelight and shadow. She clutched a broad-bladed hunting knife in both hands, her blind, scarred face tilting left and right like an owl's. When Stone took a step toward her, she began to scream and slash wildly at the air, and he snatched up Jack Walker's Colt revolver and shot her dead.

Men and women were crouched behind low walls and fallen rubble along the edge of the cave, firing into smoke boiling up from the box canyon. They turned one by one as Stone walked between them with the body of Jack Walker limp in his arms, the hot wire of his wound twisting in his belly with each step, his shirt wet with blood and sticking and unsticking to his skin, blood running down his left leg into his boot.

A profound silence hung at his back as he staggered down the steep path. He made it past the curved overhang and then he stumbled and fell to his knees. He set Jack Walker's body on the ground and discovered that he was too weak to get up. Tom Waverly darted from cover then, and dragged him through halls of fire and smoke to the spot where he'd tethered two horses.

"He'd come in with the local guy Walker's people had captured," Stone told Linda Waverly. "As far as the Company was concerned, I was already dead, so he couldn't get any official support for my rescue. Only the brother of one my guides volunteered to help him. It took them two days to follow the trail left by the guerrillas who'd caught me. They were scouting the perimeter of the camp when the brother was caught by one of the patrols. Tom sat tight, listening to him being tortured and waiting for the cover of darkness, so that he could set up his little package of surprises. He triggered the charges he'd planted and used the confusion to pick off the perimeter guards, and he was getting ready to go in and kill everyone else when I walked out."

Stone didn't tell her that Tom had wanted to call in air support to clean out the nest of guerrillas, or that he'd persuaded Tom to spare them. Most disappeared into the mountains; the rest were evacuated to Las Vegas and were swallowed up by the refugee camps. It was possible that some of them were recruited into the army, like so many young men in postnuclear sheaves, and were sent through the mirror to fight for truth, justice, and the American way in other sheaves. In any case, without their leader, the guerrillas quickly abandoned their campaign.

Jack Walker had been wrong. Ideas are not woven into the fabric of the world: they live only in the minds of men, and when men die, their ideas die too. But Stone never forgot what the boy had said about the immorality of obliterating the variety of all the different Americas in the name of freedom, and that was why he was relieved, really, when he was called to testify in front of the Church Committee. When, for the first time since he had been recruited into Special Operations, he could speak the truth about what he had done.

Linda dozed as the road descended through forested hills in lazy switchbacks. She'd had a hard time of it, Stone thought. She must have found it impossible to sleep the past few days, worrying about whether her father would be brought in alive or dead, she'd been being briefed and bugged at first light this morning, and then he'd pulled the switch on her. . . . But she'd hung in there. She was inexperienced and too ready to defer to the authority of her superiors, but she was determined to do the right thing by her father.

Stone drove past fields and patches of trees, past houses with porches raised three feet off the ground—snow would be deep here, all through the winter. At the edge of a small town, he passed a sign that stated, with touching precision, *Pottersville, Pop.1748*.

White clapboard houses, a green, the white spire of a Colonial church rising behind a row of young maples that had already turned, their leaves the colour of old blood in the glow of the dim street lamps. Yet even this quiet little town, sunk in a deep reverie of its own history, had been touched by war. The Stars and Stripes hung above the porch of almost every house. There were yellow ribbons tied around gateposts or trees, and in the windows of some of the houses pictures of fresh-faced young men were lit by flickering night lights and framed by black crêpe, memorials to casualties of the Texas War.

Stone drove past a diner and a string of factory buildings that ran alongside railroad tracks. There was a little motel on the far side of the railroad crossing, a short, single-storey string of rooms with an office at right angles to them, woods rising steeply behind. An illuminated sign sat on the office's flat roof: *The Crest Inn*.

As Stone pulled into the parking lot, Linda stirred, looked around.

"This town is where your father was born," Stone told her. "And this motel, it's where he told me to wait for him."

# 9.

While Linda Waverly took a shower, Stone used the room phone to place an order with the diner across the railroad tracks, then sat on the end of one of the twin beds and watched the late-night news he'd found on a local channel.

The TV stood four-square on the green shag-pile carpet, wood-cased and the size of a sideboard, the black-and-white picture on its fourteen-inch screen fuzzy with ghost images. Stone felt that he was beginning to get a feel for the Johnson sheaf's recent history. Technology had stalled after the nuclear war. Twenty years on, cars were still made with quarter-inch Detroit steel, secretaries used typewriters instead of word processors, telephones had dials instead of push-buttons, TVs were powered by vacuum tubes, and you had to change channels by getting off your ass and turning the selector dial.

Half the news was about the war in Texas. Most of the rest was concerned with local issues: produce and livestock prices, an early frost that had damaged the apple harvest, the winner of a local beauty contest, a two-headed pig born all alive-o on a farm near Rockingham. After the grandfatherly anchor handed over to the weatherman, Stone clicked through channels and settled on a movie—a piece of patriotic nonsense about the Army Engineering Corps, Richard Widmark trying to do his best as a stern colonel who wouldn't admit that the idea about a floating harbour put forward by his secretary—Kim Bassinger in big hair and big glasses—could be crucial to the success of the invasion of France in World War Two. They'd had Nazis here, then. A Second World War instead of the Russian Campaigns.

Linda came out of the bathroom in a puff of fragrant steam, barefoot in blue jeans and checked shirt. "Is this what we're going to do? Sit and watch TV?"

"Your father told me to wait for him here. I'm waiting. Besides, there's no point trying to look for him in the dark, is there?"

Linda sat cross-legged on the other bed and combed her damp hair with her fingers. After a minute or so, she said, "This has to be one of the corniest movies I've ever seen."

"I'm learning a lot from it."

"Such as?"

"She's cutting up that dress so she can remodel it and make a big impression at the Christmas dance, show her boss she's really Kim Bassinger, not some mousy secretary. And if you'd been watching this ten minutes ago, you would have seen that her rival is the spoilt general's daughter who swans around in designer clothes. In other words, it's more virtuous to make do and mend than buy new. And did you notice what was missing from every single ad?"

"I can't say that I paid them any attention."

"Telephone numbers for credit card purchases. Five years after contact with the Real, this still hasn't become a consumer society. If you want to get up to speed as quickly as possible on current affairs in a sheaf, you should read the *New York Times*. But if you want to get under its skin, if you want to know what people are thinking, how they live, what they fear, what they dream about, then you should watch TV. It's a direct line to the subconscious of the nation. The ads, the set-dressing of sitcoms and movies, the monologues of talk-show hosts, they all give you a feel of a place, of how people want to live their lives."

"So this is what you did back in the old days, when you were scouting out all those different sheaves for the first time. You weren't cracking safes, planting bugs, listening to chatter piped direct from the Oval Office. You were watching TV."

"When I started out with the Company, before I was recruited into Special Ops, I was put to work in the Foreign Broadcast Information Service. I was part of a team that monitored BBC radio. Our key show was *Four-Way Family Favourites*. It allowed families to broadcast messages and dedicate songs to soldiers, sailors, and airmen stationed in bases in the European Union protectorates. Every serviceman mentioned, we entered his name and his unit and current place of service into a cross-referenced database. We analysed the messages and dedications for signs that would indicate the disposition, morale, and state of readiness of troops—"

There was a knock at the door. Stone looked through the spyhole in the door, saw that it was a woman carrying a tray, a waitress from the diner, and stuck his pistol in his waistband, under his shirt. After he had asked the waitress several questions about the town, tipped her, and relocked the door, Linda said, "Did you see the way she stared at us? Like we were a couple of gangsters on the run."

"It isn't too far from the truth," Stone said, taking the covers off the plates. A chicken salad for Linda, and a fully loaded cheeseburger and fries for himself.

"The clerk gave us a good eyeballing, too. Ten to one he's been on the phone to the cops, telling them about a couple of strangers who pitched up in the middle of the night with no luggage."

Stone dipped a fry in the ketchup and took a bite. It wasn't the best he'd ever had, but after three years without fast food it was pretty damned close. "If the local cops come by to check us out, I'll show them my ID and tell them we're on a top-secret mission."

Linda said, suddenly quiet and serious, "Do you think he's all right?"

"Your father? He seemed calm when I talked to him on the phone. Focused on the matter at hand. Rational. And he knows how to take care of himself in Indian territory."

"We checked in almost an hour ago. Why hasn't he shown up? Suppose he ran into some kind of trouble?"

"If I were him, I would have been keeping watch on this place from somewhere in the woods out back. And after I'd seen us arrive, I wouldn't have gone down to meet us straightaway—I would have waited to see if there was any sign we were being tailed. He'll come see us when he's absolutely sure it's safe, Linda. Meanwhile, we should rest up. It's been a long day, and it isn't over yet."

"We eat junk food and watch TV."

"Why not? Don't you want to see how the movie comes out?"

Stone was halfway through his cheeseburger when there was a faint sound from the bathroom: the toilet flushing. Linda watched, quiet and still, as he picked up the Colt .45 and flattened himself beside the bathroom door. He reached for the handle with his left hand and in a single smooth move swung the door open and put his pistol on the man who was sitting on the toilet under the open window.

"Hello, Adam," Tom Waverly said.

"Are you trying to get shot, Tom?"

"I'm trying my best not to."

Behind Stone, Linda said, "Dad?"

Tom Waverly sat on the bed beside his daughter while Stone explained how David Welch had hooked him up with Linda, how they had escaped from New York and thrown off the people tailing them by dumping their car in the woods and stealing another. He skipped the part about Linda wearing a bug. She'd thought that she was doing the right thing, and Tom didn't need to know about her mistake.

"As far as I know, we got here free and clean," Stone said. "No one knows we're here."

"No one intercepted your waitress, at any rate. That was a nice touch, by the way. See," Tom explained to his daughter, "if someone had been keeping watch on you and Adam, they would have had one of their own bring the order, so they could scope out the situation."

"I was wondering why you asked her all those questions," Linda said. "You were trying to catch her out in an obvious lie."

"That, and curiosity about your father's home town," Stone said.

"Who gave the authorisation to bring you into this?" Tom Waverly said.

He was dressed in combat trousers, a black T-shirt, and an army-surplus forest camo jacket, reeked of woodsmoke and old sweat, and had a grim, gaunt, desperate look. His hair was chopped short and dyed black, its fringe pasted to his forehead by sweat. Salt-and-pepper stubble stood out against his paper-white face. There was an ugly bruise on his jaw, his eyes were reddened by broken blood vessels, and there were blood-spotted bandages under the sleeves of his jacket.

"David Welch told me that some bureaucrat by the name of Ralph Kohler was in charge," Stone said.

"I don't know him. You?"

"We haven't been introduced yet."

"You dealt exclusively with Welch. He persuaded you to come in, he briefed you. . . ."

"He gave me a file and told me he was there to make sure I got anything I needed."

"And you were happy with the arrangement. You didn't mind being bait for their trap."

"I knew I could get out from under if I needed to. And that's exactly what I did before I came here."

"I met with Mr. Kohler," Linda said. "He wants to help you. So do I."

"I know you do, honey." Tom looked at Stone and said, "Mind waiting outside for a minute? I want a private word with my daughter."

Stone looked at Linda.

"I'll be all right, Mr. Stone," she said.

After he had stepped into the chilly night and closed the door behind him, Stone heard the TV come back on, drowning out whatever father and daughter might have to say to each other. An ice machine burbled to itself a few doors down. Stone pressed the bar and caught a couple of ice cubes, pressed one to his forehead and sucked on another to slake the dryness in his mouth. The TV was still blaring; presumably Tom and Linda Waverly were still talking. That was okay, Stone thought. That was a good sign. Tom looked like a thousand miles of rough road, but he'd handled the surprise of finding that his daughter had come along for the ride pretty well, he'd accepted Stone's assurances, and he seemed ready to talk.

Stone crunched the ice cube between his teeth and let the cold gravel dissolve on his tongue. He was beginning to think that this might work out. The hard part—getting here uncompromised, making contact—was over. It was Tom Waverly's show now. All Stone had to do was let his old friend talk and find out what he wanted to do. If he didn't want to come in, Stone wouldn't push it; if he did, they'd work out a way of doing it safely. And then Stone would be able to go back to the First Foot sheaf, to the little farm. He would tell Susan how he felt, ask her should he stay or go. If she told him to go, he'd get in his boat and sail away. And if she said she wanted him to stay . . .

A green-and-white patrol car pulled into the drive of the motel. Stone stepped back into the shadows and watched a lone cop ease out of the car and saunter into the lighted office, then rapped on the door of the room, hard enough to be heard over the TV. A moment later, Tom Waverly cracked open the door, holding a snub-nosed .38 pistol up by his face.

Stone told him about the cop.

"He's alone?"

"He's alone, and he's talking with the clerk."

"Wait there," Tom said, and shut the door.

Stone heard Linda making some kind of protest, loud enough to cut through the noise of the TV, and had to swallow the impulse to burst in on them. After a minute, the TV went off and Tom came out, saying, "We can do this together, right?"

"What about Linda?"

"We'll keep my daughter out of this. The cop and the clerk—you in or not?"

"Don't kid around."

Tom's smile was all teeth and tendons. "Either you give me some help, or I'll have to go in there on my own and put both of them out of their misery."

"Give me a minute with the cop," Stone said. "I'll get rid of him."

When he walked into the office, the cop gave him a bored look with something mean behind it and said, "You're the fella from New York, uh?"

"Yes, sir. Is there a problem?"

The cop had a flushed face and a snow-white crew cut. His Garrison belt, a holstered pistol hung on one side, a nightstick on the other, rode low under a potbelly that strained the buttons of his blue short-sleeved shirt. He said, "Well, I'm kinda wondering why you came all the way out here from New York with that young woman. Mind explaining yourself?"

"She's my colleague."

"This is a nice quiet God-fearing town, mister. As anyone who comes here for immoral purposes quickly finds out. How about showing me your papers?"

"My colleague and I are here on business," Stone said, and pulled the little wallet from his shirt pocket and flipped it open to show the FBI badge.

As the cop took it from him, Tom Waverly barged through the door, leading with his .38, telling the cop to keep his hands away from his weapon, telling him to kneel.

"You're making a mistake, mister," the cop said.

It was exactly what Stone was thinking.

"On your knees. Or I'll shoot the clerk and then I'll shoot you."

The cop dropped Stone's badge wallet and went down carefully, clasping his hands on the back of his head and saying that he'd called in this stop on the radio. "Dispatch will send a backup unit if I don't call back in a couple of minutes."

"Bullshit," Tom said. Telling Stone, "This guy is the town constable, the only law here. If he needs help, he calls up the County Sheriff's Department or the state troopers, but I bet he didn't bother to tell either one that he was going to run a routine check on a couple of strangers."

"I was dealing with it," Stone said.

"If you really want to help me, find a place to stash him and the night clerk."

The clerk was standing behind the counter with his hands spread wide. A nice-looking kid with horn-rimmed glasses and an ink-stained thumb who was probably working nights at the motel to help pay his way through college. Stone told him to take it easy and asked him where the maid kept the stuff for servicing the rooms.

The kid led him to a linen cupboard at the back of the office. Stone tied him up with a couple of strips torn from a sheet and Tom brought in the cop, hands fastened behind his back with his own handcuffs, made him sit inside the cupboard with the clerk, then locked the door and jammed a chair under the handle.

"I guess we still got it," he said.

"If you'd given me another minute that guy would have been on his way," Stone said.

"Yeah, and he would have called in that ID you showed him, and next thing you know your friends would have been all over this place. Park his car by the side of the office, why don't you? Make sure it can't be seen from the road."

After Stone had dealt with the patrol car, Tom said that there was something he should see, and unlocked the door of the room nearest the office. Stone looked inside. Electronic equipment was spread across one of the twin beds and a man lay on his belly on the other, out cold and snoring irregularly, a goose egg raised above his right ear, wrists cuffed behind his back. A second man sat on the floor, right wrist handcuffed to his left ankle, left wrist handcuffed to his right ankle, his gaze dark and furious above a gag.

"Meet officers Piven and Corning," Tom said.

"They knew you were here? They knew I was coming here?"

"Hell, no. The Company knows I was born here, but it doesn't know that *I* know. Still, I guess someone decided to cover all the bases, and sent these two losers here just in case I showed. As far as they were concerned, it was a coffee-and-doughnuts assignment. Stake out the only motel in town, cruise the streets, tell the local law a bullshit cover story about being military police looking for deserters believed to be passing through the area. Strictly routine. They were flat-out astonished when I paid them a visit," Tom said, and shut the door and locked it. "We should get going. Sooner or later someone is going to wonder where the cop is."

"What about Linda?"

"I don't want her to get hurt, Adam. I gave her something to put her to sleep. By the time she comes around, it'll all be over."

Stone was angry enough to think about reaching for his pistol. "At least let me check up on her."

"She's my daughter, Adam. I resent the implication that I'd harm her." Tom pointed his .38 at the Chevy. "How about you and me go for a little ride? There's something I want to show you."

# 10.

As Stone drove out of the motel parking lot, Tom Waverly said, "Your standard Company unit, all you're likely to find in it is half a roll of breath mints and one of those air-freshener pine trees. This heap of junk, though, has character."

The half pint of Four Roses that he'd taken from the glove compartment was clamped between his thighs. He was unscrewing the cap with his left hand and holding the .38 in his right, not quite aiming it at Stone.

"I guess that's because it's stolen," Stone said.

"How does it feel to be on the run, by the way?"

"I'm not running from anything, Tom."

"Sure you are. You just don't know it yet."

Tom took a couple of pills from the breast pocket of his camo jacket, chased them down with a swallow of Four Roses, and immediately started to cough, spitting most of the bourbon down the front of his jacket. The coughing fit went on for a little while. He bent forward, his whole body shuddering as he hacked into his fist. When he could speak again, he said in a rough, choked voice, "Pull over."

Stone parked under a big chestnut tree that stood in front of a big, dark house; Tom opened the door and leaned out and threw up. "I can't seem to keep anything down lately," he said. There was blood on his chin, black in the dim glow of the car's interior light.

"Maybe we should hijack the local doctor, Tom. Get you fixed up."

"It's not the kind of thing that can be fixed," Tom said. He wiped his chin with the back of his hand and climbed out of the car.

Stone climbed out too. The house loomed dark and silent in its weed-choked lot.

"I'm serious about finding a doctor," Stone said.

"We're not here to talk about my health." Tom picked up a couple of rocks from the untidy verge. "Ever knocked out a window in an old haunted house, trying to scare up the ghosts?"

"Is that why we're here? To talk about ghosts?"

For a moment, Tom's grin was exactly as Stone remembered it. "In a way. One of the reasons I came here was to make up for the childhood I never had."

"So you're camping out in the woods because you never got to do it when you were a kid."

"I see I can't get anything past you."

"It's an easy reach. Your clothes stink of woodsmoke."

"Well, I couldn't hardly stay anywhere in town with Piven and Corning on the prowl."

"Hiding out where you were born, maybe it's not the smartest move."

Tom Waverly was lit by the car's headlights, his face pale, his eyes hollow. "Back in the state orphanage, did you ever wonder what it would be like, growing up like an ordinary kid in an ordinary family living in an ordinary town?"

"Just about every day," Stone said. "And then I was fostered, and I got to see what it was like."

Stone had been the last of Karl and Hannah Kerfeld's foster children. He'd spent six years with them in New Hamburg, Minnesota, the happiest years of his life. When the old couple had died in an automobile accident, just after he'd graduated from college and joined the Company, it had been as if his real, unknown parents had died.

"I forgot you had a family upbringing," Tom said.

"Part of one, anyhow."

"How was it?"

"Matter of fact, it was pretty good."

"I bet you were a regular red-blooded All-American boy," Tom said. "Letting off cherry bombs at the Fourth of July parade, tying tin cans to a cat's tail, making an outlaw's hideout in the woods. All kinds of good old-fashioned fun."

Stone believed that Tom was taking a circuitous route to what he really wanted to discuss, and decided to go along with it.

"One thing we did every spring was pick rocks out of Erwin Slominski's cornfields after school," he said, remembering how he and the other kids had tramped over the previous year's wheat stubble under the big Minnesota sky, following Erwin's ancient John Deere, plucking rocks from the black dirt and tossing them into the trailer. "If you asked Erwin if a rock was big enough to pick, he'd say leave it, it'll be bigger next year."

"Sounds too much like work. I'd've preferred hanging out in the drugstore, trying to be cool around the girls," Tom said.

"We did some of that, too."

"Any girl in particular?"

"There were one or two."

New Hamburg's teenagers had spent most of every summer out at Lake Louise, where the boys hung out on the dock and pretended to ignore the girls lying in their swimsuits and tight shorts and T-shirts on towels and tablecloths spread on the grassy bank. Stone remembered trying not to stare too hard at Suzy Segler in her polka-dot bikini. Suzy Segler, with her cute pout and the little bounce she put in her walk. He remembered how he'd spent a whole hour outside Suzy's parents' house, working up the courage to ask her to the high school prom, remembered his amazement when she'd said yes. Remembered making out with her after the ball in the car he'd borrowed from his foster parents, the same car they would die in four years later. The smell of her perfume in the hot summer night. The deep-sea smell of her on his fingers.

Tom tossed one of his rocks to Stone and said, "How's your throwing arm?"

Stone weighed the rock in his hand and looked at the big clapboard house, its black empty windows and sagging porch and steeply pitched roof. "It looks like plenty of kids beat us to this one."

"Yeah. Maybe one of them was me."

"Is that why you came here, Tom? To check up on your doppel?"

"There's one on the second floor looks like it's mostly intact. See it?"

"Sure."

"Count of three."

They counted, threw. There was the brief music of glass falling in the darkness.

"How about getting rid of your pistol?" Tom said. He was aiming his .38 at Stone now.

"What is this, Tom? You asked me to come here. And I came because I want to help you."

"Take your pistol out and toss it into the weeds. If you don't, I'll have to shoot you, just like you shot me that time."

Tom looked like a desperado who'd barely escaped a lynch mob, but he was holding the .38 rock-steady, his finger curled inside the trigger guard, the hammer cocked.

"I'll do it to show my trust in you," Stone said, and pitched his pistol a good way into the darkness beyond the car's headlights. "I hope you'll show me the same courtesy."

"Not to trust anyone, that's the whole of the law. Turn around, assume the position. Hands flat on the roof, feet wide apart."

116

As Tom quickly and thoroughly frisked him, Stone said, "You still haven't told me what you are doing here. Did you look up your family? Check out scenes from your lost childhood?"

"Except it wasn't really *my* childhood, was it? It was my doppel's. Speaking of which, there's something I want to show you. Get back in the car, you can drive me to the church."

They drove through the town. Tom hummed a tune, watching the Chevy's reflection slide over the windows of a row of shops, watching houses go by, dark and quiet behind white picket fences and neatly manicured lawns. Stone thought of and suppressed a dozen questions. He wasn't here to interrogate his old friend. He was here to listen. At the church, he cut the car's motor and headlights and drifted to a halt under the row of young maples. A breeze rummaged in their dry leaves. Apart from a single light burning in an insomniac's bedroom, the little town seemed to be fast asleep.

Tom took a slug of bourbon and handed the bottle to Stone. "Remember those physics lectures we had to endure, back when we were young and innocent?"

Stone took a small sip, just enough to taste, and passed the bottle back. "Did you really bring me all the way out here to talk about the old days?"

Tom smiled his gaunt, ghastly smile. "Be patient, Adam. I'm giving you what I can."

"So this is going somewhere."

"Sure it is. What was the name of the guy who tried his best to initiate us into the mysteries of quantum physics? It's been on the tip of my tongue the last two days, bugging the hell out of me."

"Professor Lehman. Fred Lehman. I was thinking about those physics lectures the other day. About how you derailed Fred Lehman with that remark about the cat."

Tom said that he didn't remember. After Stone told him the story, he smiled and said, "I had a smart mouth, didn't I? Always the class clown."

"You liked to stir things up."

"I was full of piss and vinegar back then, eager to prove how fucking good I was. There was this cat in one of the orphanages where I spent my childhood. This old stray that wandered into the basement and was tolerated because she kept down the mice. I was one of the kids who looked out for her. We'd bring her milk, scraps of meat. She got pregnant about half a dozen times, and each time the super would deal with the kittens. He always told us he'd found homes for them, but I reckon he tossed them in the furnace.

The cat would search for them for a week or so, nosing around in every corner, and then she'd seem to forget."

Tom was looking through the windshield at the church spire, pale as its own ghost against the night sky.

"The last time she got pregnant, she was pretty old for a cat. Something went wrong when she gave birth. She dragged herself under a pile of broken furniture, and that's where I found her a couple of days later. She was dead, and there were three dead kittens and one just barely alive, trying to get milk from its mother. We tried to nurse it, but it died too. . . . Maybe that's what I remembered when Professor Lehman started talking about that thought experiment, the cat in the box that was half alive, half dead. Maybe I was wondering if that poor old cat had been in the same either/or state until I collapsed it by finding her. That if I hadn't gone looking for her, she might in some sense still be alive."

"As I remember it," Stone said, "being dead or alive isn't an intrinsic property of a cat's elemental quantum constituents, the atoms and electrons and everything else. If you tried to combine the quantum state of a dead cat with the quantum state of a live cat, the dead half would be free to evolve into other dead states, and the live half would be free to evolve into other live states. They'd both evolve away from each other. They'd decohere, just like daughter sheaves split by some significant change."

Tom Waverly hacked into his fist, then drank from the half pint of Four Roses. It was almost empty now. "You always had something of the geek about you, Adam. If I'm honest, that earnest literal-mindedness of yours used to drive me fucking nuts sometimes, but I admit that lately I've been missing it. For maybe five minutes here and there, anyway."

"I guess we aren't here to talk about quantum states."

"The thing I want to show you? It's in the cemetery."

It was over in the far corner, a grave so new that it still lacked a marker. Wreaths and bunches of wilted flowers covered a mound of raw dirt that hadn't yet settled. Tom Waverly stood on one side of it and told Stone to stand on the other.

"In case you get a dumb idea about trying to wrestle the gun away from me."

"I wouldn't do that, Tom."

Stone was pretty sure that he knew whose grave this was. A coldness had crept over his entire skin.

"I guess me and the poor schmuck lying here in his grave began to evolve away from each other a long time ago," Tom said. "We definitely have our differences now. He's exploring all the different ways of being dead, and I'm still trying out different ways of being alive. Trouble is, I'm running out of options."

He was a shadow in the shadowy dark. The glow of the streetlights seemed very far away, another country.

"He died two weeks ago. A traffic accident, according to the local newspaper. They gave it the front page, gave him a nice obituary, too. He had a job selling farm machinery, he was married to the same woman for twenty-two years, he had three kids. He was in the Rotary Club, he was on the school board, he served a term as a selectman, organising scrap drives, paper drives, rubber drives. They got to be very big on recycling and making-do here, in the long economic slump after their nuclear war, and now there's the war in Texas. If the Real wants to make this America a power in its own history, it has its work cut out. Anyway, he was a solid John Q. Public citizen. And a couple of weeks ago he's driving along one of the back roads to visit some farm, his brakes fail at the top of a steep grade, and he hits a tree at about sixty miles an hour. Flies through the windshield, that's all she wrote."

Stone said, "I have the feeling that you're going to tell me it wasn't an accident."

"The wreck is out back in the local garage. I snuck in two nights ago and took a look at it. The brake lines had been cut, fucking local cops didn't even bother to check. I guess they found out about him from the voters' register, or maybe from his army service. He spent three years helping clean up around the edges of San Diego—the Soviets hit the naval dockyards there with two big bombs. Maybe they're killing them all off. All my doppels in all the sheaves. Poetic justice, wouldn't you say?"

"Because you're killing off the doppels of Eileen Barrie?"

"Now we're getting down to it."

Tom Waverly's face was no more than a pale blur floating in the near dark, but Stone could hear the smile in his voice.

Stone said, "Did you start off by killing the Real version?"

"I'll have to take the Fifth on that."

"But you knew her, didn't you? That's where it began."

"Again, I'm not about to incriminate myself."

"I came here to help you, Tom, any way I can. Maybe you don't know it, but the locals have a shoot-on-sight policy because you killed that cop. Turns out he wasn't just any cop. He was also the nephew of the mayor of New York."

"Oops."

"It isn't funny."

"I guess not. What did Welch tell you to offer me?"

"He told me to bring you in alive. After that, I guess it's between you and Ralph Kohler."

"I bet. How about you, Adam? Do you have any say in my . . . disposition?"

"I retired, Tom. I came here because you asked for me."

"I don't recall asking you to bring my daughter with you."

"When I shook off the tail, I gave her the choice to stay behind. She wanted to come along with me because she wanted to see you, Tom. Because she hasn't seen you for more than three years, and she thought you were dead."

Tom Waverly cocked his head, suddenly alert as a car went past in the distance. "And you let her come along out of the kindness of your heart. Not because you thought she might help you talk me into giving myself up. No, it's okay. You don't have to explain. I'm kind of glad you did it, Adam. You and Linda . . . maybe it'll work out better this way."

"You don't have to stay here. You can come back with me. You can come in, Tom. You can talk it over with me, or with whoever you want."

"The poor schmuck in this grave, you think he had a good life?"

"From what you told me, it sounds like he did."

"How about me? You think I did good? You and me, do you think we did good? That we lived good lives, doing what we did?"

"I think that we served our country as best we could."

"I bet you still think that Jimmy fucking Carter is right. That we shouldn't have meddled in the politics of other sheaves. That we've created more problems than we've solved. I used to think that was so much bullshit, Christ knows I did. I really believed that we were working for freedom, liberty, the pursuit of happiness and all the rest of that good American horsepuckey. Now . . . now, it looks like I was just as much a schmuck as this poor guy. We were supposed to be protecting places like this. American families in little American towns. There's no better way of living, right? We wanted everyone in the world, hell, in the entire multiverse, to be able to enjoy it. We wanted to give our freedom, our way of life, to every counterpart of America we could find. And you know what? Most of them hate us for it. They envy what we have, and when we try to give it to them, they hate us for our presumption.

"People back in the Real, ordinary people living their quiet lives in quiet little American towns exactly like this, except they're a little more prosperous and a little less radioactive, you think if they knew about everything that's been done in their name, they'd still believe we were heroes? The Company received a big black eye after the Church Committee published its findings, but we both know that its public report didn't reveal one-tenth of what it found in the dungeons. At the time, by the way, I thought you were a fucking fool for going up in front of the committee and speaking out the way you did instead of taking the Fifth. But now, I can't help thinking that you were right to do it. And Carter, he may be a weak president who probably won't win another term, but I reckon now that he was right too, when he tried to put a stop to the endless expansion, the endless wars and postwar insurrections. . . ." Tom Waverly shook his head and said, "If I poured some bourbon on my doppel's grave, you think it would make him rise from the dead?"

"I think it would be a waste of good bourbon."

"I think you're right." Tom took a last swig and threw the bottle away with a stiff-armed toss. Saying, as it thumped on grass somewhere in the dark, "There are other ways of bringing back the dead—if this works out you'll see what I mean soon enough. Besides, in some other sheaf, the poor schmuck is still alive. He missed that tree, or the fucker supposed to cut his brakes had a heart attack on the way, or I didn't start this thing, or they caught me early and disposed of me. We made a difference? Maybe in a dozen or so sheaves, but what's that in the face of infinity? You might as well try to raise the sea level by taking a piss in the ocean."

"I don't know what you're talking about, Tom."

"Suppose I told you that there are people in the Company doing things far worse than anything the Church Committee ever accused us of?"

"Let me bring you in, Tom. You can talk about everything then."

"I took a big enough risk luring you out here. You and Linda. I asked her, what do people in the Company say when they discover she's the daughter of Tom Waverly? Know what she said? If they're smiling, she tells them that she's very proud; if they aren't smiling, she tells them it's none of their business. And if they push it, she tells them to go to hell."

"From what I've seen, she has the makings of a good officer."

"Help her out, Adam. That's all I ask."

"Is this something to do with what you guys were talking about, back in the motel room?"

"You want to know why I've been killing Eileen Barrie's doppels? It isn't because of what she did to me, although that was bad enough. What it is, I'm trying to make a difference. I'm trying to save myself from myself. I'm trying to make sure that when you lift the lid on that dumb box Professor Lehman told us about, the cat'll be alive and well. Are you afraid, Adam?"

"Of you? A little."

"I've killed eighteen people for the Company. Sometimes I was close enough to feel their last breath on my face. And I've killed other people too. After I got you back from Jack Walker and his grim little band of ecowarriors, I killed General E. Everett McBride. Poisoned his whiskey with ricin. The fucker went out a lot more quickly than some of the teenage girls he raped and murdered."

In the quiet dark of the cemetery, Tom Waverly was calling up all his ghosts. Stone, afraid that his friend was looking for judgement or had already passed judgement on himself, said, "I'll help Linda any way I can, Tom. And I can help you, too, if you'll let me."

"Knightly found out about McBride, he also found out about a little something I had going on the side, and he made me an offer I couldn't refuse. Either I went to work for him, or I'd be hung out to dry. All the people I killed, it was the one who deserved it most, General E. Everett fucking McBride, rapist, murderer, self-righteous scum of the earth, who fucked me up. Want to know why I killed Nathan Tate? Because he'd gone over to the dark side. He was one of them. And God help me, I was one of them too." Tom looked at Stone across the grave of his doppel. "Know why I wanted you to come here? Because this is all your fault. Because, back when SWIFT SWORD kicked off, you shouldn't have stopped me. You should have let me go out in a blaze of glory."

Stone understood. "You were running away from Knightly."

"You got to ease your conscience in front of the Church Committee," Tom said, bitterness colouring his voice for the first time. "You got to retire. I got Knightly, telling me I could work for him or spend the rest of my life in jail."

"You staged a disappearance because you were working for Knightly on some black op within the Company, something the DCI doesn't know about. And you carried on working for this black op after Knightly was indicted, and had his stroke."

"Something like that."

"And Eileen Barrie was part of this thing too."

"I wish I could tell you everything, Adam. But if I do it might not work out the way it's supposed to. Besides, I believe we've run out of time. Listen."

Stone heard it: the faint wail of a siren twisting somewhere in the night. "I guess Linda woke up."

"My little girl wouldn't turn me in."

The siren was growing louder, getting closer.

"Come with me, Tom. I can get you out of this."

"I wish you could."

Stone knew with sudden cold certainty what Tom Waverly was planning. "Let me help you. We'll talk everything through, figure out what to do."

"It isn't any big thing. A couple of gates, a clandestine research facility, a question of delivering a few good men and a few megatons to the right place at the right time. . . . You don't believe me. You think I'm crazy. You want to know more, ask Welch about Operation GYPSY. Ask Kohler."

"I'm not here to pass judgement on you, Tom."

Blue lights whirled beyond the trees at the edge of the cemetery.

"We did some good work together, Adam. That's really why I wanted you to come out here. Because here at the end I've become a sentimental son of a bitch. Because I know you're a good, capable operator. Because I know you'll help Linda."

Stone shifted his stance, lifting onto the balls of his feet. Sweat pricked his palms. "Don't do this to me, Tom."

"Listen to her. Trust her. Help her."

"I won't let you do this to me."

"I wish I could have told you everything. I wish I could have told Linda everything. But I'm pretty sure this is the way it has to be," Tom said.

Stone made his move, but although Tom was sick and drunk, and much slower and weaker than he'd been in the good old days when he'd trained the rest of the cowboy angels in hand-to-hand combat, he was still a formidable opponent. He pivoted as Stone crashed into him, used Stone's momentum to swing him around and send him sprawling, and gave him a love tap on the back of his head with the grip of the .38 as he went down. Stone rolled, and came up in a crouch, dizzy and dazed, his head ringing from the blow. He saw Tom stick the .38 under his chin, saw an orange spark and heard the shot. Something spattered across the grass and Tom collapsed across the grave of his doppel.

As Stone lifted his friend's wrist, trying and failing to find a pulse, a spotlight ignited in the dark beyond the cemetery. Its beam swept across rows of headstones and flared in his eyes. He let go of Tom Waverly's wrist and stood up slowly, raising his hands above his head.

# 11.

**B**y the time David Welch arrived, in the first of two Company helicopters that touched down on the green in front of the church, the scene had turned into a circus. Police vehicles, a pair of ambulances, and the town's fire truck were parked nose-to-tail alongside the cemetery. State troopers and sheriff's deputies were holding back a crowd of rubbernecking citizens in dressing gowns and overcoats. The county sheriff had arrived, his uniform buttoned over pyjamas, and was threatening to arrest Stone for refusing to cooperate.

Welch turned his charm on the sheriff and shook hands with the town constable. As far as the locals were concerned, the man was the hero of the hour. Despite being handcuffed, he'd managed to break down the door of the cupboard in which he'd been locked by Stone and Tom Waverly, and had put out a call on his radio that sent every available police officer racing to his aid. Welch listened to his story, shook his hand again and said something that made him smile, then took Stone aside and asked for his version of events.

When Stone was done, Welch said, "We didn't want it to go down like this, but I guess we'll have to play it as it lays."

"Meaning I screwed the pooch, so I'll be blamed for any blowback," Stone said.

"You're upset. It's completely understandable."

"Tom shot himself right in front of me. Of course I'm upset. But that doesn't mean I can't think straight or see what's going on."

A white sedan drew up and Linda Waverly and a woman in a black skirt suit climbed out. When she spotted Stone, Linda broke away from her escort and ran to him and started to hit him, hard shots to his ribs and breastbone.

"Tell me the locals shot him! Tell me it was some fucking Company sharpshooter!"

Stone caught her wrists and told her how sorry he was.

Her hot gaze searched his face for a moment. Then she let him gather her into his arms and said in a fierce whisper, "You have to make sure we leave this sheaf together."

"It's over, Linda. I did what I could, and I'm sorrier than I can say that it wasn't good enough, but there it is. It's over."

"It isn't over. Not yet. Promise you'll come with me, Mr. Stone. Please. Help me help my father."

"What did he ask you to do, Linda? Back at the motel, after he asked me to leave the room, what kind of story did he spin?"

Linda had been convinced that the only way to save her father's life was to turn him over to the Company. That was why she'd told Welch about Stone's plan. That was why she'd worn a bug. And now, after she'd spent a few minutes alone with Tom, she was asking Stone to go on the run with her.

"I can't explain everything, Mr. Stone," she said. "Not yet. But if you come with me, if you trust me, you can help me make things right."

"Whatever it was, you should give it up. It can't hurt him now. It can only hurt you."

Linda shook her head and pulled free, saying loudly, "You let him die, you son of a bitch!"

Right behind Stone, Welch said, "I'm truly sorry to have to ask this, Linda, but the local ME wants you to identify your father's body."

Stone told Welch to give them a few minutes, but Linda said she wanted to get it over with. Her gaze met Stone's for a moment, cool and determined and unforgiving, and then she allowed Welch to lead her toward the floodlit corner of the cemetery where her father's body sprawled aslant the grave of his doppel.

One helicopter took away Linda Waverly and her father's body; the other flew Stone and David Welch to New York. As it cut through the night, Stone tried his best to make sense of everything and work out all the angles. Assume that for whatever reason—coercion, blackmail, misplaced idealism—Tom had been recruited into a black op run by a circle of plotters inside the Company. He'd been unhappy, he'd been looking for a way out, and then he'd fallen terminally ill, decided that he had nothing to lose, and gone on the run. Okay, but why had he been killing Eileen Barrie's doppels? Maybe he'd wanted to draw attention to the conspiracy in which they had both been involved, or maybe he'd been killing them simply for revenge, because of something the Real version of Eileen Barrie had done to him. . . . But neither explanation seemed quite right. If Tom had wanted revenge, why hadn't he simply killed the Real Eileen Barrie? And if he'd wanted to expose the conspiracy, why hadn't he turned himself in and started talking?

Perhaps Tom had found out that the Company already knew about the conspiracy, Stone thought. Perhaps he didn't want to spend what little time he had left being interrogated by a debriefing team. Or perhaps it had something to do with whatever it was Tom had refused to tell him.

*I wish I could tell you everything, Adam, but if I do it might not work out the way it's supposed to.*

Tom Waverly had let Stone know that he hadn't told him the whole story, he'd had a private conversation with his daughter. . . . Chills chased each other up and down Stone's spine. Chains of tiny cold lightnings. Suppose Linda was a cutout? Suppose Tom had given her a vital piece of information that only Stone could understand?

By now, Stone was having trouble connecting one thought to the next. He was bone tired, recent memories he didn't want to look at crowded the edges of his mind like shadows around an unsteady candle flame, and in any case he wasn't sure how much of Tom Waverly's story was true. Well, if Tom had been trying to set something up, it didn't matter now. Tom had killed himself, and Stone was bitterly sorry for it, but he wasn't going to let himself be drawn into his old friend's paranoid games. He would give up everything at the debriefing interview, try to protect Linda as best he could from the consequences of her father's last throw of the dice, and then he'd go home and try to put it all behind him.

At last, the heaped lights of New York rose out of the dark. The helicopter followed the black curve of the East River, flew over the Triborough Bridge and the Queensboro Bridge, and stooped toward the spotlit helipad on top of the Pan-American Alliance Assembly Building, a glass-and-steel skyscraper that stood on what had once been the United Nations Plaza.

Ralph Kohler was waiting for Stone on the windy rooftop. A tall man wearing gold-rimmed bifocals and an immaculate grey suit, he stepped out of a knot of aides and shook Stone's hand and said he hoped that Stone would be able to make a preliminary statement right away.

"I'm ready to talk, Mr. Kohler," Stone said. "I'm ready to talk about everything. Especially Operation GYPSY."

Kohler's face gave away nothing. "I expect full candour," he said, and several large men closed around Stone and escorted him to the elevator.

They rode down to a subbasement where a pair of officers, Carol Dvorak and Joseph Carella, were waiting in an interview room. Stone made only a token protest when it became clear that neither Kohler nor Welch were going to sit in on the debriefing; he was certain that they would be watching from the other side of the mirrored window in one of the green cinder-block walls.

Carella set a cup of coffee in front of Stone and switched on the video camera, Dvorak studied her palmtop computer for a moment, and then they were off. It quickly became clear that the two officers weren't interested in why Stone had fled the scene in the Port Authority Bus Terminal, why he'd taken Linda Waverly with him and changed cars to lose the people tailing them, or what Linda had whispered to him in that final clinch outside the cemetery where her father had killed himself. They were interested only in what Tom Waverly had told him during their brief reunion. Stone took them through it slowly and carefully, giving them everything he could remember, but he ran out of patience after he finished his story and Dvorak insisted on going over it again.

"I've told you everything Tom told me. Unless you want to read me my rights and turn this into a formal interrogation, I believe we're done."

"We need to make sure we have everything squared away," Dvorak said. "Mr. Waverly told you that Dr. Barrie was part of this mysterious black op."

"Operation GYPSY," Stone said. "And he didn't exactly say she was involved. I asked him if she was part of it, and he said, what do you think?"

Dvorak made a mark on the screen of her palmtop, as if crossing off an item on a shopping list. She was generically attractive but prim and self-contained, completely lacking any sexual presence. One of those people who look exactly like their ID photograph. Her light-brown hair was done up in a French braid and Stone could see an earpiece in her left ear, with a coiled wire running inside the collar of her blouse. He was certain that Kohler was watching the interview behind the two-way mirror and feeding her questions.

"Did Mr. Waverly say anything about Dr. Barrie's role in this so-called black op?" she said.

"No, he didn't."

"Did he tell you where he first met her?"

"No."

"Did he tell you how long he had known her?"

"No."

"Did he know her before he disappeared and allegedly joined the black op?"

"I don't recall that he ever mentioned her name before today," Stone said, and suppressed a yawn. His exhaustion had taken on a voluptuous weight, and the air in the little room was stale and stuffy. "I really want to help, but I think we've pretty much wrung the juice out of this."

"Bear with us for just a little longer, Mr. Stone," Carella said. He was in his thirties, with a relaxed manner and sharp blue eyes and black hair brushed straight back from his forehead.

Dvorak said, "Mr. Waverly told you that he was killing Dr. Barrie's doppels because he wanted to make a difference. Do you have any idea what he meant by that?

"No, I don't. I *do* know that this black op, GYPSY, has something to do with a couple of gates and a research facility. And Tom mentioned something about delivering a few megatons somewhere, so a nuclear weapon may be involved. . . . But you already know all about this, don't you?"

"It's not a question of what we do or do not know, Mr. Stone," Dvorak said. "It's a question of reconstructing your conversation with Mr. Waverly."

"Tom told me he killed Nathan Tate because Tate was part of GYPSY. What about the rest of Knightly's cowboy angels? Some of them could be involved too. Have you checked them out?"

"You can bet we'll be checking out every angle," Carella said.

"I'm not interested in flattery," Stone said, speaking to the mirrored window behind the two agents. "But I *am* interested in how much you already know about this thing. How much you already knew when you sent me after Tom. How much you kept back from me."

Dvorak glanced at her watch and said briskly, "You've had a hard day, Mr. Stone, and we've kept you up for far too long. We'll have to go over this again, of course, and work up a formal statement. But I think we're done for now."

"You did a good job," Carella said. "We really do appreciate your cooperation."

"I came here to help out an old friend, and now he's dead. What exactly do you mean by a good job?"

Stone wasn't angry with the two officers. He was angry with himself.

"You need to get some rest, Mr. Stone," Dvorak said, and with a stab of her stylus switched off her palmtop. "We'll escort you back to the Real tomorrow. You'll complete your debriefing at Langley, and then you'll be able to return to the First Foot sheaf. If you have any questions, I'm sure that the debriefing team will do their best to answer them."

"If your boss is behind that two-way mirror, I'd like to ask him a few questions right now. I'd like to talk to him about Linda Waverly."

"Perhaps you'll have an opportunity to speak with him before you leave for Langley," Dvorak said.

"I'm sure he appreciates your help," Carella said.

"Linda Waverly is young, she doesn't have much field experience, and her father just now killed himself," Stone said. "If she's holding out on you, it's either because she's in shock, or it's because she feels that she can still help him. Help redeem his honour, help finish what he started, whatever. Tom Waverly told her that I'd help her. If you let me talk to her—"

"I'm afraid that won't be possible," Dvorak said.

The two officers stood up, and Stone did too. He had a sense of things closing in around him, shutting him out. He said, "I do have one more question."

Dvorak raised an eyebrow.

"Tom Waverly was seriously ill. He more or less told me he was dying. What was wrong with him? And don't tell me you don't know. Your pathologist will have autopsied him by now."

Dvorak looked past Stone for a moment, listening to her earpiece. She said, "Apparently, Mr. Waverly was suffering from some kind of advanced cancer."

"Some kind of cancer? What kind?"

"That's all I can tell you, Mr. Stone."

"Right. Why is it I keep hearing that?"

# 12.

Stone was driven to the Plaza Hotel and escorted to his room by three officers. One of them, a lantern-jawed veteran with a salt-and-pepper crew cut, told him that they would be posted right outside the door.

"Your phone has been disconnected so you won't be bothered by locals. If you need anything from room service, give your order to one of us. We'll pass it right along."

"Am I under arrest?"

"We have orders to confine you to your room for security reasons," the officer said, returning Stone's hard stare.

"'Confine,'" Stone said. "You want to tell me the difference between 'confine' and 'imprison'?"

"It's for your own safety, Mr. Stone."

"Is there a specific threat? Does it have a name?"

"We're not at liberty to say. But don't worry, we'll take good care of you."

Stone took a shower and put on the towelling robe hung on the back of the bathroom door and sat at the window, staring at the dark trees beyond the streetlights along Central Park South. His thoughts moved in slow, futile circles. He still didn't know how much the Company knew about GYPSY, or what GYPSY was, or how Dick Knightly had been involved. He didn't know if it was still running or if it had been busted and Tom Waverly had been a loose end. He didn't much care. His part in this was nearly over. All he wanted to do before he went home was speak to Linda Waverly, persuade her to give up whatever it was her father had told her back in the motel room, convince her that it was in her own best interest to let the Company deal with it. . . .

He dozed off in the chair and was woken a few hours later by one of his guards. The man laid out a white shirt and a black suit on the bed, brought in a breakfast tray, and told Stone that he would be leaving in thirty minutes.

It was seven in the morning. Crows were busy around the corpses hung on the row of gallows. Traffic was beginning to build up, horns and distant sirens muffled by the room's triple glazing. Stone did several sets of sit-ups and squat-thrusts, took a shower, hot then cold, and shaved and dressed. He was nibbling a piece of dry toast and sipping a cup of black coffee when someone knocked at the door.

It was David Welch, uncharacteristically rumpled. He closed the door and stood with his back to it and said, "I have some bad news."

Stone's first thought was that something had happened to Linda Waverly.

Welch said, "There's been an incident at New Amsterdam. Susan Nichols was shot."

Stone jumped to his feet and Welch braced himself and said quickly, "It was two days ago. The news took a while to get through to us via the Real. I came over as soon as I heard."

Stone's body was flooded with adrenalin. His fists were raised. He was ready to defend himself from something he couldn't fight. "She was shot. What does that mean?"

He couldn't ask if she was alive or dead.

Welch shook his head and said, "I'm as sorry as hell, Adam."

"What about Petey?"

"Her son's fine. Got away without a scratch."

Stone took a deep breath, filling his lungs all the way to the bottom, and let it out slowly. He had to stay calm. He had to stay calm so that he could work out what to do next.

"Tell me everything."

It didn't take long. Two people, a man and a woman, had broken into the cabin at the farm just before midnight. Something must have alerted Susan—probably her dog, its body had been found near the barn—because she'd had time to wake her son and tell him to run to the neighbours' house as quickly as he could.

"We don't know exactly what happened after that, but there must have been some kind of confrontation," Welch said. "Mrs. Nichols shot the man dead and wounded the woman. And the woman shot her."

"Susan kept a pistol by her bed," Stone said. "Her husband was in the army—it was his sidearm."

"She knew how to use it. She killed the guy with two shots to the chest," Welch said, placing his thumb and forefinger close together over his heart.

"Who were they?"

"The dead guy is an ex-Marine. Buddy Altman. He worked for a firm of security consultants that supplies bodyguards for celebrities, that kind of thing. We're turning it over right now, investigating everyone who had any business with it."

"What about the woman?"

Welch looked at Stone, then looked away.

Stone said, "It's someone I know, isn't it?"

"Marsha Mason."

"Jesus Christ."

"My sentiments exactly," Welch said.

"Was it quick? When she killed Susan?"

"Are you sure you want to talk about this now, Adam?"

"Answer the question."

"Mrs. Nichols shot and killed Altman, and wounded Marsha in the thigh. Marsha had a machine pistol, and we believe Mrs. Nichols was killed instantaneously when Marsha fired off an entire clip."

"Susan wounded Marsha, and Marsha killed Susan. What happened after that? What about Petey?"

"The kid managed to get to the neighbours."

"Susan bought time for him. She saved his life."

"That's what I think," Welch said. "Mrs. Nichols's pistol made a pretty big hole in Marsha's thigh. She packed the wound and bandaged it, but she couldn't travel. A search party found her early the next morning, hiding in the barn. They also found an inflatable boat hidden in reeds on the river bank."

"I want to talk to her," Stone said.

"Marsha killed herself soon after she was captured," Welch said. "A cyanide pill."

"She was involved in the black op, wasn't she? In GYPSY."

"We believe it was a kidnapping that went bad. Altman and Marsha were probably planning to snatch your friend and her son, hide them somewhere in the forest, and ask you to offer yourself in exchange."

"They must have made their move as soon as I was brought into this. How did they know? Who told them?"

"Only three people were privy to the decision to ask for your help, Adam: the DCI, Ralph Kohler, and me. But a lot more knew about it after you came in, of course, and knew about that message Tom left, too. It's going to take a little time to check everyone, but if we're lucky, if we can find who ratted you out, we might be able to unravel this whole thing."

"How did Marsha and this ex-Marine get into the sheaf?"

"They could have posed as locals returning home, or tourists. They could have smuggled themselves in with a freight shipment, or they could have waited until the gate was activated when a train was about to go through and simply walked in ahead of it. We do know that an all-terrain vehicle was stolen from a farm at First Foot sometime in the afternoon. It's possible they used it to get to the East River, and then used that inflatable to get across to New Amsterdam. We haven't found the stolen ATV yet, but we're looking hard. We're checking everything, Adam."

"They planned to kidnap Susan and Petey, and offer a straight exchange. And after I surrendered myself, they were going to put me to the question, find out exactly what Tom told me. . . . Except I hadn't found Tom, two days ago. I'd only just arrived here, in New York. So either they were confident I would find him, and desperate to know what he might tell me, or this wasn't about anything I might find out. It was an attempt to force me to quit the search before it began."

"You need to calm down, Adam. Sit. Let me get you a drink."

"Susan was murdered. And the Company sat on the news until I found Tom. That's why I was confined to this room, isn't it?"

"I wouldn't know anything about that," Welch said. "And this isn't the time to be making wild accusations—"

"Fuck it, David. We both know how the Company works. This thing that Tom Waverly was involved in. GYPSY. It isn't just a few rogue operators with some crazy, half-assed plan, is it? And don't tell me you don't know anything about it, either. There are rumours that something big is going down inside the Company, and you're not only a well-connected guy, you're also my handler."

"I was brought into this on a need-to-know basis, just like you," Welch said.

"They didn't tell you anything about GYPSY? Come on."

"Well, I did hear something on the old Chinese telephone—"

"And?"

"It's only rumour, Adam. It isn't hard information."

"*And?*"

"It seems that a group of people inside the Company may have been planning some kind of coup," Welch said. "Possibly involving the assassination of the president."

"Was it something to do with a nuclear weapon?"

"I heard there was a raid on a clandestine facility, but I don't know any details."

"Tom Waverly was involved. So was Marsha Mason, and so was Nathan Tate, which is why Tom had no scruples about shooting him. And Knightly was involved, too, before he had his stroke. Who else? How deep does it go, David? What have I stepped into?"

"If I knew anything concrete, Adam, I'd tell you. But I really was brought into this knowing about as much as you."

"Tom defected from this thing, and it started falling apart at about the same time. And Kohler knew Tom had defected, knew people were after him. That's why I was brought in. That's why I was fed a bunch of bullshit and set up as bait. Not just to draw out Tom, but also to draw out any bad guys who might have been looking for him. I was used."

"I'm sorry, Adam."

"I was used. And the worst thing is, I knew I was being used, and I agreed to it anyway. I let it happen and Susan was killed because of it. Because no one thought for one fucking second to protect her. Including me."

Stone was having trouble maintaining his calm. His pulse was beating right behind his eyes, red and black. He wanted to punch out Welch. He wanted to smash everything in the room.

"I'm sorry, Adam. Truly."

"Call Kohler. Tell him I have to go home right away."

"I don't know if that's a good idea. The area hasn't been made secure."

"There isn't what you'd call a funeral parlour anywhere on New Amsterdam. When someone dies, they're usually buried inside of two days."

"I understand why you want to go," Welch said. "But suppose there are other unfriendlies involved? Suppose Altman and Marsha Mason had backup? A sharpshooter hiding out in the woods, say, waiting for you to show."

"Is that your opinion, or Kohler's?"

"I'd say half and half."

"It was most likely just Marsha and the ex-Marine, a quick in-and-out operation. Snatch Susan and Petey, hide them, wait for me to come back, and kill me. Or question me and then kill me. But they didn't reckon on Susan."

Her death was becoming real. Stone was amazed that he could say her name.

"Maybe they blew it this time," Welch said. "But you know they'll try again."

"Because they know now that I talked to Tom Waverly. Because they think he told me something important and they want to find out what it was, or they want to shut me up. David, I hope to hell you have Linda Waverly somewhere safe. They're bound to have targeted her as well."

"She's being interrogated. She's as safe as anyone can be. And you'll be safe here. There's already extra security in the hotel—"

"I'm not staying here, David. Find out when the funeral will take place. And tell Kohler that if he won't make the necessary arrangements, I'll make my own way home."

# 13.

An hour later, Stone was driven in an armoured limousine to the Pan-American Alliance Assembly Building and escorted to Ralph Kohler's office on the thirty-fourth floor.

Kohler offered his condolences and told Stone that arrangements had been made to return him to the First Foot sheaf as soon as possible. "The funeral will take place at noon, but I think we can get you there in time. I understand why you want to go, Mr. Stone. And although it places you in clear and present danger I'm not going to try to talk you out of it. In return, I hope you'll hear me out. Here, let's sit down. Is there anything I can get you? Coffee, something stronger?"

Stone knew then he was being allowed to go back because the Company still needed him, and for the first time since David Welch had broken the news of Susan's death he felt a small faint hope. "Say your piece, Mr. Kohler. Tell me what this is going to cost me."

They sat in leather armchairs in front of the floor-to-ceiling window. Neither of them paid any attention to the view across the sweep of the East River to Brooklyn's crowded hills.

"I'll cut straight to the chase," Kohler said. "According to Linda Waverly, her father stole something crucial to the success of Operation GYPSY. Something that the people involved in it would very much like to get back. And she said that she needs your help to retrieve it."

"This is what she and Tom talked about, back in the motel room."

Kohler nodded, calm and alert in his tailored grey suit and polished black wingtips.

Stone said, "After Tom shot himself, Linda told me that I could help her make things right, but she wouldn't explain how. I guess she finally saw sense."

"Up to a point," Kohler said. "She told us that her father stole something, but she can't or won't tell us what it is, or where he hid it. She also denies having any knowledge of where her father had been or what he had been doing after he disappeared three years ago. We tried questioning her under sodium amytal, but she became delusional. She told us that if it all worked out, she would find her father and he would explain everything. And she claimed that the thing he stole has the potential to change history, but she couldn't or wouldn't explain how."

"Maybe she was telling the truth," Stone said. "Maybe Tom set both of us up. He told Linda half the story, and expected me to fill in the rest."

"That's one possibility," Kohler said. "I have to say that it's also possible that he wanted to send us on a snipe hunt, to draw us away from the real action."

"You think Tom was really working for the bad guys all along? You think he was spinning some kind of fantasy story, and killed himself to make it seem convincing?"

"It's a hard reach, I know. But Waverly told you that he was involved with GYPSY, and as for his suicide, well, he was suffering from a terminal illness."

"And I suppose you think that the kidnapping attempt was part of this so-called story too," Stone said. "I suppose you think they killed Susan Nichols as some kind of *diversion*."

Kohler didn't flinch. "I think you deserve to know everything. I won't apologise for having touched a raw nerve."

Stone looked away at the blue sky beyond the window until his calm returned. He knew that he was going to be offered a choice, and couldn't afford to let anger and grief distract him. When he was ready, he said, "All right. Where do I fit in?"

"Things are very fluid right now," Kohler said. "We can't rule anything out. So although there's a chance that this could be some kind of diversion, we have to follow it up. We couldn't get any sense out of Linda Waverly with sodium amytal, and I'd rather not put her to hot questioning. She's one of our own, and she has an exemplary record. Also, breaking her could take several days, and we have to settle this as quickly as possible."

"Because you have to get hold of this thing before the bad guys do."

"If it exists, yes."

Stone ignored that. "You're going to let Linda Waverly go after it, and you want me to help her out."

"She wants you to help her out," Kohler said. "She was very insistent on that point."

"She can be very determined."

"I must tell you that in addition to the need for a speedy resolution, there are two other reasons why I have agreed to this," Kohler said. "First, as I have already said, there is a very strong possibility that this is a snipe hunt. Second, we have no evidence that Ms. Waverly is involved with GYPSY, and she has a very good reason to play this straight, because she believes that it will clear her father's name. She wants you to go with her, and I want you to make sure she comes back. You have a reputation as an honest soldier, Mr. Stone. Despite that little trick you played yesterday when you dropped your tail, I believe that I can trust you to do the right thing."

Although Kohler delivered his pitch with plausible sincerity, Stone was certain that there was more to it than he was being told, and suspected that he was probably being set up again. But as long as this gave him an opportunity to bring down the people responsible for Susan's murder, he didn't much care. He said, "How do you want to play this?"

"There isn't much to it," Kohler said. "When you've paid your respects, you'll be brought back here and put on a train with Linda Waverly. It will go through the mirror to the Real. The train will slow down, and you'll both get off and hitch a ride from there."

"As easy as that, huh?"

"So Ms. Waverly claims. A simple retrieval from a dead drop."

"Did she tell you anything at all about where we're supposed to be going? Which sheaf, which city?"

"No, she didn't," Kohler said. "We'll be watching every gate, of course, but we won't know where her father told her to go until she takes you there. Most likely, it will be one of the places where you and Tom Waverly worked together, but we can't rule anything out. So, will you help us?"

"I have one condition of my own," Stone said. "I don't want anyone following us. No tail, no backup. If I do this, I'll have to convince Linda Waverly that I'm on her side. I'll lose her trust the instant she spots someone tailing us. And I won't wear a wire, either. I found the bug you put in the heel of Linda Waverly's shoe, and I had her change her clothes, too. If she's got any sense she'll take the same precautions."

"You're asking a lot," Kohler said.

"You want my help, Mr. Kohler, and you know that I have a very good reason for wanting to help you. But you have to let me do it my way, or I guess, seeing that you can't order me to do it, you'll have to let Linda Waverly go in on her own."

Kohler thought about this for a few seconds, then smiled and said, "Very well."

"I'd appreciate a sidearm."

"There'll be one waiting for you when you meet Ms. Waverly."

"And it really would help if I had some idea of what exactly it is I'm supposed to retrieve."

"We really don't know what it is, Mr. Stone. It could be anything at all, including a figment of Tom Waverly's imagination."

Kohler's gaze was locked with Stone's, his eyes bright and sharp behind his gold-rimmed glasses. It was impossible to tell if he was lying.

"I guess you can't tell me anything about GYPSY, either."

"I'm in charge of the investigation into the murders of Eileen Barrie's doppels, not the investigation into GYPSY."

"I heard that it's something to do with a plan to assassinate the president."

"There are all kinds of rumours, Mr. Stone. I'm afraid that I'm not in a position to confirm or deny any of them."

"I guess it doesn't really matter," Stone said. "One more thing. What happens to Linda Waverly when this is over? Will she have to face charges?"

"If you're successful, it shouldn't be necessary."

"Draw up a letter guaranteeing her immunity whatever the outcome," Stone said. "If I'm satisfied with it, you've got yourself a deal."

"I told her that she can leave the Company with an honourable discharge if this goes right," Kohler said, with some steel in his gaze now. "If not, she'll be prosecuted. For disobeying direct orders, for wilfully withholding information necessary for national security, and anything else the DCI's office can think up. That's the deal I made with her. It isn't up for negotiation. How long will you need at New Amsterdam?"

"As long as it takes. That's not up for negotiation either."

# 14.

The ferry that linked New Amsterdam to the mainland was an army-surplus assault craft, a steel shoebox with a forty-foot cargo well, and a small steering platform and a powerful motor at the stern. Stone came aboard with a squad of officers in combat gear. The ferryman, Ted McDougal, ignored his greeting and busied himself with hauling up the bow ramp and casting off. Once they were under way, Stone commented on the holstered pistol hooked to Ted's belt. The ferryman looked down at him from the slight elevation of the steering platform and said, "You brought a lot of trouble on us."

"I know. And I'm more sorry for it than I can say."

"Wouldn't have come across for you if your friends hadn't insisted," Ted McDougal said. He opened up the throttle, and the roar of the motor made further conversation impossible.

As the ferry butted through the swell, Stone stood at the side wall of the cargo well and watched the wooded shore of New Amsterdam grow closer. The sky was as flawlessly blue as it had been on the day he'd left, the sun golden and benign. Another perfect day on the breast of this wild, empty world. It was probably the wind that was making his eyes water.

Willie Davis, the sheriff of New Amsterdam, was waiting with two horses on the concrete slope of the landing. After Willie had shaken Stone's hands and offered his condolences, Stone told the leader of the squad of officers that he and his men should wait by the ferry. "It's more than a mile to the church. I want to get there as soon as possible, and as you can see, we only have two horses."

"I have orders to accompany you, sir. They come directly from the DCI's office."

Stone looked at Willie and said, "Are we under martial law here?"

"Not as far as I'm concerned."

"I have my orders, Mr. Stone," the officer said helplessly.

"And I can lock you up if you cause trouble," Willie said. He was a heavily built man with dull brown skin, a shaven head, and a forthright manner. He was dressed in a blue corduroy suit and his silver star was pinned to the lapel of his jacket. The last time he'd worn that suit had been at Jake Nichols's funeral.

Stone said, "What Sheriff Davis means is that this a private affair. You guys wait here, and try not to get into any trouble. I'll be back in an hour or so."

He rode with Willie Davis through the pine forest and a belt of paper birches that had turned early after the long, hot summer. Sunlight danced through yellow leaves overhead and yellow leaves carpeted the track. Willie said that he'd asked for the funeral service to be delayed after he'd heard that Stone was coming home, but the preacher wouldn't countenance it. "You should know that some people are unhappy about you coming back."

"Ted McDougal, for one."

"Him and the preacher and about half of New Amsterdam. People are frightened, Adam. We haven't had a murder here since Pete Emerson took an axe to his wife and kids and walked out into the woods and allowed himself to freeze to death. People are frightened and stirred up, and some of them have been shooting their mouths off and blaming you for . . . well, for what happened."

"They're right. I agreed to do something without checking it out first. I stepped into a world of trouble because I didn't look where I was going. And I got Susan killed."

Willie Davis looked over at Stone. "That kind of talk won't do anyone any good. It was those two strangers who killed Susan."

"They came here because of me," Stone said. "How is Petey holding up?"

"About how you'd expect. The Ellisons have taken him in and say they're happy to look after him. I guess we'll see how that goes one day at a time."

"The worst thing about this is thinking of him growing up without a mother or father."

"The Ellisons are good people. And their boy is about Petey's age."

"It's going to be hard for him, Willie. I speak from experience."

"If you want to do something for him when you come back," Willie Davis said, "maybe you could take care of the farm until Petey is old enough to figure out what he wants to do with it. We'll have a meeting about it when things have settled down. Some people will no doubt speak against you, but I reckon the majority will be in favour."

"I'm here to pay my respects, and then I have to go finish a piece of work," Stone said. "I don't know when I'll be back."

He asked Willie to tell him exactly what had happened. The sheriff's story was more or less the same as David Welch's. He said that he'd organized scouting parties at first light and they'd ridden every square inch of cleared land. "We checked every outbuilding, every copse, we searched all along the shore. Used dogs. We found the woman pretty quickly—she'd passed out from blood loss. We found her inflatable boat, too, and that's all we found. If anyone else is still here, they're better at hiding out in the woods than any of us, and they didn't leave any tracks either, or any scent the dogs could pick up."

"I'm pretty sure there were only two people."

Willie looked relieved. "That's what I figured. I guess they thought it would be an easy job."

"Right."

"I should have gotten that woman to talk. I shouldn't have let her kill herself."

"You couldn't have known about the suicide pill."

"She was out cold when we found her. When she came around, she asked for a drink of water. She took one sip, started foaming at the mouth and jerking about, and that was it."

"There was nothing you could have done about it, Willie."

"I always heard cyanide is a painless way to go, but now I seen it I know it ain't. These must have been pretty desperate people, if they were ready to die like that rather than talk."

"They were."

Stone and Willie Davis rode out of the woods and rode up a slope of rough pasture to Broadway's white track. The little clapboard church and its cemetery stood to the east of Broadway, overlooking the broad, rush-lined pond of the Collect. Horses and wagons were parked out front and everyone in the little community was gathered inside, singing Susan's favourite hymn, the song faltering as people turned to look at Stone when he entered. A coffin of raw pine planks stood on trestles in front of the altar, a spray of wild flowers laid on its closed lid. Stone felt a swelling ache in his throat when he saw it.

He stood in the back of the church while Susan's neighbours stepped up to the lectern and talked about why they had valued her as a friend and how much they were going to miss her. Petey sat at the end of the front pew in his best shirt and jeans, his hair combed back from his scrubbed face. He was restless and kept looking this way and that, as if expecting his mother to walk in at any moment. When he spotted Stone at the back of the church, he smiled and gave a little wave, and the sudden ache in Stone's throat almost gagged him.

He kept to the end of the procession that followed Susan's coffin as it was carried out of the church to the grave newly dug beside the grave of her husband. A fresh wind tugged at clothes, snatched away the words of the preacher as he intoned the prayer for the dead, and raised cat's-paw waves out on the Collect. Several women were crying. Small children hugged their parents' legs. Petey stood dry-eyed at the head of the grave, solemn and still and small among the press of adults, clutching Nora Ellison's hand.

After the coffin had been lowered and he had taken his turn to cast a handful of dirt on its lid, Stone worked his way through the small crowd toward Petey, accepting condolences from those who came forward, doing his best to ignore the hostile stares of those who didn't. When Stone called to him, Petey ran straight to him, and he knelt and gathered the boy into his arms.

"Hey, little man."

"You came back. I said you'd come back."

They were awkward and solemn with each other because of the people around them, because they didn't know what to say about the catastrophe. Stone tried to tell Petey that he wished more than anything that he had never gone away and Petey told Stone that he was staying with Mr. and Mrs. Ellison.

"I hope they're treating you right."

"I guess. They won't let me go home."

"You'll probably have to stay away a little while."

"We can look after it together, can't we?"

"When I come back, sure."

"There are an awful lot of chores."

"Listen, Petey. I have to go away again for a little while. I have some work to do. But it won't take long, and when I've finished I'll come straight back."

"She said Mommy's gone away. Mrs. Ellison. But I know she's dead."

"I know."

"Like Daddy."

"Yes."

"When the bad people came, Mommy told me I had to run and get help," Petey said. "I ran real hard. It was dark and I fell over twice, but they didn't catch me."

"You did good. I'm proud of you, Petey. More than I can say."

"They killed Blackie," Petey said, and burst into tears.

Stone did his best to comfort the boy, but there was a ripple of agreement in the crowd when Nora Ellison stepped forward and drew Petey to her and gave Stone a flinty look and said that he'd already caused enough trouble.

Willie Davis told Stone that he was welcome to come back to his place and freshen up before he took the ferry, but Stone said that he had to ride back straightaway. He refused as politely as he could Willie's offer of company and told him that he'd leave his horse with Ted McDougal.

They shook hands. Willie said, "If you don't come back to help out, I'll send a party to fetch you."

"I'll be back," Stone said.

The slender birches tossed their heads in the wind and the air was suddenly full of their yellow leaves. It was as if he were riding away from his own wedding.

# Part Two

# LOOK FOR AMERICA

# 1.

The railcar from First Foot drew into the Johnson sheaf's version of Brookhaven station a little after three in the afternoon. The squad of officers escorted Stone across the crowded concourse toward a spur platform tucked under the curve of the dome where a chunky diesel locomotive with a single passenger car was waiting. On the neighbouring platform, handlers armed with cattle prods, whips, and shotguns were driving a shock force of big, white-pelted apemen, shackled in groups of four, out of a slatted boxcar.

As Stone and the squad went past, smoke grenades detonated underneath the boxcars. Thick jets of green vapour spurted up and flooded across the platform, enveloping the apemen; then a miniature thunderstorm of flash-bang grenades exploded, lighting up the spreading smoke. Apemen shrieked and fell over each other as they pulled in different directions. A handler vanished beneath a scrum of the white giants; two more fired shotguns loaded with rock salt in a futile attempt to drive them back into the boxcar.

The squad surrounded Stone and hustled him toward the checkpoint at the head of the spur platform. Stone grabbed the shoulder of the man in charge of the squad and yelled into his ear, asking for his sidearm.

"Keep moving!" the man shouted back. "We have to get you out of here!"

They kept moving, reaching the checkpoint moments before the apemen overwhelmed their handlers and burst out of the spreading billows of green smoke and charged into crowds of soldiers and aid workers like convicts escaping into a corn field. Soldiers fought apemen with rifle butts and knives and fists. A cacophony of shouts and shrieks and screams echoed under the dome's high canopy. A group of white-helmeted MPs battled through fleeing aid workers toward the mêlée, blowing their whistles and firing warning shots into the air.

Stone and the officers bulled through the checkpoint and jogged through tendrils of green smoke toward the passenger car, and a quartet of apemen clambered over the edge of the platform like a disarticulated albino spider. The officers felled them with a volley of small-arms fire, regrouped around Stone, and started to move forward again, and their leader spun in a half circle and collapsed, the back of his head blown away. Someone shouted *"Sniper!"* and men grabbed Stone's arms and rushed him toward the passenger car and bundled him through an open door.

The officers who had questioned Stone last night, Carella and Dvorak, were flattened on either side of the door, pistols drawn. A little way down the car, Linda Waverly crouched in the aisle between the rows of fat brown-leather seats, tending a man in a black suit. She had ripped open his shirt and was trying to stem the flow of blood from a chest wound. A sniper's bullet punched a sudden hole in a window and thumped into the back of a seat. Dvorak hit the button that shut the door and shouted "*Go! Go! Go!*" into her cell phone. The train got under way with a violent jerk. Carella lost his balance and sat down hard; Stone and Dvorak grabbed handrails.

As the train cleared the edge of the dome, Carella got to his feet, picked up a briefcase from one of the seats, and told Stone that he'd brought his pistol.

"Fuck his pistol," said Dvorak, who shot her partner in the head, knocking him back into the seat, and swung around and pointed her pistol at Stone, telling Linda Waverly to stand up and step away from the bodyguard.

"He needs medical attention—"

"Do it right now, or I'll shoot your friend!" Dvorak's voice was shrill and breathless; her face a rigid mask.

Linda got to her feet. She was wearing a denim jacket over the jeans and checked shirt that Stone had bought for her yesterday morning. Her hair was bunched in a short ponytail. She held the top of the seats on either side of her for balance as the train rocked over a set of points and picked up speed as it headed for the tunnel and the Turing gate.

"Come down the aisle toward me," Dvorak said. "Sit down, lock your hands on top of your head, and stay still."

Linda did as she was told. Dvorak ordered Stone to turn around and sit on his hands, facing the door.

Stone measured angles and distances, and said, "Take it easy. I'm unarmed."

Dvorak fired her pistol into the floor, then pointed it at Stone's leg. "I'll put the next one in your knee. Turn around, motherfucker. Right now!"

Stone began to turn, slowly then quickly, grabbing one of the handrails by the door, left hand over right, kicking off and swinging out full-length through the air. Dvorak got off one shot, the round plucking the wing of Stone's jacket, and he kicked her in the chin and felt her jaw click. She staggered backward and he landed on the balls of his feet and chopped at her wrist with the side of his hand, but she twisted sideways, raising her elbows to avoid his blow, and clouted the top of his skull with her pistol as the train plunged into the tunnel that housed the gate.

The hard blow and the black flash of translation exploded inside Stone's head. Grey light flared in the windows of the passenger car. Dvorak was smiling at him behind her pistol, showing bloody teeth, and Linda stepped up behind her and swung Carella's briefcase in a tight arc that connected with the side her head. Dvorak dropped to her knees, and Linda hit her again with a sweeping backswing and she fell sideways and lay still.

Stone and Linda grinned at each other. They were both breathing hard. "I guess she's one of the bad guys," Stone said, and knew then that Tom Waverly really had stolen something from GYPSY.

Dvorak was unconscious, her eyes half closed, her breathing ragged. Stone jammed two fingers into the nerve cluster under the hinge of her jaw, hoping that the pain would bring her around, but she was too far gone. Killing her would satisfy his anger, but it would be better to leave her to the tender mercy of the Company. Maybe Kohler could get her to talk.

He patted her down and found in the pocket of her jacket a rectangular black box about the size of an ammo clip and almost as heavy, with a pair of metal prongs at one end that snapped blue sparks when he pressed the button. There was a Colt .45 semiautomatic in a safety holster inside Carella's briefcase. Stone strapped the holster to his belt and pocketed the spare clip. Down the aisle, Linda was kneeling over the wounded man. As Stone came toward her, she sat back on her heels and wiped her bloodied hands on the carpet. "He's gone," she said flatly.

The train was rolling through the switching yard at Brookhaven, in the Real. Moving at walking pace now, exactly according to plan.

"We have to get out of here," Stone said.

"They tried to kill us—"

"They tried to snatch us, and caused all kinds of mayhem to keep Kohler's people busy. They had Dvorak, they had a sniper, and they'll have people here, too, waiting to pick us up. As soon as they realise we overpowered Dvorak, they'll chase us down. And Kohler's people will be after us too. But if we move now, we have a chance to get away and hitch a ride to wherever it is you want to go. Want to tell me where that is, by the way?"

"The American Bund sheaf. My father has an apartment there, in New York," Linda said, and stood up. "Let's do this before I lose my nerve."

Stone jumped first and hit the ground running, managing to stay on his feet as the rear end of the passenger car went past. He saw Linda Waverly jump and land awkwardly, tumbling over, rolling among tall weeds, and he ran toward her as she got to her feet, brushing gravel from her scraped palms.

The shoulder of her denim jacket was ripped and she'd torn holes in the knees of her jeans.

All around them, trains were moving through a web of tracks five miles long and a mile across. A pair of diesel locomotives hauled a string of passenger cars out of one of the short rows of grassy mounds scattered here and there like the graves of giants from some lost heroic age. Snow crested the motor units of the locomotives and the roofs of the passenger cars.

As they hurried through a broad triangle of wet, waist-high grass, heading toward the far side of the interchange, Linda told Stone that the bodyguard had been shot just after the smoke grenades had gone off. "He pushed me to the floor and then a window broke and he fell down. Carella wanted to call it in, but Dvorak told him they'd deal with it on the other side of the mirror. I should have known then that she was planning something."

"As far as I'm concerned, you didn't do anything wrong," Stone said. "You saved my life just now. Both our lives. I don't know what Tom said to you back in Pottersville, but he did a hell of a job. You went in a loyal Company soldier, and you came out a cowboy."

"You don't know the half of it," Linda said. "But he didn't tell me everything, Mr. Stone. He didn't tell me what he stole from GYPSY, or why it was so important. What I *do* know is that the trail starts in the American Bund sheaf. We have to find his apartment."

"Is that where he hid this thing? How could he be sure we'd get there before the bad guys?"

"He said it would take both of us to find it. That's all I know."

"What about the apartment? Did he give you the address?"

"He said it was in New York, and that you would be able to find it."

Stone thought for a moment. "I know someone who may be able to help us. If he isn't dead or in jail, that is. It's been a long time since I was last in the American Bund. The son of a bitch. He really set us up, didn't he?"

"He didn't tell me everything in case I was compromised," Linda said. She was limping slightly as she followed Stone through the tall grass, stubborn and indefatigable. "I know you're angry with him for dragging you into this. But this is about a lot more than clearing his name. You'll see."

"If you mean Operation GYPSY, I have my own reasons for wanting to bring it down," Stone said.

This wasn't the right time to tell Linda about Susan; maybe there'd never be a right time.

Far across the maze of railroad tracks, the train that had brought them through the mirror had come to a halt in front of the huge station. Stone pointed to the little black helicopter that was settling toward it. "Either its crew are part of the black op, or Kohler's people are about to discover just how badly things have gone wrong. In any case, we need to find a ride right away."

This side of the interchange had been the site of the original Special Operations facility, back when Brookhaven had been a research campus of white buildings scattered among grassy lawns and mature stands of pines. All that was gone now, but the pair of Turing gates that had once stood in a hangar-sized laboratory were still there, housed now in a square bunker of raw concrete slabs and served by two tracks that ran past a transformer farm caged by chain-link fencing and razor wire. Power lines slung overhead in every direction filled the crackling air with a bone-deep hum. In the distance, beyond stacks of freight containers and runs of big pipes leaking feathers of steam, was the giant block of one of Brookhaven's nuclear power plants.

Linda followed Stone as he jogged through stands of grass and fireweed toward trains waiting in dispatch loops. Off in the distance, the helicopter had come to rest beside the locomotive and its single passenger car, but it was too far away to make out what was happening.

Rusty rails began to sing as a diesel locomotive began to move, hauling a string of boxcars toward one of the Turing gates in the bunker. Stone put on speed, running hard with Linda right behind him. The helicopter was lifting away from the train halted in front of the station.

The locomotive sounded its horn as it went past. Stone grabbed hold of the handrail of the steps at its rear, swung up, hooked a foot through a rung, and clung there. Linda had missed her chance and was running alongside the train, falling behind as it moved faster and faster. The helicopter skimmed over the train with a clattering roar, so low that its downdraught flattened Stone's suit against his skin. He saw Linda clambering into one of the boxcars near the end of the train and saw the helicopter make a wide turn against the low grey sky. The train was still accelerating, but the helicopter quickly caught up with it, hunting along its length. Clinging to the steps at the rear of the locomotive, Stone could see three people inside its bubble canopy, could see the mini-guns slung on either side—and then the helicopter stood on its nose and sheered away as the locomotive sounded its horn again and plunged into the bunker, and the Turing gate took everything somewhere else.

# 2.

Adam Stone and Linda Waverly got out of the Brookhaven station as fast as they could, stole a car, and drove west, toward New York. When they were certain that they weren't being followed, they stopped at a gas station in Deer Park and Stone phoned an old friend, a former gangster by the name of Walter Lipscombe. Less than an hour later, he and Linda had been picked up and transported to a flophouse deep in the unreconstructed slums of the Bronx. It seemed that Walter Lipscombe was being investigated by several agencies, and it would take a while to arrange a safe route to his apartment.

While they cooled their heels in the mean little room, with its sagging bed and unsprung armchair and faded cabbage-rose wallpaper, Linda insisted that Stone tell her everything he could remember about her father's last hour in Pottersville. He found that he couldn't sit still while he talked; thinking about Tom Waverly's suicide was too close to the great wound ripped out of him by Susan's murder. So while Linda sat on the edge of the bed, he paced up and down and tried to give an accurate summary of what had happened outside the abandoned house and in the cemetery. There was a silence when he was finished. Then Linda thanked him in a small, choked voice and went into the bathroom and shut the door. Stone heard her sobbing, heard something smash, glass on ceramic, and broke the lock of the door and gathered her up.

"It was only a glass," she said into his chest. "I'm not going to do anything dumb."

They held each other for a moment more; then Linda pushed away and said she was okay, she just had to wash her face. Stone knew that her brittle composure might crack again at any moment, but she was a lot stronger than he'd thought. He hoped she would be strong enough to be able to face up to Walter Lipscombe's rude energy.

Before the Real had irrupted into his sheaf and kick-started a revolution, Lipscombe had been a middle-ranking soldier in one of the gangs of self-styled wise guys who, with the connivance of corrupt officers and civil servants, had bootlegged booze and merchandise across the Canadian border. He'd been responsible for organising storage space in government warehouses for clandestine loads carried by the trucks and trains of the Office of Interstate Transport, and with more than a hundred minor officials in his pocket, he'd been one of the most useful of Adam Stone's contacts during the run-up to the putsch that had toppled the American Bund. Quick-witted, capable, and street-smart, Lipscombe had refused a position in the new, democratically elected government. Instead, taking advantage of the chaotic free market that had sprung up after the revolution, he'd parlayed his political influence into a business empire that ran the docks and airport in New York City, and included four radio stations, the Metropolitan Museum, a newspaper, and a brewery. The last time Stone had seen him, he'd owned a private helicopter and an oceangoing yacht, had been maintaining two mistresses in suites at two different hotels, and had just bought the leases of the five storeys above the first setback of the Woolworth Building, one of the few New York skyscrapers to have survived the massive rebuilding programme masterminded by the Dear Leader.

That was where Adam Stone and Linda Waverly were taken, five hours after arriving in the American Bund sheaf. They rode in the back of a laundry van from the flophouse in the Bronx to the basement of a hotel in midtown New York, where they were transferred to a truck owned by an elevator servicing company. The truck took them into the garage of the Woolworth building, and after a guard insisted that Stone hand over his Colt .45 and the shock device he'd taken from Carol Dvorak, they rode a service elevator to the atrium of Walter Lipscombe's mansion apartment.

The atrium was two storeys high, glass and gold and Carrara marble spotlessly white as fresh-fallen snow. Monstrous arrangements of ferns and red and orange lilies exploded from stone urns. Water streamed down a slab of raw slate thirty feet high into a pool where a shoal of Koi carp fat as sheep endlessly patrolled. A butler in a morning suit greeted Stone and Linda, and they followed him up the sumptuous curve of the marble staircase and down a long deep-carpeted corridor to a drawing room where huge oil paintings of classical and pastoral scenes loomed over a clutter of Louis Quinze furniture. A smaller painting with a lot of gold and blue in it stood on an easel by the gleaming grand piano. Linda took three steps sideways to look at it but caught up with Stone as the butler announced them at French doors that opened onto a glassed-in terrace.

Up there, it was a world away from the queues at food stores, the concrete barriers outside government buildings, the defiant graffiti across sheets of hardboard patching broken windows, soldiers sweeping the muzzles of their .50-cal machine guns back and forth on top of patrolling half-tracks.

Up there, with the top of the Empire State Building lit in patriotic stripes of red, white, and blue, the grid of lighted streets and buildings stretching away north and east and west under the black sky, it was like being at the bridge of a Zeppelin moored above a fairyland.

Walter Lipscombe was at the far end of the terrace, talking into a cell phone, a squat bullfrog of a man dressed in a green silk gown trimmed with gold thread and green silk slippers with upturned toes. The sleeves of his gown were rolled back, showing a bleeding-heart tattoo on his left forearm. His scalp shone through the scant cornsilk of his failing hair transplant. When Stone stepped through the French doors, Lipscombe flipped up his free hand in a salute and swung away to face the splendid view, jabbing at the air with his forefinger as he made an emphatic point to whoever was on the other end of the phone. A pair of wolfhounds sprawled nearby, watching their master squint through his reflection in the thick glass that wrapped the terrace as he told the phone that he wanted it fucking well shipped tomorrow, he didn't care if it took all fucking night to crate it up, slipping the phone into a pocket of his gown and walking toward his guests, holding out his arms, saying to Stone, "My man! How long has it been?"

"About seven years," Stone said. He stood uneasily at the threshold, worried about possible watchers on nearby rooftops.

"Seven years? Get out of here!"

Stone stooped into Lipscombe's bear hug, his pungent odour of cologne and stale cigar smoke, then introduced Linda Waverly.

Lipscombe held Linda's hand after he had shaken it, and looked her up and down. "I was so very sorry to hear about your old man. He was a dear friend of mine."

"Thank you." Linda had a pinched, nervous look. She was running on anger and nerves. She was running close to empty.

"It looks like you got scuffed up some. How did that happen?"

"I jumped from a train. It isn't anything."

"I bet there's a good story to that." Lipscombe turned to the butler and said, "When Miss Waverly goes upstairs to dress for dinner, Phil, make sure to have one of the maids lay out a first-aid kit."

"It really isn't anything," Linda said. "A Band-Aid will fix it."

"Whatever you need, just ask. You're in the same kind of business as Adam, I hear. If you're half as good as you look, you'll be twice as good as this broke-down old man you're partnered up with. No offence, Adam, I'm kidding around. Adam and me, Miss Waverly, we go a long ways back. I hope I live up to whatever lies he told about me. I hope you like my apartment, too. I'm sorry I had to stash you away in that fleapit rather than bring you here direct, but at the best of times this place is a bitch to get into without being spotted. The lobby is permanently occupied by a crowd of government watchdogs, tabloid journalists, gumshoes working for my enemies—all kinds of scum. But once you're inside, it's absolutely safe. I have people check the roofs of the surrounding buildings on a regular basis, the glass is armoured, it looks like a mirror from the outside, and it's even vibrated so no one can bounce lasers off it and listen in. Which is just as well, because in addition to the usual teams of government goons dogging my every footstep, someone came looking for you guys."

Stone said, "Was it David Welch?"

"Welch? Jesus, is he in on this too? No, as a matter of fact, it was a fucker name of Saul Stein. You know him?"

"I've been out of the loop for a while, but I guess he's something to do with security, working out of the Pan-American Alliance Assembly Building."

"You *have* been out of the loop, my man," Walter said. "We're no longer a client state, thanks to your President Carter. We're fully autonomous. Independent. Anyone working for your government wants to take a shit in this sheaf—excuse me, Linda, I'm forgetting my manners in my excitement—they have to ask permission of the COILE. Saul Stein is head of the New York bureau."

Linda said, "The COILE?"

"The Central Office of Intelligence and Law Enforcement," Stone said. "It replaced the FBI after the revolution."

"Whatever they call themselves, feds are still feds," Lipscombe said. "Mr. Saul Stein sent a squad of his biggest and ugliest agents to hassle me a couple of days ago. That was when I found out Tom was still alive, and in all kinds of trouble. It seems he assassinated some woman out in California. I guess that's why you and Miss Waverly are here, huh?"

"Something like that," Stone said.

Lipscombe let that go. "I was told it was nothing personal, they were checking out all of Tom's associates from the good old days. Ever since, these gorillas have been following me everywhere I go, plus, I believe, a couple of your guys. The Real can't throw its weight around like it used to, but it still gets cooperation from the COILE when it needs it. So that was one thing, them looking for Tom, but now they're looking for you, too. Stein called by in person just an hour ago and asked had I seen you. I told him the truth, told him I hadn't seen you for a dog's age. This was after you made contact with me, so if he'd asked me had I *spoken* to you, that would have been another matter; I would have had to perjure myself. Anyway, that's how I heard about what happened to Tom. Stein told me himself. He wanted to see my reaction, the son of a bitch. So, now you understand why my guys had to be extra careful bringing you in. Did they treat you okay? Think the old switcheroo was good enough to fool Stein's gorillas and the Company guys?"

"It wasn't bad, for an amateur operation," Stone said.

"I see you haven't lost the sense of humour that was always a comfort to me in those dark days before the revolution. Let's pretend I know what I'm doing, which is why you came to see me. Which is why you need my help. No, don't tell me *why* you're here, not yet. You don't mind me saying so, you both look pretty ragged. You need to freshen up, have a drink or two, kick back and relax. Phil will take you upstairs, find you a couple of bedrooms—" Walter Lipscombe raised a shaggy eyebrow "—if you need separate bedrooms, that is. Make yourselves at home. Meanwhile, I have some people I need to shout at, make them buck up their ideas. When I'm finished, we'll catch up over dinner."

Stone soaked in a marble bath so large it had three steps down into it. He floated in an acre of eucalyptus-scented foam and tried to relax, but pictures of Susan kept crowding in whenever he closed his eyes, glimpses of happier times mixed up with scenes from the funeral. The way Petey had looked at him down the length of the church; Nora Ellison folding the little boy into herself when he'd started to cry. Stone tried to push the memories away. He didn't have the time to mourn properly, not yet. He had a job to do. He had to keep frosty. He had to stay sharp. He tried to work up a story he could tell Walter Lipscombe. He flipped through news channels on the imported plasma TV, but gleaned precious little hard information from the brief talking-head segments squeezed between five-minute-long blocks of ads.

When he emerged from the steamy bathroom, he found a tuxedo and starched white shirt laid out on the king-size bed. As he was trying to work out how to fasten his bow tie—he hadn't worn one since he'd taken Suzy Segler to the high school prom—the butler knocked on the door and told him that dinner would be served in ten minutes. Stone held out the strip of black cloth and asked the man if he knew what to do with it, while the butler expertly fixed up a neat bow under his chin, he asked what it was like, working for Walter Lipscombe.

"He's a very considerate employer, sir."

"You're a Brit, right? I heard you guys make the best butlers, and I guess Walter demands the very best these days."

"Technically, sir, I am Canadian. My parents came over as refugees in 1948 because my father was in service with the King. I had the honour of being a footman in service to the present Queen before I took up employment with Mr. Lipscombe."

"Like I said, nothing but the best for Walter." Stone was trying to remember how history here had diverged from history in the Real. There'd been a Second World War against fascism in Germany and Italy, but the American Bund had kept out of it, and the fascists had been defeated by an alliance between the Soviet Union and the British Empire. And after the war, there'd been a popular uprising in Britain, it had some kind of grim, utilitarian social democracy. . . . He said, "Last time I was here, wasn't America at war with the Brits?"

"If you mean the United Community of Europe, sir, the war ended two years ago, after your President Carter presided over negotiations in Iceland." The butler gave the bow tie a final tug and said, "I believe that does it, sir. Would you care to look in the mirror?"

Stone rattled off the names of Walter Lipscombe's bosses from before the revolution and asked if any of them ever came visiting. The butler, his bland expression giving away absolutely nothing, said that Mr. Lipscombe had many acquaintances, but he couldn't recall those particular gentlemen. Stone supposed that even if Walter Lipscombe and his old gangster pals frolicked in the blood of slaughtered virgins each and every night, his manservant would remain the epitome of tight-lipped British discretion.

He said, "Walter has gone up in the world."

"He aspires to the position of gentleman, sir. I believe that your companion is waiting next door. Perhaps you would allow me to escort both of you to the dining room."

Linda Waverly was a vision in a low-cut gown of watered green silk, her mass of red curls piled up and threaded with black ribbons, a few strands artfully dangling at her forehead. She said that she felt like a floozy in a cheap spy novel and gave Stone a shaky grin when he assured her that she was a show-stopper.

As they followed the butler down the corridor, Stone said quietly, "Walter is a generous host, but bear in mind that he's also an operator, and never passes up the chance to gather information."

"I haven't forgotten."

While they'd been waiting for Walter Lipscombe's men to pick them up, Stone had told Linda that they'd need Walter's help when they had to leave the sheaf, but he could only be trusted up to a point. If he found out that they were looking for her father's apartment, for something valuable that might have been hidden there, he'd want a piece of the action.

Now, Stone said, "If he pushes you about anything that upsets you, tell him to drop dead. He won't mind—he likes it when women stand up to him."

The dining room had stained-glass windows from the Metropolitan Museum's mediaeval collection and a huge stone fireplace flanked by a pair of stone gryphons. The long oak table, with seats for thirty guests, was set at one end with Meissen porcelain and a big gold cruet by Cellini. Stone and Linda sat with Walter Lipscombe and his wife, a cool slender brunette half her husband's age, the daughter of a congressman from Tennessee who had adroitly changed sides at the beginning of the revolution, after the army had refused to move in when student riots had set fire to campuses across the country.

"You were going to tell me the story of how you scuffed up your jeans," Lipscombe said to Linda, over the first course of salmon mousse and white truffle shavings.

Stone cut in and gave a précis of how he and Linda had escaped from the train. When he'd finished, Lipscombe said, "This woman who caused you such grief, she was working for whom, exactly?"

"That's what we're trying to find out," Stone said.

"I hear it's internal. Something to do with a conspiracy inside the Company."

"Your sources are still good, Walter."

"I try to keep up. I also heard it was something to do with your old boss, something he set up before he had his stroke."

"Like I said, we're trying to find out what exactly is going on."

"Well, you don't have to talk about it if you don't want to. I understand how it is. I'm happy to help out, no strings, no one owes anyone anything. So, how's retirement working out for you, Adam? I hear you're living in one of those wild sheaves. What are you now, a farmer? Cattle rancher? Gambler on a riverboat?"

Although Stone knew that Lipscombe couldn't possibly know about Susan, he felt a sudden chill across his skin, an ache at the back of his throat. He said, "It isn't exactly like the Wild West. Most of the time I don't do much of anything, which is the point of retirement. I fish, I hunt—"

"Ever hunt those big animals they have in those wild sheaves, the ones that are extinct here?"

"Sometimes."

"You and me, when this is all over, maybe we could arrange a hunting trip together. What's so funny?"

"I'm trying to imagine you out in the forest, Walter."

Lipscombe grinned. "It'd be an experience, right? It's good to see you back in the saddle, Adam. Really. What happened to you, what happened to all you old-time cowboy angels, the hearings, the resignations, people falling on their swords for the good of the Company. . . . It was a fucking shame. You were betrayed, you want my opinion. You shoulda risen up and got rid of that lily-livered clown calls himself president."

"Walter," his wife said. She laid a hand on his arm and said, "Let's not talk politics at the dinner table. It gets you too excited."

"He gave us full independence," Lipscombe said, "but what good is that if the commies get together and try to take us down? I met the son of a bitch once. He was on his so-called peace mission. I told him people here thanked God and the Real every night for getting rid of the Dear Leader, they would never forget that the Real had once had the guts to go to war on our behalf. He gave me the fish-eye and a clammy handshake and moved on down the line."

"Walter," his wife said again.

"I'm a passionate man," Lipscombe told Linda. "Aside from my good wife here, and my two boys, know what I'm most passionate about?"

Linda guessed that it might be fine art. "I noticed the painting in the drawing room. The one on the easel? It looks like Botticelli's *Annunciation*."

"That's because it is. Are you an art lover?"

"I remember seeing it in the Metropolitan Museum of Art, in the Real."

Walter Lipscombe's grin made him look like a frog who'd just swallowed an especially juicy fly. "That's where I got it from. *My* version of the Met, that is, not yours. And it's my *Annunciation* too, the one that belongs right here, not the one you saw back in the Real. But if you swapped one with the other, no one would be able to tell, including the guy I'm about to sell it to, a private collector in the Real. It's an everyday miracle of quantum physics, like the multiplication of the True Cross."

Linda said, trying to work it out, "You're a trustee on the museum board?"

"Honey, I *own* the place. When the Dear Leader turned tail and ran, God rot his black soul, I stood on the steps of the Met with a couple of dozen soldiers and saved the place from the looters. Later on, I bought it from the city."

"It was his single stroke of genius," Stone said.

"I've made plenty of good deals since then, but I have to admit, the time I moved in on the Met was a defining moment in my life. I know what you're going to say," Lipscombe told Linda. "You're going to say that I'm no better than the looters. That I'm pillaging a public institution for my own gain. Honey, I heard it all. If I sell off the odd painting, it's to keep the poor old place going. And besides, the museum was built in the first place by Boss Tweed, using part of the fortune he made by stealing the city blind, and more than half the stuff in it is plunder from other countries bought by tycoons who weren't much better than gangsters and pirates. Anyway, we were talking about passion. Maybe you're passionate about art, Linda, but for me, it's a business. I learned to love it, but learning how to love something is different from *being* in love, am I right? No, what I really love is history. You learn everything from history, or else—"

He grinned at Stone, who dutifully supplied the old punchline. "You learn nothing."

"He still remembers," Walter Lipscombe said. "I know a bit about your history, I know you never had what you'd call a real Second World War, that you took sides when the Russians had a revolution in 1947, and you ended up atom-bombing Stalingrad. Here, just a little earlier, the Russians and the Brits were fighting against Hitler and his National Socialism. The American Bund declared that it was staying out of the war, but of course it didn't—it supplied arms and raw materials to the Germans. That made the Brits pretty sore, I can tell you. After they invaded Europe, and the American Bund's merchant fleet lost the protection of the German U-boats, the Brits sank most of our ships and bombarded New York and Washington to drive home the point that they could do what they liked. And after they won the war, the Brits and the Russians imposed monster reparations on us. We had two decades of depression and high taxes, and if you guys hadn't come along, our Dear Leader would probably have lost a war against the United Community of Europe, we'd've had world peace, world government, everyone ground down under the same boot-heel forever. . . . Adam and me, we were part of the fight against that, once upon a time."

160

Stone said that the revolution had been about to happen anyway; he'd simply helped to give the local resistance a little boost.

"Stone and his pals trained people and brought in guns," Lipscombe told Linda. The three glasses of ashen-yellow Pinot Gris he'd drunk with the first course had lit him up. "I should know, because I was the guy helping move them. Those were good times. You lived every day, every hour, right there in the moment, because any second the FBI could arrest you and cart you off to the dungeons at Buzzard's Point, torture you to extract every bit of useful information, then shoot you, bing bang boom. They were killing a thousand a day toward the end, dumping them in the river in such numbers the politicians on Capitol Hill were complaining about the stink. Adam and your father and me, Linda, we were fighting against that."

His wife deftly turned the topic of conversation to her husband's funding of arts projects in the city, the season at the Opera House he'd sponsored, the charities she worked for. Stone saw how Walter Lipscombe waxed proud in the reflected glow of her elegance; the tough, cynical fixer was definitely in love. While the main course of rare beef and watercress sauce was being served, Linda told Lipscombe that she couldn't help noticing that he had the little finger missing on his left hand, and asked if he had lost it while fighting in the revolution.

"No, it was way before that," Lipscombe said. "As a matter of fact, it was my first real lesson in the way the world works. Adam knows all about it, and Anna has heard me tell it about a hundred times, but it's a good story. I'm sure they won't mind hearing it again."

He held up his hand and with the fondness of a retired soldier examining a campaign medal studied the silvery scar that sealed the stump of the missing finger. "Back in the bad old days, I was a raw kid driving a truck for one of the state-owned haulage companies and taking kickbacks from my immediate boss, who was connected, to run an extra trip or two at night. I'd drive across the border along the fire roads, load up, and come back. I'd been doing this for a couple of months when I was jumped coming back with a full load. The usual setup—a tree across the road, half a dozen guys in black balaclavas stepping out with machine guns and telling me to climb down. They were very efficient and knew exactly what they were doing. Hauled me out of the cab and put a gun in my ear and told me what was what, told me I'd come out of it okay if I did as I was told. So I sat nice and quiet on the tree they'd used to block the road, and didn't say a word while they took the goods.

"But the thing was, I recognised one of them. This tall skinny guy with a stutter who was one of the workgang that had loaded up the stuff in the first place. What they were doing was ripping off the outfit they worked for, the one that had sold the whiskey, as well as ripping off the outfit that had *bought* the whiskey, the outfit my boss at the haulage company was connected to. When they were finished they beat me up a little, and one of them slipped a twenty-dollar bill into my pocket and told me to say I had been held up by crooked customs officers. That kind of thing did happen, but usually the customs officers shot up the truck and killed the driver, took half the load for themselves, then turned in the rest and made themselves out to be heroes. There was a telephone number on the bill that I was supposed to call the next time I made a run. They promised me a couple of hundred if I did that.

"Anyway," Walter Lipscombe said, "I knew that *my* boss might be taken in by the lame-o story about customs officers, but I also knew that *his* bosses would think it was a crock. So I told him about the guy with the stutter. Next night, I'm pulled out of bed by two big guys in expensive black overcoats, put in a car, and driven across the border to the place where I usually loaded up. There are maybe twenty guys there, standing in a circle around six bare-ass-naked bozos all beat-up and bleeding. I'm told to identify the one I'd recognised, and although I'm sick at heart, what can I do but finger him? I mean, they'd already beaten a confession out of those guys, they just wanted confirmation from me, and if I didn't give it they'd kill them anyway. But by laying the finger on one of them, I became part of it, you see? Which was what happened. I was given a new job at a government warehouse and told to recruit drivers, and that's how I started on my long climb to where I am today, with my beautiful wife and my beautiful children and my beautiful house. All of which I owe to some poor dumb cluck with a stutter, who didn't know to keep his mouth shut."

Linda said, "But what about the little finger?"

"I didn't tell you?" Walter Lipscombe widened his eyes and struck his forehead with the heel of his hand in a pantomime of amazement. His wife was smiling at this bit of business, even though she must have seen it a hundred times. "What happened was, I kept that twenty-dollar bill that had been tucked into my pocket, and my bosses found out about it when they turned those guys over. So I was promoted for breaking open the scam, and I lost my little finger to remind me to be completely truthful at all times. And I've never forgotten that lesson—don't try to play both ends against each other, or you'll wind up in the middle, neck-deep in shit."

*

After dessert and coffee, Walter Lipscombe and Stone retired to the library while Walter's wife took Linda on a tour of the rest of the apartment. The library was panelled with fifteenth-century oak from a manor house in Kent, England, and contained more than ten thousand volumes, including one of the most comprehensive collections of pornography in the world. One wall was dominated by Jan van Eyck's *Last Judgement*. Display cases showed off drawings by Tintoretto, Pisanello, and Dürer, an illuminated page from Jean Fouquet's *Book of Hours*, rare prerevolutionary comics. Suits of ornate four-teenth-century German armour stood in shadowy alcoves.

Lipscombe poured two fingers of hundred-year-old brandy ("Liberated from the cellars of the Dear Leader's palace in Washington, DC") into two balloon glasses, and after Stone had refused the offer of a cigar and they had settled into leather armchairs on either side of a stone fireplace burning real logs, the ex-gangster made a toast to old times.

"That's why I'm here," Stone said.

"I was wondering when you'd get around to it."

In the soft red light of the fire, wreathed in the smoke of the Romeo y Julietta that was stuck in the middle of his grin, Walter Lipscombe looked like a minor devil. A nearby lamp put a shine on the pink scalp under his thinning hair.

"Thanks for holding off over dinner," Stone said.

"I know you have a low opinion of me, Adam, but even I can see that while that little girl is putting up a good front, a breath of wind could blow her clean away. Now we're alone, maybe you could tell me exactly what happened to Tom."

Stone told the story he'd put together in the bath: how he'd been recruited to try to bring in Tom Waverly, and what had gone down in Pottersville. He explained that Tom had been involved in some kind of conspiracy buried deep inside the Company, the one that Lipscombe had heard about, but didn't mention that Tom had taken something that both the conspiracy and the Company wanted to find. He knew that if Lipscombe got wind of that and found out that he and Linda were looking for it, the ex-gangster would make Stone an offer he couldn't refuse.

When Stone was finished, Lipscombe took a sip of his brandy and said, "Stein told me Tom killed himself, but I didn't know you were there. And you think Tom was dying of something."

"Terminal cancer, according to the Company pathologist. I don't know whether to believe that or not, but I do know that when we met up he'd reached the end of the line."

"The poor bastard. But we had some good times, didn't we?" Lipscombe said, and raised his glass.

They toasted Tom Waverly's memory.

Lipscombe said, "You tried your best to save Tom, and the stupid son of a bitch took another way out. But what brings you here? Why aren't you back on your farm, enjoying your retirement?"

"I'm trying to help Linda clear her father's name," Stone said. He wasn't about to tell Walter Lipscombe about Susan's murder. It was too raw and too personal, and he didn't want the man's pity.

"And you're following up a few leads, huh? Well, Tom was a good friend of mine," Lipscombe said. "Anything I can do to help, name it."

"When we've finished here, Linda and I need to get back to the Real. But we can't use a regular gate."

"Because you'd be grabbed."

"I was wondering if you still make use of the old gate at Grand Central Station."

"Funny you should mention that. The painting your girlfriend admired? I'm sending it through the mirror tomorrow afternoon, two o'clock. Or is that too early for you?"

"Not if things work out. I'd like to get out of here as soon as possible. No offence."

"None taken. Let me talk to the guys who look after this side of the gate. I'm sure I can persuade them to let you go through at the same time," Lipscombe said, rubbing his finger and thumb together.

"As long as it doesn't get you into trouble with the COILE."

"Forget about it."

"We'll need new ID, too. Something from one of the Real's agencies. Something that will get us through an interchange."

"If you go through the old gate with my name under the contract, it's strictly no questions asked. You won't need any ID."

"We might need to use other gates later on."

"You really are into some serious shit, aren't you?"

"I won't forget your help, Walter. How about that ID?"

"No problem. Army, DEA, ATF, FBI, or Carter's peacenick Reconstruction and Reconciliation Corps?"

"Army will be fine."

"You and Miss Waverly will have to give up your present ID—the guy who does this kind of work will need to copy your photographs and fingerprints."

"How quickly can he do this?"

"Hand your stuff to my butler. He'll get things organized overnight. So, is that it? If you want some company, a nice girl who can help you forget your troubles, my butler can organize that, too."

"Maybe you can help clear up a little mystery," Stone said. "Tom was in this sheaf recently, and he left in a hurry."

Walter nodded. "Right after he killed that woman. A mathematician, I believe, by the name of Eileen Barrie. She worked for the government, in the laboratories at Livermore. I heard all about it from that prick Saul Stein when he was trying to rattle my cage. He told me that Tom blew her up in her car, and they knew it was Tom because the crime scene guys had found his thumbprint on a piece of circuitry. The bomb was packed behind the plastic cover of the steering wheel column, a very nice shaped charge that decapitated her but left the bodyguard sitting next to her with no more than burst eardrums and second-degree burns to his hands. Very definitely Tom's style, don't you think? What Stein didn't tell me, what I've been trying to figure out, is why Tom wanted to kill her in the first place. You know anything about that?"

"I was brought in on a need-to-know basis, and told more or less what you were told," Stone said. Lipscombe didn't need to know that Tom Waverly had been killing off Eileen Barrie's doppels. "I do know that he managed to get out of this sheaf after he killed her. I was wondering if he might have used the old gate under Grand Central Station."

"You think?" Walter said. "The West Coast to New York, that's a long way to travel if you're on the run for murder. It would be easier to go through the mirror at White Sands."

"People would have been watching out for Tom at White Sands and at Brookhaven, just like they're right now watching out for me and Linda. The gate at Grand Central Station was his only chance of making a clean exit."

"And you think I helped him?"

"It crossed my mind."

"Especially when I admitted to using it just now. Well, I didn't help Tom. Maybe he didn't need anyone's help to get away, did you think of that? As long as you know the guys running it, and you have the cash, they'll send you through no questions asked."

"It's possible."

"He always was a lone bird. Remember, Adam, how he would take off for days at a time when he was supposed to be working with you?"

"Did you ever hear from him, after he disappeared?"

"Not a word."

"You didn't hear anything at all? I find that hard to believe, Walter, given all your connections."

"He didn't call, he didn't leave anything at any of the old drops, he didn't even send a postcard. First time I knew he'd been here was a couple of days ago, when Saul Stein sent a squad of officers around. Here, to my apartment, where my wife and children live," Lipscombe said with sudden anger, leaning forward in his chair, punctuating his words with sharp jabs of his cigar. "They tossed the place and then they arrested me. Saul Stein himself questioned me, and then they threw me in a cell and left me to sweat until my lawyer discovered where I was, filed a complaint, and sprang me. Technically, I'm out on bail, so I hope you appreciate the risk I took, harbouring a couple of fugitives from the law."

Walter Lipscombe could lie with the best of them, but Stone was pretty sure that he was telling the truth. "What kind of questions did Stein ask?"

"He showed me pictures of what was left of that woman. He told me I would go to the chair for accessory to murder if I didn't tell him how I'd helped Tom get away. I told him he was talking bullshit. He threatened to hand me over to the Company and said they'd take me to the Real, disappear me off the face of this Earth. Said there were plenty of old crimes outstanding that would put me in a special facility buried in some wild sheaf for the rest of my days." Lipscombe drew on his cigar and contemplated the smoke he exhaled. "I'm working a couple of favours right now. I intend to get the motherfucker replaced."

"The guy was doing his job, Walter. Don't take it personally."

"He sent his gorillas to my home," Lipscombe said. "They arrested me right in front of my wife and my children. You don't get any more personal than that. Mr. Saul Stein, he doesn't know it yet, but he's in a world of shit."

"How about our former associates? Do you still keep up with any of them? Do you think any of them could have been in contact with Tom?"

"The woman who acted as a cutout between you and me, Kay Francis? She killed herself a couple of years ago over a soldier boyfriend who died in some sandpit in Mexico. We got problems there with commie-sponsored nationalists. Johnny Claassen had two heart attacks, one straight after the other, and is semiretired, running a sports book down in Miami. Harry Hendricks, he's a general now, can you believe it? Four stars, very high up in the Pentagon. Even Saul Stein wouldn't think he had anything to do with this. Joe Mitchell, Tommy Kochiss, and Bobby Boyle work for me. If Tom had ever been in touch with them, I would know all about it."

"What about Freddy Layne?" Stone said, as casually as he knew how. "Is he still living here?"

Freddy Layne, one of the original cowboy angels, had worked undercover in the American Bund sheaf for three years, recruiting men and women to the cause, networking between dissident groups, setting up caches of weapons and munitions. He'd been captured at the beginning of the revolution and tortured at the FBI's maximum security facility at Buzzard's Point. Two weeks later, the First Armoured Brigade had gone over to the rebels, Washington, DC, had fallen, and Freddy and the rest of the prisoners had been freed. He'd never really recovered. After he'd been invalided out of the Company, Freddy had returned to the American Bund sheaf and married the woman he'd been using as part of his legend.

"There's another guy who doesn't stay in touch, even though he's living right here in New York City," Walter Lipscombe said thoughtfully. "When he first came back, I offered him a job, a good one. He said he wanted to put it all behind him, and I respected that. You think Freddy and Tom might have been getting together? You do, don't you?"

"What is Freddy doing these days?"

"He has a club on the West Side, a strip joint with upstairs rooms, if you know what I mean. Last I heard, he'd split up with his wife and he was drinking most of the profits. If you're going to pay him a visit, do me a favour, don't mention my name."

"You have my word. What about Eileen Barrie? She was a mathematician, and she worked at Livermore. Do you happen to know what was she working on?"

The files David Welch had given Stone had contained only scant details about the six murdered doppels.

Lipscombe smiled. "That's classified information, Adam. How would someone like me get access to information like that?"

"Amaze me."

"Well, I did hear a rumour she was the leader of one of the teams working on Ultimate Shield."

"I've been out of the loop, Walter. You'll have to enlighten me."

"It's the antiballistic missile project, a very big deal for us. The government has about two thousand physicists and mathematicians and engineers at Livermore, maybe another ten thousand in other places, not to mention the companies that are building the hardware—the radar systems and the missiles and the lasers."

"Jesus, Walter. Are you expecting to go to war against the Russians?"

"Things have gotten worse in the last couple of years. The commies, Russians and UCE both, think that we're a pushover because your President Carter wants to make peace with them at any price. He refused to give us aid for our nuclear programme, so we're doing it ourselves. We're in a race to build an effective antiballistic missile defence shield so we can make a first strike against the commies if we have to, and survive their retaliation. At least, that's what the government says. My take on it is, I have a hardened bunker forty feet under the basement of this building, I'll watch the fireworks from there."

Stone, remembering the McBride sheaf, said, "If you want my advice, you need to dig deeper."

# 3.

Freddy Layne's club was on Eleventh Avenue, two blocks north of a park that had once been the grounds of a palace owned by the Dear Leader's oldest son. After riding out of the basement of the Woolworth Building in the back of a laundry truck, Stone and Linda Waverly took an elaborately evasive route to reach it. Stone didn't entirely trust Walter Lipscombe and couldn't be sure that the elementary tradecraft of his goons had kept them from the gaze of the people watching the apartment. So he and Linda rode the A-line subway to the enormous and tremendously busy Romanesque amphitheatre that stood where Madison Square Gardens stood in the Real, took a turn around the block to make sure they weren't being followed, walked north down a deep canyon between monolithic government buildings to the soulless expanse of Times Square, caught the subway to West Ninety-Sixth Street, and rode a bus twenty blocks south.

When they strolled past Freddy's club, nine thirty in the morning, the place was closed. They took up a position in a diner on the corner of the block, a booth with a view of the street through a yellowing lace curtain and the dusty window. Stone drank thin, bitter coffee; Linda sipped a Coke, which surprised her by tasting of cinnamon.

"That's how they do it here," Stone said. He felt alert but slightly transparent, not quite properly aligned with the world. He'd had a restless night and had taken a couple of aspirin with his breakfast to deal with the residue of Lipscombe's hundred-year-old brandy.

"I thought that Coke was a constant, like gravity or Elvis," Linda said. She wore a dull green army uniform and had black hair now, a wig falling straight down her back.

"I guess fifty years of National Socialism can just about change anything."

Stone was wearing an army uniform too, with a colonel's braid on his sleeve. His hair had been given a severe crew cut by an eighty-year-old Italian barber Lipscombe had brought up to the apartment, and he squinted through eyeglasses with thick black rims as he leafed through a *New York Times* someone had left behind.

The lead story extolled the patriotism of a "hero volunteer" who'd been killed in a skirmish between American and Russian patrol boats in the

Bering Strait. There was extensive coverage of the rich and famous at charity balls, charity dinners, and charity auctions, and plenty of garish, full-colour ads for consumer goods, legal services, and various euphemisms for bodyguards and home security. Car ads emphasised armour ratings, bulletproof glass, lethal shock and gas spray antitheft devices. There were ads selling military-grade weaponry for use in "home defence," everything from shotguns that fired weighted bags to pop-up mines. There was a full-page ad for what looked like an electrified mantrap, boasting 30,000 volts for "sure-stop certainty" and "hi-power venting," presumably to remove the smoke and stink of charred meat.

Linda sipped her Coke. She watched the street. She said at last, "We can't sit here all day. Either we do this or we walk away."

Stone looked up from the newspaper. "I guess you've figured out that someone is watching Freddy's place."

She nodded, cool and businesslike. "The white panel truck parked opposite. Someone got in back just now, carrying two cups of coffee and a bag of doughnuts."

"They're confident sons of bitches, aren't they?"

"Are they locals or Company?"

"Whoever they are, they're sitting out there in plain sight to remind Freddy where his best interests lie."

"How are we going to get past them?"

"We'll wait a little while and see if an opportunity presents itself. If we miss our appointment with the gate this afternoon, Walter can arrange something else."

"Wouldn't it make things a lot easier if he arranged a meeting with Freddy Layne, too?"

Stone shook his head. "Walter agreed to arrange transport out of here because we were friends once upon a time, and because he owes me and he always honours his debts. But with men like him there's always a point where friendship stops and business begins."

Linda thought about that. She said, "Anna Lipscombe told me about this company her husband gave her as a wedding present. It seems that there are always food shortages here because so many people moved to the cities after the revolution, so anyone who volunteers to try their hand at farming gets a grant from the government. And there's also a big problem with homeless people. Mrs. Lipscombe's company, it recruits homeless people for the farm resettlement programme, it gets a cut of their grants, and it also rents them

170

twenty-acre parcels of what was once state-owned farmland. They have to buy their seed and their tools and fertiliser from company stores, and sell their crops to the company, too. Everything they do, the company makes a profit from it. I told Mrs. Lipscombe that it sounded like sharecropping by another name and asked her if she was worried about exploiting people. She said it gave them a chance to earn a living. She actually used the phrase 'by the sweat of their own brows.' And she told me that the rent on the farmland is subsidised by the government to ensure that landowners get a twenty percent return on their investment no matter how badly the tenants do, and that it doesn't matter how many of them fail at being farmers, because there's an endless supply of homeless people willing, as she put it, to try to turn their lives around. She didn't see that her company was exploiting people who'd fallen to the bottom, Mr. Stone. She really thought she was helping them."

"You can call me Adam, Linda. We're partners in crime and fugitives from justice, so we may as well be on first-name terms."

"Do you think things are better here, now that people like Walter Lipscombe are in charge? Do you think you helped make a difference?"

"Things aren't ideal, but they were a whole lot worse before the revolution. The country was run by a military dictatorship led by a man who had killed his own father to get to power. The first winter I was here, the harvest had failed across most of the wheat belt. The government cut the rations of workers in the cities, and they let tens of thousands of people starve to death in the countryside. Tens of thousands more, mostly political prisoners, died every year in the mines and prisons in Alaska. Whole families were shipped out and worked to death inside six months. And if the bosses needed to increase the productivity of their factories or mines or steel mills, they had the local cops arrest a bunch of people and put them to work."

Stone remembered streets empty of traffic except for the armoured limos of bosses and apparatus men, and the personnel carriers and light tanks of the FBI. He remembered long lines of scarecrow people waiting to receive a daily ration of two ounces of mystery meat and a loaf of black bread that had the texture of ground glass bound by wallpaper paste. The show trials on TV, mass hangings of traitors and saboteurs. The hopeless gazes of starving children begging on the streets while posters everywhere boasted of record harvests. The military parades in Times Square, phalanxes of soldiers saluting the Dear Leader and his trio of psychotic sons in their armoured-glass podium, missile carriers and tanks creeping between monumental buildings under a blizzard of ticker tape, accompanied by military bands and phalanxes of blonde, blue-eyed cheerleaders. He remembered the slave farms, and the vast death camp he and Tom Waverly had found in South Dakota: a discovery that had been instrumental in convincing President Davis, at the beginning of his first term, to approve LOOKING GLASS, the covert action that had led to the revolution.

Linda said, "And now people like Anna Lipscombe swan around charity balls in furs and diamonds bought with stolen art, writing cheques on money swindled from the aid programme."

"There are people like the Lipscombes in the Real, Linda. I think that this is one of the sheaves where we did some real good."

"We won the war, and we installed a kind of democracy. Good for us. Trouble is, we didn't follow through. We let this America be taken over by a kind of gangster capitalism that only benefits people on the make."

Stone smiled. "Is that what they teach you in the Company these days? I guess things have moved on a lot since I quit."

"And I guess you think I'm young and naive and idealistic."

"I think you want to make a difference, just like I did when I first joined the Company. And back then, we didn't know what we were getting into. We thought it would be easy to step into the middle of a mess of local politics and take over and make things right. We thought that war was the hard part of the job, not reconstruction and reconciliation. We did some good here, but in too many sheaves we made things worse. Young and naive and idealistic? That was us."

"Is that why you quit?"

"I thought I quit," Stone said. "But here I am again, back on the inside."

After a little while, a truck pulled up outside Freddy Layne's joint. A burly man came out and talked to the truck driver while a third man unloaded boxes of booze.

Stone said, "There's my way in."

Linda said, "How are we going to get past the detail watching the place?"

"We're not; I am. You're going to stay right here and watch my back, like we agreed," Stone said. Walter Lipscombe had given him Freddy Layne's private phone number. He wrote it on a strip torn from the newspaper, handed it to Linda. "If there's any sign of trouble, use the pay phone over there. And if it's serious trouble, something I can't get out of, you should take off, and don't look back. You could risk going back to Walter and asking him to help you, but I think you'd be better off returning to the Real. If you cooperate and tell Kohler everything you know, he'll probably go easy on you."

"It isn't as simple as that."

"If there's something you want to tell me, this is probably as good a time as any."

Linda shook her head. She had that stubborn look Stone was getting to know very well. "How are you going to get past the surveillance?"

Stone patted the braid on the sleeve of his tunic. "I'm going to make this uniform work for me."

*

In the hour that he and Linda had spent in the coffee shop, Stone had seen five military police patrols drive by. He didn't have to wait long, standing on the street corner, before he spotted one of their white Jeeps. He flagged it down, showed his fake ID, and pointed to the panel truck parked up the street and told the four MPs that he was pretty sure the people inside it were selling drugs to soldiers.

"Men walk right up to it, they rap on the back, the door opens, and some kind of transaction takes place. I think you boys should do something about it."

When the MPs began to whale on the side of the van with their yard-long billysticks, Stone strolled across the street and followed a man carrying a case of whiskey down a short corridor into a big room where gold-painted chairs and little tables crowded around the canvas-floored stage. It smelled of old cigarette smoke and stale booze. On one side, a bartender in a white shirt and black waistcoat was setting up behind the mahogany counter; on the other, the burly man who'd stepped outside to talk with the liquor truck crew sat in one of the plush booths along the rear wall, working through papers. He looked up when Stone walked over. He said that the place was closed right now but he'd see plenty of action if he came back after noon.

Stone let the man see his pistol and told him they were going to walk up to Freddy's apartment.

"You're making a mistake, Colonel," the man said as they went up a narrow flight of stairs behind a fire door. "We have serious protection."

"This is just a social visit," Stone said, taking off his thick-rimmed glasses and folding them into his breast pocket.

"If this is some kind of half-assed attempt at a shakedown, it's gonna be the last visit you ever make."

He was a big man but no fighter, carrying his weight on his heels rather than on the balls of his feet. When Stone cold-cocked him with the .45 at the top of the stairs, he fell straight down and groaned but didn't resist when Stone rifled his pockets. Stone found a keyring, unlocked the door to the apartment, dragged the semiconscious man inside, and bound his wrists with his belt and gagged him with his garish tie.

There was no one in the living room or the small modern kitchen, but when Stone stepped into the bedroom a woman sat up in the big round bed. He showed her the .45 and touched a finger to his lips; she shrugged, dead-eyed and unimpressed, not bothering to hide her spectacular white breasts. A little dog, some kind of poodle, jumped off the bed and ran up to him and began to yap.

"Better call off your dog before I shoot it," Stone said.

The woman shook black curls from her face. "It's Freddy's dog, mister, it don't answer to me."

"Where is Freddy?"

"In the bathroom," the woman said. "You going to shoot him?"

"I hope not." Stone caught the poodle by the scruff of its neck and tossed it to her. "Stay right there and keep hold of this."

The woman cradled the poodle to her breasts. "If you fire that big weapon of yours, I'm out of here like shit off a shovel."

The bathroom was almost as big as the bedroom, black marble and stainless steel, big mirrors, a corner tub big enough for two, someone moving in clouds of steam behind the frosted glass of the shower stall.

Stone turned on the bath's faucet, full blast; the man in the shower howled. "What the fuck are you playing at, Patti?"

"Come out just as you are, Freddy," Stone said.

Freddy Layne inched back the sliding door of the shower. He'd put on a lot of weight since Stone had last seen him. Long white hair hung in rat-tails around the scarred moon of his face. He smiled at Stone and said, "Adam, whatever brings you here? I heard you retired."

Stone locked Freddy's girlfriend in the bathroom. Freddy sat on the edge of the bed with a towel around his ample waist, calm as Buddha, cradling his poodle in his lap. He'd pulled his hair into a ponytail and fastened a black patch over the eye blinded when he'd been tortured at Buzzard's Point. Stone scraped clothes from a wicker chair and sat down, asked if the room was clean.

174

"I sweep it every day, so you don't have to worry about anyone listening in. I have a lunch appointment, Adam, so let's not waste time pretending this is a social visit, playing catch up, all that. Why don't you get straight to it?"

"Tom Waverly is dead."

"I know. And it's a damn shame."

Stone decided to try a tiny bluff. "Why I'm here, the locals told me that you saw Tom recently."

"He may have stopped by now and then."

"You knew he was listed as missing in action three years ago."

"Of course I knew. Tom thought it was a tremendous joke. There's no need to question me at gunpoint, by the way. I'm always happy to help out an old comrade, and if I may be frank, it's rather insulting."

Stone laid the .45 in his lap. "Why didn't you tell the Company that Tom was alive? Or at least let his daughter know."

"You always were a self-righteous little prick, Adam. No offence."

"None taken."

"Tom and me were buddies in the good old, bad old days. Comrades-in-arms. You really think I'd give up my buddy after he decided to go to ground? Shame on you. Besides, we were business partners."

"What kind of business?"

Freddy's smile creased the scar that ran down his left cheek from under the eyepatch.

"Perhaps you recall that after the revolution, after the state apparatus was dismantled, people were given ownership of their homes."

"Sure. Everything was made public property. People got to own their homes, workers their companies. I believe there were even shares in the armed forces."

The poodle wriggled in Freddy's grip and he chucked it under its jaw. "They were very idealistic here, after the revolution. The problem was, most people didn't understand concepts like property ownership, investment, or share dividends. What they *did* understand was the value of hard cash in their hands. Some of the so-called gangsters got rich by buying up shares at ten cents on the dollar."

"I heard about that."

"The people got cash on the nail for their shares; the businessmen got to control the companies. That's how your friend Walter Lipscombe made his fortune. That, and selling off the Metropolitan Museum of Art piece by piece."

"And you and Tom?"

"Tom came to me three years ago, right after his so-called disappearance, and said that he needed a frontman for a business venture, a little company that buys apartments and rents them right back to the people who sell them. It's a nice little arrangement. We get title to the apartments, and the people who sell them get to stay in their homes as long as they pay the rent, plus they get a nice wedge of cash. They can buy nice stuff to furnish their apartments, maybe put it into a business. . . . It frees up equity, helps keep the economy rolling along, and no one gets hurt."

"I guess no one gets hurt unless they can't keep up with the rent. I hear there are a lot of homeless people these days."

Freddy's shrug jiggled his considerable belly. "No one can legislate against human foolishness, Adam, nor should they try. If people want to behave like children and blow their money on luxury goods or drink or drugs, if they prefer instant gratification to planning for the future, they have no one to blame but themselves. It's a perfectly legal business, and we don't coerce anyone into selling to us. Frankly, we don't need to."

"No, all you have to do is wave a bunch of cash in front of people who've never had any, and let nature take its course. Was it your idea, or Tom's?"

"Tom needed money and found a way of making some. I was happy to help out."

"What did Tom need the money for?"

"I didn't ask. Old habits of self-preservation and all that. And as far as I was concerned, he was the ideal sleeping partner. He had the connections I needed, I did the work, and whenever he asked for cash, I gave it to him from the account I kept for him, no questions asked. If you want to know what Tom did with the money, though, you're asking the wrong person."

Stone found it hard to believe that Freddy hadn't made any attempt to find out about his sleeping partner's activities. He said, "You know he killed someone here, a few days ago."

"So I heard. Some scientist out at Livermore. I was as surprised as I bet she was, if she had time to be surprised before the bomb took off her head. Do you happen to know why he killed her?"

"Did Tom ever mention that he was involved in Operation GYPSY?"

Freddy's face gave nothing away. "As far as I know, he quit the Company right after SWIFT SWORD. Just like you did."

"If you know anything about GYPSY, if you know anything at all about what he's been doing for the past three years, I'd appreciate it if you told me."

"Or what, you'll shoot me?"

Freddy sat calmly in his towel, eyepatch and ponytail, tickling his poodle's ear.

"I won't shoot you," Stone said, and pulled out the gizmo he had taken from Carol Dvorak. He held it up and pressed the button that made sparks snap between its prongs. "But I will hurt your fucking dog."

"You leave Billy out of this."

Stone snapped off another spark. "Don't make me do this, Freddy. I like dogs as much as you."

The poodle yelped and wriggled when Freddy clutched it tight. "I already told you. Tom and I were in business together. If he had anything else going on, this GYPSY, anything, he didn't tell me about it."

"What about the woman he killed?"

"I didn't know anything about that, either, until the local COILE chief dragged me in."

"Saul Stein?"

"He held me incommunicado for twenty-four hours, the prick, wouldn't let me phone my lawyers or the people I pay to protect me. He wouldn't even let me find out how my little Billy-boy was doing," Freddy said, and blew into the dog's ear until it began to wriggle with delight.

"What did Stein want to know?"

"He was asking the same kind of questions as you. He said Tom had killed this woman, showed me crime scene photos. He said he knew I'd helped Tom. Said he'd give me a good deal if I gave Tom up."

"And you told him what?"

"I told him zip. He threatened to put me to hot questioning; I said I'd already been tortured by the best and never said a word, but he was welcome to give it a try. He held me for twenty-four hours, my lawyer got me out, and as far as I was concerned that was that. And then a couple of Stein's people rousted me late last night, walked right into this place without so much as a please or thank-you, and told me Tom was dead. Watched me to see if I'd blink. Told me they were making connections, told me that they'd be back. I wished them the best of luck. Poor Tom. How did he die? Stein's people didn't have the good manners to tell me."

"He got into a situation and he shot himself," Stone said, and sketched out the details.

"Poor crazy Tom."

"Crazy," Stone said. "Is that how he seemed to you, the last time you saw him?"

"No more than usual." Freddy stroked his poodle and said, "Poor Tom. He always was a wild one. Wasn't he, Billy-boy?"

"When did you last see him, Freddy? Don't tell me what you told Stein. Tell me the truth. It can't hurt you, and it definitely can't hurt Tom."

"It was before the hit. He told me he needed to fly out to the West Coast and back incognito, asked me to get him army ID and travel orders so he could hitch a ride on a military flight. I have a tame colonel who got too rough with one of my girls—he strangled her to death, if you want to know the plain truth—and had him help out."

"Did Tom tell you why he wanted to travel incognito?"

"He said that he had some delicate business out there, and didn't need the hassle of airport security. I didn't ask what kind of business it was, and that was the last time I saw him."

"What about his health?"

"You said you were there, at the end. What do you think?"

"He told me he was dying. He looked like he was, too."

"Did he tell you what he was dying from?"

"I heard it was cancer. Was it?"

Freddy shrugged. "I'm going to miss the son of a bitch. About the last thing he said to me was that he was going to change history."

"We've all changed history, Freddy. It's what we did."

"We did it here, all right." Freddy paused, then said, "He was the best of us, Adam."

"I know."

There was a moment of silence.

Freddy said, "Who are you working for, Adam? Really."

"I'm retired, Freddy, just like you. I was brought back to help find Tom. And that's what I did, but he killed himself, right in front of me. I want to know why. So does his daughter."

"Linda's in on this?"

"If you help me, Freddy, you'll be helping her too. She wants to clear her father's name."

Freddy smiled a little. "She's what? Nineteen, now? Twenty?"

"A little older."

"And you and her, you're . . . ?" Freddy wiggled a hand and winked his one good eye.

"Don't judge everyone by your standards, Freddy."

"Is she here?"

"She's watching the front door for me."

"So are a bunch of Company guys."

"Linda's watching them, too. I don't have much time, Freddy. Why don't you quit pussyfooting around? Tell me everything that happened the last time you saw Tom."

"He was in a bad way when he turned up. He looked like he was about to fall down flat on his face. When he took a drink with me, he puked it right back up. And he was self-medicating, taking Dramamine tablets, proprietary antibiotics, painkillers. . . . I persuaded him to get checked out by this doctor I know, a good man who takes care of my girls."

"And what did your doctor find?"

"He said that Tom was suffering from sores and haematomas caused by capillary bleeding over just about every part of his body, including his eyes and mouth. He had some skin darkening, too, and his blood was in bad shape. The doctor couldn't be certain, but he thought Tom was suffering from radiation sickness."

"What kind of radiation sickness?"

"The lethal kind. The doctor told Tom he should be hospitalised, and Tom said, 'Keep me going.' The doctor gave him some injectable steroids, but he told me afterward it wouldn't do much good—Tom only had a few days left."

"Did your doctor have any idea about when Tom might have been exposed to radiation?"

"He thought pretty recently. He said that most people either die of radiation sickness within two or three weeks, or they get better. Tom drew the short straw."

"Did you talk with Tom about this? Did he tell you how he'd been exposed to a lethal dose of radiation?"

Freddy shook his head. "I tried to talk to him, but you know Tom."

"Where did Tom stay when he passed through this sheaf?"

"I don't know. Different hotels."

Freddy said it a little too quickly.

"He was your business partner, but you didn't have a contact address for him? Not even a phone number?"

"Hey, be nice. I just told you all I know. What else do you want?"

The telephone on the bedside table rang.

Stone got a chill of premonition, thinking Carol Dvorak, thinking Saul Stein. He told Freddy Layne to answer it, but warned him that he should watch what he said.

"I'm not going to rat you out," Freddy said. He shifted his grip on his dog, plucked the receiver from its cradle, listened for a moment, then said, "Don't you worry about a thing, Linda. I'm an old friend of your father's—"

Stone snatched the receiver from Freddy and said, "What's the problem?"

"Carol Dvorak is here."

"Where are you?"

"In the phone booth in the diner."

"Can you see her? What's she doing now?"

"The phone's in back; I can't see the street." Linda's voice was pitched a little high but otherwise she sounded calm. "Last time I looked, she was talking with those men in the van. She's had her hair cut and she's wearing these big sunglasses, but it's her."

"Are the MPs still there?"

"They left a few minutes ago. Then a big black car drew up and she stepped out."

"Anyone else?"

"Not yet."

"Take off," Stone said. "Get to Grand Central Station and have our friend's people send you through the mirror."

"I'll see you," Linda Waverly said, and cut the connection.

"Trouble?" Freddy said solicitously.

"Can Company officers bust in here without a warrant?"

"Back in the old days, maybe, but not now. Not unless they want to risk causing a diplomatic incident. Frankly, I'm surprised they're allowed to sit out there on the street."

"How about the COILE?"

"Those two officers who talked to me yesterday walked into the club around midnight, but they weren't trying to arrest me. Before that, Stein's people picked me up on the street. If the COILE want to turn this place over, they'll need probable cause, they'll need a warrant, and they'll need to show the warrant to the people who run this block and look after my interests. You're lucky no one saw you come in, Adam, or you'd be in real trouble around about now."

"One of your guys saw me. I left him tied up in your hallway."

Freddy pursed his lips and made a kissing sound. The little dog in his lap cocked its head and looked up at him. "You just can't get good help these days. If Stein has a warrant on file—and I wouldn't put it past him—his officers could be here any moment. If you're going to ask me about a way out of

180

here that no one but me knows about, there isn't one. And there's an unmarked car parked in the alley out back with two men inside, so I advise you not to try that route."

"I'll walk out the front door after you answer a couple more questions, Freddy. We were talking about where Tom Waverly stayed when he visited this sheaf. Which of your repossessed apartments was it?"

"You have a wild look about you, Adam."

"Don't try to palm me off with some hotel, Freddy. And don't make me hurt the dog; I'd hate myself afterward."

Freddy gave an address, and the name that Tom Waverly had used while living there, adding, "I was going to tell you anyway."

"I know you were. You were also going to tell me how he escaped after he killed that woman."

Freddy looked at him.

"Those people who look after you, I bet they have an interest in the old gate under Grand Central Station. I'm sure you remember it, Freddy. It was the way we got people in and out of the sheaf during Operation LOOKING GLASS. I think that's how Tom got out of this sheaf with a little help from your gangster friends."

Freddy shrugged. "You'll have to ask them."

"I think I will."

"Keep me out of it if you do. And Adam? I hope this puts me on the right side."

"I don't know how many sides there are yet, let alone which are right and which are wrong." Stone said, and pulled a leather belt from the muddle of clothes on the floor. "I'm going to have to strap you to your bed, Freddy. Try not to take it personally."

# 4.

The man Stone had knocked out and tied up was starting to come around, jerking on the white carpet of the hallway, making a muffled growl into his gag, and giving Stone a cockeyed glare as he stepped past. Stone locked the door of the apartment behind him and at the bottom of the stairs, eased back the fire exit door, and checked out the club, relieved to see that the bartender had the place to himself. The man challenged Stone as he walked out across the dim room, but raised his hands when Stone showed him the Colt .45.

"I bet you keep a peacemaker under there," Stone said. "How about taking it out and laying it on the counter?"

The bartender produced an aluminium baseball bat and a snub-nosed .38 revolver with duct tape wrapped around its grip. Stone tossed the bat across the room, pocketed the revolver, and told the bartender to come around the counter and sit on the floor with his hands on his head.

"Whatever problem you have with Mr. Layne, it's nothing to do with me," the man said.

Stone dropped the keys in his lap. "Close your eyes and count to a hundred. When you're done, go upstairs and check on your boss and his friends."

He took a quick peek through the bull's-eye port in the front door and saw Carol Dvorak standing at the rear of the van parked across the street, talking to a tall young man wearing a shoulder holster over his short-sleeved shirt. She was dressed in a black jacket and a thigh-skimming skirt, and a big purse was slung over her shoulder. Her eyes were masked by sunglasses, and her hair had been dyed blonde and cropped close. It wasn't a bad disguise, but even without Linda's description he would have recognised the woman anywhere. He thought for a moment, then put on his thick-rimmed glasses, stuck the Colt in the waistband of his khaki pants, its grip snug against the small of his back, and took a breath and walked out into the hot sunlight.

Carol Dvorak glanced at him and looked away, and for a moment he thought he'd be able to walk away free and clear. But then she looked at him again, and reached into her purse and pulled out a pistol. He smiled at her as she trotted across the street toward him, followed by the young officer. His hands raised to shoulder height, the .38 revolver dangling by its trigger guard from the forefinger of his left hand, he said, "How are you, Officer Dvorak?"

"Stay right where you are," she said, watching him over the sight of her pistol as the young officer approached warily.

Stone said, "Is this guy with GYPSY, Officer Dvorak, or is he unwitting?"

"Lose the gun, Mr. Stone," the young officer said. He was trying to sound calm and reasonable, but there was a slight quaver in his voice and an unsteadiness in his gaze.

"Do it," Dvorak said. Her jaw was puffy and her voice congested.

Stone swung the revolver to and fro, getting the young officer's attention, then flung it in a long arc across the street. The man's gaze twitched, following the revolver, and Stone stepped in and grabbed the man's wrist, thumb pressing into the nerve cluster there, shutting it down. The man dropped his pistol and Stone pivoted on the ball of his right foot as if he and the man were partners in a dance, his left forearm in a choke hold across the man's throat as he pulled the Colt .45 from his waistband.

Dvorak stepped back, her pistol jerking in tight little arcs as she sought to aim it at Stone's face, and Stone shoved the young officer toward her as she fired, two shots that struck the man in the chest. He grunted and collapsed face down on the sidewalk, and Stone shot Dvorak in her right shoulder. Exactly where he'd shot Tom Waverly when SWIFT SWORD had gone bad. The impact spun her around and she dropped her pistol. Stone kicked it into the gutter, seeing in his peripheral vision pedestrians scattering and the back door of the white van across the street swinging open. He put two shots in the door and a man fell down behind it, and he shot out the van's nearside tires. Dvorak sat on the sidewalk, clutching her shoulder. She'd lost her sunglasses and was giving Stone a death-ray stare.

The temptation to shoot her was there and gone. No. He needed to talk to her.

"Are you going to walk," he said, "or am I going to have to knock you stupid and carry you?"

"I'm not going anywhere with you," Dvorak said, and there was a squeal of tires and a blare of horns down the block as a battered black car sped through the intersection, swerving wide to overtake a slow-moving army truck, screeching to a halt beside Stone and Dvorak. Its door flew open. Linda Waverly was behind the wheel. She'd lost her wig and her red hair was loose about her face as she leaned across the passenger seat and shouted at Stone, telling him to get his ass inside.

Stone yanked open the back door of the car, hauled Dvorak to her feet and shoved her inside, picked up her purse and swung in beside her, and slammed the door as Linda took off in a squeal of tires. She made a handbrake turn at the next intersection and accelerated down a one-way street the wrong way, working the stick shift with one hand and the steering wheel with the other as oncoming traffic swerved and flashed headlights and blew horns. She went up on the sidewalk to get around a bus, turned left against a red light, and settled into a steady stream of traffic heading uptown, finally sparing a second to glance back at Stone. Her face was flushed with excitement.

"I told you to get out of there," Stone said.

"I wasn't about to leave you behind," Linda said.

Dvorak had pushed herself into a corner of the back seat, her skirt bunched on her thighs, her face grey with shock. The right side of her jacket was wet with blood and her hand was underneath it, clutching her wounded shoulder.

"Nice disguise," Stone told her. "After our little disagreement back on the train I guess you must be travelling under an alias. Who sent you after me?"

Dvorak shook her head, then gasped when Stone punched her in the shoulder as hard as he could. "I know you're with GYPSY," he said. "I bet those guys in the van watching Freddy's place are with GYPSY too. I want to know who sent you here."

"I'm a loyal American."

Her gaze was hard and bright and full of hate.

"Who told you to kidnap me and Ms. Waverly?"

"I picked up the order at a drop."

From the front seat Linda said, "Where do you want me to go?"

"Just keep driving," Stone said, and put his pistol in Dvorak's face. "Where were you going to take us?"

"Fuck you."

"They'll have made the car," Linda said.

"We'll see about that. One last chance, Ms. Dvorak. Who sent you?"

"You won't find it so easy to get away from us this time," Dvorak said. "And if you do, we'll go after that woman's kid. Petey. We'll take the little fucker—"

She screamed when Stone punched her in the shoulder again. Linda lost control of the car for a moment, braking hard just before it slammed into a taxi. Horns blared, Stone grabbed the back of the seat to steady himself, and Dvorak pulled her hand from under her jacket, holding a little two-shot .22. Stone shot her twice in the heart, the noise tremendous inside the car, blood spray across the door, across the rear window, hot blood spattering his face and the glasses he was still wearing and the front of his tunic.

Linda got the car going again, saying "Shit, shit, shit" as she drove. Stone took off his glasses and wiped blood from his face with his sleeve, then dropped the empty clip from his Colt and shoved in the spare. He searched Dvorak's purse and found ID and travel orders identifying her as a captain in army intelligence, a cell phone with no numbers in its memory or redial, a wallet stuffed with local bills. Linda was watching him in the rearview mirror. He said, "Pull over."

"Thank you would be nice."

"For giving her a chance to draw on me?"

"For saving your neck."

"You should have cut and run, like I told you to. If this woman had more backup, we'd both be bleeding out on the sidewalk." Stone spotted a subway entrance, pointed to it, and said again, "Pull over. We need to lose this car right away."

He got out of the car and headed straight for the subway, stripping off his blood-spattered tunic and dumping it in a trash basket. He was pumped up and furious. He knew he should have checked the woman for a backup piece.

Linda caught up with him, half jogging, half walking to match his long strides, saying breathlessly, "We left a body back there."

"I left two more on the sidewalk outside Freddy's place. Want to go back and clear them up too?"

"This is how it works in the field? You shoot someone and walk away?"

"If you have to."

"My father told me I would need your help," Linda said as she followed Stone down the steps to the subway. "But that wasn't why I came back."

"You took a big risk," Stone said, and realised that he was taking his anger out on her. "You took a risk, but you did the right thing. It wasn't you that screwed up back there. It was me."

"We got away, so we did something right," Linda said, and asked if they were going back to Walter Lipscombe's place, or to the gate under Grand Central Station.

"Freddy gave me the address of your father's apartment," Stone said.

After a moment, Linda said, "Do you think they know about it? Carol Dvorak's friends from GYPSY, I mean."

"If they do, they'll be waiting for us there. Want to let it go, head for the gate instead?"

"After we've come this far? Of course not."

# 5.

The New York subway system was one of the few unalloyed triumphs of the American Bund. The stations were clean, spacious, and air-conditioned, with polished marble floors and pink granite walls decorated with enormous murals. Those featuring the Dear Leader had been smashed or disfigured, but most of the others were still intact, blazoned with brutalist propaganda: hero workers marching arm in arm with proud soldiers; atomic power stations; fleets of combine harvesters sweeping across wide wheat fields; a parade of tanks and missile carriers stretching to an apocalyptic horizon; a bevy of athletic girls in skimpy shorts and T-shirts pounding over a mountain ridge. Trains arrived every two minutes, clean futuristic designs with bullet noses and unnecessary streamlining.

As they rode uptown, Stone gave Linda a précis of his conversation with Freddy Layne. She listened with her full attention, sitting with her shoulders hunched and her hands clamped between her knees. Every now and then a shiver passed through her entire body, but she was in control, grimly determined to see this through. Doing pretty good, Stone thought, for a back-office number cruncher.

When he had finished telling her about Freddy, she said, "He didn't know how my father had been exposed to radiation?"

"I don't suppose Tom told Freddy any more than he told me," Stone said.

"It must have had something to do with GYPSY."

"I think so."

"My father said something about an atomic bomb."

"My first thought, too."

"Maybe he stole a bomb, a suitcase nuke. Maybe it wasn't properly shielded."

"Or maybe he was downwind of a bomb when it went off."

"The Company would know if a bomb had gone off."

"Maybe not. Not if it was in a wild sheaf, a long way from any civilisation."

Linda thought about that. "This is something really big, isn't it?"

"Your father claimed to have stolen something that could change history. It could be a suitcase nuke, it could be documentation about GYPSY's plans, it could be anything."

"He didn't tell me what it was, Mr. Stone." Linda brushed her hair back from her pale face and held it in a fist by the side of her neck. They were sitting side by side on orange plastic seats at one end of the passenger car, no one near them, the train rocking smoothly as it sped through the dark. "That woman mentioned a boy and said her friends would go after him," she said. "Is it your son?"

"The son of an old friend of mine, Jake Nichols. Jake died in an accident last winter."

"Oh. I'm sorry."

"Jake's wife, Susan . . . Two of Carol Dvorak's friends tried to kidnap her a couple of days ago. They planned to exchange her for me. Susan shot and killed one of them, wounded the other. And then the one she'd wounded shot and killed her."

After a moment, Linda said, "This is why you wanted to come with me."

Stone nodded. After everything that had just happened, she deserved to know the truth. "I don't owe the Company anything, Linda. Not after I found your father. Not after what happened to Susan. I came with you because I wanted to put an end to this. And Kohler let me do it because he thinks your father lied about stealing something from GYPSY and doesn't want to waste manpower on some kind of diversion or distraction."

"He didn't lie."

"I'm pretty sure he didn't. Linda, listen to me. There will be more people like Dvorak coming after us. And I can't guarantee that we'll be lucky the next time."

Linda's expression was as serious as a heart attack. "You have a good reason to go after this. So do I. We'll do it together, just like my father wanted."

They got off the subway at Amsterdam Avenue and walked three blocks north, past a bookshop with stacks of sun-bleached paperbacks crowding its dusty window, past a butcher's shop where a stout housewife in a shawl and threadbare floral dress watched a man chop a chicken carcass into four pieces on a wooden block, past shacks built from scrap wood and cardboard boxes among fire-blackened ruins. A woman soaped a toddler who stood naked and shivering in a red plastic bowl. Battered taxis and pickup trucks swerved past horse-drawn wagons. An armoured personnel carrier was parked at the corner of one block, its engine idling, its snorkel exhaust emitting puffs of black smoke.

"We were right around here just a couple of days ago," Linda said.

"That was that," Stone said. "This is this."

He was walking quickly and couldn't shake the feeling that at any moment a convoy of police cars and black limos would roar up Amsterdam Avenue in hot pursuit or a helicopter would descend from the sky, loudhailer yammering, ordering him to surrender.

The address Freddy Layne had given him was an apartment building on a quiet cross street, one of a dozen square, four-storey blocks built of yellow brick. Stone and Linda showed their fake army IDs to the fat, sour-faced old woman who sat behind a card table just inside the front door, and Stone asked her when she had last seen Mr. Anderson, if he ever had any visitors, and how long he'd been living here. She gave monosyllabic answers that more or less confirmed Freddy Layne's story, adding that two men had come to see him yesterday.

Stone touched his left eye. "Was one of them wearing an eyepatch?"

The woman nodded. "I told them Mr. Anderson has gone away, but they insisted on seeing for themselves."

"The local law is leaning on Freddy. He came looking for something he could use to make a deal," Stone said to Linda, and asked the woman how much she had been paid to let the men into Mr. Anderson's apartment.

"I don't get what you mean, mister."

Stone took out Dvorak's wallet, counted off five ten-dollar bills, and spread them on the card table. "Either you can take this and loan me your pass key, or I'll kick in the door. Do you get that?"

"Mr. Anderson's" apartment was at the far end of a gallery walkway, over-looking a courtyard where a handful of small kids were chasing each other around mounds of garbage. A sweet rotten reek packed the humid air. A fat brown rat burrowed into a burst trash bag. The wired-glass window beside the apartment's plywood door was cracked top to bottom and lined by aluminum foil. Linda used the pass key and Stone hustled in, leading with his pistol, aiming at different corners of the stale, dim room.

Freddy Layne had done a good job of tossing the place. A pull-out couch lay on its back, its brown vinyl gashed in a dozen places. Its cushions had been slashed and chunks of foam-rubber stuffing were scattered across the greasy carpet. A sleeping bag ripped from top to bottom curled in a froth of feathers. A coffee table was split in two. Science fiction paperbacks lay everywhere like dead birds. The door of the closet hung by a single bent hinge. Holes had been punched in the dividing wall of the little kitchenette in the corner. The grille of the heating register over the bathroom door had been levered away and the plasterwork around it kicked out. The toilet in the tiny bathroom was cracked and the ceramic lid of the tank lay in two pieces on the flooded tiled floor.

Linda was searching through the cupboards in the kitchenette. She told Stone that all she'd found were a couple of cans of soup and the biggest roach she'd ever seen.

"Probably a survivor from the good old days," Stone said. "They had the biggest and best of everything before the revolution."

He was standing in the middle of the little room, trying to imagine Tom Waverly camped out there, cleaning his gun, meticulously plotting his hit. He could hear the mutter of a TV through the wall, the shrieks of the children playing outside in the garbage.

"It smells of him," Linda said.

She had an odd expression on her face. Stone realised that she was trying not to cry, and got busy checking out the rest of the apartment.

He shook out the paperbacks, ripped flapping sheets of vinyl from the frame of the couch, looked in the kitchen cupboards that Linda had already searched, and found nothing but the roach flattened in one corner of a cupboard, its antennae twitching as it tested the air. It was a monster, all right. A hero roach. There ought to be a mural dedicated to it in one of the subway stations. He found a can opener and opened the soup cans. He tipped chicken soup and vegetable soup into the sink. One coffee mug, one plate, one dish, a cheap aluminium saucepan, and a spoon and a knife, all neatly rinsed, sat in the plate rack.

Linda was standing on a kitchen chair and peering inside the broken heating register. "Someone swept this clean," she said.

"If anything was hidden in there, Freddy's men would have found it."

Linda pressed sideways against the wall as she reached as far as she could into the duct behind the register. "When I was a little kid, I used to hide treasure around the house. And Dad used to hide treasure for me to find, too."

"I remember. That's how I found the message he left for me."

"We got pretty good at hiding things," Linda said. "I learned all kinds of tricks."

She jumped down and took a wire hanger from the closet and straightened it out, then climbed onto the chair again and used the length of wire to fish inside the duct. Stone perched on the edge of the upturned couch while she worked. Her face pressed against broken plaster, her arm buried up to the shoulder, the only sound in the room the murmur of the neighbour's TV and the tap and scrape of the wire. At last she tensed, then gently pulled something out and showed it to Stone: a plastic bag, wrapped tight with grey duct tape that made a loop at one end.

"He pushed it around the corner and cleaned out the dust to get rid of the track it left," Linda said. "He did something like this one time in one of our treasure hunts."

They emptied the bag onto the kitchenette counter. High denomination bills from the Real and the Nixon sheaf were mixed up with the big, colourful bills of the American Bund. There was a laminated army ID card with a grainy black-and-white photograph of Tom Waverly, giving his name as Philip Kindred, his rank as captain, 10th Airborne. There were two New York State driver's licences, both with the same colour photograph of Tom Waverly, both with fake names. Laumer. Leinster. The second name chimed in Stone's memory. There was a folding knife with a six-inch blade. There was a set of house keys on a metal ring. There was a small key wrapped in a scrap of paper, its grooves fresh-cut, its round tag embossed with a number: 48.

Stone got chills and picked up the key. "A long time ago, when your father and I were working in the Nixon sheaf, we used a proprietary company called Leinster Imports, an off-the-shelf deal set up in Delaware, to rent boxes in different cities. We used the boxes as dead drops."

Linda had a strange look on her face, as if she had just seen a ghost. "He said that it would take both of us to find what he'd hidden."

Stone smiled. "He was right."

# 6.

They threw the house keys into the garbage pile outside the apartment and tore up the fake IDs and posted the pieces down two separate sewer gratings. They kept the cash, and Linda kept the folding knife, too, as a memento. She believed that everything was falling into place, that they were just a step away from her father's vindication.

Stone used a pay phone to call the cutout number Walter Lipscombe had given him, got an answer machine and gave it the pay phone's number, and hung up. Someone rang back less than a minute later, told them to stay where they were, a car would pick them up, and hung up before Stone could reply.

A little less than ten minutes later, a low-slung black sedan pulled up beside the pay phone. Stone suspected that it was the visible tip of a vast surveillance network that had been keeping tabs on him and Linda ever since they had left Lipscombe's apartment. With a red light flashing in the nearside corner of its dash, it sped along the express lanes reserved for the vehicles of the police, army brass, politicians, and citizens rich enough to be able to afford permits for themselves and their employees.

"Isn't this a little conspicuous?" Stone said.

"Maybe you don't know it," the goon sitting next to the driver said, "but you did yourself a big favour when you went toe-to-toe with those people. It seems they neglected to tell anyone that they were staking out the premises of an honest citizen, and the little gun battle that left two of them dead and one seriously wounded caused quite a stink. The upshot is, the COILE wants you out of town as quickly as possible. Its boss, Mr. Saul Stein, has let it be known that if you happen to be given some help in that department, he will look the other way."

"I hope this hasn't caused Mr. Lipscombe any trouble."

The goon's grin showed several gold teeth. "Far from it. First, there is no evidence that he gave you shelter, so that is not a problem. Second, he is doing Mr. Stein a big favour by showing you the door, and you can bet that one day he will call that favour in. He asked me to tell you, by the way, that he had been hoping to see you off, but he has been unavoidably detained."

"Nothing serious, I hope," Stone said.

"According to Mr. Lipscombe, it's nothing his lawyers can't take care of. He also asked me to pass on his best wishes."

"Tell him from me that I hope he has all the luck he deserves."

By now the sedan was speeding down the middle of Park Avenue toward Grand Central Station. Although Turing gates had been developed in Brookhaven, the Company had decided to site its first clandestine interchange in New York City because it was the financial and cultural centre of most versions of America, and the Company's field officers could move unremarked through its teeming, multicultural population, and the Company's field officers could move unremarked through its teeming, multicultural population, and do research in its libraries and universities. But finding a site where a gate could be opened in several different versions of the city hadn't been easy; an unused basement in a building in one sheaf might be a busy office in another, or there might be a completely different building in that location, or no building at all.

A proposed open-air facility in Central Park had been written off because of the security risk; so had a plan to drop field officers in wet suits through a gate on a raft on the East River. Finally, the Company's planners had settled on Grand Central Station. The terminus had been built before the Real's history had diverged from that of all other known, inhabited sheaves, and in almost every sheaf, as in the Real, the station's powerhouse at Forty-Ninth Street had been demolished when the railroad switched its supply of steam and electrical power to Con Edison in the late 1920s, leading to the disuse of a loading platform and ancillary spaces in the two levels beneath it.

That was where a clandestine interchange with gates to five different sheafs had been built in the Real. In the American Bund sheaf, the gate was accessed by a freight elevator in the Forty-Ninth Street side of the Waldorf-Astoria Hotel, which before the revolution had housed the New York offices of the FBI. The sedan drove straight into the elevator, which clankingly descended to a loading platform one level underground where a posse of men in colourful suits was waiting.

After checking their IDs, two of the men led Stone and Linda down a spiral staircase that descended to a trucking subway that had once run between the loading platform of a freight company to the express platform of the lower level of the terminal. A steel-clad door near the end of the subway led into a low-ceilinged concrete bunker that had been much extended since Stone had first used it. Wooden packing cases of various sizes were stacked at either end; in the middle, where there had once been a wall and a cupboard full of disused electrical switching gear, was a perfect silver mirror two yards across, framed by a steel collar and reflecting a neat little electric forklift and a man in a canary-yellow suit and red shirt, who told Stone and Linda to go straight through.

"We sent Mr. Lipscombe's shipment through ten minutes ago, and our friends on the other side of the mirror do not like to keep it open long," he said. "I would suppose they dislike clocking up a fortune in power bills."

Stone stepped through first. Reflex clamped his eyes shut when he met his own reflection in the Turing gate's mirror; then black light exploded in his head and he opened his eyes and saw that he was standing on a metal platform raised in the middle of the big, brightly lit vault of the interchange in the Real.

It resembled a thirty-year-old mock-up of how the control room of a fusion power station or a space station might look in 2001. Racks of fluorescent tubes bounced harsh light off white-tiled walls two storeys high. Steel-mesh walkways and platforms were hung at different heights where technicians were tending control panels that sported acorn-sized red and yellow and green lights, dials, chunky throw switches, and cathode ray monitors filled with lines of chunky orange script. There were metal desks and black Bakelite telephones with rotary dials. There was a row of teletype printers hooded with plastic covers turned yellow and brittle.

All of this was dominated by the hulking machines that generated the Turing gates. Only a couple of steps up from the famous prototype that, in a laboratory shed in Brookhaven on January 5, 1963, had opened the first, microscopic portal to another history in another universe, the gates were massive steel-framed rectangles packed with racks of primitive electronics and skull-sized condensers, looms of wiring, and piping swaddled in silvery insulation, and were pierced by circular apertures six feet across. They stood in a miniature switching yard of narrow-gauge track in a pit that took up half the vault, two standing one behind the other to the left, two to the right, the gate from which Stone had just emerged locked down in the centre. Now Linda stepped through its silvery mirror, blinking in the bright light, grinning at Stone.

They were back in the Real. The Nixon sheaf was just a step away.

The bone-deep hum of the active gate cut off. The mirror blinked out, its aperture shrunken to a single Planck length, and held open by a trickle charge equivalent to the output of a couple of automobile batteries. Stone looked around and said, "Who's in charge here? We need to buy another ride."

*

Stone and Linda paid for their transit to the Nixon sheaf with the cash Tom Waverly had left behind: fifty thousand dollars. While technicians moved the gate through which he and Linda had just stepped, and lined up the gate to the Nixon sheaf on the identical universal coordinates, Stone asked the gate chief who he was working for now.

"The interchange was sold off to a cartel after the trouble with the Church Committee. We work for the cartel."

"Who owns the cartel?"

Stone was wondering what conspiracies and bribes were involved to keep this antique facility running and how the massive power requirements of active gates were finessed.

"Best not to ask," the gate chief said.

Linda described her father and asked if he'd recently come through. The gate chief shrugged and said that all kinds of people came through, all the time.

"Anyone who can afford to pay the fee. Businesspeople, journalists, university professors, celebrities. . . . And Company people, of course, such as yourselves."

"Who said we were with the Company?" Stone said.

"It would be pretty obvious, even if I didn't remember sending you through the mirror a couple of dozen times." The gate chief was tall and cadaverous, with thick black hair brushed back in a wave from his pock-marked face, tinted glasses, and the sour, fatalistic air of someone who has learnt from bitter experience to always expect lemons rather than lemonade. "One thing I discovered during my long, illustrious career is that when you know where all the bodies are buried, you really don't want to remember anything," he said. "Another is that you glamorous field-operative types never take any notice of the people who really run the show. That's how we get by. We're invisible, and we have the memories of goldfish."

"Maybe our friend here owns this place," Stone said to Linda. "That's why he's being so secretive."

"If I owned this place," the gate chief said, "do you really think I'd be down here getting my genes fried by virtual photons while I fielded your dumb questions? If I was the owner, I'd be living it up in a castle in some wild sheaf. Me, and thirty of California's most nubile cheerleaders."

Linda, watching the technicians who were making the final, finicky alignment of the gate, wondered why it was taking so long.

"It's taking so long because we take pride in our work," the gate chief said. "People today take Turing gates for granted, but old-school guys like your partner know they're tremendously dangerous. Right now, my people are making sure that the gate will be centred on a certain doorway on the other side of the mirror, so that the edges of its aperture will be contained within the frame of that doorway. Know why that is, young lady? Because of quantum shear. The aperture of a gate may be vanishingly thin, thinner than a hydrogen atom, but the quantum shear at its circumference is enormously powerful. Strong enough to cut diamond; easily strong enough to slice and dice you if you hit it at the wrong angle. The very first gates, we simply let the apertures hang in the air on the other side of the mirror and sent through people like your partner strapped to stretchers that ran on tracks, to make sure they didn't touch anyplace near the edge. But these days we make sure that every gate exits through a pipe or a door, a hole in a wall, anything with a frame that's smaller than the diameter of the gate's aperture."

"Listen to the man," Stone told Linda. "He's one of the original wizards."

"You know, I really resent that term," the gate chief said. "It's derogatory. It implies that what we do here is magic, that we don't really understand it. Although, of course, only three people in the world ever really understood the quantum theory, and two of them are crazy and one is dead. Have you been in the Nixon sheaf before?"

"Once or twice," Stone said.

"Then you'll know to leave through the electrical service shaft that connects the old trucking subway with the platform of the Fifty-First Street subway station." The gate chief dug in his pocket and handed Stone four keys strung on a steel ring. "These open the doors along the route. Don't use the Waldorf-Astoria exit. That platform is occasionally used by VIPs, so the local Secret Service checks it out at unpredictable intervals, and the elevator is run at least once a day. But if you go through the subway station, you shouldn't have any trouble. You have any kind of flashlight? Here, take this. We'll reopen the gate at noon tomorrow. Make sure you're there, or you'll have a long trip to White Sands, which is where the only other gate is located."

The deep hum started up again and a circle of silver light suddenly blanked the maw of the gate that had been painstakingly cranked into alignment. Stone and Linda climbed back onto the platform. After a technician used a fibre-optic probe to check out the scene on the other side of the mirror, Stone stepped through.

He emerged from the frame of a large cupboard into a small, sooty room lit only by the glow of the gate's silvery circle, this feeble light dimming as Linda emerged from it. Stone switched on the penlight that the gate chief had given him. A few moments later, the gate's mirror popped like a two-dimensional bubble, revealing thick cables and meter boxes bolted to concrete at the back of the cupboard.

It would open again at noon tomorrow. They had less than twenty-four hours to complete Tom Waverly's treasure hunt.

# 7.

"**H**ow much longer are we going to wait?" Linda said.

"We'll give it another ten minutes," Stone said. "I want to be absolutely certain that Walter Lipscombe hasn't put anyone on our tail."

He and Linda were standing on the steps of the Holy Cross Church on Forty-Second Street, hanging back, watching the street parade of commuters, hustlers, panhandlers, and bewildered tourists, the snarled tides of traffic, the plate-glass windows of the post office on the other side of the street. Linda was excited and impatient, drinking everything in with an eager, uncritical gaze. She reminded Stone of the way he'd felt on his first few trips through the mirror, of the peculiar, dreamlike dislocation of finding himself on streets at once familiar and utterly different, as if some crazy set-designer had snuck in behind his back, redressed the city, and populated it with costumed strangers acting out parts in a drama in which he was the central character but whose plot he didn't understand.

Linda had changed out of her army uniform into a pearl-grey pant suit and a pale yellow blouse with a frilly collar she'd bought with her father's dollars in Sak's Fifth Avenue. Her hair was scraped back from her face and done up in a French braid. Stone, dressed in a dark blue business suit and crisp white sea-cotton shirt and club tie, a briefcase containing his pistol and the shock gizmo set between his feet, was leafing through a late edition of the *New York Times*, looking over the top of it every now and then to check for standouts. There was one guy who'd been hanging around a magazine stand, but now a woman in a red dress walked up to him and they hugged, kissed, and walked off arm in arm through the heedless crowds into the rest of their lives. Stone was reminded of what he had lost and felt a desolate pang.

Linda nudged him and said, "See that man? Is that a phone or a radio?"

Stone shook out the newspaper and turned a page. "They don't have cell phones. At least, they didn't last time I was here."

"Maybe it's some kind of walkie-talkie," Linda said. "The thing's the size of a shoe."

Stone spotted the guy she meant. He was standing beside a traffic signal at the northeast corner of the block: slicked-back hair and a deep tan, a sharp black suit with lapels so wide you could land a jet fighter on them, talking with considerable animation into a big box he was holding against the side of his head. Cell phones. Jesus. What next, quantum computers? Turing gates? Another American empire expanding across the infinity of sheaves? It was a weary thought.

Richard Nixon had been president in this sheaf's version of America when the Real had first opened a gate into it and Stone and Tom Waverly had spent six months there, doing basic research. America had been caught up in an unpopular war in Vietnam and there'd been an air of revolution in the streets of major cities, the National Guard had been deployed on university campuses across the country, and men had just landed on the Moon, an amazing feat the Real had not yet bothered to duplicate, caught up as it was in imposing its idea of freedom in countries across the globe and in different Americas in different sheaves. When Stone had returned for a second time, some four years later, the Vietnam War had ended, but the Nixon sheaf had been embroiled in a full-blown crisis in the Middle East and (according to the game theories of the Cluster) a rapidly growing risk of nuclear war. Now Ronald Reagan, the same ex–movie actor who in the Real had served a single term before Floyd Davis and had encouraged the expansion of the Company in the early days of exploring other sheaves, was in his second term as president, fighting a not-so-clandestine war in Central America against armies of communist peasants that according to him were threatening to sweep through Mexico and topple the United States.

As in so many other sheaves, the political strategy of this version of America was shaped by fear. When Stone and Tom Waverly had been doing research there, back in 1969, Americans had been fighting in Vietnam because they'd been afraid that communists would topple countries in Southeast Asia like a series of dominoes, and they'd been fighting their own children at home because their children, grown strange and discontented, had refused to buy into the American dream. From Stone's quick study of the *Times* it seemed that little had changed. The silent majority was still brimful of patriotic sentiment, proud of the powerful presence its country had in the world, deeply indignant if anyone dared point out that other countries might feel nervous in its shadow, utterly convinced that its way of life was the only right way to live, and that the rest of the world, driven by hate and envy, was conspiring to destroy everything it stood for. In 1969, ordinary Americans had been frightened of Ho Chi Minh and his Asiatic hordes; now they were scared silly by a handful of barefoot guerrillas, and as always, they were in mortal dread of the Soviet Union, their nemesis, their shadow self. Here was an op-ed piece quoting Reagan, who called it the Evil Empire. . . .

198

"That's your ten minutes," Linda said. "If there were any lurkers, we would have spotted them by now. So please, can we go check out that box?"

Stone folded up his newspaper. "Before we do anything, I want you to listen carefully to what I have to say. If for any reason we have to split up, don't go back to Grand Central Station. The people who run the interchange aren't trustworthy; Freddy Layne wants to get hold of this thing your father stole, and I'm worried that Walter Lipscombe does too. If there's any trouble, get out of the city and head for New Mexico. There's a gate at White Sands, mostly used by comparative-culture teams en route to Los Angeles or the Midwest. You know where to find it?"

"Tell me later. Right now, I want to get this done."

"This might be the last chance we get to talk," Stone said. He gave Linda directions to the White Sands gate and told her about the caretaker who would help her go through. He made her repeat the directions until she had them word-perfect, then handed her the post office box key and said, "Let's do it."

He watched from across the street as Linda walked into the post office, remembering the times he'd come here back in '73, to pick up orders and situation reports. His hair had been long then, loose around his face or tied back in a ponytail. He'd had a beard. He'd worn blue jeans and a denim jacket with a peace symbol scrawled on its back in black Magic Marker, or a suede jacket with long fringes. . . .

Linda came out of the post office with something tucked under her arm and walked away up Forty-Second Street, toward Times Square. Stone shadowed her at a distance all the way to their agreed rendezvous point, a kind of diner called Choc Full O'Nuts. When he came in, she was waiting for him at a table with two cups of coffee, two glasses of iced water, and a padded envelope, eight by ten, the top ripped open.

"There's nothing in it," she said, as Stone sat down across from her. She looked angry and afraid.

"Nothing?"

"Not even a note."

Stone picked up the envelope by its edges. There were no stamps, and no address: it must have been delivered by hand. He looked inside the envelope and felt the padding. "You should have let me check it out first. It could have been booby-trapped. An explosive charge, nerve gas, contact poison. . . ."

"It was like that when I found it," Linda said. "Someone else knew about it, Mr. Stone. They must have broken into the box or had a copy of the key. They took whatever was inside the envelope and left it behind."

"It's possible. It's also possible that we're the victims of a practical joke. Maybe Kohler was right. Maybe your father didn't steal anything from GYPSY after all."

"He took something they want back, Mr. Stone. That's why they tried to kidnap us. He took something, and he told me he'd hidden it somewhere where you and I could find it if we worked together." Linda had the pinched look of a child kept up too late. All the bounce had gone out of her. "What are we going to do now?"

"I was hoping we'd know what to do after we recovered whatever it was your father stashed away here. Didn't he give you any kind of clue, back when you had your cosy little talk in the motel?"

"I was wondering if you'd start in on that again."

"If you're holding something back, Linda, I can't think of a better time to tell me. If your father explained why he was on the run, why he was killing Dr. Barrie's doppels . . ."

Linda shook her head, looking very unhappy. Stone was certain that Tom had told her a lot more than she was letting on, but he didn't know how to reach out to her.

"We need a new plan," he said. "I think we should go find Dr. Barrie. The real Dr. Barrie. If your father stole something, maybe she can tell us what it is, and why it's so important."

"If she's involved in this conspiracy, she'll have been arrested," Linda said. "And even if she isn't involved, she'll be under heavy protection. We won't be able to get within a mile of her. When it comes down to it, Mr. Stone, we both work for the Company. Maybe we should go back to Mr. Kohler—"

"I didn't come back just to help you clear your father's name," Stone said. "I came back because a woman was murdered. The wife of my best friend was shot dead because of this, because someone wanted to get to *me*."

His pulse beat in his head. Linda was staring at him across the table, and people at other tables and the two teenagers behind the counter were all staring at him too.

Linda said quietly, "I really, truly thought that we'd find something here."

"Tell me, Linda. Tell me everything. It'll help us work out our next move. It'll help us clear your father's name and take down the people responsible for Susan's murder."

Linda shook her head. "You'll think I'm crazy. Actually, I think I *am* a little crazy, for even believing it. But it doesn't matter now."

After a long pause, Stone said, "It's possible there's a microdot hidden under the label, or inside the padding. We need to find a place where we can pull it apart and examine every square inch."

"And if it's just an empty envelope?"

"Then we'll definitely need a new plan. I'm not giving up on this, Linda. I'm going on, with you or without you."

"With me, then," she said. "With me."

They took rooms on different floors of the Roosevelt Hotel and spent three hours taking the envelope apart. They cut open its outer layer, pulled out the grey fluff strand by strand. They opened the seam at the bottom edge. They heated its surfaces over the bedside lamps in case Tom Waverly had left a message in one of the common or garden varieties of heat-sensitive invisible ink. They didn't find anything.

Stone ordered sandwiches from room service, and he and Linda agreed that there was no point staying in New York, that they would make an early start tomorrow, hire a car and head for White Sands, and decide what they were going to do along the way. Linda retired to her own room, and Stone ordered a bottle of Wild Turkey. After it arrived, he sat on the bed, drinking from the plastic tumbler he'd found in the bathroom, watching the TV fixed on a wall bracket under the plaster ceiling.

He felt comfortably numb after a few belts of bourbon, and the garish, in-your-face simplicity of the TV ads began to seem amusing. Susan's doppel was probably living out her life right here in the Nixon sheaf, he thought; it wasn't so hard to imagine that she was also alive and well in a sheaf where she'd shot Marsha Mason dead before Marsha Mason could shoot her. It would be too close to known history to be reached by any Turing gate, but perhaps there was some other road he could take, like that highway in the song sung by the pair of strange, out-of-time musicians. A highway he could find in his dreams, a highway like a winding ribbon, a winding ribbon with a band of gold. A highway back to you. . . .

At some point Stone could no longer keep his eyes open and he fell asleep, propped up against the padded headboard. When he woke, the TV was still flickering and mumbling high in the corner of the room and two men were standing at the foot of the bed.

# 8.

Stone stayed very still, locking gazes with the larger of the men, a heavy-set guy in a sport coat and blue jeans who looked like a backwoods farmer turned fairground prizefighter. He had a nose skewed to the left, protruding ears with a touch of cauliflower, and black hair greased back in a fat wave, and he was aiming a large revolver at Stone's chest, its hammer cocked, his finger rock-steady on the trigger, his dark eyes calm and unblinking. Stone's Colt .45 lay on the briefcase, on the bedside table. He'd have to distract this klutz somehow to snatch up the pistol. . . .

"Don't even think of trying anything," the other man said. "Calvin looks dumb, but he ain't."

"Kindly reach back and take hold of those two lamps on either side of the headboard," Calvin said. "Hold them good and tight."

"Looks like Christ on the cross, don't he?" the smaller man said. Sleek and plump as a cemetery rat, dressed in an electric-green suit and a bright red silk shirt, he stepped around the end of the bed with the caution of a technician approaching an unexploded bomb, one hand inside his jacket.

"Don't move a muscle," Calvin told Stone.

His partner brought his hand out of his jacket. He was holding a fat glass-barrelled syringe with finger-grip loops, the kind of thing a veterinarian might use on a horse, and with a sudden flourish rammed its spike into Stone's left thigh and injected about half a pint of pink goo into the big muscle there.

Stone yelled more from surprise than pain, but managed to keep hold of the lamps and keep his gaze fixed on Calvin's face, asking him if they'd been sent by Ralph Kohler, if they were taking him back, suddenly finding it difficult to work the muscles of his throat and mouth, feeling as if he was pinned to the bed by centrifugal force as the room began to slide past.

"My own special mix," the small man said. "It can make a deaf-mute sing like a canary."

Calvin studied Stone for a moment, then said to his partner, "That shit works fast, don't it? Well, let's get this thing done."

"I still don't see why we can't take him through the mirror," the small man said. He had a nasal accent from somewhere in New England, a way of cocking his head this way and that like a bird. "We're asking for trouble, working here."

"It's not ideal, but we have our orders."

"I was just expressing an opinion."

"It's no good expressing it to me."

"Or to anyone else, no doubt," the small man said. "We're cogs in the machine, Calvin, cogs in the machine. I'll do my best, but in my humble opinion this is not the place to carry out this kind of work. If we attract the attention of the local law enforcement agencies, things could get messy."

The room was moving sideways with a stately slide and Stone was having trouble focusing on things. He squinted at the big man and said, "Who sent you?"

"We're just a couple of guys who happen to be very good at what they do," Calvin said, allowing a sliver of amusement to show in his battered face. He stepped around the bed and picked up the Colt .45, weighing it in his hand before slipping it into a pocket of his sport coat, then unlatching the briefcase and taking out the shock gizmo. "Word of advice. Next time you leave your stuff with someone, you should take a good look at it when you get it back. This thing, it had two big batteries inside it. We took out one and put in a transponder."

"You led us on a pretty good chase after you came through the mirror," Calvin's partner said. "We've been driving around in fucking circles for hours trying to pick up the signal. But as you're about to find out, we're the kind of guys who don't easily give up."

"He looks about ready," Calvin said.

"Give him a few minutes," his partner said and went into the bathroom.

Stone tried to keep Calvin's face fixed in the centre of the whirling room. He had the horrible feeling that if he let go of the lamps he'd fall into the magic light of the TV that all this time had been muttering to itself up by the ceiling. He said, "People are watching me. You're going to be in a world of trouble."

Calvin's grin showed a mouthful of small brown teeth. "You're a pisser, aren't you? You hear that, Al? We're in a world of trouble."

"Company guys, they're all the same," the small man, Al, sang out from the bathroom, over the sound of running water. "I've never met one who wasn't an arrogant son of bitch. But even Company guys will talk. You just have to work that little bit harder."

"Listen to my good friend," Calvin told Stone. "He's done a lot of this kind of thing. He's very good at it."

"We've both had plenty of experience with people like you," Al said, as he came out of the bathroom. He'd taken off his suit trousers and his shirt, and wore only a white vest and white undershorts, black socks with suspenders, and shiny black shoes. There was a tattoo on his right arm: a red heart dripping blood and crowned with thorns. He stood on tiptoe and turned up the volume of the TV, studied Stone for a moment, then told Calvin, "He looks nicely cooked. We'll start in when the bath's full."

"People might complain about that TV," Calvin said.

"It's either that, or we'll have to gag him. And if we gag him, how is he going to answer our questions?"

"Point," Calvin said, and started to take off his sport coat.

"Hang it in the bathroom with my stuff," Al told him. "This is going to be one of the messy ones."

They handcuffed Stone's arms behind his back and softened him up with the shock gizmo, which gave him an all-over cramp each time it was applied. Whenever he was able to catch his breath, he told the two men about the key and the post office box and the empty envelope, told them about a cache of gold, about uncut diamonds, about weird drugs, about blueprints, told them anything that came into his head.

Calvin and Al didn't take any notice of his babbling, and Al's cocktail of drugs and the exquisitely knotted agony of the cramps were making it harder and harder for Stone to think about anything but the truth. The two men hauled him into the bathroom and set him on his knees in front of the brimful bath, Calvin holding him by his hair while Al told him that they knew that Tom Waverly had left something here, something they believed to be very valuable. They wanted to know what it was. They wanted to know where it was.

Stone started to tell them about the post office box and Calvin shoved his head under water, and held it there in a rigid lock while Stone thrashed and a hard ache grew in his lungs and black spots crowded out the glare of the tub's white bottom, swarming in faster and faster. Then he was lying on his back on wet tiles, staring up at the bathroom ceiling, chest heaving.

"Good to go," Al said, and Calvin hauled Stone up and shoved his head under the water again.

When Stone came around for the second time, Al leaned over him and caressed his chest with the prongs of the gizmo and asked where Linda Waverly had gone. Stone told them that she'd run off, the bitch, and got the bath again.

On his back, coughing up water, unable to get his breath, Al in his face, saying "I know she's somewhere in this hotel. Which room?"

"She ran out on me, the silly little bitch. Said she was going to San Francisco. Or Los Angeles. Somewhere on the West Coast."

Calvin said, "She's been, what? A year on the job?"

"Eighteen months," Al said.

"And she gives this veteran the slip. You believe it?"

"I'm getting old," Stone said. "Careless."

"First true thing I've heard," Al said.

He jabbed the gizmo in the tender spot behind the angle of Stone's jaw and white fire took everything away. When Stone came back, he was on the bed. He'd bitten his tongue and his mouth was full of blood. The TV was jovial and loud; ceiling and walls threatened to swap places.

Calvin said, "Don't think you can hold out in case we don't find her. Because we *will* find her, my friend, and it won't matter if you start talking then, because we'll hurt her anyway."

"Because we'll be pissed off," Al said, and described some of the things they'd do to her.

Stone coughed blood over his chin and chest and told Al that he was a sick puppy.

"He's a craftsman," Calvin said. "I should know, I seen enough of it. Only way you can save her is to talk right now."

"What was in the post office box?" Al said. "You told us about the post office box, let's say we believe that part. What was in it?"

"A bad joke."

Al sighed theatrically and got up and went into the bathroom.

"Now you've made him mad," Calvin said. "It can get ugly, when he's mad. I were you, Mr. Stone, I'd stop with the dumb stories and start on telling the truth."

Al came back holding a lighted cigarette.

Stone said, "If that's for me, I don't smoke."

"He's a pisser, ain't he," Calvin said, watching as Al clamped a finger and thumb over Stone's left eye and peeled back the eyelid and held the tip of the lighted cigarette close.

The glowing ash filled Stone's vision. He felt its withering heat drying his cornea, felt the sizzle as it briefly touched his eyelashes. He desperately wanted to blink.

"First one eye," Al said, wiggling the tip of the cigarette a little, "and then the other."

"He'll do it," Calvin said. "I seen it before, and I wish I hadn't. The sound is pretty bad, that wet hiss, but the smell, that's worse. And the screaming, too. It hurts so bad even the toughest guy loses it."

"He ain't that tough," Al said. "He's too intelligent to be really tough. What it is, he's stubborn. He believes the mind and the body are separate, that the body can do the suffering while he stays aloof. He believes he can tell us all kinds of shit because we're just a couple of doofuses who don't know any better. Well, let me tell you something, my friend," he said, holding the cigarette rock-steady a quarter inch from Stone's eye. "This burns at five hundred degrees Fahrenheit, and when I stick it in your eye you'll fucking well know mind and body are truly one and the same."

Stone tried to spit blood in Al's face, but he was weak and out of breath, and it dribbled down his chin instead.

Al laughed and took away the cigarette. "Jesus. These old-school guys. They're hard work."

Calvin said, "What was in the post office box, Adam? That's all we need to know."

"I told you. Didn't I tell you?"

Al drew on the cigarette until its tip glowed and stuck it on different places on Stone's scalp.

Stone bit his tongue.

Al said, very patiently, "Everyone talks," and touched the cigarette to the bony ridge behind Stone's ear. "You know that. So talk to us now, and save us all a lot of work."

He waited a beat, then ran the cigarette along the rim of Stone's ear. Stone howled, letting the pain out.

"Jesus," Calvin said. "We're going to get a complaint, I know it."

The two men sat on either side of the end of the bed in their underwear and polished shoes, regarding Stone with the serious and thoughtful manner of actors trying to decide the most satisfying and effective way of winding up an impromptu performance piece.

Calvin suggested snipping off a couple of fingers, joint by joint. "Look at him," he said. "Grinning at us like an ape."

Stone wasn't aware that he was smiling. He was only half there, was trying to lose himself in a reverie of his foster father working at his bench in the dusty light of the big, hip-roofed barn, cleaning up a tenon joint with small, accurate strokes of a chisel or planing a length of pine, blond fragrant curls falling like angel feathers to the packed-dirt floor. Karl Kerfeld had been a carpenter by trade, making furniture in winter, signing up with contractors in summer to fit out or renovate houses. After he and his wife, Hannah, had discovered that they couldn't have children of their own, they'd taken in and raised half a dozen foster children. Adam Stone had been their last. Now he tried to remember the tools fixed to the pegboard behind his foster father's workbench, each sitting in an outline of red paint so you could see exactly where to put it back when you'd finished with it. A tenon saw, a bow saw, hacksaws, flat-headed screwdrivers, chisels, all kinds of wood-chisels in a row. . . .

Al came off the bed and slapped Stone to get his attention, saying, "You found something in that post office box. Where is it? That's all we want to know. You tell us, we'll go away."

They worked him over again. The gizmo, wet knotted towels. They took their time. They took turns. Stone counted off every tool on the pegboard in his foster father's vanished workshop, the ball-peen hammer and the drywall hammer and the engineer's hammer and three sizes of mallet, angle clamps and C-clamps and edge clamps and hand-screw clamps, the low-angle plane and the rabbit plane, all the way down to the wire snips and the set of hex keys, and when he was done there he tried to re-create from memory the greenhouse in winter, remembering how snow covering the glass tent of the roof and heaped up six feet high along the walls transmuted winter sunlight into a magical blue glow in which bent-backed Karl, wearing bib overalls and a heavy cardigan with the elbows worn through, expertly sifted soil into clay pots. The old man was always growing something. Early tomatoes, sweet peas. Squash, chillies. His broad thumbs tamping loam, crests of dirt under his buckled nails. . . .

Stone was crawling around the room on his hands and knees, bumping blindly into the wall, into the bed, into the wardrobe, while the TV blared a cheerful children's cartoon. Grey dawn light leaked around the burgundy drapes. The two men sat on the bed and watched him. Al was out of breath and red in the face. Calvin had sweated through his undershirt and drops of sweat rolled down his face and clung to his chin in a trembling fringe. He was drinking Coke from a can. At some point he must have gone out and bought it from the vending machine in the corridor, but Stone didn't remember it.

Stone's knees gave out and he collapsed on the wet carpet. He was naked, bleeding from the nose and mouth and ears, and as weak and trembling as if he'd just run a marathon. He curled up when Calvin kicked him experimentally in the ribs.

207

"We still got his attention," Calvin said.

A bell was ringing somewhere. It took Stone a few moments to realise that it wasn't inside his head. It was a real bell.

Al said, "Jesus. Is that what I think?"

"I'll take a look," Calvin said.

After the big man had stepped outside, Stone entertained a brief fantasy of finding a last reserve of superhuman strength and overpowering Al and stuffing the gizmo down his throat and pressing the button until the battery gave out. The bell was still ringing, for a moment as loud as the TV when Calvin opened the door and slipped back into the room.

"Can't see or smell any smoke," he said, "but this is a big place, could be ten floors below or ten above. People are going outside, using the stairs. I jammed one of the elevators. We can take it down to the service level and slip out that way."

"Uh-uh," Al said. "We have to stay here because we aren't finished with this bozo, and we can't take him with us. If there *is* a fire, we'll leave him to roast. If not, we start over on him. He's almost done, Calvin," the small man said, caressing Stone's face, patting his cheek. "He's getting ready to tell us."

"You better be right."

"We got six hours before we have to go check the gate. We—"

Someone had knocked loudly on the door. Calvin and Al looked at it and looked at each other. A man shouted something about a fire alarm and knocked on the door again.

Al put his hand over Stone's mouth while Calvin stepped up and used the peephole, saying, "A guy in one of those purple jackets staff wear here."

"If we stay quiet, he won't know we're here," Al said.

There was another rap on the door. The handle jiggled up and down.

"He'll have a guest list and a master key," Calvin said. "Let me deal with it." He unlocked the door and opened it a crack, then reeled backward and collapsed. A black knife handle protruded from his eye. Al jumped up and Stone kicked out and tangled the small man's feet in his, and a man in a purple jacket stepped over Calvin's body and shot Al in the face. The small man flopped forward with a small, sad sigh, kneeling as if in prayer with his head turned sideways, blood trickling from the scorched hole in his cheek. The man in the purple jacket kicked the door shut and bent over Stone and slapped him, quick open-handed slaps left and right.

Stone looked up at him, trying to focus.

"Do I have your attention?" Tom Waverly said.

# 9.

"They were working for Walter Lipscombe," Stone said. "One of them had a bleeding-heart tattoo, the old gang sign."

"Walter Lipscombe—now there's a guy who knows how to lead the good life," Tom Waverly said. "He had his people follow you through the mirror? You're getting careless."

"They hid a transponder in that gizmo I told you to leave behind. All they had to do was drive around until they acquired the signal."

"Pretty foxy for a couple of goons."

"Pretty dumb of me not to realise what was going on. Walter must have known all along you were in business with Freddy Layne. He found out from Freddy that you'd stolen something valuable, and he let me lead his guys straight to the prize. Except it turned out there wasn't any prize. That was a nice joke, by the way, sending us on a mission to track down an empty envelope."

Stone and Tom Waverly (if it was Tom Waverly) were riding down in the elevator Calvin had jammed open. Stone leaned in a corner like a prizefighter who'd gone ten rounds too many. His entire body ached, the cigarette burns in his scalp itched like the world's worst mosquito bites, and he had the distinct sensation that if he moved too quickly he'd topple sideways through some unseen dimension and never stop falling. In this free-floating state anything seemed possible, even talking with a dead man. A man he'd seen stick a gun in his mouth and blow his brains out not three days ago.

Tom grinned at Stone, saying, "Linda told me all about your wild-goose chase. Thing is, I didn't leave that envelope in the old dead drop."

He'd ditched the stolen staff jacket in Stone's room, was dressed in a white T-shirt under a blue denim jacket, and blue jeans and the tan workboots that Stone remembered from Pottersville. His hair, which in Pottersville had been cut short and dyed black, was long and grey now, pulled back in a loose ponytail tied with red string. He had a couple of inches of untrimmed salt-and-pepper beard and looked pretty healthy for a dead man; definitely much healthier than he'd been a few days ago.

"I guess you didn't leave the key to the box in your apartment in the American Bund sheaf, either."

Tom shook his head. "I haven't been in the American Bund sheaf for six months."

"That's not what Freddy Layne told me."

"Freddy isn't exactly my idea of a trustworthy source of information."

The elevator's door opened on a shabby corridor in the hotel's subbasement. The fire alarm clanged in the distance.

As Stone hobbled after him, squeezing past a traffic jam of service carts, Tom said, "All I know is that I got a phone call about a week ago at a number only one other person besides me should have known about. The man who made the call told me that you'd be checking out our old drop here in New York."

"Don't bullshit me, Tom. You set us up with that bogus trail to the drop, and you followed us here from Forty-Second Street."

"Matter of fact, I hired private detectives to do that for me. My mystery caller was vague about the date you'd show up; there was no way I could stake out the post office on my own. I gave them your photograph, told them to follow you, and that's just what they did."

"You're right about one thing. I've definitely lost my edge. I get jumped by Walter's guys, I don't spot that I'm being trailed by a couple of private dicks. . . ."

"Don't be too hard on yourself, old buddy. They're ex-police, good guys."

Three firefighters in heavy jackets and yellow helmets slammed through the double doors at the end of the corridor, jogged toward them. One paused, looked Stone up and down, and asked if he needed any help.

"He fell down the stairs," Tom said.

"You need to leave this place," the firefighter said, and hurried after his companions.

"Abso-goddamn-lutely," Tom said.

The double doors opened onto the platform of a loading bay. Stone limped down the steps, holding on to the handrail, saying doggedly, "You told Linda to find your apartment in the American Bund. And you told her to bring me along, because I'd know what to do when we got there. You set us up."

"I save your life yet again, and all I get is grief. We need to go this way," Tom said, leading Stone past a row of Dumpsters into an alleyway squeezed between the flanks of tall buildings.

"You also told Linda that you took something," Stone said. "She believed it would clear your name, which is why she came here. Those two goons thought *I* had it, which is why they were working me over. You took it from

GYPSY, didn't you? Or you took it from Dr. Barrie, who is working for GYPSY, just like you."

"I didn't steal anything from Eileen Barrie."

"Yeah, and you didn't kill her doppels either."

"You know, I did hear something about that. But I've been hiding out here all the time it was going down, Adam. It wasn't anything to do with me."

Stone was very familiar with his old friend's light, sly, amused tone of voice: Tom Waverly was holding all the cards, giving teasing hints, playing with him, making him work hard for every scrap of information.

"I've been beaten silly and I'm out of patience. You brought me here for a reason. If you don't have the decency to explain it, I think I should walk away."

"I really did get that phone call, Adam. And there's a plausible explanation for it, too."

"Tell me you didn't know Walter's goons were following me."

"If I'd known about them, I wouldn't have spent most of the night talking with Linda. As it was, we had a lot of catching up to do. We talked and talked, and when we were about talked out, we both kind of dozed off. I wake up, I head toward your room, and this big guy I've never before seen in my life comes out in his underwear, gets a can of Coke from the machine, and goes back inside. I tippy-toe up to the door, thinking Linda gave me the wrong room number. I press my ear to the wood and hear you talking, hear someone else talking. I hear some unpleasant sounds too, and I figure the big guy I saw isn't there to look after your health. So I pulled the old fire-alarm stunt. Worked pretty well, didn't it?"

They came out of the alley into the middle of a crowd of hotel staff, guests in overcoats or robes overnight wear and rubberneckers penned behind a police barrier. Fire trucks and police cruisers blocked the street in front of the hotel.

"There she is, my brave girl," Tom Waverly said, and Stone followed him through the crowd toward the end of the block, where Linda was leaning against the hood of a brown station wagon.

# 10.

While Linda drove the station wagon across town toward the Holland Tunnel, her father told her how he had come to Stone's rescue. When he had finished, she told Stone that she hadn't known it was going to happen, really and truly she hadn't, and asked her father, "Did you know?"

"All I know is what I was told, honey. Just like you."

"You better be telling the truth," Linda said, and glanced in the rearview mirror. "You hold on, Mr. Stone. We'll stop somewhere and get you fixed up."

Stone was sprawled on the capacious back seat in a litter of old newspapers and fast-food cartons. He coughed, tasted blood, and said, "Linda? You think this guy really is your father?"

"Of course he is."

"Jesus Christ had his Doubting Thomas; I have you. Check it out," Tom said, and pulled down the neck of his T-shirt, revealing a pale oval scar just below his right collarbone. "Remember when I got this? Want to put your finger on it, reassure yourself it's real?"

Stone ignored him and said to Linda, "How about before, in Pottersville? Was that your father too?"

"I know it's hard to take in, Mr. Stone," Linda said.

"It *was* me," Tom said, "but there's no way I'm going to end up there now. The circle is broken. We're making a split, right here. I can feel it. I bet you can feel it too, can't you, Adam?"

"I feel as if I'm tuned to the wrong channel," Stone said. "As if I shouldn't really be here."

The effort of getting out of the hotel had exhausted him, and he was still coming down from the cocktail of drugs he'd been given. He kept losing focus on the world, drifting into a state of disconnected, not unpleasant lassitude where nothing much seemed to matter.

"You're here, all right," Tom said. "And so I am, so you'd better get used to it. You and me—and Linda too, of course—we're going to split history and forge a new universe."

"We have a long way to go," Linda said.

"We're on the road, honey, that's the important thing. We're on the road, and we're operating under our own free will. So with that general principle in mind, Adam, if you want to go your own way, I won't stop you."

"Maybe I will, after I've rested up," Stone said, and zoned out for a little while.

When he came around, they were driving along an elevated section of turnpike. Across the sun-silvered sweep of the Hudson river, the spiky sky-line of Manhattan stood against a clean blue sky.

When he saw that Stone was awake, Tom said, "If you don't mind me saying so, old buddy, you look like shit. But you hang in there, we'll stop soon and get you fixed up."

"A couple of painkillers might help."

"Anything you want," Tom said. He beat a rhythm on his thighs with his palms and sang a couple of lines about cars on the New Jersey Turnpike, all come to look for America. "Everything's falling into place. We did what we had to do to get to this point, and now we're free to do what we need to do. Everything's going to work out."

"It better," Linda said.

"We have to have a little faith in the dead guy," Tom said. "But right now we're off the page. We're free." He lowered the window and stuck his head out into the rush of air. "Free at last! Great God Almighty, free at last! Man, does it ever feel good!"

They stopped in a shopping mall and purchased three different brands of painkiller and tubes of burn ointment and liniment. Stone stripped off his suit and shirt in a restroom stall and anointed his wounds, dressed again, and washed down two Tylenol with a palmful of tap water and splashed cold water on his face. Every square inch of his skin hurt, a general ache enlivened by spots of specific pain—the itchy sting of the cigarette burns in his scalp and on his ear, the hot throb of a swollen eyelid that flared every time he blinked, the bone-deep bruise in his thigh where Al had injected his special cocktail. When he limped back to the car, Tom Waverly offered him a bag of White Castle burgers, and the smell of onions and cooked meat almost made him throw up.

Tom was still in an exuberant and playful mood. He'd bought a tape cas-sette of one of Bob Dylan's old albums at the service station where Linda had pumped fifteen gallons of expensive gasoline into the station wagon's tank. He had been singing snatches of the songs and beating time to the music as he watched traffic moving in the sunlight. Linda was quieter, her face masked by the amber sunglasses her father had purchased with the cassettes.

Stone sat quietly in the back seat. He was still having trouble putting his thoughts together, but he decided that the first thing he needed to do was find out if this version of Tom Waverly could fill in the gaps in the story that the other version of Tom Waverly had told him in the Pottersville cemetery. The one who had been dying of radiation poisoning; the one who had shot himself.

"You were working for this thing of Dick Knightly's," Stone said. "For Operation GYPSY. Want to tell me exactly what you were doing for him?"

"You have to get into this now, Adam? It's a complicated story, and after all you've been through, I'm not sure if you'll be able to appreciate it properly."

"After all I've been through, I deserve to know what's going on," Stone said. "Let's start at the beginning. Knightly recruited you after SWIFT SWORD. What happened next?"

"He tried to recruit me *during* SWIFT SWORD, which is why I wanted to try for a last chance at guts and glory, and we both know how that worked out. When the dust from that had settled, right after the Conduct Board had slapped my wrist, Knightly came back to me with his offer. He said that if I didn't go work for him, he'd ring the gong, tell the Company how I'd neutralized General E. Everett McBride, and also tell them about the various little scams I had going to supplement my pension fund. The man knew just about everything, Adam. I had no choice."

"So you faked your own death and went to work for GYPSY."

"Yeah."

"Which kept going after Knightly was jailed, and suffered his stroke."

"Yeah," Tom said again, and laughed.

"Marsha Mason and Nathan Tate were working for it too. You were all working together."

"But I got out," Tom Waverly said.

"And you stole something. What were you planning to do with it, before you got that phone call?"

"Oh, you believe I got that phone call now?"

Linda said, "He was told more or less what I was told in Pottersville, Mr. Stone. He knew we were coming here, and he knew how to find us."

"You stole something that could change history," Stone said to Tom. "What is it? What does it do?"

Tom Waverly turned in his seat and looked at Stone over the top of his sunglasses. "I call it the time key. It lets you use gates to travel into the past."

"Cut the bullshit, Tom. If you can't give me straight answers, don't expect me to help you."

"He's telling the truth, Mr. Stone," Linda said. "This is what GYPSY is all about. This is what Dr. Barrie was working on. Officially, GYPSY is a clandestine research facility that's developing portable Turing gates. Gates you can put on the back of a pickup truck and move anywhere. But that's just a front for a black op. For Dr. Barrie's real research."

"Dr. Barrie is working for GYPSY," Stone said. That much he could understand. "Is that why you were killing her doppels, Tom? Were you trying to draw attention to her?"

"It won't come to that, Adam. Not now."

Another evasion. Stone wondered if the man who'd shot and killed himself in Pottersville had been a doppel of Tom Waverly tutored in every aspect of the real Tom Waverly's life. Or maybe Tom hadn't killed himself in Pottersville after all. Maybe the whole thing had been a charade, a piece of live-action disinformation involving blood-filled squibs and a gun loaded with blanks, just like the movies. But that meant Freddy Layne, with his story about a lethal dose of radiation, had to be in on it, too. . . .

He said, "Let's say I believe you stole something crucial to GYPSY, that possession of it gives you a way out of this thing you were blackmailed into working for. Why didn't you take it to the Company, Tom? Why didn't you turn yourself in? Why go to all this trouble to involve Linda and me?"

"The Company believed that I was dead. And now I'm dead all over again, and I'd kind of like to keep it that way."

"You need a middleman—is that what this is about? Did you kill Dr. Barrie's doppels just to bring me into this?"

"That's a good question. I wish I knew the answer, I really do."

"If you want me to help you out, Tom, you're going to have to be straight with me."

"I'm not playing any kind of game. I don't know why Eileen Barrie's doppels were killed because it wasn't anything to with me. I haven't harmed a hair on any one of their heads, swear to God."

"It won't happen," Linda said.

"Not in this universe, honey. Not if we can help it, eh?"

"Not anywhere, if I can help it."

There was a space of silence. The last song on the tape, a lament for lost love, played out. Tom popped out the cassette and put it back in its case, then read a couple of sentences from the liner notes.

"Listen to this, Adam. He could be speaking directly to us. 'Dylan's Redemption Songs! If he can do it, we can do it. America can do it.' Think we can do it, Adam?"

"That depends on what we're trying to do. And who we're doing it for."

"You don't trust me. I understand that. But you're going to have to learn to trust me before this thing is through. Listen: 'To live outside the law you must be honest.' Also, 'A new world is only a new mind.' Ain't it the truth? If you make enough of a difference, affect enough observers, make enough resonance in the General Quantum Field, you definitely get a whole new universe."

"Are you doing it for yourself, Tom, or for America?"

"I'm a patriot. Always have been, always will be. Do you doubt that as well?"

"You're talking about time travel and looking for messages in found text, Tom. And after all that's gone down in the past couple of days, you can't blame me for harbouring one or two doubts."

"Someone once said that poets are the unacknowledged legislators of the world. But I reckon they're the *unconscious* legislators, tapping into the background hum of the General Quantum Field, what used to be called the group unconsciousness. They don't know where their babble comes from, and as long as they can grab a few lines that echo in eternity they don't care. This guy who wrote the liner notes—Allen Ginsberg. You remember him, Adam? That crazy mission of yours right here in this very sheaf, back in 1973?"

"I remember that I was a lot younger than I am now, and also a lot more arrogant."

"Adam is partial to this particular sheaf, honey," Tom told his daughter. "It was one of the first the Company infiltrated. We both worked undercover here in 1969, and he came back a few years later. The president was in all kinds of political trouble, there was an energy crisis and a good chance that nuclear war could have broken out over a situation in the Middle East, and the Cluster decided that it was a hinge-point. Adam was in charge of a team that was working toward starting up a civil war."

"But in the end it didn't work out," Stone said. "And I'm glad that it didn't, because the locals resolved everything for themselves."

"We had a seminar about it during the trainee programme," Linda said.

"And doesn't that make you feel old?" Tom Waverly said. "Plenty of people in the Company think we missed a chance, back then."

"This version of America doesn't need our help now, and it didn't need our help back in 1973 either," Stone said. "It was already a power in the world, on its way to becoming *the* power, but the Cluster came up with a plan to bring it under our influence anyway, and we were so full of ourselves we tried to carry it through."

He and Tom hadn't seen each other for more than three years, he thought, and they were picking up right where they'd left off.

"You have to admit it was a pretty neat plan," Tom said. "Light up a civil war right in the middle of that trouble their president was having, come in and help stop what we'd started. . . ."

"A neat plan? There would have been civil war all right. Breakdown of law and order, tens of thousands of deaths, all the trouble of policing a post-revolutionary America, and for what? Another version of the Stars and Stripes flying alongside all the other versions outside every Pan-American Alliance Assembly Building in every sheaf? Another version of America forced to buy into the idea that the Real is the centre of the multiverse?"

"I said that it was a neat plan, Adam. I didn't say that it was a *good* plan. Remember our argument just before SWIFT SWORD kicked off? I was on the side of the Free Americans. I wanted to help them any way I could, and you said nothing good would come of it because they were as bad as the communists they wanted to overthrow. Remember that?"

"You supported expansionism. So did Dick Knightly."

"I *used* to support expansionism, yeah, but I wasn't as fanatical about it as the Old Man. Why I quit GYPSY? Why I didn't even want to join up in the first place? It's because I didn't like what it was planning to do. It's because, I guess, I was coming round to your way of thinking."

"GYPSY is planning covert action to destabilise sheaves, isn't it?" Stone said. "Sheaves like this one."

"It's worse than that," Linda said. "It's planning to destabilise our own history by changing the past."

Stone laughed. He couldn't help it. It came bubbling out of him.

"He isn't ready for this," Tom said.

"Show him the time key," Linda said. "Tell him everything."

"Maybe we better wait until White Sands. He'll have to believe it then."

"Fuck it," Linda said, and swerved across two lanes and braked on the hard shoulder, the station wagon rocking on its shocks as a tractor-trailer went past in a rush of wind and a howling horn blast. She switched off the motor and said, "We aren't going another inch until we get this straightened out. Mr. Stone, I want you to listen to what my father has to say. Don't ask any questions: just listen. And while you're listening, remember that my father killed himself a few days ago right in front of your eyes, and here he is again. And he isn't a doppel or some other kind of impostor. He really is my father. Dad, you show Mr. Stone the time key and explain how it works. No games. No smoke and mirrors. Just the plain truth."

Tom Waverly reached inside his denim jacket and pulled out a padded envelope folded around the shape inside it. "This is what Eileen Barrie was working on," he said, and tossed the envelope into Stone's lap.

Stone picked it up. He could feel something flat and hard inside. It was about the size and weight of a cell phone.

"Go ahead," Tom said.

Linda turned in her seat to watch as Stone reached inside the envelope and drew out a pale green, foggily translucent oblong. It felt cold and then suddenly warm. Little coloured lights flickered inside it and he had the sudden dizzy feeling that the thing was opening into a void miles deep, that baleful stars burning way down inside it were turning to look at him.

Linda said, "Mr. Stone? Are you all right?"

Stone was familiar with fear. He knew from long experience that in a tight spot fear could be your friend, that fear's little squirts of adrenalin could heighten your senses, bristle your hair, divert blood from vulnerable limbs to the centre of your body, pump you up for fight or flight. This, though, wasn't fear. This was terror: the bowel-squeezing, scrotum-tightening, mind-freezing terror of a man-ape facing a leopard on the primaeval African veldt. And terror didn't make you want to fight or flee. Terror took you by the scruff of your neck and shut you down. Terror made you ready to give up your life. You went limp in its jaws; you no longer cared that you were about to be carried off and disembowelled.

Stone's grip on the hard little oblong convulsively tightened. It felt slick and soft and disgusting, as if the rotting hand of someone long dead yet still animate had crept into his. He tried to free himself, but his fingers were cramped around it and his gaze was locked on its vertiginous depths, and then a black headache spiked straight through his skull and wiped him clean.

# 11.

I t was dark when Stone woke, and the station wagon was quiet and still, angle-parked in front of a motel room. Tom Waverly, leaning at the open door, said, "Well it's about time. How are you doing?"

"Like someone hit me in the back of the head with an ax. Where are we?"

"Someplace on the outskirts of Indianapolis." Tom stepped back as Stone pulled himself out of the station wagon. Crickets trilling in the humid night air. The faint sound of traffic on an elevated highway beyond the string of rooms. A lighted sign floating in darkness. Westward Ho.

"Linda's getting us some food from a Chinese place across the street," Tom said. "You'll feel better once you've had something to eat."

"A shower and two or three bottles of painkiller wouldn't hurt, either."

Stone took the shower cold and then hot, as hot as he could stand it, and began to feel vaguely human again. He began to remember what had happened, too—the translucent green oblong coming alive after he pulled it from the envelope, the void opening up and swallowing him whole—but was unable to make any sense of it.

When he came out of the steamed-up bathroom with a towel knotted around his waist, carrying his clothes and his shoulder holster and pistol, he found Tom and Linda sitting on one of the beds, eating Chinese food from white cartons. Linda stared at the bruises that covered Stone's torso and asked if he was okay.

"I guess I passed out. No big deal."

"You took out the key and you had a minor fit," Tom Waverly said. "Maybe you pressed the wrong combination of switches and made it mad at you. It's a tricky little gadget. The people who worked on it found that out the hard way."

"The drugs Walter's goons gave me did a number on my head," Stone said. "I'm okay now."

Tom studied him. "Want something to eat? We have Kung Pao chicken, we have deep-fried squid, beef with green peppers, noodles, fully loaded fried rice. All of it good."

Linda said, "Don't you think we should find him a doctor?"

"You want a doctor, Adam?"

"No, no doctor."

"See, honey? He doesn't need a doctor."

"I want to talk about this thing you stole," Stone said.

Stone refused Tom's offer of a carton of fried rice and sat on one of the beds, the towel still knotted around his waist and his suit jacket draped around his shoulders. Tom, straddling a chair close by, said, "What do you want to know?"

"Everything from A to B and back again."

"It has a long technical name I can never be bothered to remember, which is why I call it the time key. It has a quantum computer in it—we're pretty sure it's a self-aware quantum computer. And I guess it took an instant dislike to you."

"It's some kind of weapon, isn't it?"

Tom Waverly shook his head. "It works Turing gates."

"What do you mean, it works Turing gates?"

"It works them so you can travel into the past."

Linda said, "It's true, Mr. Stone. You have to believe him."

"I'm trying my best."

Tom said, "Someone phoned me and told me to look out for you and Linda. The man who made that call was the same guy who killed himself in Pottersville. He was a future version of me, Adam. Or at least, he's a possible future version. Call him Tom Waverly Two. Somewhere in the near future, TW Two got himself a fatal dose of radiation. He knew he was dying, and he used the time key to travel into his recent past to try to change things around. He killed a bunch of Eileen Barrie's doppels to stir things up, he got you and Linda involved, and then he killed himself. But in the middle of all that, he also called *me*, too. I'd just stolen the time key and run out on GYPSY, and I was lying low right here in the Nixon sheaf. I'd smoked my trail and made it to a safe house I set up a while back. No one knew where I was. No one but TW Two, that is, because my present was his past. He knew what I'd done and where I was hiding out because he had already done it. He told me what had happened to him: what would happen to *me*, if things weren't fixed. He said that you and Linda would be checking the old dead drop in a few days. From what Linda told me, he went on to the American Bund sheaf, got some medical attention from Freddy Layne's doctor, and killed two more of Eileen Barrie's doppels. And then you caught up with him at Pottersville, and he killed himself."

"Maybe I can believe he was a doppel. But this talk about the future—"

"It's where he came from, Mr. Stone," Linda said. "He travelled from his present, our future, into his past, our present. Just before he killed himself in Pottersville, he told me to find his apartment in the American Bund's version of New York, and to make sure that you came along. He said that he'd hidden something there, that I would know where to look for it, and you would know what it meant. He told me that it would lead to something he had stolen from Operation GYPSY, that it could change history, explain why he'd done what he'd done, and clear his name. He also said—and this is what I didn't tell you at the time—that I would meet him again. He was very emphatic about that. He said that he had travelled into his own past. He said that no matter what happened, I would meet him again."

Stone said, "And you believed him? That's why you came here?"

Linda shook her head. "I believed that he had stolen something. I believed that if I found it, it would help explain where he'd been the past three years, and why he killed those women. I believed it would clear his name. As for the stuff about him coming from the future, and me meeting up with him again . . . He was seriously ill. He was dying. And I thought it had made him delusional. But it turned out that I was wrong. He was telling the truth all along. We followed the trail he left, and it all worked out."

"It worked out so far," Tom said. "He hooked you and Adam up with me. And now we have to go forward."

Linda nodded.

"So you're going to become this guy," Stone said. "Is that what you're telling me? You're going to use the time key, travel back into the past and start killing Eileen Barrie's doppels, and end up in Pottersville."

"Not if I can help it," Tom said. "I'm sure TW Two was a great guy, but as far as I'm concerned he had one very serious flaw. He'd gotten himself a bad dose of radiation, and he was dying from it. I don't intend to make the same mistake. I'm going to break the loop. I'm going to change history."

Tom said it with such solemnity that Stone couldn't help laughing.

"He's serious, Mr. Stone," Linda said. "We're both absolutely serious about this."

"You bet I'm serious," Tom said. "I'm fighting for my life here. And for the life of Susan Nichols, too."

A hot stab of anger cut through Stone's fatigue. "All this craziness about you I can take, but don't for *one fucking minute* joke about that."

Tom didn't even blink. "It's no joke, Adam. I can use the time key to travel into the past. We all can. We can stop everything that's happened before it begins, collapse history in on itself. We can make it so you'll never need to be called out of retirement, you'll stay right there on the farm with Susan Nichols and her kid. And I won't get a lethal dose of radiation and end up killing myself."

"Go fuck yourself, Tom. If you really are Tom. And even if you're not, go fuck yourself anyway."

"I know how you feel, Mr. Stone," Linda said. "I've had a while to work this through, and I'm still having problems coming to terms with it."

"It's real, honey," her father said. "It's real, and we're right in the middle of it."

"You're both crazy," Stone said.

His anger had gone as quickly as it had arrived. All he felt now was a deep, languid weariness; even the pain of his various burns and bruises seemed to have receded to a great distance. When Tom started to explain that they had to get to White Sands and use the time key to travel into the past so that they could do a number on Operation GYPSY, Stone shook his head and said that they could talk about getting back to the Real tomorrow.

"I need to sleep," he said, and lay down and did just that. He woke sometime later to find someone had laid the coverlet over him. Tom sat close to the TV, clicking from channel to channel, the sound turned down to a barely audible murmur.

"You're really here," Stone said.

"Better believe it."

"It's pretty hard to believe, Tom."

"It's like the worm in a bottle of mescal," Tom Waverly said. "You have to swallow it whole."

# 12.

They left the motel at dawn, joining commuter traffic that was already beginning to build up along the Interstate, stopping for breakfast at an International House of Pancakes on the far side of Indianapolis. Everything seemed amazingly normal. Coffee in brown glazed mugs, pats of butter dissolving into transparent grease on blueberry pancakes, brittle strips of Canadian bacon, maple syrup in an aluminium pitcher with a hinged lid. Sunlight burned through the plate-glass windows, gleaming on blond wood and red leatherette banquettes, sharpening the haze of cigarette smoke, gilding ordinary people bent to their ordinary breakfasts, shining on Tom and Linda Waverly as they leaned side by side across the table from Stone, tracing routes on gas station road maps like a pair of regular tourists. For a moment, Stone could believe that this was the only reality, that everything else was a dream.

Back on the Interstate, the station wagon merged with the bunched rush of traffic. Linda drove with a sure, light touch. Her father slouched beside her, his cassette playing on the stereo again. While Dylan sang about a desperado on the run with his woman in the Mexican desert, Stone watched cars go past. Americans on the move, in their natural habitat. A man in a battered pickup with a yellow hard hat sitting on top of the dash. An old woman with a puff-ball of white hair in an enormous powder-blue Cadillac. Kids tussling in the back of a small red car the shape of an inverted bathtub, driven by a woman who showed every day of her life on her face. Two swarthy guys in the cab of a slat-sided truck loaded with orange pumpkins that reminded Stone of the pumpkin patch beside Susan's barn. The memory a little stab in his heart. A barechested black teenager in a rusty brown Toyota, a red handkerchief knotted on his head and one arm hung out of his open window, sped past in a booming blast of music. Look for America? Here it was: passing, repassing, changing lanes, merging, turning off. An unending stream of restless lives. A young woman steering her station wagon with one hand as she touched up her lipstick in the rearview mirror. A businessman in a white shirt and tie driving a black Volkswagen, his suit jacket swinging from a hook behind him like a ghost. . . .

The desperado died in the arms of his woman, hoping that she would escape his fate, giving her his last benediction in Spanish. *Don't cry, my love;*

*God watches over us.* Tom Waverly sang along with the first line of the next song, something about a passport showing a face from another time and place, then turned to look at Stone and said, "That's us, brother. I think we should talk about where we're heading. I tried to tell you last night, but you were pretty much out of it."

"How are you feeling, Mr. Stone?" Linda said, the third or fourth time she'd asked that morning.

"I'm fine. Rested up and ready to go." It was more or less true. His limbs and torso were stiff with bruises and the cigarette burns in his scalp and on his ears had puffed into itchy blisters, but he felt strong and alert. "We're heading for the gate at White Sands," he said. "What happens after that?"

"We're going to take down Operation GYPSY," Tom said.

"I believe you may be too late," Stone said. "There's a big flap right now. No one would come right out and tell me, but from what I've been able to put together, the Company found out about GYPSY and is in the middle of dismantling it."

"Maybe they caught some of the little guys, but I know they didn't touch the main men. And that's where we come in." Tom paused, then said, "Did they tell you what GYPSY was planning to do?"

"I heard it was something to do with assassinating the president."

Tom shook his head. "It's far more serious than that. They were planning—they're still planning—to use the time key to change history and restore the Company to its former glory."

Stone decided to play along with Tom's fantasy, see where it led. "So they're going to send people back in time and assassinate Carter before he assumes office, something like that?"

"Do I detect a mocking tone?"

"I'm interested to see how far you can take this."

"A lot further than mere assassination. GYPSY's game theorists played around with the idea, but it turns out that killing individuals, even presidents, isn't guaranteed to cause any major changes. If you went back a few years and killed Carter, there might still be some kind of investigation similar to the Church Committee, a similar humiliation of the Company, a similar reduction of its influence. No, to really change history, you have to think big. You have to use a much blunter tool than assassination."

"What kind of tool?"

"Nuclear war."

"You're kidding." But Stone remembered that in Pottersville Tom

224

Waverly—the other Tom Waverly, TW Two—had said something about delivering a few good men and a few hundred megatons in the right place. . . .

Linda said, "From what I've been told, it seems to me that GYPSY isn't much different from the covert actions the Company used to be involved in. Like the one you worked on right here, Mr. Stone, or Operation LOOKING GLASS in the American Bund. But rather than supporting opposition movements and using black propaganda and sabotage to destabilise governments, GYPSY planned to travel back in time to known crisis points in the histories of precontact sheaves and use nuclear devices to turn those crises into full-blown wars."

"How would that help the Company?"

"Everyone agrees that we should help out postnuclear sheaves," Tom said. "Especially bleeding-heart liberals like Carter. It's a major part of the Company's work, even now. The idea is, if you go back in time and create enough postnuclear sheaves, the Company would become so strong and influential that no president would ever dare challenge it. Go back in time and change history in just the right way, and there'd be no Church Committee, no black marks on the Company's history, no cutbacks in expansionism. Carter's dismal term of office would never happen, and the Real would keep expanding without interruption, spreading freedom and democracy into every corner of the multiverse."

"Are you saying that these guys were willing to kill millions of people for the sake of the Company?"

"For the sake of life, and liberty, and the pursuit of happiness. Like the old saying goes, after breaking a few eggs, you can't help but make omelettes."

"And you were part of this?"

Stone was beginning to believe that there was a kernel of truth hidden inside this fantasy of time travel and rewriting history. If you had a nuclear bomb and were prepared to use it, you didn't need to go back in time to change history. You could do it right here, right now. Use it to commit some atrocity in the Real, for instance. Blame it on terrorists, stampede the administration into attempting a quick fix by declaring war on dissidents in the Real and in every client sheaf. . . .

"He was blackmailed into helping them," Linda said. "And he got out. He's ready to do the right thing."

"But I need your help," Tom said. "I need you to front for me, Adam. I'm a broke-down renegade with a price on my head, but you're a clean-cut all-

American hero who did the right thing in front of the Church Committee. After we go through the mirror back into the Real, you can give up the time key and explain where to find the men who built GYPSY."

"Dick Knightly recruited you. And he recruited Marsha Mason and Nathan Tate, too. How many of the other cowboy angels are involved? And who are they working for?"

"All in good time, Adam. We're playing for high stakes here. I'm not about to reveal my hole card until I know I can collect the pot. But believe me, if this works out, you'll be instrumental in bringing down the biggest act of treason since Booth shot Lincoln. Carter himself will pin the Distinguished Intelligence Cross on your chest. Hell, they'll probably put up a statue of you right in front of the Allen Dulles Center."

"There's only one reason why I'm going along with this," Stone said. "I want to catch up with the people who sent Marsha Mason into the First Foot sheaf."

"You want revenge for the murder of your woman," Tom said. "I hear that. Well, don't you worry, old buddy. I'll give you that, and a lot more besides."

After they crossed into Missouri, they pulled off the highway and filled the station wagon's gas tank at a service station and bought lunch at a hamburger joint called Big Wendy's. Tom loudly asked the teenage staff behind the counter who Big Wendy was and if he could meet her—he always liked a woman who enjoyed her own cooking. The other customers looked up from their plastic trays of fast food and stared at this big grey-maned maniac; he grinned at them and asked them how they were doing. A little later, after Tom went off to use the restroom, Stone said to Linda, "What did he tell you that he isn't telling me? What's behind this dumb story about time travel?"

"It isn't a dumb story, Mr. Stone. Turing gates access other sheafs, so why can't they access other times, too?"

"I was there at the very beginning of the exploration of parallel universes, Linda. I remember how profoundly it changed everything. After it became possible to move from one universe to another with a single step, nothing was ever the same again. It was like discovering that Earth wasn't the fixed centre of the universe, it revolved around the sun like the other planets. But every sheaf we've ever accessed shares exactly the same time as every other sheaf, down to the nanosecond. Asking me to believe that you can use a Turing gate to step into the past is like expecting me to believe that I can bicycle to the Moon. Or Mars. It's easier to believe that Tom is crazy, or he's lying, or he's laying down a smokescreen. He's spun a very nice story about bringing down GYPSY, but I can't help wondering if he's planning something else. I wish it wasn't so, but there it is. And I think you have your own doubts, too."

"My father isn't lying, Mr. Stone. Maybe he is crazy, just a little, but he's also alive, right here, right now. How do you explain that?"

"Perhaps it was a doppel back in Pottersville. A doppel, or some kind of trick. A setup. Smoke and mirrors."

"You're clutching at straws, Mr. Stone."

Linda was pale and tired. There were dark pouches under her eyes. She'd picked at her hamburger and fries but hadn't eaten very much. Her hand shook when she lifted her paper cup of ice water.

Stone said, "You should rest. Let me take a spell at driving."

"You're in worse shape than me. Besides, I like driving. I'm good at it."

"I noticed that when you came blasting up to rescue me, outside Freddy Layne's club."

It won a small smile from her. Stone said, speaking quickly, knowing that her father would be back at any moment, that he might not get another chance to talk frankly, "He's taking us to White Sands. That part I have no problem with. He doesn't want to use the gate at Grand Central Station and neither do we, because Walter Lipscombe's people will be watching it, and the gate at White Sands is the only other way out of this sheaf. What we have to do before we get there is figure out our next move, so we know what to do when we go back into the Real."

"He's my father, Mr. Stone. Don't try to turn me against him."

"I want to help him, Linda. That's why I came out of retirement in the first place."

"But now all you want is revenge for the murder of your friend. And you think that my father has something to do with it."

Her words stung because they contained more than a grain of truth. "I want to find the people responsible for Susan's murder," Stone said, "and you want to vindicate your father. I don't think those two things are incompatible."

"My father needs your help to change what's going to happen, Mr. Stone. That's why he risked his life to save you from those two gangsters. Please promise me that you'll be patient. Promise me that you'll go along with this, even if you don't believe it."

Her gaze was searching his face, looking for some sign of agreement.

Stone said, "Even if this thing he stole is some kind of time machine—and I don't for one second believe it is—his story doesn't hold up. It's full of holes. For instance, Tom claims that his future self, TW Two, used this thing to go back into the past. He kills Eileen Barrie's doppels and he ends up in Pottersville. Okay, I have no problem with the part about killing Eileen Barrie's doppels because I know that's what happened. But what about the time key? What happened to that? What did he do with it?"

"Dad and I talked about that. We think that TW Two knew he didn't have long to live and didn't want the time key to fall into the wrong hands. So he ditched it."

"He stole something that cost him his life, and he threw it away? I don't think so. My guess is that we didn't find any time key because the doppel we met at Pottersville never had it in the first place."

"You'll see when we get to White Sands," Linda said, and looked up.

Stone turned and saw Tom Waverly walking toward them.

"You two have been talking about me," he said with a grin. "Don't deny it."

"Mr. Stone doesn't quite believe your story," Linda said.

Stone felt a little dip of disappointment, knowing that he'd blown it, he'd gone in too hard, had been too challenging.

"I know he doesn't. But he'll find out soon enough," Tom said. He picked up Linda's cup and drained it, ice cubes rattling against his teeth, and thumped it down on the table. "Let's hit the road."

# 13.

They drove across Missouri. They drove across Oklahoma. They pushed for long hours across the plains of Oklahoma, wind battering the station wagon while tarred cracks in the road raced under its nose like ticker-tape hieroglyphs written by a vanished race to appease their sky-gods. Tom Waverly had bought another cassette at the service station. As they drove through small towns and farmland, Dylan's sly wire-cutter voice hymned lost souls, cowboys, hoboes, and other citizens of a lost, weird republic. Mailboxes stood on planks and posts at intersections with dirt roads that ran out to the flat horizon. Red and silver mailboxes, mailboxes painted with the Stars and Stripes, black mailboxes like little houses of the dead. A ruined farmhouse was stranded like a shipwreck on a rise in the middle of a ploughed field.

Tom and Linda took turns at the wheel. There wasn't much conversation. Stone dozed, or stared out of the window at empty farmland, trying to work out the angles of this thing he'd walked into.

He was pretty sure that the man who'd shot himself in Pottersville had been a doppel. A patsy, a dupe. In the bad old days before the Church Committee, the Company had neutralized especially troublesome individuals in client sheaves by replacing them with compliant doppels; it had been a running joke in Langley that several senators and congressmen in the Real might well be doppels, too. Tom had found out where one of his doppels had lived, so why couldn't he have found another, someone with nothing to lose? As for the time key, it was clearly some kind of experimental device tricked out with a defence mechanism that he'd triggered by accident. He'd been in bad shape after his session with those two sweethearts in the hotel room, the thing had given him an electric shock, and he'd suffered some kind of fit. All the talk about time travel was a smokescreen. What this was, when you got down to it, Stone thought, was a heist, pure and simple. Tom had stolen something valuable and he was trying to figure out what to do next, whether to sell it back to GYPSY or sell it to the Company. Tom was crazed, but he wasn't crazy. There was method to his madness. He had a plan, and Stone and Linda had their parts in it, witting or unwitting.

Well, Tom could spin fantasies of changing history all he liked. Stone would travel with him back into the Real, but he had his own ideas about chasing down the people at the heart of GYPSY. It wouldn't matter if Tom refused to give up their names, because Stone already had a way in. The woman who had developed the time key, or whatever it really was, the woman whose doppels Tom had assassinated. Dr. Eileen Barrie.

Still, as he brooded about what he needed to do and how best to do it, Stone couldn't help remembering the way his hand had cramped around the time key as it opened up like a malignant flower, its seemingly infinite depth and its baleful stars. . . .

They reached the state line late in the afternoon. The road surface changed and a sign informed them that they were entering the Republic of Texas. Linda took the wheel for a spell. A few miles on, Stone saw chickens pecking among the thin grass by the side of the road. As the station wagon slowed to a crawl, he saw chickens on the road, a scatter of broken crates, and a pickup slewed nose-down in a ditch. A chicken flew at the windshield in a panicky whir, bumped against it, and fell away. Chickens strutted away on either side as the station wagon nosed through them. Chickens perched on fence posts. They were scrawny, bedraggled, and mostly white, with scaly legs and red-rimmed eyes and yellow beaks.

"Stop a moment," Stone told Linda. "I'll go check it out."

"Keep moving," Tom said. "This isn't anything to do with us."

"Someone might be hurt," Linda said, and eased the station wagon to a halt.

Stone stepped out into a thin cold wind. The pickup was tilted into the ditch like a sleepy animal. As he walked toward it, a lanky kid in a sheepskin jacket stood up, dusting the seat of his jeans. Chickens stuck their heads through the slats of crates in the pickup's loadbed. An old man slumped in the driver's seat, white hair combed back from a creased brown face that rested at an angle on the steering wheel as if peeking up at the sky.

"He's dead, mister," the kid said. He glanced at Linda, who had climbed out of the station wagon and stood watching them, her red hair flung back by the cold wind that blew from nowhere to nowhere, and added, "Reckon he had himself a heart attack. Can you believe my rotten luck?"

"You found him like this?"

"Mister, I was sitting right beside him when it happened. I was hitching and he gave me a ride. We were talking, this and that, and he all of a sudden started rubbing his left arm. He said it hurt something awful, and then he just laid his head on the steering wheel and died. I tried to grab the wheel, but I was pulling against his weight, and that's how we ended up in the ditch." The kid squinted off into the distance. "Some folks stopped half an hour ago. They said they'd report it to the cops and I should stay here. I guess the cops'll give me a ride into the next town when they're done here."

"Sounds like a plan."

"I guess," the kid said, and kicked at a chicken that had strayed close. It fluttered into the ditch with an indignant squawk. A chicken stood on the roof of the pickup's cab, square above the dead man at the wheel. "I thought I'd save money by hitching home. You believe my luck?"

When Stone climbed into the station wagon Tom said, "Satisfied your curiosity?"

"I had this odd human impulse to help," Stone said.

Linda drove slowly through a thinning tide of chickens.

"You always did have a soft heart," Tom said. "It'll get you into trouble one of these days."

"You know that for a fact?"

"Nothing's certain. If I didn't believe that, I'd just lay down and give myself up to fate."

The land rose in a long sweep. Sparse trees hunched low in the wind, clumps of prickly pear and thorn scrub, scruffy pasture fenced by barbed wire. They drove through a small town in the wake of a thunderstorm, forlorn window-lights scattered on either side of a wide street shining like cold steel under the black sky.

Five or six miles beyond, they pulled in at a two-pump gas station whose raked wooden canopy was crowned by a large sign that claimed this was the last gas for eighty miles. Stone used the restroom at the back of the cinder-block building, then walked past a tow truck and an old car with sun-faded paint and split whitewalls to a cottonwood tree that stood at the edge of a ditch flooded with fast-flowing brown water. Beyond, open country stretched to the horizon.

It was the first time he'd been alone all day. It occurred to him that he could wade or jump the ditch, find a place to hide until night fell, circle back to the town, and make his own way to White Sands. The notion was there and gone, leaving an unsettling sense that he was at the creaking centre of the world's pivot, that each and every footfall could create a new universe.

Stone walked back to the road. Linda was rooting in the ice chest by the office door and Tom was leaning against the flank of the station wagon, asking the old guy pumping gas if there was a good place to stay up ahead, when the windshield starred and a side window blew out. Stone heard the whoop of a spent slug going end over end and dropped to a crouch; then a tire exploded.

Tom was kneeling behind the station wagon now, holding his pistol up by his face. The old guy started toward the office and pirouetted ungracefully and collapsed as the faint crack of the shot that had killed him shivered across the empty landscape. Linda was sprawled flat on her belly by the ice chest. A shot knocked jagged shards from the window behind her and she rolled through the open door.

Stone did a fast crawl on elbows and knees to where Tom knelt.

"I saw a pickup heading off down a track on the far side of the road," Tom said. "He must have parked up and walked back and found a position. Sounds like it's about three or four hundred yards away, and a little to the north and east."

"Just the one guy?"

"I think he saw a chance to hit us and fucked up. Now he'll have to try to keep us pinned down until his friends arrive. You can bet he isn't the only one looking for us."

There was about thirty feet of open ground between the cover of the station wagon and the office. The old man lay there with blood puddling under his head.

Tom shouted to Linda and asked if she was okay.

"I'm fine."

"Keep your head down, honey. I'll deal with this." Tom shucked off his denim jacket, took out the padded envelope that contained the time key, draped the jacket over the nozzle of the gas hose the old guy had dropped, and pushed it out beyond the station wagon's bumper. A few seconds later a round smacked into it and he dropped it and shook his hand, saying, "He's a testy son of a bitch, ain't he?"

"He's definitely shooting to kill."

A car went by on the road, oblivious to the drama.

"He thought he could ambush us and take the time key all by himself, which means he's either inexperienced or a fool," Tom said. "What's in back? Can we get out that way?"

"We'd have to wade a ditch, and then there's nothing but open country. He may be a fool, but he picked a good spot for an ambush."

"We can't sit here. Want to give me some covering fire?"

"I've got a better idea. Give me that hose."

A round smacked into the side of the station wagon when Stone opened the door. He crouched as low as he could and wet down the front seat, the cold air suddenly full of the sweet reek of gasoline.

"I see your plan," Tom said. "But how are we going to get out of here?"

"There's a tow truck in back," Stone said. "Or we could always take the shooter's pickup."

He flooded the concrete apron under and around the station wagon, the gasoline flowing thin and quick and silvery, spreading past the body of the old man. Then he and Tom crawled backward on their bellies, and Tom took out a book of matches and scratched one into flame and set fire to the matchbook and tossed it under the station wagon. The gasoline ignited with a solid thump and then the station wagon and the two pumps were standing in a sea of bright flames that licked up higher than the top of the canopy.

Stone and Tom scrambled to their feet and ran to the office, keeping low behind the wall of flame. As Stone dived through the door a round struck the ice chest and made its lid jump. A moment later, the station wagon's gas tank cracked open and a fireball rolled up into the darkening sky and a pulse of fierce heat washed through the little office.

Tom was crouched beside Linda on broken glass to one side of the shot-out window. He grinned at Stone and said, "Pretty good for a couple of old men."

Stone drew his pistol. "If it's just one guy waiting for reinforcements, I'm willing to go after him. But I'll need you to furnish some kind of distraction."

"Use the tow truck?"

"That's what I'm thinking. Start it up, put it in drive, let it roll forward."

"And you break out in the opposite direction."

"I can follow the ditch and then circle around."

"How are you going to spot him?"

"You might want to let off a few shots in his general direction. It's growing dark. I should be able to spot his muzzle flash."

"If you two old men want to know where he is," Linda said, "why don't you ask me?"

While Stone and her father had been pinned down she'd found a pair of binoculars in the office desk and had glassed the landscape, spotting movement behind rocks and brush about three hundred yards northeast of the road. Stone took a quick peek, saw where she meant, and said, "It's definitely doable."

"Just like old times," Tom said.

"No kidding."

"I hope your stupid machismo doesn't get you killed," Linda said.

"We can't sit here," Stone said. "The storage tank could blow at any moment, and the sniper's friends must be on their way."

"Not to mention the local law," Tom told Linda. "Don't worry, honey. This is what we used to do for a living."

They ducked through the rear of the office into a small untidy room with an unmade bed, a sagging armchair, and a strong smell of the old man, then went through the back door. Stone crabbed along the margin of the ditch, keeping low. When he heard the sound of an engine turning over, he glanced back at the gas station. The station wagon was on fire from stem to stern and the canopy and its sign were burning too, tossing flames and smoke into the darkening sky. Behind the cinder-block building, the tow truck ponderously rolled away into the open ground beyond. There was the faint crack of a shot, then another. Stone jumped up and raced through scrub, his bruised legs stiff as posts, crossed the road in four long strides, vaulted the barbed wire fence, and threw himself flat among tufts of grass, his pulse pounding in his head, his breath raw in his throat.

Just like old times. Absolutely goddamn right.

Pasture stretched to the low horizon where the little town's spread of lights shimmered. Lone trees crouched here and there. Stone moved forward in little rushes, pausing behind patches of scrub or sprawling in cold dirt, working toward the clump of rocks and brush that Linda had pointed out.

He was about fifty yards away when he heard two shots from the direction of the gas station, then two more. He ran flat out, circling around the rocks, and a man sprang up not twenty feet away, raising a rifle to his shoulder, snapping off a shot that parted the air close to Stone's head. Stone braced and aimed and fired two quick shots. The man dropped and Stone charged forward, crashing through the brush with his pistol extended.

The man had fallen against a rock, slumped sideways with his head tipped back and his legs sprawled in front of him. His shirt and the waistband of his khaki pants were wet with blood. One hand curled in his lap and the other was outflung as if reaching for the rifle that lay a yard away. He wasn't much older than Linda, staring sightlessly as Stone stepped toward him and touched the side of his neck, finding blood there but no pulse.

*

"Pretty good shooting, for an old man," Tom Waverly said, when he and Linda reached the sniper's position. "Any idea who he is?"

Stone showed him the gleanings from the dead man's pockets: a pack of cigarettes and a disposable lighter, a roll of bills, a New Mexico driver's licence with a name and an address that were almost certainly false, and a set of car keys.

Tom weighed the keys in the palm of his hand. "Where's his ride?"

"All we have to do is follow the track," Linda said, and pointed north.

The pickup sat in a dip in the ground a little way down the track. It had Texas plates and a crew cabin and was brand-new, with that new-car smell and fewer than five hundred miles on the odometer.

"He didn't follow us from New York," Tom said. "They must have figured where we're headed and strung themselves out along the likely routes."

"It isn't hard to figure out where we're going," Stone said. "There are only two gates in this sheaf; all they have to do is wait for us to turn up at one or the other. Was he working for GYPSY, or is someone else looking for you?"

"It's all under control, Adam."

"All I have to do is trust you, is that it?"

"Don't sull up on me. If we're gonna get through this, we need some of that old team spirit."

"When where you ever part of a team?"

Linda was looking toward the distant flicker of the burning gas station. "I think I heard a siren," she said. "We should get going."

"We have to get rid of his body," Stone said. "We don't want the local cops finding out he's the exact double of someone."

Linda drove the pickup back down the track, and Stone and Tom Waverly lifted the dead man between them and laid him in the loadbed. Blue lights small as stars prickled near the pyre of the gas station. The two men climbed inside the pickup and Linda swung it around and drove off across the dark land toward the last of the sunset.

# 14.

After night overtook them, they drove by the scant light of a sickle moon, headlights off, bumping slowly over rocky ground as they picked a way through gaps in rolling ridges and followed the flat land between. When they reached a dry river bed that ran between stands of small juniper trees, Stone got out and walked beside the pickup, guiding it down the rough slope. It took them an hour to dig a shallow pit, loosening sand and gravel with the handle of the pickup's jack and scooping it out with their hands. They buried the man with his rifle and covered the mound with flat rocks and Linda said a few words over the grave while Stone and Tom Waverly stood with their heads bowed. They shared water from a plastic bottle lodged in the well of the driver's door, slept as best they could in the crew cabin, and set off again in the grey light before dawn, soon striking a ranch road that led south to a paved highway.

They abandoned the pickup in Amarillo, washed up and breakfasted on huevos rancheros in a Mexican greasy spoon, stole a green four-door Oldsmobile from the employees' section of a supermarket parking lot, and headed west along the I-40, passing through the Pecos into New Mexico, and taking the I-25 south toward Las Cruces. The sky shimmered blue and cloudless above bluffs of red rock and slumped fans of rubble where little grew but ocotillo and catclaw. The muddy Rio Grande snaked close to the road and bent away again.

Stone was jittery with anticipation and lack of sleep. His bruises and burns had kept him awake most of the night, and the miasma of a dream still clung to him. He'd been walking down a road that cut through vague, dark countryside and someone had been walking behind him. He could feel the warmth of her presence like sunshine on his back, but knew that if he looked around she would no longer be there. And so he kept walking through the darkness until he reached a crossroads, turned to ask which way he should go, and found that he was alone.

A dry wind was blowing through Las Cruces. Dust from Mexico hazed the air above the low buildings and left the taste of iron in Stone's mouth. Tom Waverly purchased a road map, bottles of water, and a bottle of Jack Daniel's at a general store with bars across its window and gang signs spray-painted on its walls. They ate tacos at a roadside stand hung with *ristras* of red chillies, then found a gun shop, a small place with an old-fashioned glass counter and the heads of antelope, mule deer, and a single mountain lion arrayed on its whitewashed adobe walls. They bought a twelve-gauge Winchester pump-action shotgun and boxes of double-ought buckshot shells and ammunition for their pistols, .38 hollowpoints and .45 ACP hardball loads. The clerk told them that they would need a licence if they were going after antelope and Tom gave the guy a shit-eating grin and said that they were planning to shoot rock doves.

"You'd be better off with number four birdshot," the clerk said. "That double-ought will shred a bird."

"We plan to kill 'em, not eat 'em," Tom said.

Back in the hot, stuffy car, he unfolded the map and started to show Linda where the gate was.

"I know," she said. She was tired and tense, and had been quiet for most of the day. "Mr. Stone told me all about it. There's a turnoff twenty-one point eight miles west of Alamogordo, marked by a mailbox painted red. A track leads to a cabin, and the gate is set among rocks about a mile to the south."

"The duty caretaker is one of GYPSY's people," Tom said, folding up the map. "We'll have to deal with him."

Stone said, "There may be more than one guy. By now, they must know we killed one of theirs."

"I guess there's only one way to find out," Tom said. "Let's hit the road. We've got some ground to cover. The gate opens at exactly six p.m. and stays open for just ten minutes. If we miss it, we'll have to spend a whole day hiding out in the desert before it opens again, and meanwhile our friends will be doing their best to hunt us down."

They drove through a pass in stark mountains to the desert plain spread beyond. The sun burned white through a haze of dust. Sheets of dust blew across the road and laid a fine mantle on the windshield. Broken glass glinted along the margin of the two-lane blacktop, mile after mile. They passed a military base with decommissioned missiles aimed at the sky on either side of the gate in its chain-link fence and drove through the little desert settlement of Point of Sands. When a bullet-riddled marker for Alamogordo appeared, Tom told his daughter to pull off the road. He jumped out as soon as the car had stopped and raised the hood.

"Linda will make like a damsel in distress. When the local law comes by to help her out, we take their cruiser. Then we ride up to that cabin, and when the bad guys come out to see what the local law wants, we'll draw down on them and let them know what's what."

Stone squinted in the hot whip of the wind. "Suppose the local cops don't come by?"

"Then we'll go find them," Tom said, and took a swig from his bottle of Jack Daniel's. "But trust me, we won't need to."

"Because it's supposed to happen? Because this is what's predestined?"

"Don't be sarcastic, Mr. Stone," Linda said. "It doesn't suit you."

"You still don't believe me," Tom said. "I don't mind, because I know that in a few hours you'll be singing a different tune. You'll be begging me to help your woman."

"Susan is dead, you son of a bitch. Nothing can help her now."

Stone knew that he shouldn't have let the jibe get to him, but he was tired, he was worried that he still hadn't figured out Tom's game, and he knew that he couldn't expect any help from Linda, who was clearly taking her father's side. He had to step hard on the impulse to put his pistol in Tom's face and have it out there and then; if he was going to get back to the Real, he had to pretend to go along with his old friend's plan, even it was dangerously cockeyed and probably hid some devious stratagem which almost certainly hinged on using him as a patsy.

Tom must have read Stone's intention in his gaze or his body language. He smiled and said, "You think you can take me, Adam?"

"Is it going to come to that?"

Linda said, "It looks like someone's heading this way. You two old men will have to work off your excess testosterone some other time."

Stone looked around and saw in the far distance a glittering dot bobbing in the glassy heat shimmering off the road.

"We aren't done with this," he said.

"Maybe not, but we're getting close."

Stone and Tom Waverly hid inside a circle of creosote bushes and watched the glimmering dot resolve into a battered pickup. It pulled up beside the green Oldsmobile and its driver, a lean young man with a high-crowned straw hat set square on his thickly greased black hair, got out and talked with Linda. Both of them looked under the raised hood; Linda shook her head as if refusing some offer; the driver touched the brim of his hat with thumb and forefinger and got back in his pickup and drove off toward Alamogordo.

"Won't be long now," Tom said.

He unbuckled his belt, pulled half of it out of the loops of his jeans, and began to strop the blade of his knife against it. The shotgun lay beside him, a plastic bag knotted over its muzzle so that sand wouldn't get in the barrels.

Linda sat on a ridge of dirt by the car. Stone saw a greasy flash of sunlight on plastic when she took a swig from a bottle of water. He took a long drink from his own bottle and said, "Even if we manage to get hold of a cop's car, do you really think driving up to the gate in it will give us an edge?"

"The people guarding the gate may be working for GYPSY, but they're also Company people," Tom said, intent on his work with the knife. "And it's still standard operating procedure to keep on the right side of the local law in uncontacted sheaves. We can ride right up to the place in a cop car, and get the jump on them before they realise who we really are."

"Then what? What's supposed to happen when we go through the gate and get back to the Real?"

"You mentioned predestination just now. Do you believe in it? Do you think we're no more than robots, acting out parts already written for us?"

"Of course not. If we didn't have free will, if we didn't make choices that mattered, choices that really changed things one way or the other, there would only be one sheaf."

"Exactly." Tom raised his knife and studied the edge of its blade. "It's because our choices can make a difference that nothing about the future is certain. And if the future isn't fixed, neither is the past. If you could travel back in time, you could change things around. You could fix all your mistakes."

"That's a fantasy, Tom."

Tom slipped the knife into its sheaf and buckled his belt. "I plan to blow GYPSY wide open and bring the people in charge of it to justice. I plan to make sure that I don't get a fatal dose of radiation and don't set off to kill those doppels of Eileen Barrie. And if I'm successful, you'll stay on your farm in that backwater sheaf, Adam, and never get involved in any of this."

"The problem is that I *am* involved," Stone said.

"You're involved because good old TW Two knows that I need your help to change things. He sacrificed himself, Adam, so that I would have the chance to live through this. I aim to make sure that he didn't die in vain."

"According to you, we wouldn't be here unless, sometime in the near future, you get a fatal dose of radiation, travel back in time and tell your own past self what to do, go on to murder Eileen Barrie's doppels, and end up in

Pottersville. So if we change things, there'll be no TW Two, he won't travel into his past and tell you what to do, and none of this will have happened."

"Time travel doesn't only create a new history; it also creates a new sheaf. If things work out, we'll end up in a different sheaf living through an entirely different history where none of the unpleasant stuff has to happen." Tom smiled and shook his head. "Will you listen to us? Two old-school snake-eating cowboy angels arguing about metaphysics. How did it ever come to this?"

"I guess you're the one with all the answers."

"I guess I am."

They sat quietly for a few minutes. At last, Tom looked up and cupped a hand to one ear. "Hear that? Pretty good response time, don't you think?"

Stone crouched beside him in the creosote bushes and watched as a police cruiser drove out of the haze of blowing dust and shimmering air and pulled off the road in front of the Oldsmobile. A solidly built sheriff's deputy climbed out, set a Stetson on his head, and exchanged a few words with Linda before taking a look at the Oldsmobile's engine. When Stone and Tom stepped onto the road, pistols drawn, the deputy studied them from beneath the brim of his hat, sizing them up calmly, telling them that they'd just entered a world of trouble unless they put the guns right away.

Tom said, "There won't be any unpleasantness as long as you do what I say. We clear on that?"

The deputy looked at him, then turned his head and spat on the road.

Tom told him to take out his revolver and toss it into the creosote bushes, then said that they were going to take a walk off to the side of the road.

"You don't have to worry about me, mister," the deputy said. "I'm not about to try anything dumb."

"We aren't going to do anything dumb either," Stone said, as much for Tom's benefit as the deputy's, and followed the two men into the brush.

Fifty yards in, Tom told the deputy to take off his tunic. "The hat too."

"Was a gift from my wife," the deputy said as he handed it over. "Take good care of it."

"Sit down and put your hands to the back of your head," Tom said.

He cuffed the deputy and told him to keep his head down or he was liable to get it blown off. Back on the road, he pulled the keys from the Oldsmobile's ignition and threw them into the bushes, then shrugged off his jacket, put on the deputy's khaki tunic, and swept up his hair and set the Stetson on his head.

Stone said, "The guy will walk out into the road as soon as we're gone, and flag down the first vehicle that comes along."

"You're probably right," Tom said, smiling his sly smile. He checked his watch and took a swig from the bottle of Jack Daniel's. "You ride shotgun, Adam. Put on your jacket and tie and try to look like the hard-ass government agent you used to be. In this tunic and shit-kicker hat, I reckon I stand a good chance of being mistaken for a local law enforcement officer who found you wandering in the desert."

"You think the bad guys will buy a story as lame as that?"

"It'll give us about thirty seconds. All the time in the world to do what needs to be done." Tom took another swallow of whiskey and said to Linda, "This could get messy. Are you ready for that?"

She gave a tight nod, straight up and down, and said, "Are you sure the people guarding the gate work for GYPSY?"

"I give you my word. They stand between us and where we need to go and what we need to do, so we have to deal with them."

"If we're going to do it, let's do it properly," Stone said. "Lose the whiskey, Tom. You don't need Dutch courage."

"You don't know what I need," Tom said. "Take the shotgun and lay down in the back seat of this fine law-enforcement automobile, honey," he told Linda. "We have to get moving."

Tom drove at high speed toward Alamogordo and after a few miles swung the cruiser past a mailbox on a post, scarcely slowing. The rear end of the heavy vehicle shimmied, raising a cloud of dust; then Tom had it under control and they were roaring along a track that climbed a long slope of scrub and stony sand.

The caretaker's shack was built of weathered grey planking, with a slanting tin roof weighted with rocks. A fantail windmill turned atop a wooden tower. The cruiser skidded to a halt on the rutted dirt in front, next to a brand-new pickup truck that still had the dealer's sticker in its rear window. Tom took out his pistol and worked the slide, then sounded the horn. Telling Stone, "Leave the first move to me."

Stone squeezed down his nerves and found the still, cold place in his head that allowed him to sit calmly, watching through the dusty windshield as two men came out of the shack. One hung back by the door while the other, a muscular young guy in desert camo combat pants and a cut-off T-shirt, ambled toward the cruiser, his thumbs stuck in his beltloops. Tom Waverly cranked down the window and the man looked in at him with a kind of amiable arrogance and asked if there was a problem.

Tom jerked a thumb at Stone and said, "Know this fellow?"

The man stooped to peer at Stone and Tom rammed his pistol into the soft flesh under his chin and shot him. A bloody fog burst from the top of his head and he collapsed backward. The man in the doorway of the shack reached behind himself and pulled out a pistol. Tom shot at him and missed, and Linda sat up and stuck the shotgun through the back window and fired both barrels, the noise incredibly loud inside the cruiser, and the man was knocked on his back, the plank wall on either side of the doorway gouged and splintered by shot.

Stone pushed out of the cruiser and ran to where the second man lay twitching on the dirt. He clutched his chest with both hands, blood welling up over his fingers. Blood bubbled from his mouth and there were holes ripped in his throat and face. Stone kicked his pistol away and stepped over him and checked the shack's single room, pointing his own pistol left and right, high and low. His heart was beating strongly in his chest and he felt as if he was at the centre of a humming calm. Everything—cards abandoned on the table, disordered bunk beds, dust motes floating in sunlight that burned through a window—stood out with extraordinary particularity.

Tom came up behind him, breathless, grinning like a maniac. He'd taken off the Stetson and his grey hair hung around his face. The bottle of Jack Daniel's was clutched in one fist, his pistol in the other. He stooped over the man, lifted his head by the hair, and asked him who had sent him, who he'd reported to. But the man was dead. Tom went through his pockets and found a walkie-talkie. He switched it on and held it by his ear, listening to the voice that whispered from it, smiling at Stone.

"This guy is worried about his friends. He heard the shots, isn't sure what happened," Tom said, and mashed the walkie-talkie's *speak* button. "Here's some breaking news, pal. You're in deep shit. Your friends are dead, and pretty soon we're coming up there for you."

Stone said, "Where is he? Up by the gate?"

"You bet. Don't you worry, partner, this is all going *exactly* to plan."

Tom walked back to the police cruiser and hugged Linda and told her that she'd done the right thing, he wanted her to know that he was proud of her.

She pulled away from him and said, "You didn't have to shoot him."

"Yes, I did. I couldn't risk overpowering him because his friend would have started shooting at us. It's hard, but there it is."

"Tell me one thing, and don't lie. You knew the deputy would come and check me out. Did you know that we'd have to kill these men, too?"

"I hoped it wouldn't come to it. I swear to God. But as soon as they both walked out, I knew there wasn't any other way."

"Are we going to make it through?"

"Of course we are. If you're up to it, I'd like you to walk up to that ridge," Tom said, "and keep watch on the road. A bunch of cops will be coming along any moment now, and I need to know when they show."

"You were told about that, too, I suppose."

Tom shook his head. "I'm about to tell them where to find us. Walk up there and keep watch, okay?"

Linda stared at him, a muscle jumping in her jaw. Then she snatched the bottle of Jack Daniel's from his hand and took a long drink. She wiped her mouth with the back of her hand, handed the bottle back to her father, pulled the shotgun from the back seat of the cruiser, and walked off.

Stone watched her go. He felt as if he had just seen something fine and precious smashed to pieces.

Tom lifted the radio handset from its cradle under the cruiser's dashboard and told the dispatcher there was trouble out at the Anderson place. "The property just past mile twenty, you know it?" he said. "We have two men down, looks like there's gonna be a third before too long. No, ma'am, your deputy is hogtied a ways down the road. I'm one of the bad guys who stole his cruiser and shot those poor men dead. If you want to bring me to justice, you should send your best men out here."

"Was that necessary?" Stone said.

"You've been in plenty of bad situations. You know it was."

"I don't mean the theatrics. I mean was it necessary to involve your daughter?"

"We're all in this together," Tom said, as he took off the uniform tunic. "The law should be here in ten or fifteen minutes. It's five forty now, and the gate opens at six. We're cutting it close, but I reckon we'll do it."

"If you really are Tom Waverly, something really bad must have happened to you. Because the Tom Waverly I knew would never have used his daughter like that."

"I didn't see you stepping in to help."

"I didn't know you were planning to shoot those two. And don't tell me you had to. You knew you were going to do it all along."

"I guess it's knowing what will happen to me if I fail that makes me a hard-ass," Tom said. He pulled on his denim jacket and walked past Stone and shaded his eyes, looking across the desert panorama. "They test missiles out there, the kind that carry nuclear warheads. A little further north is the spot where they exploded the first atom bomb in this sheaf, the prototype of the two bombs they dropped on Japan to end their version of World War Two. Funny, isn't it, how history can work out so differently in different sheaves, yet some things always stay the same? The equivalent of the CIG in this sheaf, the CIA, has its headquarters at Langley, just like the Company. Hell, its officers even call it the Company."

"I know."

"We stole the idea of memorialising our dead with a Wall of Honor from them, did you know that? Ideas go back and forth, histories bleed into each other through the gates, grow more and more alike. Maybe one day every history will collapse into every other history, and we'll end up with just one sheaf."

"I'm not in the mood for barroom philosophy, Tom."

"Do you think that meta-sheaf would feature the best of every history, or the worst? Think about it," Tom said, and walked a little way up the slope and used the walkie-talkie, goading the man at the gate, telling him he'd better get ready, he'd soon have to make a hard decision.

Linda stood some way off, cradling the shotgun as she stared toward the road. Stone decided that it would be better to leave her alone and squatted in shade cast by the cruiser, brushing flies from his face. The windmill made an arthritic creak as it turned in the erratic wind. A hollow feeling grew in his chest as the time at which the gate would open drew closer.

At last, Linda turned to her father and called out. "Here they come!"

Stone got to his feet and saw two cruisers chasing each other along the road, light bars flashing. They were two or three miles off, coming on fast. Tom Waverly took a drink of Jack Daniel's and tossed the bottle to one side and said it was time they dealt with the guy who stood between them and the gate.

They climbed into the pickup truck and Tom drove it up the stony slope toward a line of tall rocks that in the light of the setting sun glowed blood-red against the pale sky like a palisade hammered into the earth by aboriginal giants. There was a notch between two of them, a track wandering into

244

its vee of deep shadow. Tom steered the pickup off-road, jolting through scrub, pulling up to one side of the notch.

Downslope, the two cruisers were wallowing up the track toward the shack, a cloud of dust boiling behind them.

Tom Waverly used the walkie-talkie again. "Take a look downhill, why don't you? I bet you can see that the local cops have come to check things out. You're in big trouble, pal. My advice is you pull out before they get hold of you." He paused while the walkie-talkie squawked, then said, "Maybe you can kill 'em all, but then what? You gonna be able to wait around here until the gate opens tomorrow? You'll have to make a run for it, and we're waiting right outside. As soon as you put your head out we'll shoot it off."

Deputies were moving around the shack. Stone saw two of them run to one of the cruisers. He saw it dig out in a cloud of dust and accelerate up the slope toward them. "We've got about a minute here," he said.

Tom Waverly checked his watch and said into the walkie-talkie, "The gate just now opened, didn't it? Here's your choice. You can go through, or you can stay and hope to convince the local law of your innocence. But if you choose to stay here, you should know we're gonna surrender to the cops and tell them everything we know."

Stone saw two quick flashes in the darkness beyond the gap in the rocks and heard the hard noise of the shots echoing off the rocks. Tom stepped from the cover of the pickup and fired his pistol toward the gap, yelling, "You want some? Get some! Get some right here!"

He fired until the pistol's clip was empty and ducked behind the pickup again. A few hundred yards downslope, the cruiser swerved to a halt and the two deputies scrambled out on either side, crouching behind the notional cover of its splayed doors.

Tom jammed a fresh clip into his pistol and thumbed the walkie-talkie. "You got six minutes before the gate goes down and you got yourself a siege with us *and* the local law. Yeah? We'll see about that."

He tossed the walkie-talkie away and said, "He's going through. Says he'll be waiting for us on the other side. If only he knew."

The two deputies were coming up the slope toward them, making broken runs from bush to rock to bush.

Stone said, "Where are we going?"

"Through the mirror," Tom said, and pulled the envelope from his denim jacket and took out the pale green oblong of the time key.

Even though the thing wasn't switched on, Stone took a step backward.

Downslope, one of the deputies shouted a warning. Tom and Linda took off, and Stone ran after them. He had a bad moment when they ducked into the notch, thinking that the man guarding the gate could have been bluffing when he'd said he was going through, but the narrow cleft was empty and lit by the silver light of the gate, a circular mirror eight feet across that blocked the far end.

Tom Waverly took out a scrap of paper and handed it to Linda. She read out a string of letters and numbers and he poked at the face of the time key with his forefinger, the tip of his tongue caught between his lips. Stone watched this charade with mounting impatience, but he wasn't about to step through the gate on his own. The man who'd been guarding it would be waiting on the other side, and besides, he had to see where Tom was going with this.

"We've got about two minutes," Linda said.

"I have to get this right," Tom said, and green light suddenly struck up from the time key, turning his face into a jack o'lantern.

Stone felt as if a nail had been hammered into his forehead. A nail driven in right between his eyes, whacking through bone, jolting inch by inch into his brain.

From a great distance, Tom said, "Oh man. It really has it in for you."

The nail went in with hard sharp jolts, no end to it. With each blow, Stone's pulse pumped blood into his skull like air into a beach ball. His sight went black and he fell to his knees.

Tom pulled him up. They took a step together, and another. Stone saw through fluttering shadows their reflections stumbling toward him in the gate's mirror. Tom was aiming the time key at the gate with his free hand. A flat rock formed a step in front of the gate. Stone lost his balance as Tom hauled him onto it. He tumbled forward and the black flash of transition drove the nail clean through him.

# Part Three

# A HIGHWAY BACK TO YOU

# 1.

Half blind, punch-drunk, Stone managed to stagger halfway down the metal ramp on the other side of the mirror before his feet tangled with each other and he fell to his hands and knees. His pistol skittered away, fresh pain exploded inside his head, and his stomach twisted inside out and he threw up.

Linda and Tom Waverly stepped around him, aiming their weapons at shadows. As Stone coughed and spat and blinked back tears, Tom scooped up his pistol and said, "Like it or not, you're a bona fide time traveller now, Adam. When this is over, I'll write you out a certificate. You too, honey."

"Are you sure it worked?" Linda said.

"Take a look at the gate and tell me it didn't."

Something appalling was happening to the Turing gate. Instead of simply blinking out, its silver disk was receding down a dimension at right angles to everything else, falling away into a great distance, dwindling into a star, a spark, a speck, a mote. . . .

The hammering pain in Stone's head diminished to no more than an ordinary headache. He managed to get to his feet. It hurt a lot and his stomach performed an ominous backflip, but he managed it. He was standing in front of the black maw of the dead gate, at one end of a low-ceilinged bunker lit by a string of dim bulbs. There were two desks of quiescent electronics and a row of metal lockers, but no sign of the man who had fled through the gate ahead of them. Maybe he'd figured that three on one were bad odds, and had run off, Stone thought. But where were the gate technicians?

Linda was asking him if he was okay.

"I've had better days. Are *you* okay?"

She gave a tight little nod and said, "This is *where* we're supposed to be. What we have to do now is find out if it's *when* we're supposed to be."

"Three weeks in the past, you better believe it," Tom Waverly called out.

He was doing something to the key-operated switch box to one side of the bunker's big steel door. After a moment, the motor engaged and the door rolled back. Stone followed Linda across the bunker. He had to stop and lean against one of the control desks for a moment, and knocked a coffee mug and a slew of pens and pencils to the floor when he pushed away.

Out through the square doorway, into simmering desert night.

The bunker was one of more than a dozen dug into the top of a low ridge. Beyond the edge of the service road, the lights of the White Sands interchange stretched for miles across the desert basin. It contained the largest concentration of Turing gates on the planet, more than two hundred, serviced by three railroad marshalling yards and a dozen freight depots and passenger stations. There was an airport, two solar power plants, three nuclear power stations, six wind farms. There were hotels and military barracks, hangars and factories. Water was supplied through a dozen pipeway gates that accessed lakes in wild sheaves where the climate was warmer and wetter. There were eight hospitals, with a combined capacity of six thousand beds. Canteens with a total floor area of two square miles served more than a hundred thousand meals each day to troops and support and aid-agency personnel passing through the gates, as well as feeding the technicians, railroad workers, and ancillary staff who operated the interchange, and the soldiers responsible for its security.

All of this was laid out in nets and chains and deltas of lights beneath a sodium-orange sky where attack helicopters constantly shuttled back and forth as they monitored the trains passing in and out of the gates. Traffic flowed in opposing streams of red taillights and white headlights along broad highways that linked the marshalling yards and their service areas.

Stone was having trouble thinking around the steady pulse of his headache, but he knew that his sense of time was out of joint. Every sheaf shared the same clock time, but although the sun had been setting when he'd stepped out of the Nixon sheaf, it was long past sunset here, in the Real. Maybe I passed out, he thought, as he followed Linda and Tom Waverly past shuttered bunkers and a reef of shipping containers. I passed out, and Tom shot the guy who went through ahead of us, chased off the gate technicians, hid the guy's body. . . .

Tom said, "How are you holding up, Adam? Don't you go dying on me."

"I don't plan to," Stone said.

"Good man. You believe me now?"

"Go easy, Dad," Linda said. "That thing really hurt him."

"He has to get with the programme," Tom said.

"Maybe you should tell me what the programme is," Stone said.

"I already told you. I'm going to put a stop to everything before it has a chance to begin. I'm going to take down GYPSY and make sure no one involved in it escapes justice. I'm going to avenge my own death by making sure it doesn't happen."

Tom Waverly was pumped up, manically exuberant; Stone knew that there was no point arguing with him when he got like this. Look at him now, swaggering down the middle of the road, making extravagant gestures as he told Linda that they were definitely off the map, that they had freed themselves from the inevitable, that anything was possible. It was as if he really believed his bullshit story.

The road switchbacked down the flank of the ridge and passed through a small chemical depot: a cluster of silvery tanks with insulated pipelines running between them, a skinny aluminium chimney pumping white vapour high into floodlit air, a prefabricated office building with a Jeep parked to one side.

Tom took the shotgun from Linda, saying that he didn't want to have to explain it to perimeter security, and tossed it in a Dumpster and dropped Stone's Colt in after it.

"What about your pistol?" Stone said. He didn't like the way that Tom had more or less bushwhacked him and taken charge of the situation.

"We need some insurance. Think you can hot-wire that Jeep, honey?"

Linda didn't need to; the keys were in the ignition. As they drove away downhill, Tom rapped the dashboard clock with his knuckles and told Stone with a sly grin that everything was looking good.

According to the clock, it was twenty after eleven. Stone had lost five hours somewhere.

They drove past a railroad yard where long rakes of passenger cars stood side by side, and took an on-ramp onto a busy eight-lane highway. Tom fiddled with the Jeep's radio, surfing through civilian and military stations, through snatches of rock, country, and gospel music, then switched it off and told Linda to take the next exit. The off-ramp looped under the highway to a road that ran between trenches and fields of concertina wire and tank traps, past spotlit billboards that warned of minefields and the use of terminal force against intruders, to a plaza where soldiers with lightsticks directed traffic toward a dozen brilliantly lit checkpoints. Snipers were posted in watchtowers above each checkpoint and armed soldiers patrolled the lines of vehicles waiting to go through. Atop a hundred-foot flagpole, a big Stars and Stripes fluttered in the electric glow of crossing spotlights.

Tom told Linda to stay calm, it was only a routine security check. "It's three weeks before you and Adam were brought into this, and I have good cover—a security adviser who passes through here all the time. But just to be on the safe side, you two should use those fake army IDs Walter Lipscombe gave you," he said, and turned to look at Stone and asked him if he was going to behave.

"I want to see where you're going with this," Stone said.

"I expect you do," Tom Waverly said, and tucked his pistol under his thigh.

When they reached the checkpoint, a sergeant in combat fatigues downloaded data from their ID cards to his palmtop while another soldier used a mirror mounted on a pole to scrutinize the underside of the Jeep.

Tom said, "I'd appreciate it if you could move us right through. I need to get these two debriefed, and my friend in back is in need of some medical attention."

"You might want to turn around," the sergeant said. "There's a clinic a couple of miles along the east perimeter highway where the colonel can get himself fixed up."

"Thanks for the advice, but I prefer to use my own people."

For a moment, the sergeant looked as if he might say something else, but then he handed over the IDs and the steel barrier dropped into its slot. Linda drove the Jeep through the checkpoint, and Tom told her to take the highway toward downtown Alamogordo.

"Where exactly are we going?"

"To see a friend of mine. Everything will become clear when we get there. Meanwhile, you'll just have to trust your father. Will you do that for me?"

"I wouldn't be here if I didn't trust you."

"We're almost there, honey. I promise. How about you, Adam? Tell me that you're not going to give me any trouble. Tell me that you're going to trust me to do the right thing."

Stone was feeling a lot better now—his nausea had passed and the rush of warm dry air was blowing away his headache—but he figured that it wouldn't hurt to let Tom think that he was still woozy, and said that as far as he was concerned finding a doctor wasn't a bad idea.

"We don't have time," Tom Waverly said. "You'll just have to hang in there, old buddy."

"You could at least stop someplace and get me a bottle of painkillers," Stone said. "I lost all my stuff when the station wagon went up."

Despite Tom Waverly's bragging, despite the clock on the Jeep's dash, Stone didn't believe that the so-called time key had taken them back three minutes, much less three weeks. He knew that perimeter security at White Sands had a hot link with the Company's network and knew that the scan of the biometrics encoded in his fake ID would sooner or later ring bells with Ralph Kohler's people. It was possible that Kohler would order local agents to put a moving tail on them to begin with, to see where they were heading and if they were going to meet up with anyone from GYPSY. But it was also possible that Kohler would have them arrested straightaway, and if that happened, Stone would lose his chance to track down the people who had ordered Susan's murder. And besides, he was tired of jumping when Tom Waverly said jump. He was tired of being drip-fed information that was ninety percent bullshit. It was time to break free of Tom and Linda Waverly's *folie à deux*, and make some moves of his own.

They drove down the Strip, the long six-lane street that ran through the heart of Alamogordo, where a dozen histories and pop cultures collided in a flood of neon signs and the clashing pulses of music pumped from car stereos and the open doors of bars and casinos. Stone counted three places advertising floor shows featuring the genuine Elvis—all of them no doubt doppels, press-ganged into imitating the original. Although it was close to midnight, pedestrians crowded the wide sidewalks. Most of them were in uniform. A posse of teenage girls crammed in the front and back seats of a convertible waved their hands in the air and sang along to music booming from the radio. Two barechested men stood in the open sunroof of a white Cadillac, taking heroic swigs from cans of beer. In the parking lot of a burger joint shaped like a flying saucer, a pickup with a garish pink paint job shudderingly jacked itself up on hydraulic shocks. There were bars and fast-food restaurants, strip clubs and dance clubs. An electronics bazaar took up an entire block. Motels advertised rooms for rent by the hour, cable TV, waterbeds, Jacuzzis. A wedding chapel boasted that notaries were available twenty-four hours a day. A bar offered genuine apemen death matches.

Stone pointed to a convenience store up ahead. "A lousy bottle of painkillers. That's all I ask."

"You better not be faking," Tom said, and told Linda to pull over. When she'd bumped the Jeep into the parking lot beside the store, he asked her to buy a newspaper while she was at it. "It won't hurt to check the date."

"I'll go with you," Stone said as Linda swung out of the Jeep, but when he grabbed hold of the roll bar and hauled himself up, Tom drew his pistol and advised him to sit right there and take it easy.

"I wouldn't like to have to shoot you because I thought you were trying to get the jump on me."

"The way I feel, I couldn't jump your grandmother," Stone said. He fell back heavily on the rear seat and slumped down, shaking his head when Tom Waverly asked him if he was going to barf.

"Next time through, you should follow my example," Tom Waverly said. "If you get a half pint of booze inside you, the time key won't be able to do a number on your head."

"It didn't seem to affect Linda."

"Some people are more sensitive than others. If I'd've known how hard it was going to hit you, I would have insisted you share my Jack."

"Maybe you could share your plans with me instead."

Tom laughed. "Man, you don't give up, do you? Trying your lame-o segues even though you're sick as a dog."

"You could at least tell me who we're going to meet."

"Try to be patient. We're going to blow GYPSY wide open, but it has to be done my way because I have to make sure I don't get caught up in what's going down. That's why I need your help, partner. Linda's too."

"Bullshit." Stone spoke softly, trying to put a little quaver in his voice, trying to sound sick and at the end of his strength. "If you really wanted to give up GYPSY, you would have done it already."

Tom shook his head. He was resting his .38 in the crook of his left arm, aiming it at Stone's midsection, his finger lightly curled around the trigger. "I've been on the run for too long. No one would believe a word I said. And even if they did, I don't have time for hearings and trials and the rest of that crap. I have a life to live, and plans that don't include the faintest possibility of ever going to jail. But you're an honest broker, Adam. You're Mr. Clean. You stood up in front of the Church Committee and told the truth. Anything *you* say, they'll take seriously, especially if you have some hard evidence. You can help me change things around, Adam. You can save my life, and save the life of your woman, too. But you have to trust me. You have to stick with my plan."

"You're going to kill Eileen Barrie, aren't you? The Real version, that is."

"Why would I want to do that?"

Tom was smiling that sly, infuriating smile of his. Stone wondered if he could knock the pistol out of his hand without getting shot. Probably not, even though the man was half drunk.

"Why did you kill six of her doppels?" Stone said.

"That wasn't me."

"I forgot: it was one of your doppels who murdered all those women."

"Yes it was. Tom Waverly Two. I know it's hard for you to understand this, Adam, but we really have travelled back three weeks. None of that bad stuff has happened yet, and I intend to make sure that it never does."

"By killing Eileen Barrie."

254

"No one has to get killed if everything works out."

Linda came out of the convenience store. She was carrying a paper bag and a newspaper, and looked worried. Tom glanced at her, and Stone used the moment of inattention to palm the screwdriver he'd taken from the desk in the bunker. When Linda reached the Jeep, she tossed the newspaper onto the driver's seat and said, "Look at this."

"What is it, honey?"

"Look at the date."

Tom studied Stone for a moment, then picked up the newspaper and squinted at it in the orange glow of a nearby streetlight, saying, "Jesus Christ."

Stone made his move. He reared up and clamped his right forearm around Tom's throat, locked his wrist in the elbow of his left arm, and hauled back with all the strength he'd earned from working on the railroad and the farm. Tom clawed at the choke hold and tried and failed to get his hands under Stone's forearm, then tried to jab his elbows in Stone's face, but Stone ducked down and held on. Linda tried to climb into the Jeep and get between the two men as they bucked and reared, but one of Tom's elbows caught her in the temple and knocked her to the ground. Stone jammed his knees into Tom's spine through the back of the seat and tightened his grip. Tom kicked a diminishing tattoo against the Jeep's dash and went limp and dropped his pistol into the footwell, and Linda snatched it up and rolled away and stood up, holding it in a two-handed grip. Stone pressed the blade of the screwdriver against the corner of Tom's eye and looked straight at her and told her that if she didn't drop her weapon he'd punch the screwdriver into her father's brain.

"How about you let him go and we forget this?" Linda said.

She was staring straight at Stone, but the muzzle of the pistol was trembling. She was clever, brave, and resourceful, but she hadn't been trained as a killer. Stone believed that she wouldn't be able to shoot someone she knew. He was betting his life on it.

"I can't do that, Linda," he said. "Put the pistol on the driver's seat. Do it now, or I swear I'll kill him."

Linda did as she was told. Tom was a dead weight now, completely out of it. Stone eased his grip and let Tom slump forward, then snatched up the pistol and pulled Tom's knife from the sheath sewn inside his denim jacket.

"What now?" Linda said.

"The time key is in your father's pocket. I want you to take it out for me."

When she offered it to Stone, he shrugged out of his jacket and told her to wrap it up.

"You're being used, Mr. Stone," she said. "The time key got inside your head. It's using you."

"All that thing did was give me a headache."

"Why don't you read the newspaper?" Linda said, and held it up, folded to the headline. "Take a good look, and see that I wasn't lying."

It was the late edition of the *Los Angeles Times*. The date on the masthead was August 31, 1984.

Stone imagined and instantly dismissed some impossibly elaborate plan involving an officer working undercover in the convenience store, fake newspapers. We really did it, he thought. We really travelled into the past—but only a shade over two weeks into the past, not the three weeks that Tom had claimed. We're at the beginning of the road that runs right to Tom's suicide. To Susan's murder.

Linda was saying, "We're in the right place but at the wrong time. We haven't gone back far enough. We have to go back to White Sands, and try again. We have to go back another week."

"And let your father do whatever it is he wants to do? I don't think so."

"He wants to break the circle, Mr. Stone."

"So do I." Stone felt calm and cold. The initial shock had passed. He was in unknown territory, but he'd been in all kinds of unknown territory before. He could deal with it. And for the first time since Tom had burst into the hotel room and killed the two goons, he felt that he had the advantage.

"That's good," Linda said. "Because if we stay here, there's a strong chance that my father will end up murdering half a dozen different versions of the same woman, get a fatal dose of radiation, and shoot himself to death in Pottersville. And your friend, Mr. Stone, she'll die too. We have to go back to White Sands."

"How can you be sure the time key will to do the right thing the second time around?"

"Maybe we didn't get the code quite right. This time we can make absolutely sure we do."

"We can't be certain it will cooperate," Stone said. "According to your father, it has a mind of its own. No, the only way to stop this is to take out the people in charge of GYPSY. I know your father has said that's what he wants to do, but frankly, Linda, I don't trust him. I think he has his own agenda. I think he's been playing both of us. He wouldn't give up the names of any of the people involved in GYPSY, but I know someone who will. What we're going to do right now is go find her."

He told Linda to get behind the wheel, said that if she tried anything funny he'd shoot her father, and sat right behind her while she drove, figuring out his next move. In the shotgun seat, Tom coughed and gurgled, started to pluck at the safety belt Stone had buckled around him. He stiffened when Stone put the muzzle of the pistol in the tender spot at the base of his skull and told him to behave.

"You're making the biggest mistake of your life," Tom said.

"Just keep quiet," Stone said. "No more bullshit."

Tom massaged his throat, then said to his daughter, "Did you show him the newspaper, honey?"

"Yes. Yes, I did."

"You think that's bullshit, Adam?"

"I think I need a second opinion. Linda, you keep driving. Take the next right. We need to get off the main drag. Tom, you shut the fuck up, or I swear I'll do you some permanent damage."

They were waiting in the turn lane when Stone heard a siren. He glanced around and saw a military police cruiser a couple of blocks down the street, its light bar flashing as it bulled its way through nose-to-tail traffic. A scenario flashed across his mind: someone at the chemical plant making a call to the military police after discovering that their Jeep had been stolen, the MPs checking security camera footage, finding that the Jeep had passed through one of the security gates, heading for Alamogordo. . . .

Tom must have had the same idea. He said, "If they take us in, we'll never get to fix this."

Stone saw the light change and told Linda to make that turn now.

She pulled out of the turn lane and swerved across the intersection just as a pickup truck ran the red light in the opposite direction. Stone saw headlights heading straight toward him and managed to grab the roll bar and brace himself. The impact was as loud as a bomb and sprang the Jeep's hood and shattered its windshield and spun it around. As soon as it stopped moving, its engine stalled, steam spitting from under its buckled hood, Stone swung down to the street and tucked his rolled-up jacket under his arm. He had to kick the door on the driver's side to spring it open, and grabbed Linda's wrist and dragged her out.

She was limping badly. Grains of safety glass glittered in her hair. She came with him docilely enough at first, but when they reached the crowded sidewalk she began to scream for help. Three soldiers stepped toward them, but froze when Stone showed them the pistol. Linda tried to pull away, shouting that this man was going to kill her, saying, when Stone put the pistol to her head, "You're going to kill us all, so why don't you go ahead?"

People backed away on every side; Stone and Linda stood at the centre of a clear wide spot like a pair of street performers. The hard noise of the impact was still ringing in Stone's ears, but he could hear the siren of the military police cruiser growing closer. The Jeep sat alongside the pickup in the intersection, lit by streetlights and the headlights of stalled traffic. Tom Waverly was gone.

"Make sure your father doesn't do anything stupid," Stone said, and shoved Linda away, fired two shots into the air to discourage anyone thinking of trying to intervene, and ran straight across the street. He dodged through the stalled traffic and ran under a marquee announcing in flashing red LIVE ELVIS LIVE into a plush foyer. A teenage usher shrank away as Stone slammed through double doors into some kind of club. Subdued lighting, couples at little round tables with shaded lamps, and Elvis Presley kneeling at the front of the stage in a white jumpsuit and tinted aviator's shades, crooning "Love Me Tender" in a husky, slightly off-key baritone while a ten-piece orchestra sawed away behind him.

Elvis stood up as Stone barged through the tables, stepping forward when Stone clambered onto the stage, saying, "Hold on there, fella," and going down hard when Stone kicked him in the knee. The orchestra trailed off in discord. Stone dodged around Elvis, pushed past a gaggle of chorus girls in spangles and feathers standing in the wings, crashed through a fire door, and ran through the parking lot at the back of the theatre, into the unknown.

# 2.

The Company's field office in Alamogordo was in a mini-mall off the northern end of the Strip, disguised as an information technology consultancy. Stone took off his brand-new Stetson and leaned on the buzzer and held his army ID up to the camera on the bracket above the door. After a long minute, a tall man wearing black suit pants and a white shirt with its sleeves rolled high on his biceps let him into a cramped reception area, saying as he relocked the door, "I bet you don't remember me, Mr. Stone."

Stone stepped on a jolt of alarm. "I don't believe I do."

He'd taken a risk coming here—if the military police had passed the data from the fake army ID to the Company, they'd know who he was by now—but he needed to find Eileen Barrie as quickly as possible, and this was his best bet. He'd stopped at a shopping mall and purchased a change of clothing—a pale silver John B. Stetson hat, a blue shirt with pearl snaps, jeans, Tony Lama cowboy boots—as a rough-and-ready disguise. He was carrying a Macy's bag in which he'd stuffed his suit, the time key, and the pistol he'd taken from Tom Waverly.

The man's smile showed a lot of white teeth. His skin was matte black and his head clean shaven. "Back in '73 I had hair—a *lot* of hair—and I guess I was shy fifty pounds," he said. "Not to mention I was wearing some pretty wild clothes. Stuff like bell-bottom jeans, tie-dyed T-shirts, and what they called love beads."

Stone took a few seconds to get the reference. "You worked on the Nixon sheaf operation."

"Richard Garvey," the man said, and held out his hand.

Stone shook it. "It's been a while."

"Meaning you still don't recall me. That's okay. It was eleven years ago, and we met just the once, when you briefed us."

"You were in the Washington team."

"Yes, sir. We were supposed to provide backup for the people who were going to make the hits, but the op got cancelled in the last minute of the eleventh hour on account of that bomb factory going up. I did get to see some action later on—"

"Richard, I need to use a computer with a connection to the Company net. You have one here?"

"We have four in back. Excuse me for asking, but I heard you retired. Did they reactivate you?"

"I'm kind of passing through on a job."

"The old need-to-know. Say no more."

"Exactly. It would help," Stone said, "if you logged in for me."

"Because you're not really here."

"You got it."

"Step this way, Mr. Stone. I'll fix you right up."

Garvey led Stone around the receptionist's desk into a square windowless room with a row of workstations down one side and storage racks and filing cabinets and two steel desks down the other. He fired up a computer, logged in, and told Stone to take as long as he needed—the other two guys on the night shift were staking out a bar where soldiers were rumoured to be selling museum-quality artifacts stolen from a war zone.

"We kind of slip between the cracks here. The FBI thinks it's in charge of policing the Strip because it's on American soil; the army thinks it's in charge because ninety percent of the people who use the Strip are military personnel, there's the Sheriff's office, state troopers. . . . The Company likes to maintain a presence, too, but we don't advertise. You want coffee? The day-shift guys are cheapskates who drink generic supermarket crap. I buy Colombian beans and grind them myself."

"Coffee sounds good."

It was strong and black, in a chipped mug printed with an old Company joke: *E Unum Pluribus.* Out of one, many. Stone stirred three packets of sugar into the coffee and sucked it down while he used the computer. Across the room, Garvey sat sideways to one of the desks, reading a fat paperback with his feet crossed on the lower drawer. Either he was the world's best actor, or Stone's luck was holding and no one had yet thought to alert the field office about three fugitives in a stolen Jeep.

Linda Waverly had told Stone that GYPSY's real work was disguised as a research programme developing portable Turing gates, and he was pretty sure that, like most Company employees assigned to clandestine projects, Eileen Barrie would be working under some kind of cover. He didn't have clearance to access the Science and Technology Directorate's blue book, but after ten minutes' work with the computer's powerful search engine he turned up an obscure reference to a security briefing that identified Dr. Eileen Barrie as director of research in an army laboratory engaged in development of Turing gates with low energy requirements, close enough to Linda's story to make no difference.

He spent several futile minutes searching for the location of the laboratory and at last turned up a contact number with the Alamogordo area code.

The number wasn't listed in the phone directory of the White Sands interchange or in the business pages of the Alamogordo phone directory, and there wasn't a listing for Eileen Barrie in the white pages, but Stone knew that she had to be somewhere close by. Despite the office's fierce air-conditioning, there were saddles of sweat under his arms, and sweat stuck his shirt to his back. He was running on adrenalin and caffeine, unable to shake the stupid idea that at any moment a posse of military police and Company officers would break down the door in hot pursuit. He studied the original reference again. E. L. Barrie, PhD. It didn't give her rank, but maybe that was because she didn't have one. Maybe, like many Company operatives who disguised the true nature of their work with army credentials and documentation, she was a civilian employee. He asked Garvey if there was a directory of home addresses for civilians working at White Sands, and Garvey told him to hit F3 on his keyboard and type in the day code.

"You'll have to give me the code," Stone said.

Garvey looked at him over the top of his paperback, no particular expression on his face.

"I've been working all night. I didn't have time to phone in for the update," Stone said, hoping he wouldn't have to pull the pistol to get what he wanted.

"Sinaloa cowboy," Garvey said, and went back to his book.

That got Stone to a menu; two levels down were the residential listings of all the civilian employees of the White Sands division of the army's Development and Engineering Office. He committed Eileen Barrie's address to memory, searched the rosters of military personnel serving at White Sands and memorised a telephone number, then shut down the terminal and set his Stetson on his head and asked Garvey if he had a spare pair of handcuffs.

The tall man rummaged inside a drawer, found a pair of steel cuffs, and tossed them across the room to Stone. "You need any help bringing in your bad guy, I'd be happy to ride along."

"You have a key for these?"

"Take mine. I'm serious about the offer of help. We don't get too much action here."

"If I need any help, I know where to call."

"It was a good op," Richard Garvey said, "but I'm kind of glad it didn't work out. We had no business subverting that sheaf, or any like it."

"Absolutely," Stone said, startled.

"You're a stand-up guy, Mr. Stone. I thought so back in '73, and I thought so when you went up before the Church Committee and said what you had to say. Good luck with your work."

Stone had stolen a Ford compact from the parking structure of the shopping mall where he had bought his change of clothes. Its underpowered engine pulled badly on uphill grades as he drove through suburban tracts that extended into the foothills of the Sacramento Mountains above Alamogordo. Dingbat apartment buildings, ranch houses with two-car garages, gas stations, mini-malls. The close proximity of the time key, wrapped in his suit jacket inside the Macy's bag on the passenger seat, gave him the spooky feeling that someone intent on doing him serious harm was sitting beside him.

It was one thirty in the morning. The winding streets were quiet and empty. Stone left the suburban developments behind and drove past executive houses set in big, landscaped lots separated by stands of pine trees. Every third or fourth curve revealed the lights of the White Sands facility, a complex grid that stretched away to the horizon like a UFO landing strip.

The house he was looking for was a modern design of interlocking cubes of white concrete and glass set on top of a ridge and partly cantilevered over a steep drop. As he drove past, Stone saw a black late-model sedan with tinted windows parked just inside the steel-bar gate. After the next bend, he pulled off the road, parked among pine trees, and slipped through a strip of rocky woods to the chain-link fence at the rear of the property. A dog barked somewhere far off in the night. The uncurtained windows of the house dropped rectangles of light over the garden and the short, steep drive. Stone could see that someone was sitting in the driver's seat of the sedan, face laid sideways on the steering wheel as if he'd fallen asleep.

Stone checked the fence for alarm wires and sensors, swung over it, and crept through a Japanese garden of bamboos and moss, moving from shadow to shadow. The irrigation system had recently been on. The cool air smelled of wet earth and wet vegetation.

The man slumped inside the sedan didn't stir when Stone tapped the window with the muzzle of the pistol. He opened the door and saw that the man had been shot at close range by a small-calibre weapon that had left a neat hole above his ear. It had happened very recently. The man's skin still held some warmth and the worm of blood that slanted across his cheek to his chin had not yet dried.

Standing in the yellow light that dropped from the house's windows, Stone felt as exposed as a bug in a jar. He sprinted around the side of the house and found a sliding glass door that stood half open. When he stepped through, leading with the pistol, he nearly tripped over the body of a woman sprawled just inside. She had been shot with a small-calibre weapon too, and wore an empty shoulder holster under the jacket of her black pants suit. Stone found a cell phone in one of her pockets and a little flashlight and a set of handcuffs in the other, but if she had been carrying any ID it had been taken with her gun.

He stood in the shadows by the door, scoping out the dark, sparely furnished living room, listening to small noises elsewhere in the house. He eased off his boots and in white socks walked carefully across the living room into the hallway beyond. A room to the left had been made over into an office. Books lined one wall, a mix of glossy art-photograph albums, technical works on quantum theory and computing and system engineering, and a small run of self-help and management theory manuals. The desk was a wide curve of laminated ply fitted between the angle of two walls, empty except for a state-of-the-art computer and a glass case in which a big tarantula spider sat motionless on a litter of bark and dead leaves. The top drawer of a filing cabinet had been pulled out and papers were scattered underneath.

The small noises were coming from a room at the far end of the hallway. The door was open and light beyond threw a faint moving shadow on the wall opposite. Stone flattened beside the door and risked a quick peek inside, saw a suitcase open on a platform bed, saw a woman in jeans and a grey T-shirt rummaging in a closet. When Stone stepped into the room, Eileen Barrie turned toward him, clasping a folded sweater to herself, her stare rising from his pistol to his face.

# 3.

As Stone walked her out of the house at gunpoint, Eileen Barrie told him that she'd shot the man and the woman because they'd broken into her property and meant her harm. Stone asked her why she hadn't called the police and she said that she'd panicked and thought that the police might get the wrong idea.

"I expect they would," Stone said, "because no housebreaker would leave his car in plain sight. It's obvious that those two were bodyguards, or were keeping you under some kind of house arrest."

Eileen Barrie said he could think what he liked. She had the same square, pugnacious face, framed by glossy black shoulder-length hair parted with surgical precision down the centre of her scalp, that he remembered from the photographs David Welch had shown him. She'd put on a leather jacket as thin and supple and fine-grained as baby's skin, and was carrying an attaché case full of papers and computer disks. She claimed that it was information about Operation GYPSY that she would be willing to hand over to the Company in exchange for immunity from prosecution.

Stone shorted the starter solenoid of the stolen Ford with a wire he'd ripped from the dash radio. The engine caught with a roar that seemed loud enough to wake everyone for a mile around. He shut the hood and told Eileen Barrie she was going to drive; warned her to calm down and keep to the speed limit when she swerved out onto the road in a spray of dirt and pine needles. The road climbed past big houses that stood further and further back until at last all that could be seen of them were high stone walls or drives wandering away into the woods, and then there were only trees. Stone kept quiet, letting her stew, letting her imagination work on her confidence. She drove with her hands at ten and two on the steering wheel and her gaze fixed straight ahead. She didn't question Stone when at last he told her to turn off the road and park at a picnic area.

They walked past tables and barbecue pits into the trees beyond. Stone was carrying the Macy's bag, lighting the way with the flashlight he'd found in one of the dead woman's pockets. A short flight of stone steps led down to a paved viewing area that looked across a dark, narrow valley to a rock ridge that gleamed pale and bare in the light of a half-moon hung behind runners of thin cloud. Eileen Barrie sat at one end of a stone bench and Stone sat at the other, aiming his pistol and flashlight at her face. The bag sat between them.

"Let's talk about what you were doing when I found you," Stone said. "You'd shot your guards, you'd stuffed an attaché case full of valuable papers and computer disks, and you were packing a suitcase. Any reasonable person would have to think that you were getting ready to make a run for it, Dr. Barrie."

"Who are you working for, Mr. Stone? Perhaps you have some ID you could show me."

"I used to work for the Company, just like you. Right now, I'm working for myself. Did Tom Waverly tell you to make a run for it, or was it your own idea?"

Eileen Barrie showed no reaction when Stone mentioned Tom's name. She was calm, cool, and controlled, trying hard to show that she wasn't scared and doing a pretty good job. Stone wondered how someone who lived in the desert could stay so pale. Perhaps she only went out at night, spent the days working in some windowless maximum-security subbasement.

"I should have figured it out as soon as Tom told me what he'd stolen," he said. "I should have known that he would have had inside help, someone he could trust. Someone like you, Dr. Barrie. How did he get in touch with you while those two agents were dogging your every move? Was it the old wrong-number trick?"

"Why would he call me?"

"I used to work with Tom. I was persuaded to come out of retirement because he'd landed himself in a good deal of trouble. He'd stolen something, he was on the run from the people who wanted it back, he was moving from sheaf to sheaf, and he was killing your doppels wherever he could."

That got her attention. After a moment, she said, "If he was doing . . . what you claim he was doing, why haven't I heard about it?"

"When I found Tom, he was in a pretty desperate state. Matter of fact, he went ahead and killed himself, Dr. Barrie. He shot himself dead. He put a gun in his mouth and blew his brains out, right in front of me. The funny thing is, he was already dying of radiation poisoning. Would you know anything about that?"

"How could I?"

"You don't believe me because you know Tom is here, in Alamogordo. He phoned you a little while ago, didn't he? That's why you killed your guards, that's why you were packing, that's why you think my story is crazy.

But here's the twist. A few days after Tom killed himself, I ran into him again. The very same man, only not quite so desperate looking, and healthy as a horse. I've been travelling with him ever since. You're a smart woman, Dr. Barrie, so I'm sure you can tell me how all this is possible."

"It's an amusing story, Mr. Stone, but not very believable."

"I had a lot of trouble believing it myself until tonight. I thought the guy who blew out his brains in front of me was a doppel, or that it had all been some kind of stagecraft. But then I saw what the thing Tom stole, he calls it a time key, could do to a Turing gate."

"I really don't know what you're talking about."

"You want to know what I'm talking about, it's right in here," Stone said, resting his hand on the bag that sat between them. "Why don't you take a look for yourself?"

"Why don't you show it to me?"

Stone gave the bag a hefty shove. It skidded about a foot along the bench and tipped on its side, spilling the sleeve of his jacket. Eileen Barrie jumped, just a little. Stone said, "It made a connection with you, didn't it?"

"I don't know what you mean."

"Tom told me that it had a mind of its own. He told me the people who worked on it found that out the hard way. It's wrapped in that jacket. Why don't you take it out for me?"

Eileen Barrie didn't move.

"All you have to do is switch it on," Stone said. "If you can do that, it'll do a number on me. It'll more or less knock me out. You'll be able to take this pistol from me and shoot me in the head, like you did your two guards."

She still didn't move.

Stone raised the .38. "How about I put it another way? Take the device out of the bag right now, or I swear I'll put a bullet somewhere that'll seriously inconvenience you."

"You're being insulting, Mr. Stone," Eileen Barrie said, with enough venom in her voice to kill half the population of Alamogordo.

"You'd do it in a moment if you could," Stone said. "You'd just love to reach in there, switch it on, and watch me do a funny dance to its tune. But you can't, because you know it likes you about as much as it likes me. You know it'll fuck you up too. Why did you and Tom steal it from GYPSY?"

"You seem to think you know everything, Mr. Stone. Perhaps you could tell me what this has to do with me."

"I know about half of everything, Dr. Barrie, if that. I do know that you're one of GYPSY's key workers. *The* key worker, according to Tom. You're part of GYPSY's cover, the research programme into portable Turing gates, but you're also part of the black op hidden behind the cover story, and so is Tom. That's what he's been doing ever since he faked his death and dropped out of sight three years ago. That, and cooking up a plan with you to steal the time key. Don't waste my time by trying to deny it, Dr. Barrie. One way or another, you're going to tell me everything you know."

"I'm willing to talk to the proper authorities. Not to a hoodlum who has kidnapped me."

Stone raised and fired the .38, knocking a fist-sized chunk out of the fieldstone wall behind Eileen Barrie. She jumped to her feet as the hard flat sound of the shot rolled across the dark valley. Dust flung into the air defined the beam of the flashlight.

"All right," she said after a moment, staring at the pistol centred on her face. "All right."

"Sit down, Dr. Barrie."

She did as she was told, her hands shaking as she brushed dust from her leather jacket.

"Let's start over," Stone said. "The two people you killed weren't intruders. They were guards."

Eileen Barrie nodded.

"The people in charge of GYPSY have put you under guard ever since Tom Waverly stole the time key."

"Ever since he vanished, yes."

"Were you under house arrest, or was it for your protection?"

"I was told that it was for my protection."

"When are they due to be relieved? Tell the truth, Dr. Barrie. I'll know if you're lying."

"Eight o'clock in the morning."

"Then we have plenty of time to get things straight. Did you kill your guards because Tom Waverly contacted you?"

"What can you offer me?"

"What do you mean?"

"To begin with, I need a guarantee that I won't be prosecuted, and that my name will not be used in any proceedings the Company might bring against anyone else."

"I'm not here to make any kind of deal with you. I'm here to find out everything you know about GYPSY. I need the names of the people you're working for. I need to know where to find them. I need to know what they are planning to do."

"I'll only make a full disclosure in exchange for a guarantee of immunity."

Stone raised the .38 again. "You'll make it to me. Right here, right now."

"And then you'll let me go?"

"I'll hand you over to the Company. I'm sure they'll want to know everything you can tell them about GYPSY. I'm sure you'll be able to cut a deal with them."

"Very well."

"Just like that, huh? What guarantees can you give me?"

"What to you mean?"

"How will I know you're telling the truth?"

"You have made it clear that I have no choice in the matter, Mr. Stone."

Stone realised then what he'd walked in on, why she'd killed the bodyguards, why she'd decided to bail. He said, "I guess it helps that you've already decided to run out on Tom Waverly."

She hesitated, then gave a tight little nod.

"He talked to you tonight. What did he say?"

"I have a cell phone that no one in GYPSY knows about. He sent me a text message an hour ago. I knew at once something had gone wrong because he was not supposed to be in this sheaf and we weren't supposed to contact each other until it was all over. He sent me a telephone number and asked me to call it at once. We talked. He told me that he'd lost the time key, but he wouldn't explain how. He said that I wasn't in any danger and he had a backup plan. I was to go to work tomorrow as if nothing had happened, and download certain files."

"About GYPSY."

"About the operation inside Operation GYPSY. He said that he would intercept me on my way home and kill my guards. We'd go into hiding, and we'd offer the files to the Company in exchange for an exemption from prosecution."

"But you already had those files, didn't you? You had your own backup plan all along. And after he contacted you, you decided to make a run for it."

"I couldn't trust him, Mr. Stone. He sounded . . . agitated. Agitated, drunk, and not at all like the man I knew. I decided that his so-called plan was too risky."

"So you decided to betray him before he could betray you."

"I decided to take action of my own," Eileen Barrie said primly.

"But you did trust him, once upon a time. You helped him to steal the time key."

"That's what Tom calls it. I prefer a simpler, less specific term: the device."

"Why did you help him?"

"It was my idea, Mr. Stone, not his. I wanted to put an end to GYPSY. I found that I no longer agreed with its aims."

"That's the same bullshit Tom fed me. He also told me that he couldn't take it to the Company because he'd been on the run for three years, he'd done too many bad things, and no one would believe him. Maybe that's true, maybe not. But you're a respectable scientist, Dr. Barrie. If you really wanted to put a stop to GYPSY, you could have gone straight to the Office of the Director of Central Intelligence. You could have blown the whistle any time. But you didn't, did you? So why did you and Tom steal the time key?"

Eileen Barrie looked past Stone for a moment, then said, "Money."

"Money?"

"Money."

"You and Tom stole the time key because you wanted money?"

"We wanted a life together. We wanted out of GYPSY. We needed a good deal of money to accomplish those aims."

Stone made a connection he should have made a long time ago. "You were lovers."

"Yes."

"And you cooked up a scheme to steal the time key and blackmail the people who run GYPSY for its return."

"Tom took care of the blackmail. I gave him the information he needed to steal the device. He took it and went into hiding, and a third party was going to make the arrangements for the exchange."

"A third party by the name of Freddy Layne."

"I'm unfamiliar with the name," Eileen Barrie said, as unblinking as an owl in the beam of the flashlight.

"Freddy Layne was Tom's business partner in another sheaf. Why didn't you go with Tom?"

"We agreed that it would be best if I stayed behind. That way they wouldn't know who had stolen it."

"But they suspected you had something to do with it, didn't they? That's why you were under guard."

Eileen Barrie didn't deny it.

Stone said, "I think you stayed behind because if things went wrong it would be Tom and not you who'd take the fall."

She didn't deny that, either.

"You're quite a piece of work, Dr. Barrie."

"After the device went missing, I was interrogated and I was put under guard, but so was everyone who had access to it. They knew Tom had something to do with it because he had disappeared, but they didn't know about us. About our . . . connection. And I was quite sure that, if he was caught, Tom would not tell them about me. He loved me, you see."

"Don't kid yourself, Dr. Barrie. If you and Tom were indulging in extracurricular activity, you can bet your colleagues in GYPSY knew about it. They didn't do anything to you because they were using you as bait. They were waiting for you to make a move. Waiting for Tom to get in touch."

She thought about that for a moment. "He wasn't supposed to get in touch with me. I didn't even know where he went after we liberated the device. He was supposed to make all the arrangements for the exchange, and then I was going to join him."

"But he turned up here instead. He told you that he'd lost the time key, but he had this nifty, brand-new plan, and he needed your help. You didn't like it, so you decided to make a run for it before he found you. When did he steal the time key, by the way?"

"A week ago." Eileen Barrie hesitated, then said, "Tom told me that he has been hiding out for three weeks. He told me that he had used the time key to travel two weeks into his past. Is that true?"

"He was aiming for three weeks, Dr. Barrie, but the time key didn't cooperate."

"He wasn't supposed to use it at all. Without the proper precautions it can be . . . dangerous. You said that he was aiming for three weeks. Did he tell you why?"

"He said he was going to put a stop to everything before it began. He didn't explain how."

"Unless the device is used in exactly the right way, Mr. Stone, it tends to go its own way. We know that it's highly intelligent, and we have good evidence that it is self-aware. We believe that it has free will. It makes choices that can affect the direction of history. So when it is necessary to make use of it, it must be forced to make the correct choice."

"You have 'good evidence'? You 'believe'? I thought you built this thing."

270

"It's very flattering that you should think so, Mr. Stone, but I'm afraid that I didn't."

"If you didn't build it, who did?"

"Time travellers."

Stone laughed. He couldn't help himself.

"If you found a spaceship sitting in the desert, Mr. Stone, you'd think at once that it had been built by space travellers. You have had a practical demonstration of what the device can do, so why is it so hard for you to believe that what is in effect a time machine was built by time travellers— by people who travelled back in time into their past, our present?"

Stone thought about this for a moment, then said, "Where did these time travellers come from? What were they doing?"

"From somewhere in the future—we're not sure how long. There were three of them. They were shadowing some field officers in the Nixon sheaf. When our people realised that they were being watched, they set a trap. Perhaps the time travellers were no more than observers, perhaps they were engaged in their own version of a covert operation; unfortunately, we have no way of knowing, because they died in custody. Not under so-called hot questioning, nor from injuries received when they were caught. They simply died."

"They killed themselves?"

"Their hearts stopped. We believe that they willed themselves to die."

"They were carrying this thing, the time key."

"The device."

"You were given the task of finding out how to make it work. That's what GYPSY is all about."

Eileen Barrie nodded.

"And it did a number on your head while you were examining it, which is why you don't even want to look at it."

"We had to devise a way of interrogating it. Like any self-aware entity, it tried to defend itself."

"But you found a way around its defences. You know how to make it do its little trick with time and the Turing gates."

"I found out how to operate it. Or at least, how to make it cooperate. And I was part of the team that discovered the principles of its operation."

"If you've duplicated it, why is the original so valuable to GYPSY? Why would they pay you and Tom to get it back?"

"We have some understanding of what the device can do, Mr. Stone, but we do not yet completely understand how it works. Our best guess is that it is the physical manifestation of a highly complex emergent phenomenon distributed within the General Quantum Field of the universe."

"The thing that makes the universe intelligent."

"We're what makes the universe self-aware, Mr. Stone. Our brains are physical constructs that are sufficiently complex to be able to interact with the General Quantum Field, and that interaction generates consciousness. That's why the choices we make can affect the quantum state of the entire universe and cause one sheaf to split into two. The device is at least as complicated as the human brain, but it is merely the interface for operations that take place within the General Quantum Field itself."

Eileen Barrie was growing animated, getting into her explanation.

"The multiverse contains a vast number of alternate histories. We can travel between some of them using Turing gates. What's not so well known is that for each alternate history, each sheaf, there is a very large number of different states. Our minds read these states in a sequence that establishes time's arrow, like the pages of a book, or the sentences on a page. In one state, I'm saying this sentence. In the next, I'm saying *this* sentence, and we both have an extra moment of memory about the first sentence. We experience the so-called passage of time because we move from one state to the next in an unbroken sequence, but in fact, all possible states exist at every moment. The time key not only allows movement between different sheaves but also between different moments in those sheaves."

"Turing gates link different sheaves. But the time key does something to a Turing gate that enables it to link different states—different times—within a single sheaf."

"You're a quick study, Mr. Stone."

"I guess it helps that I've had firsthand experience. So this thing is very complicated. It's self-aware. How did you make it give up its secrets? Did you torture it?"

"I did some reverse engineering. GYPSY needs the device, Mr. Stone. With my help, you could sell it back to them. You could make a great deal of money."

"You want me to be your partner, huh?"

"Why not?"

"Who would I be selling it to, Dr. Barrie? Who is in charge of GYPSY? I know that Dick Knightly had something to do with it before he was sent to prison and had his stroke. He recruited Tom and at least two other people I served with in Special Ops. Who else?"

"If I tell you, I won't have anything to bargain with when you turn me over to the authorities."

"You burned your boats with GYPSY when you killed your guards and went on the run. Right now, I'm the only person who can get you out of this safely. I'm the only person you can trust. If you want me to help you, you're going to have to help me." Stone let the woman think about this. When she focused on him again, he said, "The people in charge of GYPSY, Dr. Barrie. Who are they? Give me some names."

"Mr. Knightly put Victor Moore in charge of the day-to-day running of GYPSY."

Stone knew the name. Victor Moore hadn't been one of the original cowboy angels, but had been recruited from the Science and Technology Directorate to take charge of a programme that assessed technology brought back from other sheaves.

"Is he in charge of the cover, or the real operation?"

"Mr. Knightly is in overall command. Victor Moore is his deputy."

"But Knightly is stroked out, a vegetable, so I guess that makes Moore number one. He'd be the guy who'd give the order to kill someone if GYPSY was in danger of being compromised."

"I wouldn't know, Mr. Stone. I was in charge of the research programme. I had little to do with the operational side of things."

"Who else?"

Eileen Barrie named names. Stone recognised a few from the good old days, not many. She said that they were loyal to the Company and wanted to restore it to its former glory. She more or less confirmed Tom's story about travelling back in time and starting nuclear wars in precontact sheaves to create client states that needed the Real's help, expanding the Real's hegemony, making the military and the Company too powerful for any president to control.

"Nuclear war has the greatest effect on the greatest number of people, the biggest resonance in the General Quantum Field. If you want to shake things up, if you really want to change history, the best thing to do is to start a nuclear war," she said, but claimed that she didn't know which sheaf GYPSY's operational team had targeted.

They went around and around, but Stone couldn't break her. Perhaps she was telling the truth, perhaps she was holding back information that she hoped would help her to escape prosecution after Stone turned her over to the Company. It didn't really matter. He had a name now. Victor Moore. He had the beginning of a thread that, when pulled, would unravel GYPSY and save Susan from her fate.

# 4.

While Eileen Barrie drove, taking a route north and then west back toward Alamogordo, Stone gave her an abbreviated version of how he had become involved in Tom Waverly's plan. He described meeting him in Pottersville and told her that Tom had been dying of radiation poisoning and had shot himself when the local cops had moved in to arrest him. Eileen Barrie listened without showing a trace of emotion. When she said that she didn't know how Tom could have suffered a lethal dose of radiation, Stone believed her—after all, as far as she was concerned, it hadn't happened yet. And if Stone had his way, it wouldn't ever happen. Tom wouldn't receive his lethal dose, he wouldn't set off on his rampage through sheaves, killing Eileen Barrie's doppels and killing himself in Pottersville, and operatives working for Operation GYPSY wouldn't be sent to the wild sheaf, and Susan wouldn't be murdered.

He said, "I'm here, which as far as I'm concerned is two weeks in the past, and there's also a version of me, two weeks younger, living in a pioneer sheaf. It seems to me that if I stop the cycle repeating itself, that earlier version of me won't be called in to help find Tom. He'll stay right where he is. He won't become me."

Eileen Barrie unravelled the paradox with ease. "You travelled back in time, and now you are moving toward the point where you set out, two weeks in the future. If everything happens the way it has already happened, you will complete a closed loop, your younger self will be sent off to find Tom, and he will end up here. But if you're able to make a significant difference, you will create a new sheaf where history plays out differently."

"And the younger version of me won't be reactivated. He'll stay where he is."

Stone had to be certain that there really was a chance that he could save Susan, even if it meant that he had to ask the advice of a woman who was part of the conspiracy that had murdered her.

"If you do the right thing and break the loop open, you can think of the younger version of yourself as a doppel," Eileen Barrie said. "He'll go on to live his life, and you'll go on to live yours."

"But I won't be able to go home."

"No, you won't. If you make a significant change here, you will unmake the future—the place you came from."

They stopped at a McDonald's in High Rolls, a dormitory town of mini-malls, fast-food joints, and cheap apartment complexes for technicians and service workers at White Sands. After an early breakfast of Egg McMuffins and sugared coffee, Stone stood guard outside the bathroom while Eileen Barrie freshened up, then escorted her across the parking lot to the gas station next door and used its pay phone to call the number he'd pulled off the Company system.

He got through to an aide who wanted to know where Stone had obtained the number for General Ellis's office.

"From the command and control list. I'm an old friend of the general's. I need to talk to him urgently."

"If you have a message for him, sir, I'll pass it on."

"I need to talk to him myself. Right now wouldn't be too soon," Stone said, but the aide was wedded to protocol and wouldn't give way. At last, Stone gave his name and said that he would be visiting the general's office shortly. "I want to talk about Tom Waverly and SWIFT SWORD—be sure you tell General Ellis that," he said, and hung up.

"What now?" Eileen Barrie said.

"I'm giving you what you want, Dr. Barrie. I'm taking you to a place of safety."

Stone opened the hood of the stolen Ford and fired up the engine. After they had climbed inside, Eileen Barrie said, "You like this Boy Scout stuff, don't you?"

For a moment, Stone thought she was actually going to smile.

"Used to be what I did for a living. Turn right, Dr. Barrie."

She turned right, neatly merging into the thin flow of traffic heading toward Alamogordo. Sunrise was still an hour away, but the sky was already turning blue above the steep bare ridge to the east. After a few minutes, she said, "The Company office at White Sands is compromised. If that's where you're taking me, you might as well shoot me dead right here."

"I know the guy in charge of perimeter security. He'll take good care of you."

"I don't want to talk to some army officer, Mr. Stone. I want to talk to the director of Central Intelligence, no one else. And before I do that, I have to discuss my position with my lawyer."

"When my friend hears what you have to say, he'll put you on the next plane to Washington. If you behave yourself, he might even let your lawyer ride along."

"Or he'll put me in front of a firing squad. Or you'll take me out into the desert and shoot me."

Stone didn't blame her for getting the jitters. Officers usually spent many weeks cosying up to potential defectors, gaining their confidence, becoming their best friend, slowly and surely bringing them around to the idea of going over to the other side. But he'd taken Eileen Barrie prisoner at gunpoint and threatened to kill her if she didn't answer his questions, and now he was forcing her to betray Operation GYPSY. He knew that he couldn't make her trust him, but told her that she was doing the right thing, that she would feel better once she had been taken into custody.

"You'll be able to talk with your lawyer," he said. "You'll be able to start to put your deal together. You'll be able to move forward."

"That's easy for you to say."

"I'm in as much trouble as you, Dr. Barrie. More, probably. You'll get a sympathetic hearing from the DCI. The best I can hope for, after I've dealt with Victor Moore, is a hot debriefing, probably in handcuffs."

But for the first time since Pottersville, Stone felt that he was in control. That he was making things right. If he could bring down GYPSY right now, Susan would be saved, and so would his other self, his doppel. They'd live out the rest of their lives on the farm in New Amsterdam and never know anything about this, he thought, and remembered with a pang the summer's day when he and Susan had rambled through the woods, with Petey running ahead of them, running back to show them the treasures he'd found—a black pebble, a bird's feather, an oyster shell dropped by a gull—and he had resolved to talk to Susan about what was happening between them when the right time came, when the raw wound of Jake's death had healed. Maybe in six months, maybe a year: he'd been prepared to wait as long as it took. There'd been a moment when they'd been walking back from the Harvest Home dance a couple of weeks ago, and he'd thought *now, speak to her now*, but he'd lost his nerve. And there'd been another moment when Susan had been watching him getting ready to leave with David Welch, but before either of them could say anything Petey had burst in on them. . . .

Knowing now that he'd never be able to go back to the First Foot sheaf and tell Susan what he felt, that when this was over he would have to walk away and start afresh, a defector from his own life, was as hard and cold as anything Stone had ever faced. But there was some small comfort in knowing that it would mean his doppel, his secret sharer, would have the chance he'd lost.

They were driving through the edge of Alamogordo's sprawl now, past gas stations and tire depots, generic restaurants and warehouse retail units, dingbat apartment blocks offering no-deposit rentals and cable TV. Billboards overtopped each other like rainforest trees struggling for sunlight. Amoco. Midas Mufflers. Winston Tires. A fast-food restaurant got up to look like a wooden fort was offering a super-saver deal on mammothburgers.

Stone said, "Have you ever thought we're the wrong kind of people to be spreading our influence throughout the multiverse?"

"There's no wrong or right," Eileen Barrie said. "There's no manifest destiny. There's only chance and probability. We just happen to be the sheaf where the probability of quantum computing coming into existence is highest. The one where Alan Turing emigrated to America, where he invented the concept of the universal quantum computer, where Richard Feynman provided the theoretical background for manipulation of single supercooled atoms, where the first quantum calculation was performed at Bell Labs in 1962. There's nothing special about us, Mr. Stone, it's just that in other sheaves a host of factors conspired against those key events. Take the Nixon sheaf, for instance. They had a Second World War in the 1940s, and Alan Turing was an important part of the British war effort, taking a lead in a top-secret operation to decipher German code. He stayed in Britain after the end of the war, and that's where he killed himself, in 1954. He was hounded by the security services because of his homosexuality, and one day he injected cyanide into an apple and took a bite. Highly symbolic, don't you think?"

Stone, remembering the cemetery in Pottersville, remembering Willie Davis describing how Marsha Mason had died after she'd swallowed her poison pill, tried to get away from the subject of suicide. "It sounds like you've done some research on Turing and his doppels."

"When I was growing up, Alan Turing was something of a hero to me. Other girls had pop stars or movie stars. I had the man who made it possible to walk between worlds."

"You mean you had a poster of him on your wall, stuff like that?"

"As a matter of fact I did have a photograph. Also a form letter his secretary signed when I wrote him once. And copies of his papers, of course, and a first edition of his autobiography. You think that I'm some kind of android, Mr. Stone, but I can assure you I'm as human as anyone else."

"You risked your career for love, so I guess you must have a human side."

Stone had a brief image of Eileen Barrie and Tom Waverly moving over each other on some hotel bed. He couldn't imagine any tenderness in the act. It must have been like spiders mating.

"My career was effectively killed off a couple of years ago, Mr. Stone. They used me, and when they had what they wanted they sidelined me. They put me in charge of the research that was covering up the real purpose of GYPSY. They made it clear that I couldn't go anywhere else, or my life would be forfeit. I had offers to work in Livermore, in Princeton. I was offered a senior professorship at the University of Chicago—the very same position that Alan Turing held. I was forced to turn everything down."

"Tom gave you a way out," Stone said, understanding now how Tom had turned Eileen Barrie, how he'd worked on her dangerous mix of arrogance and naivety.

"Perhaps this isn't the way it'll be," she said, almost to herself. "Perhaps this path has a very low probability. Perhaps it'll collapse, and all that'll be left are trace memories of what might have been."

"Don't put yourself down, Dr. Barrie. What you're doing right now is world changing."

She glanced over at him. "Don't you feel a certain transparency, Mr. Stone? Do you get increasing attacks of déjà vu? Do you feel as if you're walking on thin ice?"

"We're on the right road, Dr. Barrie. Straight ahead, all the way."

"Maybe we're a transient loop. A footnote rather than a new page. A change that won't take."

"What I have in mind," Stone said, "is a lot more permanent than that."

They turned onto the Strip and drove through the centre of Alamogordo. In the stark early morning sunlight it looked shabby and two-dimensional, like a movie set waiting to be struck. Eileen Barrie slowed down as they drove past a string of motels. A black sedan and a squad car were drawn up at the curb outside the entrance to one of them, the El Dorado. In front of a fake stone monolith carved in pseudo-Aztec style, two uniformed cops were talking with a man in a black suit.

Stone got a bad feeling and said, "Keep going, Dr. Barrie. There's no help for you here."

Eileen Barrie reached inside her leather jacket and tossed a cell phone into Stone's lap. "That's the phone my handlers didn't know about. I palmed it when you were searching my attaché case. Back at the McDonald's, I used it to call Victor Moore."

Stone looked at her, at her cool defiant smile. "If you warned him, it won't help your case."

"I didn't tell him about you. But I did let him know that Tom Waverly was hiding out somewhere in Alamogordo."

Stone's hard-won confidence vanished. Dropped straight into a black pit and vanished, just like that. "You think they found him."

"We used various motels for our trysts," Eileen Barrie said. "The El Dorado was the first. Tom's fatal weakness is sentimentality—my guess is that it has let him down again. You wanted to end the cycle, Mr. Stone. Well, I've done it for you."

They were coming up to the end of the block. Stone jammed his pistol into Eileen Barrie's side and said, "Make a right, park in the first space you find."

She made the turn. "I didn't betray him when he contacted me because I thought he loved me. But your story convinced me otherwise. You told me that he'll murder as many of my doppels as he can—"

"That was in another history."

"I had to do it, Mr. Stone. I had to make sure that he wouldn't be able to come after me."

Stone saw a service alley that ran along the back of the string of motels and told Eileen Barrie to drive into it and park. "If Tom was staying in that motel, his daughter was probably staying there too."

"Linda's here?" Eileen Barrie was genuinely startled.

Stone grabbed her wrists and handcuffed her to the steering wheel. "I'm going to check things out. I won't be long."

"Take me into custody before you do this. I'm a noncombatant, Mr. Stone. And I can tell you everything you need to know about Operation GYPSY."

"You can wait in the car while I check out the motel. Then we'll do the other stuff."

She tugged at the handcuffs. "What if you don't come back? What do I do then? Sit here until they come for me?"

There was more than a hint of panic in her voice now.

"Maybe this isn't anything to do with us. Maybe Tom and Linda were staying at some other motel. Sit tight, Dr. Barrie. I'll be back in ten minutes."

Stone locked her attaché case and the Macy's bag in the trunk of the car, set his brand-new Stetson on his head, and moved down the alley, past parking lots, past cinder-block walls topped with razor wire, past steel gates stencilled with the names of different motels. The El Dorado's gate was painted green. He climbed over it, dropped down between a pair of Dumpsters, and edged along the back wall of the motel. At the corner he took a fast peek and saw service carts parked under a steel stairway, a swimming pool inside a chain-link fence, cars and pickups angle-parked along a two-storey L-shaped block, and a man in a black suit standing about twenty yards away.

Stone pulled the brim of the Stetson low on his face and walked out into the early morning sunlight, holding his pistol behind his back and waving his army ID, saying loudly, "Maybe you can help me. A couple of people used false papers at one of our checkpoints last night. I understand you might be looking for them too."

"There's nothing for you here, pal," the man said, and reached inside his jacket a moment too late as Stone swung the .38 in a short arc and clubbed him behind his ear.

Stone stashed the man's pistol in a planter, heaved him over his shoulder, and carried him to the service area under the stairs and sat him down. He found a spray-bottle of bleach hooked to the handle of one of the service carts, unscrewed the top and held it under the man's nose until he stirred, slapped him to get his attention, and asked him where the two fugitives had been taken.

The man was about half Stone's age, with a blond crew cut and bright blue eyes. He gave Stone an arrogant stare and said he didn't know anything about any fugitives.

Stone put the .38 in his face and asked him again.

"Fuck you."

"You work for GYPSY."

The man denied it, but Stone saw a telling flicker in his gaze.

"Where did you take Linda and Tom Waverly?"

The man studied him for a moment, then said, "I guess you must be Adam Stone."

"Where did you take them?"

"You're too old for this, Mr. Stone. Give it up now and we'll go easy on you and the girl—"

Stone cocked the .38 with his thumb. "Last chance. Where are they?"

The man saw something he didn't like in Stone's expression and said quickly, "Take it easy. We only found Waverly's daughter."

"Where is she?"

"Somewhere you can't reach her."

"She was taken to GYPSY's facility, wasn't she?"

"I have friends right out in front. If you shoot me, they'll be all over you."

The blond man put up his hand when Stone clubbed him with the .38 again, got his fingers mashed against his skull, and howled. Stone gave him another tap. This time his eyes rolled back and he slumped sideways.

Stone tied him up with strips torn from a hand towel, clambered onto one of the Dumpsters, and checked the alley before vaulting over the wall.

He jarred his knee when he landed; as he limped down the long service alley, he thought ruefully that the crew-cut guy had been right—he was definitely too old for this.

Someone was standing by the Ford, a panhandler it looked like. Ratty denim, long grey hair tangled around his face, something flashing in his hand. A knife.

Stone realised that it was Tom Waverly and started to run. He saw Tom jerk open the car's door and lean inside. He heard Eileen Barrie scream.

Tom turned when Stone shouted his name. Stone stepped forward, watching Tom over the front sight of the .38. Eileen Barrie was slumped halfway out of the open door of the car, hanging from her handcuffed wrist, her throat cut to the bone. Blood soaked the front of her leather jacket and there was blood spray on the windshield.

"Lose the knife, Tom," Stone said, maintaining eye contact as he stepped closer, hoping that he wouldn't have to shoot.

After a moment, Tom opened his fingers and let the knife drop point first into the dirt between his feet. "You should have trusted me," he said. "This would never have happened if you'd trusted me."

# 5.

When Stone kicked the knife under the car and told Tom to assume the position, Tom said, "Listen to me, Adam. Listen carefully. They snatched Linda. It looked like a clean job, I don't think she was hurt—"

"They're from GYPSY."

"Of course they're from GYPSY," Tom said, and inclined his head toward the car and Eileen Barrie's body. "She sold me out, didn't she?"

"You shouldn't have taken a room in the motel where you two used to rendezvous. Turn around, Tom, and put your hands flat on the roof."

"You're kidding."

"No, I'm not. You just killed an unarmed woman. It's made me kind of twitchy. If I'm not one hundred percent sure you aren't carrying, I just might accidentally shoot you if you look at me funny."

"This is all I have," Tom said, and hitched up his denim jacket to show the Remington .45 semiautomatic stuck in the waistband of his jeans.

"Pull it out slowly. Keep your fingers away from the trigger."

Tom did as he was told. When Stone took the pistol from him, he said, "I know exactly where they're going to take Linda. We'll go in together. We'll blast our way in if we have to, but we'll get her back."

"We won't be going anywhere but jail if we don't get out of here right now. Where did you get this pistol?"

"This is a military town," Tom said. "There's a guy in just about every bar can get you anything you need. Don't throw it away. I'm going to need it."

Stone unlocked the trunk, lifted out the Macy's bag, dropped the Remington inside, and told Tom to take Eileen Barrie's attaché case. "Do you have transport?"

"Linda hot-wired a pickup last night. But it's parked at the motel, and there are cops out front."

"I saw them. Start walking. We need to steal a car."

"We need to catch up with the people who took my daughter."

"One thing at a time. How did it happen? How did you manage to escape?"

"I couldn't sleep," Tom said as they headed down the alley. "When it got light, I went out to find us some breakfast. I was in the Denny's across the street, waiting for my take-out order, when I saw three black sedans pull up outside the motel. I phoned Linda, but it was too late. There was nothing I could do, Adam. There were too many of them, I couldn't risk a gunfight in the street, and then the cops turned up. I guess the manager called them. I had to watch them take her out. I had to watch them *drive her away. . . .*"

"Keep walking, Tom."

"I hung back, waiting for the cops to leave. A couple of knuckledraggers had been left behind to watch the place. I figured I could take them down and use their car to get to where I need to go. But then you arrived, and as soon as I saw Eileen I knew. I didn't even have to talk to her. As soon as I saw the way she smiled at me I knew she'd given us up. I guess I snapped, went crazy for a second—"

"Bullshit, Tom. You planned to kill her all along. That's why you made that call last night. That's why you set up a meeting with her. That was always the plan, wasn't it? That's why we came here."

Tom shook his head. "Back in the Nixon sheaf, TW Two warned me that Eileen was compromised, that I would be ambushed if I tried to close the deal with GYPSY. That's what happened to him, you understand? I thought I could fix things by going back three weeks, to the day before I stole the time key. It would have given me the chance to start over. I would have taken Eileen away, and left you and Linda with enough evidence to bring down GYPSY. But the time key fucked things up by taking us back just two weeks instead of three, and then you fucked things up even more. I knew you'd go after Eileen, so I tried to warn her, and she sold me out. She told GYPSY where to find me. The coldhearted bitch. I knew it as soon as I saw her. She would have given up everything to save herself. That's what happened before. That's why I had to do her, Adam. Don't you see? It was the only way to break the cycle."

"Tell me exactly what happened last time, Tom. No more smoke and mirrors. No more bullshit. Just the straight truth."

"I'll tell you when we've found some wheels. If we hustle, we might get there before they take Linda through—"

Stone dropped the bag and grabbed Tom's arm and yanked it up behind his back, spun him around and slammed him against a utility pole, and jammed the muzzle of the .38 under his jaw. "We're not doing it your way," he said. "Not anymore."

"Jesus Christ, Adam, this isn't the time or place—"

"Tell me everything," Stone said, screwing the pistol's muzzle into soft flesh. "Tell me everything. Right here, right now. Or I swear I'll leave you here for the cops and do what I have to do on my own."

"All right, all right." Tom's head was tipped back and he was standing on tiptoe. "Whatever you want to know. But how about easing up with the fucking gun?"

Stone let go of Tom's wrist and stepped back, trembling with anger and disgust and fatigue. He had to stay frosty. He had to keep on top of this. "How did she sell you out, the first time around?"

Tom massaged his jaw with thumb and forefinger. "Eileen and TW Two stole the time key. TW Two hid out in the Nixon sheaf while he arranged a deal with GYPSY through an intermediary—hard cash for the time key's return. But the people running GYPSY figured out that Eileen Barrie was involved, they confronted her, and she sold him out. When he came back to make the deal, she steered him into an ambush. The bitch dumped him in the shit to save her own skin."

"And?"

"Adam, we really can't get into this here. The area is crawling with spooks and cops—"

"*And?*"

"Jesus Christ. All right, but you have to understand that I only know what TW Two told Linda and me. He got away from the ambush, but he didn't realise that Eileen had sold him out. He went after her because he wanted to rescue her. The poor sap. GYPSY has a black facility hidden in a wild sheaf. That's where he went. He found Eileen and discovered that she'd sold him out to save herself, and he killed her and did some serious damage to GYPSY's facility."

"That's where he got his fatal dose of radiation."

"The facility has a nuclear reactor. He fucked it up and got a lethal dose. Adam, we can talk about this later. I'll confess everything. But right now we have to get moving."

Stone picked up the Macy's bag. "I need to know everything you know, Tom. I need to know how I can stop the loop closing. I need to know how to make things different."

"Things *are* different. For one thing, I killed the bitch right here. For another, as near as I can figure it, she isn't supposed to sell me out for a little over two weeks. The ambush and TW Two's dumb rescue attempt, all that, it happened a couple of days before you and Linda turned up in the Nixon sheaf."

"Bullshit. Freddy Layne saw him a few days before we were brought into this, and he was already suffering from radiation sickness."

"He used the time key, Adam. He blew the fuckers to Kingdom Come, or at least I hope he did, and he used the time key to escape into the past. You know the rest."

Stone thought about it as they walked. "He went back two weeks and killed six of Eileen Barrie's doppels. He was trying to change things."

"Of course he was. Maybe he tried to kill the Real version of Eileen Barrie, too, but she was put under guard after the time key was stolen."

"He killed the doppels, he passed through the Nixon sheaf and gave you a call and told you when Linda and I were going to turn up—"

"And he ended up in Pottersville. But that isn't going to happen this time around."

"What about the time key?"

"He dumped it."

"Tell the truth, Tom. I'm at the end of my patience."

"I'm telling you what he told me. That post office box, the one where you found the empty envelope? Our old drop? I was using it for one of my little businesses. I got the idea from your old buddy Walter Lipscombe. I found rare books in the American Bund sheaf, where prices are low, and brought them through the mirror and sold them in the Nixon sheaf, where prices are high. It made a nice contribution to my retirement fund."

"This doesn't explain where the time key went. Unless you took it."

"I looked, of course, but it had already gone. My guess is that TW Two stashed it there, all right, but he left it switched on so the people who owned it could find it and take it back. The real owners, not anyone from GYPSY," Tom said. "Did Eileen happen to mention them?"

"She spun a story about GYPSY taking the key from a bunch of time travellers."

"It isn't a story. Why do you think there's only one time key? Why do you think GYPSY wants it back so badly? Eileen hasn't been able to duplicate it, but she figured out some fundamental principles and used them to modify Turing gates. There are three of those gates in the black facility, back doors into the past of three different sheaves. If we don't move fast, the major players will disappear through one of them as soon as GYPSY begins to unravel. They'll take Linda with them, and they'll take their fucking nuclear bombs too. No lie, Adam," Tom said. "I swear on my daughter's life I'm telling you the truth."

Stone thought for a moment. "If we go after GYPSY, we're not doing it on our own," he said. "We're going to do it my way."

# 6.

The soldiers guarding Adam Stone and Tom Waverly snapped to attention when General Bruce Ellis and his aide entered the office. Bruce Ellis was wearing a yellow sweater and checked slacks. He strode across the room and took Stone's hand in a two-handed grip, saying, "Good to see you back in active service, Adam."

"Good to see you, too, Bruce. Congratulations on the promotion. And I guess I should apologise for interrupting your game."

"I'm strictly a Saturday hack-and-slicer, and you gave me a great excuse to bow out of a game I was bound to lose. I was seven points down at the fifth hole when I was told that you had actually turned up."

Stone's army ID had got him into the administration building of the division responsible for perimeter security at White Sands, where he'd discovered that he was expected: Bruce Ellis's aide had passed on his message.

Bruce glanced at Tom Waverly and said to Stone, "I guess this isn't a social visit."

"Take a look in there," Stone said, pointing to the Macy's bag. It sat on a desk next to Eileen Barrie's attaché case. "It's wrapped in my jacket."

The duty officer said, "We fluoroscoped and chem-sniffed both items, sir. They're clean."

Stone flinched when Bruce lifted out the slim jade bar. "Don't touch any of those little depressions. They're switches."

Bruce asked his aide if he'd ever seen anything like this. The aide, a young captain with steel-rimmed glasses and traces of acne on his cheeks, said that he hadn't.

Stone said, "It's at the heart of a clandestine op, Operation GYPSY, which has research labs right here in White Sands. That sort of makes it your responsibility, doesn't it?"

Tom said, "I can tell you all about it while you're getting your men together."

He'd sat quietly enough while he and Stone had waited for Bruce Ellis to arrive, but he was fired up again now, wild-eyed and eager and impatient.

"We need the army's help," Stone said. "The people in charge of this clandestine op have taken Tom's daughter prisoner."

"We need to get moving right now," Tom said. "We need to hit them hard and fast."

Bruce set the time key on the desk. "You guys need to take a couple of deep breaths and slow down. You come here to ask me to hit a Company facility because of something to do with Mr. Waverly's daughter? Is this Company business, or is it some kind of personal beef?"

"It's about fifty–fifty," Stone said.

"We don't have time to do things by the numbers," Tom said. "GYPSY's labs in White Sands are a front. There's a gate that leads to a wild sheaf and a black facility where the real work is done. If we don't move right now, the main players will disappear through that gate and shut it down."

"We're in a tight spot and time is of the essence," Stone said. "But I won't ask for your help until I've explained everything."

Bruce Ellis studied him for a moment. "You have enough to make a credible case against this clandestine op?"

Stone smiled. "I'll do my best."

"You're willing to go on record?"

"Absolutely."

"We don't have time for this shit," Tom said.

"You can try to go it alone," Stone told him, "but I think you know how that works out."

"Your way or the highway, huh? Meanwhile, *right now*, those fuckers are probably putting Linda to the question."

"They won't mistreat her, Tom. They want to use her as a bargaining chip, offer to exchange her for the time key."

"You don't know that, you son of a bitch."

"I know we can't do this on our own. Bruce, will you listen to what we have to say?"

"Come through to my office, gentlemen," Bruce Ellis said. "Do your worst."

Stone told his story as quickly and concisely as he could, from David Welch's arrival at the farm in the First Foot sheaf to the point when he'd escaped from Tom and Linda Waverly. Then Tom Waverly explained about his involvement with GYPSY and its chief research scientist, and the plan to rewrite the history of the Real by starting nuclear wars in other sheaves. Bruce Ellis listened with his full attention while his aide made notes on a palmtop. He swallowed the talk about time travel whole, like an oyster, and said, "Why come to me? Why not go directly to the Company?"

"The Company offices at White Sands could be compromised by GYPSY's presence," Stone said. "I'd have to go all the way to the top, to the DCI's office. It would take time, and in the end they'd need the army's help anyway. So it made sense to come straight to you."

"If we don't move quickly," Tom said, "the main players behind GYPSY will fumigate their cover and disappear."

Bruce picked up the time key again and held it in the sunlight that fell through the window behind him. "I can accept that this is some kind of classified device. But time travel? Really, gentlemen, don't you have a better cover story than that?"

"All you need to believe is that we're the good guys," Tom said.

"I think you should take a look at the stuff in the attaché case," Stone said.

Bruce leafed through Eileen Barrie's papers. Classified studies of geopolitical destabilisation plans, details of laundered funds, read-and-burn operational orders, intelligence reports, service management orders, memos, payrolls. She had collected evidence against GYPSY with forensic and fanatical care.

"I can't move on a Company facility without authorisation," he said at last. "My superiors would give me a permanent posting in some ice age sheaf."

"Go talk to your superiors, Bruce," Stone said. "But before you do, maybe you can provide Tom with a phone and a tape recorder. He can buy time for his daughter and provide evidence that she is in clear and present danger."

Tom said, "Yeah? How am I going to do that?"

"By calling Victor Moore, and telling him that you're willing to negotiate. That you're willing to swap the time key for your daughter."

Tom made his call. He didn't get through to Victor Moore, but talked to someone who claimed that he could arrange a deal and agreed to a meeting at a spot out in the desert in four hours. Bruce Ellis said that it gave them plenty of time to organize a strike force, but he would have to do some fast talking with his superiors. While Tom described the layout of GYPSY's black facility to the colonel who would be running the front end of the operation, Stone sat in front of a video camera in Bruce Ellis's office and made a sworn deposition, and then had nothing to do but wait while Bruce talked to the Joint Chiefs and people from the DCI's office.

The aide brought him coffee he didn't want to drink and sandwiches he couldn't eat. Bruce's office smelled of furniture wax and floor polish and a hint of industrial disinfectant, an obscurely comforting institutional odour that reminded Stone of the orphanage where he'd spent his early childhood. He kicked off his boots and stretched out on the red leather sofa and dozed, waking at once when Bruce returned. It was almost noon; more than two hours had passed. Bruce was in uniform now.

"Bottom line, I have a green light to move on GYPSY's facility," Bruce said. "What I need to know now is that you'll trust the army to get the job done."

Stone felt relief fall clean through him, like sunlight through glass. He smiled and said, "I'm in your hands, Bruce."

"You bet you are. We're going in hard and fast to take control of both the facility here in White Sands and the facility on the other side of the Turing gate, and we don't know what we're going to run into. You and Tom can ride along as advisers, but only if you agree to follow the instructions of my men at all times. We have to be clear on that."

"Absolutely."

"However it falls out, it's going to give the Company a serious black eye," Bruce said. "And when this is all over, Tom is going to have to answer for killing Dr. Barrie. A good lawyer should get it pled down to man-slaughter, but he could be facing some serious jail time."

"If GYPSY is everything he claims it is, he'll probably get a presidential pardon," Stone said. He was pleased and excited. Things were very definitely different now. Everything was in the air; nothing should come out the way it had before.

Bruce pulled a bottle of Jim Beam from a desk drawer, poured two meas-ures into paper cups from the water-cooler in the corner, and handed one to Stone. They toasted old times and drank.

"I've been in charge of security at White Sands for just over a year," Bruce said. "It's an important job, a necessary job, but it's police work, not sol-diering. This is soldiering. This is what I'm trained to do, and what my men are trained to do." He smiled at Stone. "Don't tell my superiors, by the way. They think I'm enjoying my promotion. But if this goes wrong, I'll go down and you'll go down with me. You won't ever get to go back into retirement and play at being a farmer in your cosy little wild sheaf. Hell, even if it goes right, you probably won't get back there for several months."

"I can't ever go back," Stone said, "because in a manner of speaking I'm already there."

"Yes, you are. Your deposition, the papers, and Tom's phone conversation were pretty persuasive. It also helped that Company officers were dispatched to check Dr. Barrie's house and found and arrested several people who were tearing up the place. But the fact that you are in two places at once was a major factor in convincing the Joint Chiefs to move against GYPSY."

Stone felt a prickle of alarm. "You sent someone into the First Foot sheaf to check on me?"

"Don't worry. It was done discreetly. A Company officer went through the mirror and phoned the sheriff of New Amsterdam from First Foot, and the sheriff confirmed you were at home. He wanted to know what it was all about, of course, but he was told it was just a routine background check. We checked with the transit authority at Brookhaven, too. You haven't been back through the First Foot gate since you quit the Real, two years ago. Either you're a ghost, or a doppel, or you're telling the truth." Bruce downed the last of his bourbon and tossed the paper cup into a wastebasket. "I'll take you over to the quartermasters and get you kitted up, and then you can talk to the man in charge of the assault team. He'll run you through the plan."

# 7.

I t kicked off with a frontal assault on Operation GYPSY's research laboratory: fifty acres of desert scrub fenced with electrified razor wire, a spur line that ran through a Turing gate hidden inside a concrete bunker, and a two-storey office block and a couple of workshops, tucked away in the sprawl of storage yards, industrial sheds, vehicle parks, and maintenance facilities at the northern edge of the White Sands interchange. A jump-out crew in a delivery van secured the guards at the checkpoint in the perimeter fence, and three attack helicopters swooped in above the parking lot in front of the office block, the downdraught from their rotors blowing a storm of sand and litter as ropes flopped out from their hatches and soldiers in combat armour slid down and scattered in every direction. One squad kicked down the door of the prefab shed where the gate controls were located and tossed flashbangs and gas grenades inside; the rest combed the offices and workshops, marching out men and women at gunpoint.

When the Jeep carrying Adam Stone, Tom Waverly, and General Bruce Ellis drew up outside the control shed, soldiers were standing over three men who knelt with their hands secured behind their backs by plastic ties. The air stank of tear gas and bits of paper blew everywhere; the raid had disrupted an orgy of computer smashing and document shredding. Colonel Rebhorn, commander of the counterinsurgency team that formed the core of the assault force, saluted Bruce Ellis and told him that they'd found more than a dozen fresh bodies behind one of the workshops, every one of them shot in the head.

"They were definitely spooked before we arrived," the colonel said. He was a sturdy, compact man with a red handkerchief knotted in the open collar of his camo jacket and an unlit cheroot stuck in one side of his mouth. "They were destroying files and smashing up equipment in the offices and workshops, and we caught these geeks trying to activate a suicide sequence in the quantum computer that controls the gate. They didn't move fast enough, though. It's still up and running."

"It wouldn't have made any difference if they had managed to shut it down," Bruce said. "We have our own gate into that very same sheaf, a weapons-testing range only a couple of hundred klicks away from their dirty little secret. These guys were left behind to sacrifice themselves for no good reason. They should be reminded of that when they're being interrogated."

Tom said, "If the gate's still working, why aren't we going through?"

"How about it?" Bruce said to Colonel Rebhorn.

"The gate was shut down to minimum aperture, sir, but we're bringing it back online. It'll be wide open in five minutes, and the train's standing right outside the perimeter, ready to go."

Bruce smiled at Stone and asked him if he was ready for some real soldiering.

"Let's hope it won't come to that," Stone said.

Colonel Rebhorn's men were battle-hardened veterans who in addition to the usual gear toted a variety of unconventional weapons, from combat shotguns to crossbows. They rode through GYPSY's Turing gate in a short train of boxcars. Stone braced as it accelerated toward the gate, but the black flash of transition was no worse than usual. There was a brief roar overhead as a robot drone launched from its cradle on the roof of the leading boxcar. A sergeant handed Colonel Rebhorn a palmtop that displayed the drone's video feed, and a few moments later the train began to brake hard in a shuddering screech of steel on steel.

"Something's wrong," Tom told Stone. "The railroad runs all the way into the facility."

They were both wearing camo fatigues, heavy Kevlar vests, and flak helmets. Tom was unarmed; Stone had an army-issue Colt .45 in the holster on his right hip, and orders to shoot Tom if necessary.

Colonel Rebhorn studied the palmtop's screen for a few moments, then sang out to his men. "They blew the track. Get ready to roll—we're a sitting target out here!"

Men got busy inside the confined space of the boxcar, readying their weapons, unclipping the straps that held down a Jeep and four quad bikes, hauling back the sliding door of the boxcar, dropping a metal ramp. Colonel Rebhorn swung into the shotgun seat of the Jeep, Stone and Tom Waverly climbed in behind him, and the sergeant took the wheel and gunned the sturdy vehicle down the ramp.

The climate of this sheaf was warmer and wetter than the Real's. Rolling grassland stretched away under a slate sky and blowing drifts of rain. Quad bikes, Jeeps, and two squat armoured personnel carriers drove out of the other boxcars and lined up alongside the little train, which had stopped about a hundred yards in front of a huge crater of raw, upturned dirt. On the other side of the crater, the railroad track ran toward thickly forested mountains whose peaks were lost in low cloud.

Rebhorn angled his palmtop so that Stone and Tom could see the grainy video feed. He pointed to a cluster of buildings in a rectangular clearing, and a brilliant white gem in the forest about half a mile to the southeast. "Am I right in thinking that's their nuclear reactor?"

"It powers the Turing gates they've hidden here," Tom said. "If you can shut it down, you can stop them from escaping."

"This was taken in infrared," Rebhorn said. "The reactor is running hot, and the drone has detected radiation, too. I think the unfriendlies have sabotaged it."

"They've done what TW Two did," Tom said. "Lifted the core rods, and started a runaway reaction. It's an obvious move, Colonel. The ultimate in deniability. A core meltdown would render hundreds of square kilometres uninhabitable for at least a century. If they've sabotaged their power source, they've either gone through one of the gates or they're about ready to go through."

Rebhorn scowled around his cheroot. "Any idea about how long we have before it blows?"

"Could be hours, could be minutes," Tom said.

"Then we better get moving," Rebhorn said.

He stood up and waved his hand in a circle above his head and pointed forward. Engines revved, and the column of vehicles accelerated alongside the railroad toward the tree line. Braced in the back of the command Jeep, Stone tried not to think about the nuclear reactor sitting just a few miles away, its core growing hotter and hotter. He felt that he was riding an avalanche he'd accidentally triggered. Just one wrong step could wipe him out. A reactor was about to go critical, right here, right now, and the version of Tom Waverly who'd been killing Eileen Barrie's doppels had been dying of radiation poisoning. . . .

As the edge of the forest resolved out of the rain, muzzle flashes flickered in the shadows beneath the trees. A bullet cracked past Stone's ear, and then the mini-guns on top of the APCs on either side of the command Jeep opened up, hosing rounds into the tree line. Trees tossed as if caught in a gale, shedding leaves and shattered branches, and a ragged line of figures stood up and charged through the long grass.

They were a species of apeman that Stone had never seen before, wiry creatures about seven feet tall, clothed only in greasy red fur and leather harness. They carried assault rifles and rocket-propelled grenade launchers, and their small heads were cased in fat white helmets: a battle computer in some remote bunker was controlling them through encrypted radio links to electrodes in their brains. They charged without fear, firing their weapons as they ran straight toward the column. A gout of smoke and red dirt burst in front of the pair of quad bikes that led the command Jeep. The bikes tipped over and spilled their riders, hot dirt rattled down as the Jeep slowed and swerved past the raw crater, and Tom swung out of the vehicle, fell down, picked himself up, and ran back toward the overturned bikes.

Stone jumped out too, fell, rolled, scrambled to his feet and drew his pistol, and ran after Tom. Wet grass immediately drenched him to the waist. Something reared up to his right, beyond the smoldering crater, and he turned and fired. The round knocked the skinny giant onto its back but didn't kill it. As it climbed to its feet, Stone braced his right wrist with his left hand, took careful aim, and put a second round through its white helmet. It fell bonelessly, a puppet whose strings had been cut, but more apemen were already running toward him. He picked his targets and fired off the rest of the clip, taking two of them down. He dropped the empty clip and snapped a fresh one into the hot pistol, and the rest of the apemen vanished in a storm of dirt and flying foliage as a soldier standing in the rear of a Jeep hammered them with the heavy machine gun mounted on its roll bar.

Tom righted one of the quad bikes and accelerated away in a spray of wet dirt. Stone ran to the other bike. Its rider sprawled beneath it, head twisted around, blood all over his face, no pulse behind his jaw. Stone used all his strength to heave the heavy machine onto its four all-terrain tires. Its engine started at the first press of the button, and Stone pursued Tom toward the trees, the two of them peeling away from the railroad and Rebhorn's team.

Stone realised with sick dismay that they were heading toward the nuclear reactor. He opened up the throttle of the quad bike, gaining on Tom as he disappeared into the trees, leaning into turns, leaning *out* of turns when the tough little vehicle tipped sideways and two of its fat tires lifted off the ground. A big animal crashed away, a ground sloth with a shaggy grey pelt and the build of a bottom-heavy bear, glimpsed and gone as Stone bounced and slithered down a corduroy track that dipped into a draw filled with mist that rose from the swift river running through it: the outflow from the reactor.

The reactor loomed ahead, a squat, windowless blockhouse built across the draw. Smooth torrents of steaming water shot out of three huge outflow pipes at its base, sluicing through a concrete basin that emptied into the river bed. Tom was racing his quad bike along a track above this cauldron, cutting toward the flank of the reactor. Stone chased after him, saw him jump off his bike and jog up a steel stairway, and swerved to a halt, shouting Tom's name.

When Stone gained the second landing of the stairway, three loud shots made him crouch low. Tom was leaning over the rail, two flights above. He'd lost his helmet. Strings of grey hair hung around his face as he angled an assault rifle downward and shouted at Stone, telling him to get the fuck out of here right now.

"Don't do it!" Stone shouted back. He had drawn his pistol but couldn't get a clear sight through the grid of steps.

"It's my fucking destiny!" Tom screamed. He rattled off three more shots and disappeared from view.

Stone went up the rest of the stairway slowly and carefully, leading with his pistol. There was a short walkway to a locked steel door set in a deep recess. He pounded on it impotently, then ran back down the stairs, started his quad bike, and sped up the switchback trail that climbed past the reactor, blasting through mist, jolting along a track between dense trees, emerging at the edge of a wide strip of pounded earth. Railroad sidings fanned out in front of three hangar-sized buildings. Rain blurred the lights inside the hangars and the floodlights on tall pylons alongside the tracks.

Colonel Rebhorn's team was stretched across the far end of the sidings, firing at groups of apemen that rushed toward them through squalling rain. A string of boxcars burned fiercely. Mini-guns on top of the two APCs swivelled this way and that, firing short deadly bursts that churned dirt, disintegrated sandbagged emplacements, and vaporised apemen.

Stone heard rounds snap past and saw apemen moving toward him, shooting from the hip. He gunned the quad bike, planning to cut across the tracks, but more apemen popped up from a trench right in front of him. He swerved sharply and the bike tipped and skidded away on its side as he jumped clear. He rolled three times and hugged the ground, reaching for his pistol, as rounds cut the air above his head. The apemen were climbing out of their trench and he took aim and shot two of them and jumped up as the rest charged, firing at their white helmets, their blank leathery faces. Beyond the sidings a line of power transformers exploded in great fountains of sparks, and floodlights and the lights inside the hangars all went out.

The apemen screeched and dropped their weapons and clutched at their white helmets. Stone shot one down and the rest turned tail and fled. Across the wide space in front of the hangars, apemen were standing mute and still in the rain or wandering aimlessly this way and that, jerking and falling over as Rebhorn's men picked them off, the soldiers' gunfire slowly dying down as they realised that the battle was over.

Stone caught up with Rebhorn in one of the hangars. The colonel had lit his cheroot and was puffing on it as he stood with his hands on his hips in the middle of the huge space, studying the three Turing gates that loomed above him. Their empty maws were each twenty feet in diameter, big enough to take a truck. Soldiers were spraying foam at the burning Airstream trailer that housed the gate controls. Black smoke rolled out of its broken windows and rose into the hangar's high roof and flushed out of its square doorway. Smashed equipment lay everywhere. Dead men and women sprawled in a pool of mingled blood.

Rebhorn told Stone that his men hadn't found Linda Waverly yet, but they were still searching. "Looks like the sons of bitches killed everyone they didn't need and went through one of these gates. We don't know which one, and we don't know where the gates went because they're all stone-cold dead. We heard explosions as we were fighting our way in. I lost five men to those goddamn apes, twice that many wounded. I would have lost more if the battle computer hadn't been taken out."

Stone told him that the power surge was probably down to Tom Waverly. "He got inside the reactor and locked the door in my face. We have to find another way in, Colonel. We have to get him out."

Rebhorn said that he'd do his best, but he was waiting on a specialist team that would be able to deal with the reactor.

"Give me a couple of shaped charges," Stone said. "I'll blow the door and drag him out by his hair."

"Can't let you do that, Mr. Stone. That reactor could go critical at any time, and we need you to help us understand what happened here. Let's hope those specialists can help your friend before he gets himself a lethal dose."

"It might be too late already," Stone said.

When he'd taken the time key and set out to confront Eileen Barrie, Stone had believed that he had been setting out on a path that was straight and true, but the path had betrayed him, had looped back to a place very like the one he'd been trying to escape. He wondered with a bitter weariness if he'd gone around the loop before, passing through minor variations and flourishes but always arriving at the same outcome.

Rebhorn said, "It could have been a whole lot worse. My men found three small nuclear devices in various states of assembly. None of them were ready to go, fortunately, or I doubt we'd be having this discussion right now."

"This isn't over," Stone said. "These people may have taken an armed bomb with them. Maybe more than one."

"You're going to have to discuss that with General Ellis back in the Real," Rebhorn said. "My job is to secure this place, not to worry about imponderables."

"I'm not going back until I know what happened to Tom Waverly."

As they walked out of the hangar toward the command Jeep, Rebhorn got a call on his radio; a couple of his men had spotted movement in an outbuilding.

It was a small concrete cube that stood at a corner of a field of smoldering, truck-sized transformers. One of the soldiers keeping watch from behind a boxcar told Colonel Rebhorn that someone was inside, and at the same moment the building's door cracked open and a white shape—a T-shirt tied to the barrel of an assault rifle—fluttered like a ghost in the narrow aperture. A familiar voice shouted that he was coming out and he was unarmed. Stone told Rebhorn and his soldiers to hold their fire, and ran forward as Tom Waverly stepped out into the rain stark naked, hands held high.

# 8.

Two of Rebhorn's men drove Stone and Tom Waverly back to the train. Tom told Stone that he'd had to go onto the floor of the reactor and reinsert its control rods manually, and then he'd fed a killing surge through the power lines to the facility. He'd been suited up, he said, but he wasn't sure if the suit had given him enough protection.

"We'll get you checked out as soon as we get back to the Real."

"They took Linda with them, didn't they? They took her through their back door." Tom was slumped in the shotgun seat of the Jeep next to Stone, his wet hair hanging in rat tails, one blanket wrapped kiltwise around his waist, a second draped over his shoulders. "This didn't exactly go according to plan. Linda's gone; I got a lethal dose. You ever read Dante? There's a circle of Purgatory where the damned are condemned to live through the same thing over and over. But I can't for the life of me remember what they'd done to deserve it."

"We'll take care of you," Stone said, but he felt a cold hopelessness. This really is still the same loop, he thought. We haven't changed anything important. Maybe it isn't possible to change anything: we're fated to go around in a circle. Tom will die. And Susan will die, and we'll come back here, and start over, no end to it. No end.

"If we don't do something soon, we'll be headed for Pottersville," Tom said. "They want to exchange Linda for the time key. That's how we'll get to them. They still want it. They still need it. They need it so very badly they'll risk everything to get it back."

"You aren't going anywhere, Tom, except straight to a hospital. I'll take it from here. I'll get Linda back. All you have to do is tell me where these guys have gone and what they're planning to do."

Tom shook his head. "There's no point going to a hospital. I know I caught a lethal dose in the reactor. I know I'm gonna die this time around, like I did the time before. I know it, and you know it too. They'll want to take me away for debriefing, and then they'll throw me in the deepest, blackest hole they have. But you can't let them do that to me, Adam, not if you want to save the life of your woman. We still have work to do, old buddy. One last op."

"I don't think they'll let you go anywhere, Tom. But if you tell me what needs to be done, I promise I'll do my very best."

"I'll tell you this: they took a suitcase nuke through one of their gates. They're going to try to start a war sometime in the past of another sheaf. They're going to try to change its history, and if they succeed they'll change *our* history too. The Company is going to have to let me go because I know where the bomb is going to be planted. I helped scout it out and set it up, and I know how to stop it, too. You're coming with me, Adam. We'll find the bomb, we'll find them, we'll find Linda. Otherwise, they'll change history. They'll change everything."

"Where did they go? Which sheaf?"

Cold rain blew over the Jeep as it sped along the muddy track. The train stood in the distance, small and black in the wide, empty grassland.

"We'll go after them together," Tom said, and wouldn't say anything else.

Back in the Real, Stone told Bruce Ellis, "Linda, Tom, and me, we're caught in some kind of loop. It's about two weeks end to end. We travelled back to the beginning, and now we're going forward. And if we don't figure out how to stop it, Tom will end up killing himself in Pottersville and Linda and I will go on to meet another version of Tom in the Nixon sheaf, and we'll all end up back here."

Bruce said, "If you catch up with these bad guys, will it stop this loop of yours?"

"I hope so. Colonel Rebhorn found three partially assembled nuclear devices at that facility. If they abandoned those in place, it's likely that Tom was telling me the truth when he said that they took a suitcase nuke with them when they fled through the mirror. If we don't catch them, Bruce, they'll change history. Strictly speaking, they may have already done it."

Stone was jittery and exhausted. When he lifted his cup of coffee, the disk of black liquid inside it shivered and shook.

"Let me bring you up to speed on what's been happening here," Bruce said. He was sitting in the leather chair behind his desk, his back straight, his hands folded on the blotter in front of him, the creases in his uniform sharp enough to draw blood. "Most of the people we arrested at the facility on this side of the mirror aren't talking, but we managed to convince a few of the smarter ones that they wouldn't have to face the most serious charges if they made statements right away. We've heard a lot about the time key, but no one seems to know anything about the operational side. It seems to have been rigorously compartmented. Research here in White Sands; black ops run from the facility in the wild sheaf."

"How about Victor Moore?"

"We have his wife. She told us he left home in the early hours of this morning, and she isn't saying anything else. We're trying to bargain a plea, but our lawyers think we have a pretty weak case because we can't prove that she had anything to do with this. We're examining the documents we rescued from the facility and the documentation you took from Dr. Barrie. And although most of the people we arrested seem to be pretty low in the pyramidal organisation of this thing, it's possible that they'll lead us to bigger fish. The DCI's office is sending teams to continue the interrogation process, and to investigate every square inch of GYPSY's facilities. They'll want to talk to you, too."

"We don't have time for that, Bruce."

"I'm sorry, Adam. It's out of my hands."

"There is something you could do for me. One more big favour, my last. You remember what I told you about Susan Nichols? What happened to her—what might happen? She and her son have to be moved from her farm in the First Foot sheaf and placed in a safe house in the Real. I can't do it myself because I have to do this thing with Tom—"

"I wish I could help," Bruce said. "I really do. But the DCI's office is in charge now, and I can't do anything without talking to them first. I do know that they're taking this extremely seriously, Adam. I'm sure your friend and her son will be looked after."

"The guy in charge. It's Ralph Kohler, isn't it?"

"You know him?"

"Yeah. I met him a few days ago, two weeks in the future. . . ."

Bruce studied Stone, then said, "I think you need to get some rest, Adam. You're going to need your wits about you when you talk to his people."

# 9.

**B**ruce Ellis's aide escorted Stone to a bleak little room in the unmarried officers' quarters. He stretched out on the narrow bed, convinced that he wouldn't sleep, and woke six hours later. He was still tired, but his thoughts were moving more easily now.

He used the phone beside the bed to call Bruce's office, hoping to get an update. The man who answered told him that the general was away from his desk, but two men from the DCI's team wanted to talk to him.

"I guess they know where to find me," Stone said.

He did several sets of crunches and sit-ups. There was still some stiffness in his left leg, but the exercise eased it. He took a shower, and was eating a hot meal in the mess when the two Company officers found him.

They interviewed him in his room. One of the officers was tall and pale and not much older than Linda Waverly; the other had a cool, hooded stare and a Brooklyn accent that could score glass. Stone told them at the outset that he wanted protection for Susan Nichols and her son, and they assured him that measures had already been taken.

The officer from Brooklyn, Bradley Cramer, said, "We've locked down the Turing gate to the First Foot sheaf. No one can get in or out without passing through two layers of security."

His partner, Preston Echols, said, "We have people watching the New Amsterdam ferry too."

"For all you know, some of the officers on the security detail could be part of GYPSY," Stone said. "And the people behind GYPSY definitely know I'm involved in this—one of them recognised me after I took him down at the El Dorado Motel. It puts my friend and her son in immediate danger. You should move them out of First Foot and put them in a safe house."

"I agree we don't yet know how many people are involved in this thing," Cramer said. "We've discovered links to cells in every part of the Company, and we're still tracing contacts, trying to work around cutouts and other precautions. Those names you and Waverly gave us are a big help in that respect. So far none of them are talking, but we think that the ex-Marine, Buddy Altman, is close to telling us what he knows. We'll bring this whole thing down, I guarantee it. Meanwhile, we have army units stationed on either side of the First Foot gate in addition to our own guys. Every train that goes through is checked out top to bottom. The same goes for the ferry."

Echols said, "Even if we took Mrs. Nichols and her son to a protected facility, it's possible that some sleeper will get to them. They'll be safer where they are, Mr. Stone. And so are you—or rather, so is the earlier version of your good self."

Stone said, "Does he know about this?"

Thinking about this other version of himself, two weeks younger but otherwise identical, made Stone feel like a ghost haunting his own life.

"He knows that there's a situation, but he doesn't know about you," Cramer said. "And neither he nor Mrs. Nichols wants to move out."

Stone smiled a little. "I don't suppose they do."

"We'll look after Mrs. Nichols and her son," Echols said. "And we will be taking very good care of the doppels of Dr. Barrie, too."

Cramer said, "We're going to do our level best to make sure that this loop or circle of whatever it is doesn't swallow its own tail. For that, we need your help."

"To begin with, we need to know everything you know," Echols said, and opened his briefcase and took out a small video camera and a folding tripod.

"I've already made a deposition," Stone said.

"Then you won't mind making another," Cramer said. "You can start at the beginning, and take it from there."

It took three hours to get through the entire story. Stone bottled up his impatience and anxiety and answered every one of the two officers' many questions and requests for clarification. At the end, he spoke straight to the camera. "Colonel Rebhorn found three partially assembled nuclear devices at the facility. I believe that the people in charge of GYPSY escaped through one of the Turing gates and took with them a fourth, functional device. I believe that they intend to use it, and I believe that Tom Waverly knows when and where. I am willing to go with him and do whatever is necessary to stop them."

"Duly noted," Cramer said, and Echols switched off the camera.

Stone said, "Where will that go?"

"We report directly to the DCI," Cramer said.

"Promise me he'll see that last part."

"He already knows about it," Cramer said. "That's why we're here. You rest up now. Take it easy. You can bet we'll be wanting to talk to you again very soon."

Although Stone wasn't under arrest, he couldn't leave the compound and was dogged by two large men in black suits everywhere he went. An army doctor treated the fading bruises and minor burns inflicted by Walter Lipscombe's goons. He was interviewed by a Company psychiatrist, and briefed four frighteningly young civilian advisers who planned to use game theory to predict GYPSY's next move. He ran laps around the track in one corner of the compound. He had dinner with Bruce Ellis in the officers' mess. They talked about everything but Tom Waverly and Operation GYPSY, and did their best to ignore Stone's bodyguards at the next table. At last, two days after the assault on GYPSY's clandestine facility, Cramer and Echols paid him another visit.

"Tom Waverly wants us to help him get his daughter back," Echols said.

"The cocky son of a bitch knows we have to go along with his goddamned story about a suitcase nuke," Cramer said.

They were on the running track. Stone, in a khaki T-shirt, khaki shorts, and running shoes, was blotting sweat from his face with a towel.

"We'd like to investigate it thoroughly before we decide what to do," Echols said. "Unfortunately, there's a time factor."

Stone felt a chill at the back of his neck. "He's dying, isn't he?"

Echols nodded. "He received a bad dose of radiation when he secured the nuclear reactor."

"How long has he got?"

"At the moment, he's recovering from severe bouts of nausea and diarrhea," Echols said. "Once he's over that, he'll appear to be quite healthy for a few days. But then he'll begin to experience bleeding of his gums and his intestinal lining. His teeth will loosen in their sockets, his hair will start to fall out, and his skin will bruise as his blood vessels began to degenerate. He'll lose his appetite, and then his motor control. He'll suffer uncontrollable internal bleeding—"

"*How long?*"

"Maybe a week, maybe two," Cramer said. "Three at the outside."

"It sounds about right," Stone said. "It took him fifteen days to kill six of Eileen Barrie's doppels."

"It must get confusing," Echols said, "waiting for the rest of the world to catch up with what you already know."

"I don't know everything. Things aren't exactly the same this time around. But I do know that we can't afford to sit on our hands and hope it will come out right. My offer to help still stands, gentlemen. I hope that's why you're here."

Stone had spent the last two days working out angles in his head. He was determined to do everything he could to make sure that the loop didn't close.

"You have to understand that we're the tip of the iceberg," Cramer said. "Everyone is going balls-out on this thing. We have a team that's trying to reconstruct half a ton of shredded documents. Another team is trying to retrieve data from smashed computers. We even have people down at Lompac trying to question Knightly. The guy is the next best thing to a vegetable, no way he had anything to do with GYPSY after his stroke, but he was in at the beginning and there's a faint chance he'll tell us something useful."

"A committee of experts chaired by Richard Feynman is trying to work out the implications of Waverly's story about time travel and changing history," Echols said. "Feynman won the Nobel Prize for Physics. If anyone can make sense of this, he can."

"But Tom knows you won't be able to find where that suitcase nuke went without his help," Stone said.

"We did try to interview him while he was under the influence of truth drugs," Cramer said. "It didn't go anywhere useful."

"We were trained to resist interrogation," Stone said. "And in any case, Tom knows that he's dying. He knows that he has nothing to lose."

Cramer nodded. "Bottom line, the clock's ticking. Waverly's got us, and he knows it."

"He said that there would be no discussion about or variation of his terms," Echols said. "He was very calm about it, laid it right out and sat back and let us think about it."

"He wants to use the time key to chase after the people who have kidnapped his daughter," Cramer said. "I'll say this for him, the guy has big balls."

Echols said, "He doesn't have long left, and we can't wait for the scientists to get around to building a Turing gate that can do this trick with time. We have to go now. And we wouldn't ask this if we hadn't exhausted every other option."

Cramer said, "What my partner means, Mr. Stone, is we're going to accept your offer to help."

# 10.

Tom Waverly sat at a metal table in a brightly lit interrogation room, bare-legged in a green gown. A plastic sack of clear fluid hung upside down on a steel pole beside him, connected by a line to his left forearm.

Stone watched from the other side of the room's mirrored window as Cramer and Echols told Tom that they were willing to let him go after the people who had kidnapped his daughter on one condition: he had to tell them where the bad guys were hiding.

Tom considered this, taking his own sweet time, grandstanding in front of the two weary interrogators. At last he said, "Take me to Brookhaven. Then we can talk all about it."

He smiled at the mirrored window: smiled straight at Stone.

# 11.

They flew to New York in an executive jet. Tom Waverly was secured in the bedroom at the rear, with three doctors working to stabilise his condition with a cocktail of drugs and a whole-blood transfusion; Stone sat in the lounge area with Cramer, Echols, and the four young civilian advisers. Once the plane was in the air, Echols handed Stone his palmtop and played a video clip from the interrogation of one of the technicians who had been arrested at GYPSY's White Sands facility.

Stone watched the little screen as the man talked about time travellers. "That's more or less what Eileen Barrie told me," he said.

"There's more," Echols said. He took the palmtop from Stone and jumped to another video clip and handed the palmtop back.

". . . didn't know that the device was self-aware at first," the technician said.

He was a small man in a loose-fitting orange jumpsuit, his face and bald scalp as pink as a boiled shrimp. His hands shook when he extracted a cigarette out of the packet on the table in front of him, and he flinched when one of the interrogators leaned across the table and snapped a flame from a lighter.

"We found out when we were doing lab tests," he said. "We started out by sending clocks a little way back in time. We used clocks because they showed the time when they were sent through. A clock would pop out of the mirror, an exact duplicate of one of the clocks we had in the laboratory. We'd note the time it arrived and the time it displayed, which gave us the time it had been sent through, and then we'd wait until that exact second, and send the original clock back. Completing the loop, you understand? One day, all kinds of objects started popping through, and we had to scramble and find out where they came from, so we could send the originals back. It was like playing hide-and-seek with the future. And then we got more ambitious. We started doing experiments that could split the sheaf in two. By, for instance, receiving an object from the future, but refusing to send it back to the past."

The two interrogators spent some time questioning the technician about this. He asked for paper and pencil, sketched loops labelled with subscripted $T$s. "What happens when you receive something from your future self, let's say a clock, you end up with two identical clocks. One of them is the original, showing the correct time, $T_1$, and the other is from some future time,

$T_2$. Okay? So now you wait until the original clock reaches $T_2$ and you send it back into the past, to $T_1$. That means you've completed the loop and you've stayed on the same time line. But if you *don't* send the original clock back, if you keep it, it means that the clock you received from the future must have come from an alternate sheaf where the original *was* sent back. . . . You understand? By refusing to do what you're supposed to do, you exercise free will, and that splits the sheaf into two. One sheaf ends up with two clocks, the other with no clocks.

"We played dozens of variations on that kind of game. For a while, it was like Practical Quantum Mechanics 101. We were having a lot of fun, but we got carried away. We became careless, and left the device switched on for hours at a time. And after a couple of weeks it made its move. We'd been working in shifts, and luckily for me I wasn't there. It struck down everyone in the lab, blinded them with headaches worse than any migraine or gave them seizures, and then it altered the settings on the gate. Two men came through. We can't be certain, but we think that the device sent some kind of signal into the future, and the two men were sent to rescue it. What they didn't know was that the lab was being monitored from a remote location. The security people shut down the gate and locked the doors and ordered the two men who'd come through the mirror to surrender. They looked at each other, and they died."

One of the interrogators asked how the two men had died.

"Like the others, the ones who were caught with the device in the first place. They willed themselves to die. I heard that the surgeon who autopsied them said it was cardiovascular collapse," the small man in the orange jump-suit said. "After that, everyone who worked on the device began to suffer from bad headaches and nightmares. One guy killed himself sleepwalking. Walked straight into the electric fence. Another drank a half pint of liquid nitrogen. We didn't think too much of it at the time. I mean, we were all pretty stressed. We were working twenty hours a day, eating junk food, strung out on coffee and speed, snatching catnaps. It wasn't surprising that a few of us went crazy. But then people started to have seizures every time the device was switched on, and we realised that it was somehow getting inside our heads. After that, we didn't dare switch it on again until Dr. Barrie worked out how to control it. She designed a bridle that forces it to do what you tell it to do, but it can still hurt you when it does it. It can still get inside your head."

Stone thought about that as the plane flew east. He wondered what the time key might have done to him, wondered what it might have done to Tom Waverly after he'd stolen it. He thought about the story about people from the future, and Tom's claim that TW Two had left the time key switched on in the drop in the Forty-Second Street post office in the Nixon sheaf, so that it could be retrieved by its owners. . . .

But that would only happen if the loop swallowed its own tail and ended up more or less where it had begun, and Stone was determined to stop that from happening. He racked his seat back as far as it would go and tried to relax, half listening to the four advisers argue about the scenarios they had constructed. They were eager young college kids with too much intelligence and not enough experience, wearing short-sleeved shirts or T-shirts, pleated slacks or expensive jeans, penny loafers, high-top baseball boots. One wore a bow tie. Another had a row of pens in his shirt pocket. They wielded palmtops like six-shooters. They scribbled on pads of yellow legal paper. They drank coffee and Diet Coke and jabbered back and forth unceasingly, treading on the ends of each other's sentences, trying to outthink the people who'd fled GYPSY's black facility and figure out where they had run to, arguing about the reasons to select one sheaf over all the others. They talked about tipping points and esoteric statistical sieving techniques. They talked about emergent properties of history. Then they started over from first principles.

"We're still looking at everything."

"Because we can't rule out anything."

"We can rule out client sheaves."

"We can't rule out anything."

"We can rule out client sheaves because they're already client sheaves. And we can rule out post–nuclear war sheaves because they've already had a nuclear war. That leaves precontact sheaves. There are only a dozen, and we should be gaming all of them intensively. I mean, what's the point of gaming post–nuclear war sheaves?"

"Some of those sheaves had their war thirty years ago."

"What are you saying? They're ready for another?"

"They're pretty much reconstructed. Maybe the point is to tear it all down and start over. Maybe the point is to *make it worse*."

"We're talking about the past, not the present. We have to focus on precontact sheaves because we have to place these guys *somewhere*, and without hard information to the contrary, precontact sheaves are the most likely targets."

That remark got Stone's attention. He opened his eyes and said, "Place which guys?"

Someone said, "Now you've done it, Howie."

Someone else said, "You'll have to tell him. Otherwise he'll break your fingers one by one until you do."

"What do you have to tell me?" Stone said.

Cramer, who had also been trying to sleep, opened his eyes but otherwise didn't move. Echols looked up from his palmtop.

Howie had a wet bottom lip and black-framed glasses that kept sliding down his nose. His Adam's apple bobbed when he said to Stone, "I don't have clearance to tell you."

Stone felt sorry for the kid. "You don't have to tell me anything, Howie. It's pretty clear you want to work out which sheaf GYPSY is going to hit because the Company wants to insert undercover officers—people Tom won't know about. I don't have a problem with that. I understand why the Company doesn't trust Tom and me to get the job done on our own. But *where* GYPSY is going to hit is only half the problem. You also have to figure out *when*."

The four advisers looked at him with a mixture of pity and contempt, as if a chimp had ventured an opinion on experimental brain surgery.

Howie said, "I really can't talk about it."

"Too late, Howie," someone said.

"*When* doesn't matter, because we're giving you a resource," someone else said. "Howie will explain."

"Quit it, you guys," Howie said. "This is strictly need-to-know stuff."

"I think he needs to know more than most, don't you?"

Cramer yawned and said to Echols, "I guess we'll have to tell him now."

Echols said, "He's supposed to be briefed at the gate."

"I know. But if these boys try to make him guess, he might get mad and kill them all."

Stone said, "Briefed about what?"

Cramer said, "You and Waverly will go through with a technician and officers from Special Operations. The technician and three of the officers will guard the gate and take care of the time key while you and Waverly go look for the bad guys. The other officers will shadow you, and step in if you need any help."

"Tom knows about this?"

"Waverly didn't want to go through with anyone but you," Echols said. "But we soon disabused him of that notion."

Cramer said, "We made it plain that we'd rather he didn't go through at all than trust him with the time key. We told him that if he didn't agree, he could forget about saving his daughter. He called us all kinds of names, but he gave in."

Stone said, "I guess that means you figured out how to use the time key."

Echols smiled. "Not exactly. One of GYPSY's technicians decided he didn't want to spend the rest of his life in a maximum-security prison. He's going through the mirror with you."

"Even if you can trust this technician, the time key isn't reliable," Stone said. "It has its own agenda. It didn't do what Tom wanted it to do, so how do you know it will do what you want it to do?"

"Because we have Dr. Barrie's bridle," Echols said.

"We found it in a safe in GYPSY's facility in White Sands," Cramer said. "Luckily, none of the bozos who were trying to trash the place knew how to get the safe open. Our technicians have done all kinds of tests, and the thing works exactly as advertised."

"In laboratory conditions," Stone said.

"We don't trust it any more than you do, even with the bridle," Echols said. "That's why we are providing you with additional backup—a resource that Mr. Waverly won't know about. As soon as we find out which sheaf GYPSY has targeted, we will insert two of our people. Not in the present, but in the past. All the way back to the first week the gate into the sheaf was opened, in fact."

"This is in case Waverly or the time key tries some funny move that puts you and him in one time, and the technician and the Special Ops guys in another," Cramer said. "Our two people will stay under deep cover for as long as it takes, and we'll give you a way of making contact with them in case you find yourself stranded with Waverly."

"We sent the time key on ahead of us, in an air force jet," Echols said. "It'll get there two hours before we do. As long as these bright young things can work out where you'll be going, there will be ample time to set this up."

"In my opinion, you should place officers in all the precontact sheaves," one of the advisers said.

"Spoken like someone who's never worked in the field," Echols said.

"Maybe we should send *these* guys back," Cramer said. "See how they cope when they're cut free from everything they know, and have to build new lives and wait ten or fifteen years in deep cover for a call that might never come."

Stone said, "So my backup depends on these kids making the right guess."

"If things work out, you can call in an army division if necessary," Cramer said. "You'll only need the deep-cover guys if the time key futzes things up."

"Well, that's exactly what it did the only time I saw it used."

"One of the doctors looking after Mr. Waverly is a psychologist," Echols said. "He will be doing his best to trick him into letting something slip."

"Tom will know you'll try something like that," Stone said. "If he does let something slip, you can bet it will send you in the wrong direction."

Cramer gave him a sour look. "You old-school guys always did think you were hot shit."

"We've been around the block," Stone said. "Tom won't talk because he knows he doesn't have to talk. He'll play you all the way to the wire."

# 12.

The plane was cleared straight in at Brookhaven, and taxied to a hangar where an ambulance, a black limo, and a small fleet of NYPD squad cars and motorcycle cops were waiting. Tom Waverly and his doctors were escorted off the plane by a squad of soldiers and put in the back of the ambulance; Cramer and Echols led Stone to the limo. Echols carried a briefcase and Cramer was using his cell phone, listening to someone at the other end, saying "yes, sir" several times, folding the phone shut as he climbed into the limo, telling his partner that everyone was scrambling to redeploy. A helicopter went up as the column of vehicles moved off with motorcycle outriders front and rear. Cramer, hunched on the fold-down seat across from Stone, said, "Just before he came off the plane Waverly told us to head into Manhattan instead of Brookhaven. The son of a bitch is playing games with us."

"He wants to use the Grand Central Station facility," Stone said.

"We think so too," Echols said. He sat next to Stone, his briefcase in his lap.

"Right now the attorney general is writing a search-and-seizure warrant that will give us complete control," Cramer said. "It's going to cause an almighty stink, but we have no choice."

"At least it narrows it down to just five gates," Echols said. "Five sheaves, three of them precontact."

"It's the Nixon sheaf," Stone said. "Tom and I worked undercover there, and he told me that he'd been working there for Knightly after he disappeared. Also, that's where he was hiding out after he stole the time key."

Cramer said, "Why would he hide in a sheaf whose history GYPSY wants to change?"

"Because it's always a good idea to hide in the place you know best," Stone said. "You have contacts there, you've probably established several different identities and hidden caches of money and documents, you know how to blend in. . . . And if GYPSY manages to do what it plans to do, it won't just change their target sheaf. It'll change everything."

"He has a point," Echols said, "and I believe that the Nixon sheaf was one of the favourites of our advisers. It's a good tip. We should pass it on."

Cramer took out his cell phone, punched a number, and immediately got into an argument with the person who answered. Echols opened his briefcase and took out a set of keys and handed them to Stone, telling him that they were for the doors between the gate and the subway station, then gave him a steel ballpoint pen that was a little heavier than a pen should be.

Stone weighed it in his hand. "This is what? Plastic explosive?"

"Click it once and it works like a normal pen," Echols said. "Click it three times in a row and it will fire a needle tipped with nerve toxin. It has five needles and has a range of a couple of feet, but it works best if you hold it against the target's skin."

"A sidearm will do just fine."

"You'll get a sidearm at the gate. This," Echols said, handing Stone what looked like a watch battery strung on a fine chain, "contains a radio transmitter with a fractally folded aerial. Squeeze it like so, the top pops up, and you twist it ninety degrees to the left to activate it. It'll send an encrypted signal every five minutes. The people we're sending through ahead of you, the embeds, will have receivers that can pick up the signal from up to twenty miles away."

"As long as they're still alive, or haven't lost their receivers," Cramer said, folding away his cell phone. "And as long as they've been sent to the right sheaf."

"They're both good men," Echols said. "They'll be there for you if you need them, Mr. Stone."

"Let's hope you don't need them," Cramer said. He reached into the briefcase on his partner's lap and handed Stone a waterproof capsule the size of his thumb. "You can hide this where the sun don't shine. It contains diamond-tipped wire cutters that can deal with the links in standard police handcuffs. There's a set of lock picks, too."

"Very thoughtful," Stone said, taking the suppository. "What else have you got? A gun that looks like a toothpaste tube? A trick comb? Exploding cigars?"

"Your suit will have a sewn-in lapel dagger," Echols said. "You'll also get official ID for the three different precontact sheaves. Anything else you think you might need, you better ask now. We don't have much time."

Cramer leaned forward, all business. "Listen up, here's what we want you to do. As soon as Waverly divulges the location of the nuclear device, you'll neutralize him, you'll make your way back—"

"Hold on. What's this about killing Tom Waverly?"

"He's as deeply involved in this conspiracy as anyone else," Cramer said with exaggerated patience. "He's only divulging information because he's trying to play us. So let's be clear. Once you've learned the location of the nuke, you must neutralize him. Terminate him if necessary, but at the bare minimum you have to make sure that he can't interfere with the rest of the operation. It's a shitty thing to spring on you, but it has to be done. He's an outlaw. He can't be trusted."

"He's gone over to the dark side," Echols said.

"If you don't do it, the people shadowing you will," Cramer said. "After that, you'll make your way back to the insertion point, and we'll get you out and take it from there."

"Tom's doing this to get his daughter back. What about her?"

"We'll do our very best to trace her," Echols said.

"They have a whole sheaf to hide in," Stone said. "And they'll probably kill Linda as soon as they realise their plan's been blown."

"She's one of our own," Echols said. "We'll find her."

Cramer said, "I have the authority to shut this down if I think you're not going to follow the script."

"I'll do what I have to do," Stone said.

"I need to tell you how to set the time key so that you can return to the present if things don't go quite as planned," Echols said. "It's very simple. And I have some paperwork. We can work through it now, and then you'll be good to go."

They were racing along the red-surfaced government lane of the twenty-lane expressway, squad cars and motorcycle outriders fore and aft of the limo and the ambulance, lights and sirens on, speeding past civilian traffic as they swept toward the Williamsburg Bridge. The towers and tents and domes of Manhattan glittered in late afternoon sunlight and dirigibles moved above them like fish drifting over an exotic reef.

The towers of the Pan-American Trade Center rose twice as high as any other skyscraper, straddling the tip of Manhattan like a mountain, parks spilling dabs of greenery down its lower slopes, the spiky cluster of television and microwave masts that crowned its tallest peak raised half a mile above the city. It generated its own electricity from thermal shafts drilled two thousand feet into the bedrock. Vaults in its thirty floors of basements and sub-basements contained gold reserves, libraries of government and commercial confidential documents, fleets of antique cars, and several museums' worth of loot from client sheaves. It was serviced by a railroad station, three subway lines, a heliport, and a docking point for dirigibles, and housed offices where half a million people worked, crèches and schools for their children, shopping malls, apartment complexes, a hospital, and a police station.

As the limo sped across the Williamsburg Bridge, Stone recalled visiting the Company's suite of offices up on the two hundred and twentieth floor of Tower Four, above a domed preserve where mountain goats and ibex grazed among crags planted with forty species of conifer. The elevator he'd taken from the cathedral-sized lobby had at one point travelled through a transparent tube at the edge of a void that cut a rectangle out of fifty storeys and framed a view clear across New Jersey. He thought of Susan and Petey, alive at this very moment, the little farmhouse among the trees on the rise above the empty sweep of the Hudson, the stony fields. Its site somewhere beneath the enormous footprint of the Pan-American Trade Center, its reality as remote from him now as Babylon, or Troy.

The limo followed the ambulance and the squad cars and motorcycle cops down the off-ramp onto Delancey Street and sped past apartment blocks. Cramer's cell phone rang. He answered it and told Stone, "Waverly just told his handlers to head toward Forty-Ninth Street and warm up the Nixon-sheaf gate. You guessed right."

Stone said, "So we know where. Do we know when?"

"Not yet. Like you said, he's playing us all the way to the wire."

Stone changed in the restroom of the Grand Central Station facility. He shrugged the shoulder holster over his white shirt and put on the black suit jacket, then picked up the brand-new Colt .45 he'd been given, checked its action, and slid it into the holster under his left armpit. He opened the suppository and pocketed the wire cutters and lock pick and dropped the capsule in a trash basket. He studied his reflection in the speckled mirror above the sinks but it had nothing to tell him.

In the main room, technicians were busy at their desks and old-fashioned computers. There was no sign of the saturnine gate chief. The officer in charge of the operation, Lewis Meloy, was a burly former marine with salt-and-pepper hair and a bone-crushing handshake. Stone had met him years ago, when he had been in charge of field operations in the postrevolutionary American Bund sheaf, and knew that he was a tough old boy with a brisk no-nonsense attitude. As Meloy introduced Stone to the Special Operations officers who would be going through the mirror with him, Tom Waverly was escorted through the room by a press of soldiers and officers.

Stone followed the little party to the platform in front of the active gate;

it was the same gate he'd gone through the last time he'd been here, two weeks in the future.

Tom smiled and said, "Ain't this just like the good old days?"

He was wearing his usual uniform of denim jacket and blue jeans. There was a hectic flush in his cheeks and his eyes were reddened by broken blood vessels, but otherwise he was his old self.

A deep hum started up. Stone could feel it through the soles of his polished black shoes, in his bones. In his heart. The gate was about to open. He said, "Those days are long gone."

Tom's smile widened into a grin. "Maybe so, but we're headed right back to them."

Cramer stepped up and said, "You two will be handcuffed together for the transition. That acceptable to you, Mr. Stone?"

"I don't have a problem," Stone said.

"I'm not going to try to make a run for it," Tom said. "I have more than enough motivation to make sure everything happens the way you guys want it to happen."

Cramer ignored the remark and deployed the handcuffs. Echols told Stone that returning should be straightforward as long as they used the same gate and didn't alter the settings on the time key. "All you have to do is switch it on, and it will reel you back."

"You mean that's all your technician has to do," Stone said. He had no intention of ever using the time key. Even the thought of touching it made his scalp tighten.

"You need to know this in the remote event that things go bad," Echols said. He explained that the gate would be closed as soon as it had inserted them into the past; after that, they wouldn't be able to return to the present until it was opened by contemporary operators in the Real.

"We pulled the records," he said, and gave Stone a laminated card with dates and times printed on it. "In some years it was open every day; in others just once a month, or even less. Let's hope you don't have too long a wait."

Tom said, "Hey, Adam, why don't you let me have a sight of that?"

"I'll hang on to it. If you want to come back, you better stay right with me."

"Wouldn't have it any other way, old buddy."

The circular mirror of the gate flicked on, reflecting the room and everyone in it. Cramer gave a signal and a small, scared-looking man in an orange jumpsuit—the turncoat technician from Operation GYPSY—was brought forward. An army captain opened a steel attaché case and took out a sleeve of black plastic. The time key's jade tablet was fitted inside, so that only its face showed. There was a microswitch in one corner of the sleeve, a red pinlight shining next to it.

Although the time key was locked in its electronic bridle, although it wasn't even switched on, Stone felt as if he had suddenly come face to face with a venomous snake.

Cramer said to Tom, "What date do we program into it?"

Tom smiled at him. "You realise that the date by itself won't help you find where the bad guys have hidden the bomb."

"We have a deal," Cramer said, "and we're gonna stick to our side of it. You and Stone will have your chance to play cowboy."

"I'm not playing any kind of game," Tom said. "I only want to make sure that I can save my daughter."

"You already have our word," Echols said.

"You won't get that chance unless you tell us what to program into the time key," Cramer said.

"October 5, 1977," Tom said, and winked at Stone. "Let's say about half past seven in the morning. Should give us plenty of time."

The technician took out a notepad and scribbled on it, then tore off the page and held it out. "This will get us there. It's a simple alphanumeric code, and I'll make sure whoever's going to input it gets it right."

Cramer said, "You said you'd do it."

"I said I'd give you the code," the technician said. "Look, I've been around that thing for too long. It *knows* me. The bridle will force it to do what it's supposed to do, but it won't stop it putting the hurt on me if I use it."

"Man," Tom said, "aren't you all a bunch of pussies? Give it to me. I'll do the deed."

Stone said, "You're enjoying this too much, Tom. I hope you're not going to try anything stupid."

"And risk Linda's life? Not me."

His cheerful insouciance deepened Stone's foreboding.

"All right," Cramer told the tech. "Show one of our guys how to do it."

"As long as I don't have to touch it," the technician said. "It's going to be bad enough as it is without me touching it."

Stone watched as the technician and one of the officers bent over the time key. The technician had sweated through the back of his orange jumpsuit and sweat beaded his pink scalp.

The face of the time key lit up inside the bridle.

The hot black nail slammed into Stone's head with tremendous force: he would have fallen down if Tom hadn't caught him. Everyone around them—everyone in the room—had collapsed where they stood or were clutching their heads and howling. The technician was hitching and jerking on the floor, eyes rolled back to show their white undersides, slobber seething out from between clenched teeth. The time key lay beside him. Tom snatched it up, and hauled Stone through the gate.

# 13.

Linked by handcuffs, they stumbled into a bare, sooty room lit by a couple of shielded bulbs and the lunar glow of the Turing gate. As Tom Waverly aimed the ensleeved time key at the gate and the gate's mirror slipped sideways and vanished, Stone fell to his knees, clutching his head with his free hand as if to protect himself from the spike driven through his skull into the agonised jelly of his brain. He could scarcely see around the pain, but when he felt a hand moving inside his jacket he caught Tom's wrist and hauled himself up and smacked Tom square in the chin with his forehead. Fresh pain slammed through his head like a stick of dynamite exploding in a sump of pressurised oil. Tom swung a wild uppercut that connected above Stone's ear, and then they were waltzing around each other, linked wrist to wrist by the handcuffs, trading swift blows.

Stone tried to stamp on Tom's instep, and Tom pushed him off balance and drove him backward. Stone went with it, slamming into a wall and swinging Tom around and planting a solid uppercut under his ribs. Tom grunted and pulled Stone close and loosed a volley of punches, reigniting pain in old bruises, driving air from Stone's lungs, rattling his heart. When he fell down, Tom came with him, snatching the Colt .45 from Stone's shoulder holster and firing a single shot that lit up the room for an instant.

Stone's left arm flopped free: the shot had severed the handcuff chain. He rolled over and tried to catch his breath. His ribs ached. The nail thump-thump-thumped through his skull, and then Tom switched off the time key and most of the pain went away.

When Stone stood up, Tom stepped back and raised the pistol. He spat something thick and black and said, "Son of a bitch. I think you cracked one of my teeth."

"Well, I think you cracked a couple of my ribs."

They stood like two old and exhausted prizefighters, breathing hard, heads hung low. Stone started to laugh, and Tom laughed too, both of them howling, raising echoes in the sooty concrete box.

"This doesn't change anything," Stone said.

Laughing hurt. His chest yielded a creaking pang with every breath and his right elbow throbbed with vivid heat—he'd bruised it when he'd fallen down.

Tom spat again and wiped his mouth on the back of his hand. "I could shoot you right here, take the time key to the bad guys, get Linda back and vanish into America. That would very definitely change things, don't you think?"

"I hate like hell to bring it up, but you won't have long to enjoy your freedom."

Tom's smile showed the blood on his teeth. "Good point. I want to save my daughter, you want to save your woman, and we don't have long to do it. Let's agree that we're in this together, and get going."

"If we're in this together, maybe you won't mind giving back the pistol."

"I reckon I'll keep it, just in case your friends in the black suits asked you to kill me after I led you to GYPSY's nuclear surprise," Tom said, and stuck the .45 in the waistband of his jeans, under his denim jacket.

"As a matter of fact, they did ask me to neutralize you. But I didn't say I'd do it." Stone found the handcuff key in one of his pockets and unlocked the bracelet around his left wrist. His hands were shaking badly. He tossed the key to Tom and said, "Now you have the advantage, maybe you won't mind telling me where the bad guys are planning to plant their bomb."

"They've already planted it, right here in New York. Take a look at that card they gave you, Adam. Tell me when the gate is due to open again."

Stone took out the laminated card and held it up in the yellow light of one of the caged bulbs. "If that technician got the settings right, we're in luck. It should open every day at six p.m."

"If we're in the right place, if it's the morning of October 5, 1977, the bomb is set to blow a little before noon," Tom said. "There's no way back before then, so I think we should get going, don't you?"

They followed a trucking subway and a service shaft to the Fifty-First Street subway station, climbed to street level in a tide of commuters, and walked south along Third Avenue, Stone in his black suit, Tom Waverly in his denim jacket and jeans, his grey hair loose down his back. It was a crisp, clear morning. Sunlight bathed the upper storeys of tall buildings rooted deep in shadow, slanted low across intersections, and glittered from the windshields and roofs of cars and vans and yellow taxis. According to the papers on the newsstand next to the entrance to the subway station, it really was October 5, 1977. The time key had lashed out at everyone in the interchange except for Tom Waverly, but it had also done exactly what it had been programmed to do.

The sidewalk was crowded with office workers heading toward their offices. Traffic was jammed nose-to-tail, horns playing impatient arpeggios. Stone saw blue-and-white squad cars at each intersection, police patrolling on foot, police on horseback. The east side of the Forty-Sixth Street intersection was barricaded; the empty street sloped toward the steel-and-glass skyscraper of what they called the United Nations Building here. Flags of all nations fluttered in front of it.

Stone asked Tom if the UN was the target.

"The president is the target."

"Carter? They're going to assassinate Jimmy Carter?"

"They're going to assassinate his doppel, although you'd be hard-pressed to tell them apart. He's a peacenik and appeaser in the Real, and he's a peacenik and appeaser here. Right now he's finishing his breakfast, getting ready to meet the mayor and take a tour of the South Bronx, to show how sympathetic he is about urban poverty. After that he'll visit the UN, sign a human rights document, and make a brief speech about it. When he steps up to the lectern at eleven thirty-five a.m., downtown Manhattan will vanish in a mushroom cloud."

"Christ, Tom. You're playing it close."

"I know exactly what I'm doing. I worked here, grooming some fall guys. The people in charge of GYPSY think they had everything compartmented, but I made it my business to find out about the big picture." Tom was pumped up, walking and talking quickly, his face shining with sweat. "They plan to take out the president, the UN, and any number of foreign heads of state, and then they'll expose the fall guys: a gang of radical communist Arabs with a fierce set of grievances we've been carefully nurturing over the past couple of years. I guess you know what that signifies, seeing as you helped set up a black op in this very sheaf in the early seventies. Matter of fact, they used some of your research when they war-gamed this scenario. Kind of ironic, don't you think?"

Stone had a good working knowledge of the Nixon sheaf's recent history. After its version of World War Two and a holocaust as bad as anything in any known version of history, an independent Jewish nation had been set up in British Palestine. It had been a potential flashpoint ever since, the focus of Arab resentment and geopolitical rivalry between America and the Soviets. If Carter's doppel was assassinated by a nuclear device that destroyed most of New York, and the blame was pinned on an Arab communist faction, the American government would have no option but to strike at the Soviets. The beginning of World War Three was only a few hours away.

"If you have a plan, you better tell me now," he said to Tom.

"Getting hold of the nuke isn't the problem. I know where it is, and I know that only a handful of crazy wannabe martyrs will be guarding it until it goes off. For a couple of hard cases like us, relieving them of the nuke won't be much more difficult than taking candy from a baby. What happens afterward, *that*'s gonna be kinda tricky."

"One thing at a time. Where's the nuke?"

They were standing at the edge of a crowd of people waiting for the light to change, at the intersection of Second Avenue and Forty-Fifth Street. Tom said, "See the office building, more or less midblock? The one advertising all-day parking?"

"Sure."

"GYPSY has a proprietary company in there," Tom said. "It's an import/export shoe company, A&A International Services, Inc., Suite 409. I'm telling you where to go if I get into trouble. You ready to do a stroll-by, partner?"

They walked past the building on the other side of the street. Stone spotted a man smoking a cigarette near the lobby entrance.

"I see him," Tom said.

"What about the cop in front of the parking garage ramp?"

"You still got it, don't you? He's Khudora Ghanem, a Palestinian I happen to know."

"You recruited him?"

"He's a nice young guy, an engineer who studied in Egypt, which is where he got radicalised. He believes me to be a double agent working for the Soviets, helping him and his friends strike a blow against the Yankees."

"He knows you. Will that get us inside?"

"He'll wonder what the hell I'm doing here, and then he'll reach for his gun. Let's go find a set of wheels."

Stone stole a van parked outside a building site. The ignition was pre-electronic; all he had to do was rip out the wires and spark the engine. He drove the van around the corner and picked up Tom, who sat in the back among a litter of paint cans and ladders as they drove down Lexington and back up Third Avenue. It took fifteen minutes in the bad-tempered, bumper-to-bumper traffic; Stone had sweated through his shirt by the time he reached the office building. The fake cop, Khudora Ghanem, was posted by the pole barrier at the top of the ramp to the basement parking garage. When Stone stopped the van, he stepped up and asked Stone for his ID.

Stone gave the man his best blank stare. "What's the problem, officer?"

"Extra security for the president," Khudora Ghanem said.

He was very young, with a dark complexion and a nick on his chin where he'd recently shaved. He started to turn when Tom appeared behind him, and Tom shot him in the face and caught his dead weight as he folded forward.

"Give me a hand," Tom said. "I don't want to get blood all over the uniform."

They slung the dead man into the van, raised the pole, and drove the van into the basement. It had taken less than two minutes.

They rode the service elevator up five floors. Stone was wearing the heavy blue serge tunic and cap they'd taken off Khudora Ghanem's body, and was carrying his service revolver. The tunic's collar was soaked with blood and the cap had a hole in its crown where the bullet had exited, but Tom said it would pass muster.

The fourth floor's narrow corridor was quiet and cool. Tom hugged the wall beside the door of Suite 409, and Stone pulled the bill of the cap down over his eyes, knocked on the door, and looked down at his shoes when he saw a shadow pass behind the spyhole. After a moment, the door opened on its chain. Stone fired a single shot through the gap and kicked the door open as the man behind it went down. He shot him again, the noise loud in the small anteroom, where display shelves along one wall held rows of women's shoes. A man in his undershirt ducked away through a door to the left; Stone fired a shot that splintered the frame, chased after him into a room stacked with cardboard cartons, saw him scoop up a submachine gun from a camp bed, and blew his brains across the wall.

"Not bad," Tom said from the doorway.

Stone turned, looked at the Colt aimed squarely at him, and looked at Tom. "What are you going to do? Shoot me?"

"I will if you don't drop that gun."

Stone saw that he was serious. He let the revolver slip from his grasp and stepped back when Tom Waverly told him to step back.

Tom kicked the revolver across the room and said, "Let's take a look at what these two heroes died for."

The bomb was housed in an aluminium case four feet long, a foot and a half across, and a foot deep. The case's hinged lid revealed square and oblong steel panels neatly fitted together inside. No protruding sheaves of multi-coloured wires, no LED timer usefully ticking away the hours and minutes and seconds, just an electronic circuit buried somewhere inside mindlessly counting down toward 11.35 a.m. and its own end.

"The yield is a fraction under a kiloton," Tom said. "More than enough to take out the UN Building and everything else for half a mile around."

Stone felt his heart thump against his chest. "Do you know how to defuse it?"

"Didn't the boys from the DCI's office tell you?"

"I was supposed to kill you after we found the bomb, go back through the mirror, and bring in a team of specialists," Stone said.

Tom shut the lid and latched it. "If we let them have this bomb, they'll kill me, and they'll almost certainly kill Linda too, when they go after the bad guys. And what about Susan Nichols?"

"I know how to save Susan."

"Do you really think they'd let you save her when her death led to the downfall of GYPSY?"

"You smart-ass son of a bitch."

"You know I'm right."

They stared at each other across the aluminium case. Stone said, "You want to find these guys? Okay, let's go find them."

"Give me a hand with this thing," Tom said. "We can't hardly leave it here."

They lugged the heavy case to the elevator, rode down to the basement, and set it in the back of the stolen van, next to Khudora Ghanem's body. Stone took the wheel, keenly aware of the bomb's presence every time the van bounced over a pothole. It took over an hour to reach the Lincoln Tunnel. After they passed through the toll plaza on the New Jersey side, Tom told Stone to take the next exit, hit the surface streets, and find a phone.

"Better hurry, partner. We have less than two hours before our little treasure chest is due to blow."

"Don't I know it," Stone said.

He turned off the main highway at the next junction and stopped at a gas station. The pay phone outside the gas station's convenience store was an old-fashioned mechanical model: no screen or credit-card reader, just a coin slot, push-buttons, and a greasy plastic handset. Before he could use it, Stone had to buy an odd-looking can of Coke to break a dollar bill peeled from the slim roll of low-denomination notes he'd been given back in the Real. The quarters were thicker and heavier than quarters in the Real, but they had the same profile of George Washington on one side, the same eagle on the other. Tom gave him the number to dial. The phone at the other end picked up on the first ring, emitting a staticky crackle; Tom told Stone what to say.

Stone recited the brief set of directions, hung up, and said, "That was a cutout, wasn't it?"

"A tape recorder in an empty apartment, with a relay that rings another number after it receives a call. I used it when I worked for these fuckers."

"Will they be listening?"

"If they aren't, there's going to be a perfectly circular and highly radioactive lake where the Hackensack River used to be." Tom Waverly sniffed, wiped his nose on his forefinger and examined the streak of blood on it, then gave Stone a sombre look. "Do you trust me, partner?"

"You're not the kind of man anyone in their right mind would trust."

"I believe my ex-wife said exactly that, once upon a time. And it's true, I never was what you'd call responsible. Yet here I am, responsible for just about everything in the Real, and a couple of dozen other sheafs besides, and I won't even get to live to enjoy the fruits of my labours. If there is a God, he's either the worst kind of practical joker or he's pretty fucking pissed with me. What do you think?"

"I think we should bring in that team and let them deal with the bomb. I also think you're in no condition to go through with whatever it is you're planning."

"Don't fret, partner. I have a couple of weeks left. You should know."

"We still have time to drive back into Manhattan, get to the gate—"

"Two weeks isn't what I'd call a whole lot of time any way you cut it," Tom said, "but I'll have a whole lot less if I let you call in those boys, and so will Linda. I guess it doesn't matter if you trust me or not. This is the only dance in town. Like it or not, you're my partner until it ends."

# 14.

They drove past the outskirts of Union City and Meadowlands Stadium and turned off the highway onto a service road, passing desolate parking lots and abandoned factories and pulling up at a crossroads with cattail reeds on every side. This was where Stone, following Tom Waverly's instructions, had told the tape recorder he'd be waiting with the bomb.

They climbed out of the van into bright sunlight. A warm wind blew through the tall reeds, and their brown tassels bent and swayed with a dry whispering.

"What if they don't come?" Stone said. He was thinking of the circuit in the bomb counting down to oblivion, and was finding it hard to suppress the urge to start running for the horizon.

"They'll come," Tom said. "If they're going to change history, they need the bomb to kick-start a nuclear war, and they need the time key, too, so that they can get back to 1984. Don't sweat it, partner. They'll come after us, all right. And when they do come, you have to trust me to do the right thing."

"You know where they are, don't you? You know it's within an hour or so of where we are now."

"Yeah, but it isn't the kind of place you can drive into unannounced, even if you are packing a nuclear weapon. That's why you have to let them take you in."

"You mean let them take us in."

Tom smiled and struck his forehead with the heel of his palm in mock chagrin. "Man, did I forget to tell you about this part? You're going to surrender to them and explain that you're working on your own. They'll take you in to find out what you have to say, and while they're listening to you spin some bullshit tale I'll sneak in behind you and set up a diversion. When that kicks off, I'll take down the man in charge and bring you and Linda out."

"What kind of diversion?"

"Whatever's to hand. Preferably something big and noisy, so you'll know what it is when it happens. Basically, it'll be a rerun of that little action in the McBride sheaf. I got you out then, and I'll get you out now. Only this time, try not to get shot."

"If you know the layout of the place, you better show me."

"It's an old farm GYPSY bought last year," Tom said, and drew a rough diagram on the van's dusty windshield. A house and a barn and a few small outbuildings, a fallout shelter in woods behind the property, and a track running through the woods to a highway.

Stone studied the layout, remembering that David Welch had wanted to lure Tom to an old farm the Company had used for covert entry into the Johnson sheaf, and wondering if this could be its counterpart. He and Tom agreed on a rendezvous point, and Tom erased the diagram with his sleeve.

"What about the bomb?" Stone said. "What's to stop them from driving it back to New York?"

"They'll have to reset the detonation mechanism first. Don't worry about the bomb, or anything else. All you have to do is keep them interested in your story. I'll do all the hard work."

Stone thought about how satisfying it would be to sock Tom Waverly right in the middle of his silly smile. "You planned this all along, didn't you? You knew the time key would knock out everyone in the interchange, you knew where the bomb was, and you knew you could use me as a sacrificial pawn."

"I never did get the hang of chess—checkers is about my speed. Listen, partner, I'm taking a big risk, letting them take you in. You might shoot off your mouth, tell them about me, and put Linda in danger. So what you have to do right now is promise you won't do that. You have to tell me that you trust me."

"You know I can't do that," Stone said, "and you know why, too."

Tom studied him for a moment, then shrugged. "I guess it doesn't matter. I know you want to end this here so that you can save your sweetheart. We may not be on the same team, but we're pulling in the same direction." He looked at his watch and said it wouldn't be long until they had company, then took out the Colt .45, checked its clip, and asked Stone if he had a spare.

Stone shook his head. "You have just five rounds left. Is that going to be a problem?"

"I guess I'll have to make them count."

"It isn't too late to come up with something better."

"I thought long and hard on how to do this. There isn't any other way," Tom said, and started to walk away.

Stone called after him. "What do you want me to tell them? What's my story?"

"You can tell them anything you like as long as you don't tell them I'm here," Tom said, and parted the tall reeds like a curtain and disappeared into them.

Stone walked around to the far side of the van and lifted the little signalling device from inside his shirt and twisted the button until it popped
up. The two men who'd been sent into this sheaf's past as his backup had
been here for more than eight years. They might have gone crazy and killed
themselves, or perhaps their covers had taken over their lives—they'd settled
down and forgotten all about the call they were supposed to be waiting for.
But they were about the only shot left in Stone's armoury, and he figured that
it wouldn't hurt to try to reach out to them.

He paced up and down the road and thought about what he needed to
do, always aware that Tom Waverly was watching him, always aware that the
bomb in the van was ticking off the last hour of its life. That was, if Tom had
been telling the truth about the time it was set to go off. On every side, reeds
swayed and whispered. Traffic twinkled along a raised highway a couple of
miles away, its bumble-bee drone coming and going on the warm wind.
Stone thought about making a break for it, hitching a lift that would take
him out of the blast zone, vanishing into America and letting history take
care of itself, forgetting all about Susan. Yeah, right. He drank the Coke he'd
bought at the service station. It was warm and too sweet, and sat heavily in
his stomach.

With thirty minutes left until the bomb was due to detonate, Stone
heard vehicles approaching. He walked out past the rear of the van, shaded
his eyes against the sun's sharp glare, and saw three of the big boats they
drove here heading toward him at speed, moving ahead of a rolling dust
storm. The lead car blew straight past him, so close that its side mirror
clipped the pocket of his jacket. The second skidded to a halt with the shark's
grin of its radiator grille just inches from his knees, its doors flying open and
three knuckledraggers in black suits pitching out and levelling their pistols.
The third car had drawn up at a distance, parked sideways across the road. A
man stood behind it, leaning a short-barrelled assault rifle on its roof, aiming
it straight at Stone.

He was told to kneel and lock his hands behind his head. One man pointed
his pistol at Stone while a second patted him down, tossing the lock pick and
cutting tool and lapel knife into the dirt, ripping the signalling device from his
neck and tossing that away, too. The third man opened the back doors of the
van and looked inside and reported that the bomb was there.

"At least, it looks like the bomb. There's a dead guy too."

The man who'd patted Stone down, a burly man with a black crew cut,
told him to stand up and asked him who the dead guy was.

"One of your patsies."

"Did you kill the others?"

"Two of them."

"Did you touch the device, try to do anything to it?"

"It's still armed, if that's what you mean. Are we going to stand around talking, or are you going to do something about it?"

The man slapped him in the face with his open palm. "Who are you working for? Who else came through with you?"

Stone rode the blow, spat blood, and said, "I want to talk to Victor Moore."

That got him another slap, and a repeat of the question.

"My name is Adam Stone. I was one of the original Special Operations field officers. Ask Victor Moore about me. And while you're at it, tell him I have what he needs to get back to 1984."

"Where is it?"

It hurt when Stone smiled; his cheek was swelling. "You think I'm going to tell a bunch of apes? I know you have orders to take me in, so why don't you carry them out instead of playing silly games in plain sight?"

The burly man stared at Stone for a moment, then went back to his car and talked on a radio handset. An overweight, balding man got out of the third car, pulled a tool box from the trunk, and carried it to the van and clambered inside. Stone watched as he opened the top of the bomb's aluminium case and took an Allen wrench from the tool box and started to work on an access panel; then the burly man called to him and told him to get in the car.

"Sit on your hands in the middle of the back seat and don't give me so much as a funny look."

Stone did as he was told. Two men got in on either side of him, the burly man swung into the shotgun seat, and the driver did a three-point turn and blasted away from the scene. Framed in the rearview mirror, the van dwindled between banks of reeds, and then the car swung around a turn and it was gone.

# 15.

The burly man hitched around in his seat, told Stone to lean forward, and pulled a canvas hood over his head. It smelled of someone else's sweat and clung heavily to his bruised face, but it gave him a small measure of reassurance. His captors didn't want him to know where they were taking him, which meant that they weren't planning to kill him. At least, not right away. There was a chance that he might survive this.

He wondered if Tom knew where he was being taken.

He wondered if Linda was still alive.

He wondered if Tom really was going to follow through, or if he was going to kill the technician and the other bad guys and let the bomb go off in a final grand gesture.

He counted off seconds. He counted off minutes. The men around him were quiet; another good sign. Amateurs were nervous and unpredictable. They talked too much and brutalised or killed their hostages at the slightest provocation. Professionals were careful and calmly lethal, but they were also methodical in their habits, which meant they were easier to manipulate. Stone constructed and discarded various scenarios, realised that he wouldn't know what to do until he faced whoever was waiting for him at the end of this ride, and tried to relax.

He had counted past the time when the bomb was due to go off, a little over forty-three minutes, when the car made a sharp turn and jostled uphill along a rough track, bushes or tree branches scratching at its sides. The track levelled out and the car slowed and stopped, easing on its springs as the two men on either side of Stone got out. Stone sat where he was until someone dragged him out of the car and pulled off the hood.

The car was parked in front of a house with clapboard walls and a front porch enclosed by screens. Every window was blinded by sheets of hardboard. Trees clad in the vivid colours of fall crowded up a hillside behind the house toward a distant ridge; in front, an unkempt lawn studded with clumps of wild garlic sloped down to a small, rock-strewn river. Stone saw a man armed with an assault rifle walking among the trees on the far bank. A short track led to a large barn and a paddock with a split-rail fence where vans and cars were parked in a row, the layout exactly as Tom had diagrammed it.

The burly man shoved Stone forward and followed close behind him as he mounted the steps into the shade of the porch, where two men sat in high-backed cane chairs. One of them, about fifty pounds heavier than Stone remembered, his sandy hair receding from an island of freckled scalp, was Victor Moore. The other was the former deputy director for Special Operations, the Old Man, Dick Knightly.

"You led me on a merry dance, Adam," Knightly said. "But now that you have delivered yourself into my hands, perhaps you'll be good enough to tell me what kind of game you're playing."

"He had the bomb," Moore said. "He also claims to have the device. It's pretty clear he's playing the same kind of game as Tom Waverly."

Knightly hushed his deputy with a fly-brushing flap of his mutilated hand. He looked exactly as he had the last time Stone had seen him, when he'd been answering with considerable style and wit questions shouted at him by a pack of reporters on the steps of the Capitol: lean and vital, his silvery hair trimmed in a military brush cut, his seamed face ageless as an Egyptian mummy. He was dressed in one of his trademark tweed suits and a primrose-yellow waistcoat, a matching handkerchief folded into his breast pocket. He smiled at Stone and said, "No doubt you're wondering how I come to be here when I am supposed to be languishing in jail."

"Not really," Stone said. The shock of seeing his former boss was still fizzing in his blood, but he felt calm and clearheaded. "It's pretty obvious you substituted a doppel."

"I'm pleased to see that you still have your edge, Adam. The unfortunate incarcerated in Lompac is indeed a ringer. We plucked him from a sheaf where he won't ever be missed—I was very disappointed by how that particular version of my private history turned out—and removed two of his fingers and gave him a stroke and made a simple switch. I know that standards have fallen badly since the appeasers took over the Company, but I'm surprised no one ever spotted it. Or perhaps they did, and decided it would be best to cover up the inconvenient fact that they'd been duped."

"I wouldn't know."

"That's right—you retired."

"After ratting out his colleagues to the Church Committee," Moore said, glaring at Stone. He was dressed in a safari suit and had the puffy eyes and broken veins of a dedicated drinker.

"No doubt he did what he thought he should do," Knightly said. "Personally, I admire a man who sticks to his principles, even if he is horribly misguided. I believe you went off to live in some rural retreat, Adam, and the Company reactivated you to help find our mutual friend Tom Waverly. Do I have it right?"

"I'm not here to talk about Tom. He's out of the picture."

"You'll talk about whatever I want you to talk about," Knightly said. His pleasant expression didn't change, but his voice and his gaze suddenly sharpened. "You knew where to find the nuclear device, so I must suppose you also know our intentions, but you were kind enough to leave us time to carry the day. The president of this pissant version of America will have made his speech by now, but he's still at the UN, lunching with . . . Who's he lunching with, Victor?"

"A bunch of Asian foreign ministers and heads of delegation to the UN. And then he has meetings with foreign heads of state all afternoon."

"We were able to take a look at Carter's daily diary," Knightly told Stone. "We know his every move. He doesn't leave New York until after seven this evening, so we still have plenty of time to nail him. That's why I've given you the chance to speak up for yourself, instead of shooting you in the fucking head."

"Which is what you deserve," Moore said.

"Which is *all* you deserve if you don't tell me right now what game you're playing," Knightly said. "Are you here on your own, Adam, or did you bring Tom Waverly with you? Don't waste my time by denying that you've been working with him. I know all about it."

Stone stepped on the impulse to ask about Linda. "Tom made himself known to the Company, and I was brought in to find him. And that's what I did, but there were complications—frankly, he got the better of me for a little while. Until a couple of days ago, I was his hostage."

"And he brought his daughter along for the ride, too. Is she working with him, or is she the loyal Company drone she claims to be?"

"She wanted Tom to turn himself in. He had other ideas."

"He had both of you prisoner, he was forcing you to travel with him from sheaf to sheaf. . . . I find that very hard to believe, Adam."

"I went with him because I wanted to know what he was up to. And, like Linda, I spent a lot of the time trying to convince him to do the right thing."

"You knew all along what he was up to," Moore said. "You and Waverly are in cahoots."

Knightly made the fly-shooing gesture again and said to Stone, "You certainly know about the device."

"He told me what it was and what it could do, but I didn't believe him until he used it."

Knightly steepled his index fingers and touched them to his lips. "Mmm. It *is* rather unbelievable, isn't it? Where is it, by the way?"

"It's safe," Stone said. He wondered for a moment just where Tom was, and hoped that no trace of the thought had shown in his face.

"It better be," Knightly said. "It's one of a kind, and I wouldn't like to lose it."

"Especially not now," Stone said, seizing the opportunity to change gear, to try to put Knightly on the back foot. "Not when you're stuck in the past, with no quick way back to where you came from."

"Now we're getting down to the reason why you delivered yourself to me, aren't we? How did it come into your possession?"

"I took it from Tom. At gunpoint."

Knightly's stare was compelling.

Stone said, "It was after we came through the mirror at White Sands. I saw my chance to get the drop on him, I took the time key, and I got away."

"And then?"

"Then I went to see Eileen Barrie. I knew she was partnered up with Tom, and I forced her to confirm everything he'd told me, and made her show me how the time key worked. What I didn't know was that on that very same night she tried to save herself by selling Tom to you."

"I suppose you helped her get away from her guards," Knightly said. "What happened after that?"

"She turned herself in to the Company, and by now I guess she must have given up everything she knows about GYPSY," Stone said.

He wasn't about to tell Knightly that Tom Waverly had killed her. Let the bastard sweat a little. Let him wonder about all the secrets Eileen Barrie might have spilled.

"You handed Dr. Barrie to the Company, but you didn't give up the device."

"She turned herself in," Stone said. "She was scared that your people would find her. I had my own agenda. I used it to come here because I want to make a deal."

"Did you, now? But why did you come to me? Why didn't you take it to the Company, like the good little errand boy I know you are?"

334

"Maybe I'm working for myself," Stone said.

"You're suited and booted, son, and when you surrendered you were carrying several items of Company kit. Also, if you don't mind me saying so, you always were mindlessly loyal to the government of the day."

"I'm loyal to my country, Mr. Knightly."

"Good for you, " Knightly said, and patted his hands together in mock applause. "That's exactly why I don't see you going over to the dark side. I don't see you falling in with an outlaw like Tom Waverly."

"I learned a lot from my time with Tom. I learned all about the time key, what it does, and how to use it. And I learned that it is very valuable to you, which is why I'm here."

"You're a fucking liar," Dick Knightly said, quite without venom or rancour, as if making a casual observation about the weather. He looked at Victor Moore and said, "Am I right?"

"No question," Moore said.

"I think you took the device from Tom Waverly, Adam, and I think you confronted Dr. Barrie," Knightly said. "That much may be true. But I think that you arrested her yourself, you turned her in, and then you came storming into my private facility with a bunch of soldiers."

"We saw you just before we quit the place," Moore said. "We had video feeds from our apemen. You staged that raid, you son of a bitch, and Waverly was with you."

Stone ignored him, telling Knightly, "The Company caught up with Tom after you snatched his daughter. That's why I had to go in with Dr. Barrie—I knew Tom would tell them about me sooner or later. But I hid the time key before I did, and if you saw Tom and me with those soldiers, you must know that we were under guard, and you must have seen us make a break for it."

Knightly allowed himself to look amused. "And where is Tom Waverly now?"

"He caught a bad dose of radiation when he went into the nuclear reactor and reinserted the control rods," Stone said.

"Lethal?"

"Very. He was trying to shut down the power. Trying to stop you escaping with his daughter."

"And now you turn up here," Knightly said. "You tell me that you have the device, that you're working for no one but yourself, and you want to cut a deal."

Stone looked straight into Knightly's x-ray stare. "Why else would I be here?"

He was beginning to believe that Tom had screwed up, that he'd been shot dead or taken prisoner when he had tried to deal with the technician and Knightly's foot soldiers, that Knightly knew it and was cat-and-mousing him, trying to tease out exactly how much the Company knew.

"What kind of deal?" Knightly said.

"You have Tom Waverly's daughter. If you let her go, I'll tell you where the time key is."

"That's all you want?"

"Yes, sir."

"You came here to save her. No other reason."

"That's it."

"I don't think so," Knightly said. "You came here because you're working for the chicken-hearted sons of bitches who closed down the best hope of a thousand Americas, and all this talk about changing your mind and wanting to dicker with me over the return of the device is so much bullshit. You were a disappointment to me when you testified against everything I built, and you're a disappointment to me now. You can't even work up a decent cover story. I don't doubt you used the device to come after me, but my best guess is that you were brought here by some government flunky who has charge of it and is waiting somewhere to take you back. I intend to find out where you're supposed to rendezvous with him, and it isn't going to be pleasant."

A board creaked as the burly man who all this time had been standing behind Stone took a step forward. Stone kept his gaze locked on his old boss and said, "Where did it go wrong?"

"As far as I'm concerned, the Real took a wrong turn and headed down the wrong road three years ago, when Carter was elected," Knightly said. "But we're keepers of the flame, son. We're going to bring history back on track. When we've finished our work here, we'll have created a brand-new sheaf, and in the process we will have remade the Real. The old version of the Real, the one that took the wrong turn, the one that caught the disease of appeasement and insularity, will wither like a vine whose roots have been cut away. And a new vine will thrive in its place and send up many new tendrils into the sunlight. Out of one, many: there's some truth in that old joke. We'll raise up the weak and make them strong. We'll liberate every American who labours under the yoke of tyranny. We'll spread democracy like the wise farmer in the parable. I came to you once upon a time because I wanted to give you the chance to help us, to come over to the right side. Because this *is* right. This is right, and you are wrong."

"If people can't choose freedom for themselves it isn't freedom, it's just another form of tyranny," Stone said. "And what you want to do here in the name of freedom is a thousand times worse than any of the terrorists who've attacked the Real."

"The terrorists are wrong," Knightly said, "and I'm right. It makes all the difference. I know you'll probably prefer to die under questioning than give up the device—I trained my cowboy angels well. But I happen to know that under your tough exterior beats the bleeding heart of a liberal. Perhaps you won't mind paying the price for your silence, but I think you'll mind it very much if someone else has to." Knightly looked past Stone at the burly man behind him. "Take him away, Mr. Fitzgerald. Prep him. And prep Linda Waverly too."

# 16.

Fitzgerald and a guard in combat fatigues marched Stone into the house, through a door under the stairs, and down wooden steps into a root cellar walled with rough stone and lit by three floodlights on metal stands. A tin bath brimful of water stood in front of a scarred table on which various domestic items were laid out like surgical instruments. A car battery with starter cables clamped to its terminals and an assortment of knives. Pliers, a claw hammer, an aluminium baseball bat, an electric drill. A roll of plastic wrap. Folded sheets of white plastic.

Linda Waverly sat in a kitchen chair to one side of these sinister props, bound by many loops of thin cord wound around her body, her arms caught behind her back. Her eyes were wide and unblinking above the duct tape over her mouth as she watched the two men shove Stone forward so violently that he missed the last few steps and fell to his hands and knees on the clay floor.

Fitzgerald stepped around him and the guard stood near the bottom of the stairs, pointing his rifle at him. "Stand up and lose your clothes," Fitzgerald said.

Stone climbed to his feet slowly and warily. The burly man was aiming a stainless-steel semiautomatic pistol at him, standing with his back to the table, six o'clock to Stone's twelve. Stone took a couple of steps forward, not quite toward him, and said, "Suppose I want to talk right now?"

Fitzgerald moved sideways out of reflex conditioned by rigorous training, maintaining a good distance, the pistol aimed steadily at Stone's chest. He said, "You can say what you like. But we still have to make sure that what you tell us is the truth."

"Do what you want with me but leave her out of this," Stone said. He heard the creak of stressed wood as the guard took a step down the stairs behind him.

"It's not up to me, pal," Fitzgerald said, moving two steps sideways as Stone moved forward again. The man was a professional. He was used to pointing guns at people and making them do what he wanted them to do. He thought that he was in control. He didn't seem to realise that he was part of a dance, that he was being forced into a vulnerable position. He gestured with the pistol and said, "Lose your clothes."

Stone looked up at the black oak beam that ran under the rough board ceiling. He took another step, as if to get a better view of the butcher's hook screwed into it, and said, "You're going to hang me from that? What is this, amateur night?"

Fitzgerald stepped sideways again, moving on the balls of his feet, moving with surprising delicacy for a big man. He was standing in front of Linda now. He said, "Goddamn right we're going to hang you up. Get undressed right now or I'll shoot you in the knee."

Stone took off his jacket, folded it and laid it carefully on the floor, slowly unknotted his tie, began to unbutton his shirt.

"I'll work you over to get you in the mood, then Mr. Knightly will go to work on your girlfriend," Fitzgerald said. "I'm pretty good, but the Old Man, he's amazing. Very inventive. It'll be a very instructive session."

"Everything's going to be all right, Linda," Stone said.

"Don't talk to her," Fitzgerald said.

"What are you going to do?" Stone said. "Hurt me?"

He was looking at Linda, trying to convey with his gaze what he needed her to do.

"I'm going to hurt you bad," Fitzgerald said, watching as Stone knelt to untie the laces of his shoes. His eyes were dark and flat above his thin smile. "I'm going to fuck you up. And then I'll staple your eyelids open so can you watch every single thing Mr. Knightly does—"

The sound came from upstairs, a percussive noise followed by the pop and crackle of gunshots. Without taking his gaze from Stone, Fitzgerald told the guard, "Find out what the fuck's going on, Mike."

After the guard had turned and started up the stairs, Stone threw a shoe at Fitzgerald, hard and fast. The burly man warded it off with his arm, his pistol moving off Stone for a second, and Linda jacked up one leg and kicked him in the back of the knee. She went over backward, still strapped to the chair, and Fitzgerald fell against the table, scattering knives and tools. Stone was on him before he could recover his balance, butting him hard under the chin and grabbing his gun hand and slamming it against the edge of the table. The pistol went off when Stone ripped it from Fitzgerald's hand, discharging harmlessly into the clay floor, and Stone hammered its grip into the man's face and felt the cheekbone snap. Fitzgerald dropped to his knees and Stone reversed the pistol and shot him in the head. The guard was coming back down the stairs in a hurry. Stone shot at him and missed and shot him as he raised his rifle and shot him again as he fell forward and tumbled to the foot of the stairs and lay still, head twisted at a sharp angle, feet tangled in the steps.

The noise of the shots sang in Stone's ears. The air was hazed with blue gunsmoke. He stepped over Fitzgerald's body and checked that the guard was dead. Linda was making a muffled noise, rocking to and fro in her overturned chair. Stone stripped the tape from her mouth and used one of the knives from the table to saw through the cord and plastic cuffs that secured her to the chair.

Guns popped and snapped somewhere above. Smoke drifted down the stairs and rolled across the plank ceiling.

"I think your father has turned up," Stone said as he pulled on his shirt.

"It's about time," Linda said. She was rubbing the weals that the rope had left on her wrists.

"Are you okay?"

"They were model hosts until an hour ago. They showed off their fully equipped fallout shelter in the woods behind the house, and they took me up to the hilltop to watch for the flash when New York was vaporised. They had smoked glasses and they had slathered themselves with factor fifty sunblock. One of them had a video camera. They were ready to have a little party. And then," Linda said with a grim smile, "they got your phone call."

Stone shrugged his jacket over his unbuttoned shirt. "We're going to have to make a run for it. Through the woods to the highway."

"That's your plan? We run?"

"Your father is the one with the plan. Let's hope it survives contact with the enemy."

Stone gave Linda the stainless-steel pistol, searched Fitzgerald's body and found a spare clip and tossed it to her, then scooped up the guard's assault rifle and climbed the stairs. The hall was full of smoke and the front part was on fire. A man sprawled on his back near the flames. He was clutching a pistol and had been shot in the chest and had a look of surprise on his face. Stone pulled the pistol from his hand and stuck it in his waistband, walked out through the kitchen, and took a quick peek around the edge of the back door before sliding down the steps and along the side of the house. Linda was right behind him.

The porch was on fire from end to end. The white van that Stone had stolen in New York was slewed behind the car that had delivered him to the farm, and a man was slumped over its steering wheel. The barn was on fire too. Men crouched among old farm machinery in front of it, shooting into smoke that poured from its gaping door; others were advancing through the vehicles parked in the paddock.

340

Stone dashed across open ground to the van, Linda at his heels. The back doors hung open. The body of the fake cop was gone. So was the aluminium case of the bomb. Stone went around the side and opened the door and pulled the dead man out by his arms. It was the overweight guy who had attended to the bomb. The keys were in the ignition.

Linda, watching the barn over the sight of her pistol, said, "There are sixteen of them."

"We have four confirmed kills," Stone said. "And your father must have taken out the other guys who were left behind to deal with the bomb."

"You brought it along?"

"What else could we do? It was in the van, but it isn't there now. I hope that means Tom has hidden it somewhere safe. How are you holding up?"

"I'm good," she said, but flinched when a long burst of automatic fire sounded from the direction of the barn. Her red hair spilled over her shoulders. There was a curled length of duct tape stuck to it. "He's in there, isn't he?"

"It looks like Knightly has got him pinned down. I'm tempted to leave him, but he has the time key, and only he knows where the bomb is. Stay with the van, and be ready to pick us up and make a run for it when we come out. If anyone comes near you, shoot them. Don't give them any warning, don't tell them to drop their weapon, just do it. If there are too many of them or if they start shooting back, don't try to defend your position. Drive away if you can, or beat it into the woods and head west, toward the highway."

"How are you going to get him out?"

"Any way I can."

Stone slid into the driver's seat of the car, the rifle across his lap, fired up the engine, and stamped on the gas pedal. The car jolted sideways, wheels spinning uselessly because its rear bumper was tangled with the bumper of the white van. Two men were running toward him. One stopped and aimed his pistol and fired. The round punched through the windshield and exited through the roof about an inch from Stone's head. He selected reverse and slammed into the van, then selected drive and floored the gas pedal again. Metal tore and the car ripped free and shot forward. Stone steered straight at the two men. One threw himself out of the way, but the other, it was Victor Moore, stood his ground and got off two shots before the car struck him with a solid thump. He flew across the hood and smashed into the windshield and lay there, caught in a cracked cradle of laminated glass, one foot punched clean through. Stone leaned sideways to peer through the only clear patch in the wrecked glass and aimed the car at the barn door.

The men in front started to shoot at the car as it raced toward them. Knightly stood among them, firing his pistol as calmly and methodically as if this was an exercise at one of Camp Perry's ranges. Rounds ticked into metal and knocked gouts from Moore's body. A tire blew and the car lurched sideways through volumes of drifting smoke and struck the doorpost a glancing blow. Stone slipped the selector into neutral and cranked the wheel in the direction of the skid and pulled hard on the emergency brake. Moore's body rolled away as the car spun through a hundred and eighty degrees and stopped with its nose aimed at the door.

The barn was full of white smoke that gushed from a long stack of hay bales burning inside a wall of fierce yellow flame. Drifts of smoke rolled across the underside of the pitched roof and poured out of the door or down the far wall. Tom Waverly dashed out of this waterfall of smoke after Stone hit the horn, a ghost suddenly gaining solidity. He held a pistol in one hand and a long-handled axe in the other. He slung the axe away, wrenched open the passenger door, and fell into the shotgun seat.

"A couple more minutes, I'd've cut my way out the back," he said. "Where's my daughter?"

"She's safe," Stone said, and handed Tom the assault rifle and mashed the gas pedal.

The car shot forward, gushing steam from its broken radiator and yawing on its flat tire. Tom stuck the rifle out of the open side window and fired a raking burst; Knightly and his men fired back and shot out the rear window and punched holes in the bodywork. Then they were left behind as Stone accelerated toward the house, wrestling with the wheel. He slammed to a halt beside the van, shouldered the door open, and rolled out, drawing his pistol. His heart was bumping inside his chest and he was out of breath.

Linda stood behind the open door on the driver's side of the van, shooting at the men running toward them. Tom fired the rifle from waist level and one man tumbled over and the rest threw themselves flat. Linda swung up into the van and Stone ran around the front and climbed in beside her. Tom fired again, a long burst that emptied the clip, and threw the rifle away and jumped into the van as Linda put it in gear. She accelerated in reverse, cut the wheel sharply and swung the van around, then stepped on the gas and sped away down a track that slanted through scrubby woods.

"My little girl," Tom said.

# 17.

The burning barn and house were soon lost behind trees as the van bucked down the rough track. A dead man was tumbled in weeds beside an ungated gap in a fieldstone wall. Tom told Linda to turn left, and the van swerved out onto a four-lane highway. Two threads of smoke hung above the tree line behind them, diminishing into the cloudless blue sky. Stone checked his watch. It was five after three. The gate opened at six.

"I didn't know you guys were in the house, or I wouldn't have set fire to it," Tom said, "but aside from that it worked out pretty well. After they took you away, Adam, I waited until that technician turned off the bomb, and then I capped the two bad boys who were with him, stuck a gun to his head, and told him to take me in."

"And then you shot him," Stone said.

"You bet. I set fire to a gallon can of turpentine and tossed it onto the porch as a diversion, and I went looking for you and Linda in the fallout shelter they have in back, which I admit was a dumb move. They chased me into that barn, but what the fuck, you had the balls to come get me. We made it, partner," he said, and thumped Stone on the shoulder. "We fucking made it."

"We're not home yet," Stone said. He still had to find out where Tom had hidden the bomb, and he had to stop him from making off with the time key and returning alone to 1984, taking the road that would lead him to Pottersville and to Susan's murder.

"You did good. And Linda, you did pretty good too." Tom looked across Stone and said, "You *are* okay, aren't you, honey?"

"I'm holding up," Linda said.

"My brave girl."

Linda didn't say anything. She was gripping the steering wheel so hard that her knuckles had turned white.

Stone said, "Let's get something straight, Tom."

"What's that, partner?"

"I'm not your partner."

"For a few minutes back there, it sure seemed like it."

Tom's laugh turned into a cough. He wound down the window and spat into the slipstream.

"You got me into this, but I was never your partner," Stone said.

"Why don't you lighten up? We all got out safely. We have the bomb. We have the time key. It's a lovely day. . . ."

The urge to shoot him was so strong that Stone could taste it. He said, "You know I'm not going to let you run off. You have to come back with me."

Tom shook his head. "I'm not going to spend my last days in custody, being asked ten thousand different damn-fool questions. We'll go back to the day before we left. Just one day. I can slip away, and you and Linda can take the time key and leave it switched on in the old dead drop right here in this sheaf, so its rightful owners can find it and retrieve it." He looked at Stone and said, "You know how it fell into our hands in the first place?"

"Eileen Barrie told me that you took it from a bunch of time travellers."

"That's right. And it happened here, in this very sheaf. The future it comes from isn't *our* future, Adam—it's the future of the Nixon sheaf. Don't you think that's where it should return?"

"You want me to leave it behind because some guys from the future will come get it? I don't think so."

"Apparently that's just what I did, the first time around. You found that empty envelope, didn't you?"

"An empty envelope doesn't prove anything."

But Stone was wondering if the reason why Tom had been unaffected when the time key had knocked down everyone else was because the thing knew, somehow, that he had set it free at the end of the first loop. Eileen Barrie had said that it was self-aware; if she had been telling the truth, it was possible that it had been attempting to manipulate events all along. Sending them back two weeks instead of three. Making sure that Tom Waverly took it with him when he went back to 1977. Trying to make sure that the loop came out more or less the same, so it would end up in an envelope in the old Forty-Second Street drop. . . .

"I know you're not going to let me use it," Tom said. "Fine. But don't for Christ's sake let the Company have it. Do what good old TW Two did. Switch it on and leave it behind. Let it go. Because if you give it to the Company, it'll be just as bad as letting Knightly have it."

"I doubt that."

"Think about it, Adam. Do you really believe that any politician who has the time key could resist the temptation to use it? He makes a mistake in policy, he sees that he's going to pay for it in the next election, so he sends someone back to change things around, or to give his former self the benefit of hindsight. I bet not even the saintly Jimmy Carter could resist that option.

Back in the Real, in 1984, he's coming up for reelection. If he had the time key and saw his popularity slipping, do you think he'd leave it in a vault?"

"Stop it," Linda said. "Stop trying to pretend you're on the right side."

"I'm thinking of the big picture now, honey. I'm not thinking of myself. Leave the time key behind, Adam. Leave it switched on so its rightful owners can take it back. That's all I ask."

"It isn't going to happen," Stone said.

"So that's how it is," Tom said. "The two of you are working against me because you're both blindly loyal to the Company."

"It ends here," Linda said.

She slowed the van and turned off the highway into the weed-strewn parking lot of an abandoned diner with boards over its windows and a half-collapsed roof. She switched off the engine and told her father that she wanted to talk to him and climbed out. When Tom turned to open the passenger door, Stone put his pistol in his side and said, "Hand it over."

"What are you going to do, shoot me in front of my daughter?"

"I'll shoot you in the heart. She won't know about it until it's over, and you won't know about it at all."

"It's in my jacket pocket."

Stone scooted back on the bench seat, told Tom to put his pistol in the footwell, then told him take off his jacket.

"You're taking a risk, Adam. If I happened to switch it on, it would fuck you up."

"It probably would, but I reckon I could still shoot you. Do it, Tom."

Tom shrugged out of his jacket and folded it up and laid it on the seat between them. He said, "This doesn't mean anything. I was going to give it to you anyway."

"I'm taking you in," Stone said. He was sure now that Tom was planning to go back and start things over again, the whole weary cycle from Pottersville to White Sands, in another attempt to save himself. "I can't let you start killing Eileen Barrie's doppels or do whatever else it is you're planning."

"You know why I killed them? I'll let you into a secret. That woman back in the Real, she wasn't the real Eileen Barrie. The original, the Real version, died in a lab accident while she was trying to figure out how the time key worked. Knightly had already groomed one of her doppels as a replacement. He brought her in, and she picked up where her predecessor had left off."

"This is another of your stories," Stone said.

But he was remembering something David Welch had told him. That in almost every sheaf where she was alive, Eileen Barrie was a mathematician working on some aspect of quantum theory. That she was more stable than Elvis.

"I was the guy who brought her through the mirror into the Real," Tom said. "I was the poor sap who fell in love with her. She was a real piece of work, Adam. Brilliant and beautiful and venal, like one of those man-eaters from the old black-and-white crime movies. I know about her doppels because Knightly built up files on possible replacements, and most of them are involved in stuff that's either at the edge of the law or on the wrong side of it. The doppel in this sheaf, for instance, was a university professor—*is* a university professor, right now, but in a few years she'll be working for a big Wall Street company. She came to work for us later on because she was about to go to jail over a scam involving junk bonds."

"She was an outlaw, like you. Is that what you're saying?"

"That's why I loved her. It was kind of like being the male partner of a mantis, or a black widow spider. Or, you know the story of the frog and the scorpion, caught in the flood? She was like that scorpion, couldn't help stinging the people trying to help her, even if it meant that she got hurt too. But man, was she irresistible. Now, can I have a moment with my daughter, or are you intent on taking me straight to jail?"

"I guess a couple of minutes won't matter."

"You have all the time in the world now, Adam. Think about it."

Stone watched through the windshield as, in white T-shirt and blue jeans, Tom walked up to where his daughter stood. He spread his arms to embrace her, saying, "Sweetheart—"

Linda slapped him in the face, the sound loud as a gunshot. She reared back and tried to slap him again, and he grabbed her wrists and pulled her close, whispering in her ear. She fought in his grip and he held her, still whispering, and she went suddenly limp.

Stone pulled the keys out of the ignition and climbed out of the van with Tom's denim jacket tucked under his arm. Tom looked at him over the top of Linda's head.

"We have less than three hours before the gate opens," Stone said, and walked away to the edge of the parking lot to give them a little privacy.

Traffic went past on the highway. Cars, trucks, tractor-trailers. Tons of metal battering past in a slipstream wind. Stone saw the blank faces of drivers and passengers behind glass, saw a little girl turn in the back seat of a car to stare at him. Saw himself as she might see him, raggedy and exhausted and smoke-smudged, his shirt pulled out of his trousers, a bundle under his arm. A drifter lost and forlorn among the dried wreckage of summer's weeds, a long way from the home he'd lost.

Linda was coming across the parking lot toward him. Her eyes were red-rimmed and her cheeks were wet, but there was a flinty determination in her gaze and an angry flush in her cheeks. "You know, don't you? You know he's dying, just like the last time."

"He went into the core of the reactor of GYPSY's facility," Stone said. "He manually reinserted the control rods, stopped the runaway chain re-action, and shut down the power source to the gates. He was trying to stop Knightly from escaping, and he also saved a lot of lives. Including mine."

Linda's gaze searched his face. She looked like she was a moment away from either tears or some serious violence. "He didn't tell you—"

"Back in Pottersville? No. Whatever else he is, Linda, whatever else he's done, there's no denying his bravery. A lesser man would have used it to jus-tify himself. He didn't say a word."

"There's a lot he didn't tell us. Things he should have told us from the start. The Company would have gone after Knightly and his merry crew and put a stop to this without having to involve us. None of this would have happened."

"He wanted to save himself. You can't blame him for trying."

Linda kicked at dead weeds while she thought about this. She looked at Stone and said, "Do you think we've done what we're supposed to have done?"

"We have to make sure he doesn't end up in Pottersville."

Linda kicked at the weeds some more. She said, "Just now, he asked me to help him. He told me where the bomb is—"

"He told you?"

"He said it was to show he trusted me to do the right thing. I had to tell him I couldn't."

Stone realised that Tom Waverly was willing to give up the location of the bomb because he knew it didn't matter now. But he couldn't tell Linda that her father had tried to buy her trust with worthless coin.

"I thought my father died three years ago," Linda said. "I mourned for him and tried to get on with my life. And then I find he isn't dead after all, and the next moment he commits suicide. And then he turns up *again*. . . ."

She turned away. Stone waited while she sniffed and gulped.

When she had regained her composure, she said, "He wasn't there a lot of the time when I was a little kid. But when he was around, he was everything a father could be. It was like the circus had come to town. You never knew what he might do next. He was funny, charming, mysterious, exciting. . . . He'd say, out of nowhere, let's go for a ride. And we'd end up eating lunch in some fabulous backwoods barbecue place two hundred miles from home. Now, well, maybe I've grown up and I can see through his bullshit. I still love him for what he was, Mr. Stone, but I hate him for what he's become. Knightly has his principles, however twisted they are, but my father was only after the money. And I hate myself too," Linda said, "because I know I have to turn him in. Because I can't do anything to help him."

"You did all you could, Linda. You did all right."

She turned and gave Stone a raw look. "Did I?"

"We have to get back to the Real and tell the Company about Knightly and what's left of his crew, to make sure they're brought in before they can do any more damage. If it's any consolation, your father will probably come out of this a hero."

"There's a problem," Linda said. "Knightly has the components for a gate."

"What kind of gate?"

"The same kind he used to get here."

"A gate that allows time travel?"

"We came through the mirror in four vans. Three were full of crates. We rode in convoy all the way across the country to New Jersey. I've been here three weeks while they finished assembling their nuclear bomb and talked to their local contacts. I heard all kinds of things, and I think I've made some kind of sense out of it. What they brought with them is the equivalent of the time key, only a whole lot bigger, and not as versatile. Once they've bolted it onto a gate, they can travel back in time to any point after that gate was opened. But they can't travel forward, to 1984. For that they need the time key."

Stone thought about that for a moment and said, trying to get it straight in his head, "If they want to use this gizmo, they have to get back to the Real. They have to get back to where the gate mechanisms are. But even if they do that, they can't use the gizmo to get back to 1984. It doesn't sound like much of a threat."

"If they get back to the Real, they can go into hiding and start over. Build up GYPSY again. Work out some other way of changing history."

"So we find a way of warning the DCI's office about them, right here in 1977."

Linda shook her head. "We can't do that. Because if we do, *we'll* change history, and things might work out worse than they already are. And besides, this is long before the Church Committee. Right now, in the Real, Knightly's younger self is in charge of Special Operations. He's a power in the Company, and the government thinks just like he does. Even if we do manage to warn the DCI's office, they'll probably stick us in jail."

"I'm not good at thinking like this," Stone said.

"I've had plenty of time to work it out," Linda said. "We have to stop Knightly and his crew here, before he gets back to the Real." She looked across the parking lot at Tom Waverly, looked at the sky, looked at Stone, and took a breath. "But first of all," she said, "we have to take care of my father."

They drove toward New York. Tom was quiet, sombrely ruminative. Stone hoped that he was facing up to his fate, that he was beginning to accept that he had nowhere left to run and wouldn't be able to start things over. When they neared the intersection that led to the George Washington Bridge, Tom broke his silence and told Linda to take the 95 south, and a few miles later they turned off onto the service road where he and Stone had waited for Knightly's men.

He'd stashed the nuclear bomb in the yard of an abandoned factory building, under a tent of rusty iron sheeting.

"I didn't have time to find a better hiding place," he told Stone as they lugged the case back to the van. "I was in a righteous hurry to come rescue you and Linda."

"And I'd thank you for it," Stone said, "if it wasn't for the fact that you put me in danger in the first place."

They put the case in the back of the van and drove on toward New York.

"You don't trust me, Adam, but do you trust Linda?" Tom said, after a little while. "Would you put your life in her hands?"

"I put my life in your hands more than once, Tom. It isn't something you think about. It's something you have to decide when the moment comes."

"The moment's fast approaching. And you're going to have to trust Linda, Adam, because you can't use the time key. It's fucked you up pretty bad three times now, and it'll probably fuck you up again. What I was thinking, maybe Linda could use it to send you back to 1984, and she could stay here, take care of what needs to be done."

"Stay here with you and a nuclear warhead? I don't think so."

Linda said, "I'm sitting right here. Why don't you two old men ask me what I want to do?"

Tom said, "Adam has the upper hand, honey, that's why I'm asking him. But you're right. In the end it's your decision. If he agreed to it, would you help me out?"

"You ran away because you wouldn't face up to the consequences of what you did," Linda said. "Now you want me to work for you. I don't think so."

"You don't have to listen to me. But if you don't, I can't promise you that it'll come out right," Tom said, and sat with his arms folded, staring out at the stony prow of Manhattan as they headed toward the Lincoln Tunnel.

# 18.

They left the van in a parking lot on Third Avenue. It was five o'clock. The Turing gate would open in an hour. As they walked toward the subway station at Fifty-First Street, Tom said, "If someone thinks to take a good look inside the van, or if some punk steals it, the history of this sheaf is going to take a giant fucking leap into the unknown."

"We'll be back for it in a New York minute," Stone said.

He was scanning the faces of passersby and watching the traffic, alert for anything out of the ordinary, certain that Knightly had sent people after them.

"No, we won't," Tom said. "As soon as we step into the Real we'll be arrested. And I'll get to spend what's left of my life in some windowless room being questioned by civil servants."

"We can't let you go," Linda said.

"If I walked away from you right now, what would you do? Shoot me? Well, go ahead. It would be a mercy."

"We're making things right," Stone said.

"You're making a mistake."

"I'm going home," Stone said. "We're all going home."

He held his pistol inside his jacket pocket as the three of them went down the steps of the subway entrance into a hot tunnel full of strangers hurrying past each other. Linda bought tokens at the booth and they passed through the turnstiles and walked toward the end of the crowded platform and the door that led to the electrical service shaft.

There was the growing rumble of an approaching train. People folded their newspapers and got up from the benches along the wall. People moved toward the edge of the platform. Stone checked his watch. In less than forty minutes the gate would open, and they'd step through it and return to the Real, to 1984. He would tell Cramer and Echols that if they wanted to know where the bomb was and where the remnant of Operation GYPSY was hiding out, they'd better get their boss to agree to a few things. He wanted to visit the First Foot sheaf. He wanted to talk to his younger self and tell him what he needed to know, tell him to look after Petey and Susan, ask him if it wasn't about time he did the right thing by her. . . .

The train breasted out of the darkness in a rush of air and a metallic screech. Overlapping splashes and scribbles of hectic colour stretched along the steel flanks of its cars, blinding their windows. Cartoon faces and exclamations, stretched and shaded signatures framed by electric jags. Doors slammed back, people getting off pushed through dense knots of people trying to get on, and someone stepped out from behind one of the red girders that supported the low ceiling. A man in a tweed suit and a yellow waistcoat, Dick Knightly, pointing a rolled-up newspaper at Stone, calling out his name.

Stone threw himself at Linda, knocking her into a shallow embrasure as Knightly fired his concealed weapon. Shotgun pellets smacked dust and fragments from the tiled wall. People screamed and flinched away, or stood frozen or knelt down. The driver of the train stared through the window of his cab, then ducked out of sight as Knightly whipped his arm to one side, the burning newspaper flying away to reveal a sawn-off pump-action shotgun.

"This is the end of the road, Adam," he shouted, his voice lifting above the bedlam screams of the passengers. "You've nowhere left to run."

Two men showed themselves. One was half hidden by a girder support and the other was shielded by a stout black woman in a flower-print dress, his arm around her throat, his pistol at her head.

Stone was flattened in the embrasure, pointing his pistol toward Knightly. Beside him, Linda aimed her pistol at the two men, moving it back and forth in quick but steady hitches. Tom knelt behind a trash basket fifty feet away.

"If you wanted to beat us to the gate," Knightly said, "you should have taken the George Washington Bridge. But I suppose you had to stop off and pick up the bomb."

"Where are the rest of your men?" Stone said. "On their way to New Mexico?"

"If you throw down your weapons and surrender, I promise that I'll let Ms. Waverly live."

"Put down your gun, Mr. Knightly, or none of us will get out of this alive."

"Do it now," Knightly said, and turned and shot a long-haired young man who crouched in one of the open doors of the train, shot him in the chest and knocked him down. People inside the passenger car screamed. At the far end of the platform, people were fighting to escape through the turnstiles.

"They're nothing to me, Adam," Knightly said. "They're dust in the wind. They're the walking dead. But how many can you afford to lose?"

Tom rose to his feet and stepped forward. "You want the bomb? I'll take you to the bomb."

Stone saw a man wearing a blue sport coat push through the panicky crowd at the turnstiles and cross the platform in three quick strides and disappear into the train.

"I'll take you right to the bomb," Tom said. "After that, you can kill me or you can let me go, I really don't care. All you have to do is promise you'll let me daughter live. Let her walk away now. Let her go back through the mirror."

"I won't do it," Linda said loudly, right by Stone's ear.

"Adam Stone has the device," Tom said, "and I can show you where the bomb is. Let Linda go—she doesn't have anything to do with this."

Stone could see the man in the sport coat moving through one of the cars of the train, appearing and disappearing behind graffiti scrawled across window-glass. He touched Linda's hand and said quietly, "There's a guy just got on the train. I think he's our backup. When he makes a move, so do we."

She gave a tight nod.

"If you do have the device, Adam, I suggest that you give it up now," Knightly said. "Or would you rather see more innocent people die? Their lives, such as they are, are in your hands."

"Don't shoot anyone else," Stone said and threw the denim jacket onto the platform.

"Is the time key in there?" Knightly said.

"And its bridle."

"Put down your weapons."

"Have one of your men come get it. Do you think I'll shoot him and risk the life of an innocent hostage?"

"I'll have her shot if you don't lay down your weapons right now," Knightly said, and the man in the blue sport coat stepped out of the open door of the car and shot the man holding the black woman. He stumbled forward and fell down and the man in the sport coat grabbed the woman and pulled her into the car. Knightly turned, lifting his shotgun, and Stone stepped out of the embrasure and took his shot. He saw paint chips fly from the girder, corrected his aim a fraction, and shot again. Knightly stumbled forward, and Stone's third shot took him down. Linda's pistol went off behind him, dropping the other man.

Stone started toward Knightly's body, and Tom Waverly slammed into him and pinned him to the wall. One of Tom's hands caught Stone's chin and smashed his head against sooty tiles; the other snatched away his pistol and swung its grip against his temple. Stone fell to his knees and Tom scooped up the denim jacket and pulled out the time key and switched it on.

Pain thumped in Stone's skull. Its black pulse beat in his sight and locked his muscles. He felt Tom's hands on him, felt him pluck the set of keys from his pocket. Linda was down too, clutching her head. Stone saw Tom pull her up, pull her close, heard him shout to the man in the sport coat that he'd kill this woman, he'd kill her if he didn't put his gun down right now. The man hesitated, then dropped his pistol and raised his hands. As Stone levered himself to his feet, Tom unlocked the door at the end of the platform and shoved Linda away, then stepped through the door and slammed it behind him.

Most of the pain in Stone's head lifted at once. He stumbled down the platform as Linda braced and shot up the door's lock. Stone pushed her out of the way and kicked the door just beneath the shattered lock, a good solid kick that made it shiver in its frame, then stepped back and shoulder-charged it, but it wouldn't give way. Tom Waverly had jammed or bolted it from the inside.

The man in the sport coat jogged down the platform, saying breathlessly, "I'm Harvey Shiel, Mr. Stone. Your contact."

"Follow me," Stone said, and ran for the exit, pausing to scoop up a pistol dropped by one of the dead men. Linda and Harvey Shiel chased after him as he ran up the steps, straight into the arms of two cops who were descending toward the platform with their guns drawn. One spun Stone around and pressed him against the wall; the other covered Linda and Harvey Shiel with his revolver.

"I'm a Secret Service agent," Stone said, as calmly as he could. "Look in my jacket, the inside pocket."

The cop was a brawny veteran. He held Stone's hands at the back of his neck and wanted to know if Stone had anything to do with a report of shots fired in the subway.

"I'm chasing fugitives," Stone said. "Three are down. One got away. Check my ID, officer."

"Take it out nice and slow," the cop said, and stepped back and aimed his revolver at Stone as he took out the badge case he'd been given back in the Real. The cop studied the photograph on the card and the embossed gold shield, showed it to his partner, and asked Stone what was going on.

"It's a matter of national security. I want you to secure the area and call up ambulances—there are civilian casualties. My partners and I have to go get backup," Stone said, and turned and ran up the rest of the steps before the cop could think to ask why Stone's partners didn't show their ID.

Stone ran two blocks down Lexington Avenue and turned left onto Forty-Ninth Street. His nose was bleeding and he snorted blood into his hand and wiped it on the leg of his trousers without breaking stride. As in the American Bund, as in the Real, the north side of the Waldorf-Astoria Hotel took up the whole block. The brass-faced double doors of the freight elevator and the door to the service stairs were next to the entrance to the hotel's underground parking lot. Stone shot out the lock of the door to the stairs and kicked it open. Linda was running toward him, her face flushed, her hair like a banner. At the far end of the block, Harvey Shiel turned the corner, labouring mightily.

Stone went down the spiral stairs two at a time; Linda's footsteps clattered somewhere above him as he unbolted the grated door at the bottom. As he hauled it open, he heard another shot echo far down the white-tiled passageway and ran toward it.

Pain suddenly thumped in his head, growing sharper as it knocked through his skull.

He was getting close to the time key.

A sooty bulb burned above the iron door that stood open in the side of the passageway and two dead men lay on their backs just inside. When Stone stepped over the bodies, the pain in his head doubled, doubled again. Shock waves of hard sharp pain hammering through his skull, pain so bad it didn't seem possible he could survive it. He stumbled forward and crashed into the edge of the doorway and clung there like a drowning sailor. He saw through a kind of black pulse the tarnished glow of the gate filling the meter cupboard on the other side of the small, sooty room; saw someone silhouetted against it.

The mild-faced man in a business suit, the time key glowing in his left hand, looked straight at Stone, then reached inside his jacket. Tom Waverly's body was sprawled at his feet. Another man sat against the wall next to the silvery mirror of the gate, his face shot away. The man in the suit pulled out a pistol and Stone tried to lift his own weapon, but it seemed to weigh about a thousand pounds. Then something exploded right by his head.

Stone fell down, convinced he'd been shot. Linda stepped past him, shot the man as he crawled toward the gate on hands and knees, shot him as he collapsed and shot him again, the hard noise pounding the nail through Stone's skull.

The man fell on his face and stayed down. Linda dropped to her knees beside her father's body. Stone found his gun and began to crawl forward. The time key lay on the floor next to the body of the man in the business suit. Stone's sight was full of black rags that pulsed with the pulse of the pain in his head. All he could see was the time key, a faint green rectangle that suddenly inverted, opening into a vast void in which baleful stars rushed at him like angry hornets. He felt its full force drive through him and with a convulsive effort lifted his pistol and set it against the time key and squeezed the trigger. The pain in his head blew out and the gate vanished like a burst soap bubble.

## WHITE SANDS, OCTOBER 1977

Harvey Shiel and his partner had been sent all the way back to 1969, the year when the gate had first been opened onto the Nixon sheaf. Shiel's partner had been killed in a traffic accident four years ago, but Shiel had continued to live in deep cover, scrupulously maintaining the radio receiver, keeping it charged and carrying it with him wherever he went out of habit so deeply ingrained he'd almost forgotten the reason for it. He told Stone that when the receiver had begun to vibrate it had taken him a while to remember what he was supposed to do.

"I tracked the signal to a back road in New Jersey," he said. "North of Secaucus. I found two cars there all shot up, three bodies dumped in the reeds, and the transmitter lying in the dirt. I knew something had happened, but I didn't know what. I couldn't think of anything else but to hang out near the gate and hope I spotted you. It was pure dumb luck that I did."

They were driving out of New York in the van. They'd had to leave Tom Waverly's body and the bodies of the other men in the squalid room where the gate to the Real opened. It had been an awful thing to do, but there had been no choice: they'd only just got out ahead of the local cops.

Stone still wasn't quite sure what had happened. He was certain that the three dead men had been Dick Knightly's, left there in case the ambush in the subway station failed. And he was also certain that Tom Waverly had killed them, because he'd heard only a single shot as he'd been running down the tunnel toward the gate—the shot that had killed Tom, fired by the man in the business suit.

He imagined Tom standing in the little room with the time key alive in his hands, waiting for the gate to open. And when it had opened, the man in the business suit had stepped through the mirror and shot him. But where had the man come from? He'd carried no identification, no money, nothing but a spare clip for his pistol. Was he a Company assassin, sent back in time from 1984 to deal with Stone and Tom Waverly after the Company had managed to build a time gate from the plans left by Eileen Barrie? Or had he come from much further in the future?

Maybe he would be able to figure it out later, Stone thought. Right now, he still had to dispose of the nuclear bomb and deal with the rest of Knightly's men.

Harvey Shiel said that taking care of the bomb wouldn't be a problem. He had a converted fishing boat, a forty-footer with twin GM marine diesels that he rented to deep-sea fishing parties.

"We can take her out and dump the thing in ten thousand feet of water if that's what you want. You're absolutely sure you don't want to make contact with the Real, bring in specialists to deal with it?"

"Absolutely," Stone said.

"Then we can load it up tonight," Shiel said, "and go out at first light. What are you going to do after that?"

Linda stirred and said, "Some of Knightly's people are still alive."

She was possessed by a brittle calm that Stone found more unsettling than raw, unreasoning grief. He felt as if he was sitting next to a bomb with a mercury-tilt trigger that was liable to go off at the slightest disturbance.

He asked Shiel how much cash he was carrying.

"A couple of thousand dollars. I emptied my checking account after I got the signal, thought it might come in handy. I can get more, but it'll take a little time."

Stone was grateful that he had this competent, good-hearted man on his side. He said, "I'll need all of it. Think you can handle the disposal of the nuclear device by yourself?"

"No problem. Who are you chasing? Can I help you with that, too?"

"I have to go after Knightly's people. They want to take three vans full of equipment through the mirror, back to the Real. It's too much to smuggle through the gate in New York, and in any case the area's swarming with local cops. That means there's only one place they can go. I reckon I'll have a couple of days to get ready if I fly out there, as long as I leave right now."

"It doesn't stop," Linda said.

"This one last thing," Stone said, "and then it's done."

She took a breath and let it out. "All right. What do we have to do?"

"You're going to stay with Harvey. You can give him a hand with the bomb, if you're up to it."

"I'll come with you—"

"You're in shock, Linda. You don't know it, but you are."

"They killed my father. I want to come with you and kill them. Kill them all. . . ." Her face twisted, and then tears came. She swiped at them with the heel of her hand, but they kept coming. She said in a tight voice, "He didn't want to be saved, did he? He'd gone all the way over. He would have gone through and left us behind, he would have gone after Dr. Barrie's doppels, he would have started the whole thing over, just to save himself. . . ."

"I'm sorry," Stone said. After a moment he put his arm around her shoulders. She leant against him and wept silently, angrily. He said, "He's still alive, Linda. Right now, in the Real, in 1977, he's still alive."

"You think that makes it any better?"

Stone thought of Susan. "I guess not."

Harvey Shiel looked straight ahead as he drove, giving Stone and Linda the space they needed. After a little while he said, "I have a cabin on the shore. You can stay there as long as you like."

"I'd like that," Linda said.

"It's pretty basic, but it's peaceful." Shiel hesitated, then said, "What about me? Will the Company want me back, now that I've completed my mission?"

Stone said, "You want to go back?"

"I've been here eight years. I've made a life for myself here. I'm married, I have kids, a business. . . . You think they'll want me to return to active service?"

"I can't see any way for you to return to active service without waiting for 1984 to swing by," Stone said. "You can ask them then, if you feel the need, but don't ask me. They reactivated me for this, but as soon as it's done I'm going back into retirement."

"I'm not going back either," Linda said. "I'll help Mr. Shiel get rid of the evidence, and that'll be the last thing I do for the Company."

"This is a good place to live," Shiel said. "It has its problems, sure. There's a nuclear standoff with the Soviets, and just now we have an energy crisis, rolling power cuts, and gas shortages. But on the whole it's one of the better Americas. If you work at it, you can make a life here, any kind you want."

"I look forward to finding out about that," Stone said. "They have New Jersey airport here?"

"They call it Newark."

"Take me to Newark, Harvey. I have an appointment to keep at White Sands."

Stone flew ahead of the sunset and landed at Albuquerque a little after five p.m. local time. He stole a car from the long-term parking lot, claimed he'd lost his ticket at the exit, paid the fine, and drove south along the I-25 to Las Cruces, riding a floating sense of déjà vu. He reached the little town after sunset. After checking into a motel, he ate a beef burrito at a truck stop and in the pungent restroom bought a dozen uppers from a fat biker with wreaths of jailhouse tattoos on his arms.

The gun shop was more or less exactly as Stone remembered it from just a few subjective days ago. He waited until after midnight before short-circuiting the alarm and using the jack from the car to lever a security grille from the back window. He was in and out in five minutes. He stashed the stolen goods in a Dumpster behind the motel, slept exactly six hours, showered, ate breakfast in the diner across the street, and bought beef jerky and plastic jugs of water in the general store where in seven years he would shop for provisions with Tom and Linda Waverly—no, that was in another time-line of this sheaf. Things would be different now.

Stone retrieved his stolen booty from the Dumpster and hid it among the clubs in the golf bag in the trunk and headed out of town. Two black-and-white cruisers were angle-parked outside the gun shop. A deputy leaning against the wing of his vehicle and drinking coffee from a foam cup gave Stone the eye as he went past, but when Stone checked his rearview mirror the deputy was ambling toward the open door of the gun shop.

Through the dry mountains, then, into the heat-haze and burning light of the desert. Stone drove past the turnout where the track to the cabin met the road, parked the car behind a billboard advertising a place that sold Indian jewellery, and hiked up a stony slope. He circled wide, coming at the cabin from the west, holing up in a circle of creosote bush and scoping it out through the twenty-power binoculars he'd stolen from the gun shop.

A pickup truck was parked in front of the cabin, but for a long time nothing moved but heat shimmer. It was so hot sweat evaporated straight from Stone's skin as he lay on sand and gravel under dry brush with a T-shirt tied like a scarf over his head. Apart from chewing strips of jerky and taking sips of warm water from a plastic jug, he kept so quiet and still that a jack rabbit loped within a yard of him.

He had plenty of time to think about what he needed to do, and think about everything that had happened in the past few days. He remembered saying goodbye to Linda Waverly at the airport. Linda, still possessed by that cold calm, had told him to come back to New York when he had done what needed to be done.

"Promise me you won't go through the mirror."

"No promises, Linda."

"You're thinking of the woman you left behind. The one who was murdered."

"It's complicated."

"Right now her son isn't even born, Adam. Her husband isn't dead."

She had never before used his first name.

"I wasn't thinking of trying to find her, but I was wondering about trying to save her husband, when the time comes. He was a good friend to me, Linda. The least I can do is warn him off the duck-hunting trip that killed him."

"When did it happen? Will it happen?"

"In a little over six years. Right now he hasn't even moved to First Foot. He's still in the army."

"You have plenty of time," Linda had said. "And so do I, if I'm going to try to save my father from himself all over again. We could both wait it out here. It's as good a place as anywhere else."

Remembering this and everything else, Stone felt a growing sense of freedom, as if gravity was loosening its hold on him. After this one last task he would be released from the wheel of fate. After this, he would be able to do anything. Send covert messages to the DCI, rat out Knightly and GYPSY early. Help Linda save her father. Warn Jake about the wolves, when the time came. Anything was possible, anything at all.

Close to six o'clock, with the sun westering toward the mountains, two men came out of the cabin and drove the pickup to the rocks where the gate was located. A little later, they drove back down again. Knightly's men, no doubt about it, left behind to guard the gate after the crew had escaped from 1984, checking it out when it opened each day. Stone wondered about the caretaker.

The temperature dropped quickly after the sun set. The cloudless desert sky was full of stars. The luminous smoke of the Milky Way, sky-spanning constellations. In every sheaf that Stone had ever visited the stars were always the same, but elsewhere it was entirely possible that sentient bears or wolves or creatures outside any human experience or dream had built strange civilisations under different stars. So many different Americas. An infinite variety, for all practical purposes. In all that unimaginably vast array, did the Real and the few sheaves stitched to its time-line by Turing gates really count for all that much? Would it really make any difference if a few of those sheaves vanished, or were changed so radically and violently that they forced all the others connected to them to change too? Maybe not. After all, in the infinite array of Americas, there must to be any number of versions of this particular story. In some, Tom Waverly's blackmail scheme succeeded and he escaped with Eileen Barrie; in others, Knightly's black op failed to take the nuclear bomb back in time, or Tom was in prison and his daughter was safe and Stone had returned to the farm and Susan and Petey, or he had never left in the first place. How did he, one of so many different versions of one person, count in all this?

He counted, he thought, in the way that everyone counted. Every individual was only a single drop in an infinite ocean, but every drop sparkled with particularity. This moment was never quite the same as any moment before or since, in any of the multitude of sheaves. He was the sum of millions of such unique moments.

Stone remembered the Harvest Home dance at the Ellison place, two weeks before he'd lit out from New Amsterdam and the First Foot sheaf with David Welch. Tables set up in the yard behind the house had been crowded with bowls and platters of food. Jars and bottles of homemade apple cider and beer cooled in clay pots brimful with water. Neighbours talked with neighbours; blue smoke boiled up above the men around the barbecue pit; small children chased each other around the tables. After sunset, a fiddler and an accordionist had struck up and people had moved onto the floor as white-haired Ben Shepherd called out dance steps, beating time with a tambourine, beating time with his hands. That was when Susan had dragged Stone from his chair. Mischief in her eyes and her dirty-blonde hair loose about her flushed face as she told him where to put his feet, when to turn, when to turn her, when to clap, both of them laughing as they capered to "Dogs in the Ashcan," caught up in the music and the moment, caught up in each other, dancers inseparable from the dance.

Stone snapped out of his reverie when he saw a scrap of light move away from the cabin—one of the men was using a flashlight to navigate to the outhouse. Stone covered the four hundred yards quickly and quietly and grabbed the man as he left the outhouse, clamping a hand over his mouth, dispatching him with a single thrust of the hunting knife. He lowered the dead man to the ground and drew the Colt .45 that he'd stolen from the gun shop and crossed to the cabin, took a quick peek at the window, then walked straight in. The second man was sitting at the table in his shirtsleeves, spooning peaches from a can. He stared at Stone, reached for the pistol on the table, and Stone shot him twice in the chest, a quick double tap that knocked him out of his chair.

There was a fresh grave behind the cabin. Stone laid the bodies of Knightly's men beside it and covered them with a tarpaulin sheet and shovelled dirt over it. He allowed himself a few hours' sleep, woke at dawn, and worked through a set of exercises in the clean cold air, his muscles loosening sweetly and easily, his mind absolutely centred on the task ahead of him.

He made coffee and scrambled a couple of eggs and ate them with the ham he found in a coolbox, then circled the cabin and found a good spot near the top of a ridge three hundred yards to the south, where two boulders leaned together like the heads of lovers, leaving a wide notch beneath. He rigged a hide with a couple of chair legs and a blanket and plenty of cut brush, swallowed an upper to stay sharp, and sat in the shade of one of the boulders. With shoes planted in gravelly sand and his elbows resting on his knees, he used the binoculars to track every vehicle that moved along the highway cut across the bleached plain. Knightly's people would be pushing it, driving nonstop across America. A ragged army in retreat, anxious to cross back to the Real and start over, make another attempt to change history. Stone figured that they would arrive by the end of the day, early tomorrow morning at the latest.

They came just after five in the afternoon. Three vans materialising out of the shimmering compression of dust and heat haze, small black bullets running close together, appearing and disappearing as they rode through inversion layers shimmering in dips in the highway. No doubt about it.

Stone wriggled inside the hide, settled the stock of the hunting rifle against his shoulder, and laid its heavy barrel on the dirt-filled pillow behind the screen of thorny branches. It was a good rifle, a heavy-barrelled .50 on a Ruger bolt action, with a checkered walnut stock and a twelve-power telescopic sight. One of its 660 grain rounds could smash an engine block or kill a man by hydraulic shock if it hit him anywhere in the body. He'd tested it that morning, working out the drop of rounds over hundred-yard intervals, marking off distances and memorising landmarks in a killing zone spread on either side of the track to the cabin. He was confident that he could hit a target no bigger than a man's head at five hundred yards.

The three vans came on fast, making the turn onto the track to the cabin one after the other, two miles away and closing, moving in a storm of dust as they roared up the slope. Stone pushed off the rifle's safety with his thumb and tracked the vans through the cross-hairs of the sight. His mouth was dry, but that was only the amphetamine. He felt cool and clearheaded.

The lead van was in range now. Stone could see its driver behind a flare of sunlight on the windshield. He curled his forefinger around the trigger. He was ready. Anything was possible. Anything at all.

Universes waited to be born.

# ABOUT THE AUTHOR

**P**AUL MCAULEY's first novel won the Philip K. Dick Award, and he has gone on to win almost all of the major awards in the field. For many years a research biologist, he now writes full-time. He lives in London. Visit him online at unlikelyworlds.blogspot.com.